A WREATH OF SERPENTS

ALEX CONNOR

First published in Great Britain in 2024 by Merisi Publishing. https://www.merisipublishing.com

A CIP catalogue record for this book is available from the British Library.

ISBN 978-1-7385363-6-8 (PB)
ISBN 978-1-7385363-5-1 (EBOOK)

A WREATH OF SERPENTS

ALEX CONNOR writes contemporary thrillers, always with a link to the art world. She has been published and translated in sixteen countries, had a world No 1 for CARAVAGGIO SAGA, and won the Rome Prize for Fiction. She is a working artist, historian, and FRSA.

A WREATH of SERPENTS is No 7 in her series of art thrillers.

Also by Alex Connor

THE CARAVAGGIO CONSPIRACY
ISLE OF THE DEAD
THE REMBRANDT SECRET
THE BOSCH DECEPTION
MEMORY OF BONES
LEGACY OF BLOOD

ARTEMISIA

BOOK ONE

PROLOGUE

London.
11.20pm, 19th November.

I could make a run for it.

She paused, hunkered down in her coat, looking out at the rain.

Was it worth it? Or would she be soaked by the time she got to her car?

A glance upwards. Mouthy sky spitting rain. Water underfoot, gutters bloated.

Maybe she'd wait until the rain stopped. Her boyfriend knew she was coming. And even though she had left her mobile in the car and hadn't rung to say she would be late; he'd wait for her.

She looked up. What was the point of wrecking her hair and outfit? It was an expensive dress; why risk spoiling it? She wanted to impress him because tonight was special. She could sense that. He was going to ask her tonight.

So, she'd wait. The rain would stop soon.

Yeah, she'd wait.

-o0o-

What's she doing? He wondered, staring out from behind the hoarding, his tall, awkward body cramped in the narrow, shadowed space. He thought the bitch was going to her car, but she wasn't, she'd taken cover instead. Frustrated, he raked his fingernails along the back of the hoarding, listening to the rain falling. He'd had it all planned. He knew her car and had been watching and waiting for the opportunity for weeks. But the fucking rain had started, and she had taken cover instead.

Taken cover instead of running past him to her car.

He couldn't get her until she crossed his path. Couldn't move out and grab her on the street. Even on a quiet city backstreet. Even in pelting rain, someone might spot him. He'd been so close to her only the day before. Near enough to notice that her hair had needed washing. Close enough to see all the grubby secrets of a beautiful young woman: the beginning of a spot on her chin, the souring of perfume. Close enough to smell a minuscule breakdown in her deodorant after a long day.

He was breathing heavily - not that she could hear him. The rain was smothering every sound. He tensed and could see a quick flash of her sleeve as she moved around in the doorway. She was getting agitated, probably looking down the street to her car, wondering if she should make a break for it, wondering if she could make it before she was soaked.

Go on, he willed her, run.

o0o-

Would her boyfriend wait for her? She paused, worried. Maybe he'd think she had got cold feet. Maybe he'd think she'd stood him up. If only she'd kept her mobile with her instead of leaving it in the car, she could have called him and told him not to worry. Stay where you are; stay at the restaurant rehearsing your speech. I'm on my way.

Her gaze moved down the street, nervous, eager to be gone. And she wanted to pee so badly. She'd never make it to the restaurant without relieving herself. God, what a night, she thought, looking around and noticing the hoarding.

She could go behind there. No one would see her there.

A sudden, low noise made her jump, her gaze fixing on the hoarding and the dense black shadow behind. Narrowing her eyes, she struggled to see more, but the shadow remained closed off, impenetrable.

And still the rain kept falling.

-o0o-

Oh, he was cursing himself now. Knocking into one of the struts at the back of the hoarding, how fucking clumsy was that? He knew at once that she had heard him. Her head popped out of the doorway and glanced over. She didn't see him in the darkness, even though he was looking right at her. But she sensed something, her instinct was working overtime. He could see that in her expression and the way she held her breath. He knew what she was doing because her shoulders froze, as they always do when someone inhales and holds.

She was scared.

Come on, he willed her, run for your car. Run past me. Run, run.

And then suddenly, she did just that. She left the doorway, diving out onto the road, startling him. But she wasn't going to pass him. Instead, she was running, her right arm outstretched, towards a taxi that had just entered the street. He tensed, outmaneuvered. The bitch was going to get away. She had broken cover like a pheasant ducking the gun.

He had never expected that, never suspected that some random cabbie would save her. Thwarted, he drove his fingernails into the hoarding, tearing at the wood. She was flagging the taxi down. Clever bitch, he thought bitterly; she was going to leave her car behind and make a run for it.

Desperate, he moved towards the edge of the hoarding, just in time to see the cab drive **past** *the woman. Leaving her on the side of the street, in a ruined dress, in the pouring rain.*

He decided then that luck was on his side, and ran out from behind the hoarding, looping his arm around the woman's neck. Pressing against her windpipe, he could barely hold on to her as she jerked about, struggling frantically. But he was quick, feeling her shock as the knife went into her spine. He knew it would work. He had practised on animals many times, severing the spinal cord to paralyse his victim, leaving only the mind working.

When he lifted her over his shoulder, there was no resistance, and when he dumped her in the boot of her car, he took her keys out of her pocket and slammed the lid closed on her agonised face. He then slid into the driver's seat and started the engine. He had the whole night to spend with her. Uninterrupted.

When the woman's mobile rang suddenly on the passenger seat, he threw it out of the window and drove on.

1

Maida Vale,
London

Thomas de Souza is a man to be reckoned with. An investment banker with a reputation assiduously built up over seventeen years. A man who lived well and had the apartment and car to prove it. A man made more handsome by wealth, relaxed with women. Envied, admired, London's finest.

In the space of a week, he had lost everything.

Now, that is the public version. It tells the bare facts. but it doesn't explain how a man loses his status and survives. It doesn't describe the humiliation of being fired, having an apartment repossessed, and a wife walking out. If you passed Thomas de Souza on the street, he was still upright, looking straight ahead, defiant. But inside, a belly used to the best food rumbled with acid; a mind accustomed to clever and fluid thinking faltered against the emptied days.

No one returned his messages, nor replied to his emails. Where once people had clamoured to hire Thomas de Souza, there was only the eerie silence of indifference. And then Fate decided that she would change his career for him and turned him into a carer overnight. A massive stroke had felled his father, leaving an impressive man floundering like an octopus on a griddle, and there was only Thomas available to take care of him. Because, after all, he had the time, didn't he?

It always worked better if he fed his father with small amounts, Thomas realised. If he fed him too much at once, he would struggle to swallow, and some of the pap would escape the corners of his lips. You learn these things, he thought; you think yourself into the other person's shoes and imagine being afraid to choke. Because eating was dangerous. Or had been since Peter de Souza's stroke.

Before, his father wouldn't have thought about eating; you ate, talked, and drank; it all went down into the digestive tract and was dealt with later. Nothing to think about. Nothing to worry about. That was until you had a stroke, and the left side of you was suddenly as floppy as a landed carp. Until your speech sounded like someone hiccupping through the alphabet. The stroke had made a doily out of his father's satin eloquence, the speech therapist sitting with Peter de Souza and forcing him to make shapes with a mouth that someone had unpicked on one side.

Thomas leaned down towards his father. "Have another spoonful."

"Enough." He replied, putting up his right hand, warding off the slop.

He would be able to eat proper food before long. One day. Soon. Maybe. You get used to that too, Thomas thought, used to the medical profession handing out platitudes like Maundy money. He paused, looking at his parent, his responsibility. It was no good wondering how he got here. He *was* here. Carefully he wiped the sides of Peter de Souza's mouth and left the sitting room. It had been his parents' home until his mother had gone. Not died, nothing so respectable, but run off with another man. It had never occurred to Thomas that his mother might leave, even though his father had been nearly seventy, and she, although fifty-five, looked a decade younger.

His own marriage had failed, but that was inevitable as he was a ruined man, an embarrassment to any ambitious professional woman. But Thomas hadn't expected his mother to follow suit in such a splashy, brutal fashion. To admit to adultery with a friend of the family, then to accuse Peter de Souza of being *too old* had been savage, and not something he could change. Instead, she had wielded his age like an axe to their marriage. Of course, it nearly killed him.

But that had been a month ago, and he was rallying. Peter de Souza might recover with constant, round-the-clock professional care, which was excruciatingly expensive, and the amateur nursing provided by his newly available son. Care that stripped bank accounts and beggared people. Care that gobbled into pensions and ate at Thomas's final pay cheque. A cheque that had been intended to provide for him until he had decided what to do next. A six-month ballast which had already damn near gone.

Unfortunately, Peter de Souza had loved his adulterous wife and willingly agreed to put the home and money in her name because she was so much younger. He had wanted to make sure she would be provided for. She didn't feel the same way, and when Peter needed help, she stepped back and Thomas was drafted in.

His life was hijacked. From power to powerless. From prestige to penury. Thomas told himself that when his father recovered, he would start again. He was ambitious and determined, clever and tenacious. He could do it; of course he could. But he couldn't do it *yet*. At present, he was manacled.

Until someone unpicked the lock.

2

Heathrow Airport
20th November

He had to admit that she had been a disappointment to him. What was the use of going to all that trouble and planning when the bitch died on you? Preoccupied, Sam Purchass emptied the bins in the airport departure lounge, thinking back to the previous evening. It had seemed so promising that he got an erection at the thought of it, and struggled to control himself, staring out of the window at the whalelike body of a plane bound for Moscow.

The sexual excitement finally fading, he gripped the handle of the trolley he was pushing and moved into the main reception area of the airport, making for the staff toilets. Sitting down in a cubicle, he stared at his hands. At the fingernails he had ripped against the hoarding, the fingernails he had tried to file back into order.

He had really thought it was going his way after the taxi didn't stop and left his victim stranded. Vulnerable. That had been the best moment of the whole night, sheer pleasure. He drummed his fists lightly on his knees, then rubbed his fingers and thumbs together as though relishing the feel of her skin again.

What he hadn't counted on was the suffocation. That by cutting her spinal cord and paralysing her, he had also depressed her breathing. The noises should have given it away, but he had been so preoccupied with touching her that he had ignored the wheezing and rasping gasps. Without looking at her face, he had undressed her and was just clambering on top when he realised she had wet herself. Revolted, he had slapped her. Once. Hard. But she hadn't reacted. Just stared at him with glass eyes, bead eyes.

Well, it was over then, wasn't it? He couldn't fuck a corpse. What kind of man did that? He wasn't a pervert. Not him. Angered, he had pushed the dead woman off the kitchen table. She landed heavily on the floor, one arm twisted under her, her head to the right. Dead fish eyes staring. It was no longer sexual. Smelling of piss, lying at an odd angle that had made her look ugly. It wasn't attractive or sad. Just ridiculous.

That wasn't how it was supposed to be. He had dreamed of it, planned it, rehearsed it in his head for eighteen months. All that practise with the animals, all those myriad little tortures refining his technique. Wasted. All wasted because she had died on him. Cheated him. He wouldn't make the same mistake next time. Next time, he would make sure she stayed alive for a few days, anyway.

After the killing, he hadn't slept much and, in the early hours of the morning, had woken and gone downstairs. The blood had been settling in the girl's body, making her belly discoloured and underarms purple. Repelled, he had rolled her up in a soiled rug and staggered out to the car. No one saw him. The farmhouse was set back, more than a hundred yards from a disused lane, trees surrounding it, not even a sign to say that it was there. Which was just the way he liked it. It was the way the whole family had liked it, until, one by one, they had died off.

He had been a baby born to late middle-aged parents; his elder brother seventeen years older than him. It was inevitable they would die before he did, but that didn't make it right. To leave him, the baby of the family, on his own. He got lonely in a house that had once been busy. Even though there had only ever been the family. No friends, no other relatives.

People had never mixed with the Purchasses. There had been too many rumours about the wretched farmhouse, now presumed abandoned. As for Declan Purchass, the old man had come over from Ireland and worked the docks, earning extra as a bare-knuckle fighter until someone landed a punch that scrambled his brains. That was the story he told away. So, he would mutter as he paced around the ruined outbuildings, shadowboxing bales of hay that had mildewed from being left too long in the wet. And he would half starve the animals, so they were short on fat and muscle, tough to eat after he'd killed them.

It never bothered him killing things. It was once said he had killed a goat by punching it on the side of the head; he damn near killed his wife the same way. Only the old woman fought back and cut him with the bread knife instead. It made Declan Purchass laugh, that did, saying the only person on earth who'd scared him had tits.

Memories of his dead family kept coming back to him. Purchass remembered a sister from a long time ago, but she had run off with some man. He hardly ever thought about her anymore and had burned all her clothes in the garden. He couldn't even remember her name.

Surprised that he had been thinking so much of the past, Purchass forced himself to relive the murder instead, remembering how he had left the farmhouse carrying a rolled-up rug with a body in it. Opening the car boot, he had dropped the corpse in, thrown the handbag on top of her, then slammed the lid closed. For a while, he had leaned against a nearby tree and stared at the car, his head on one side. Then, he glanced across the yard. There were six other cars lined up, all in various stages of decay, one sporting a buddleia grown through its broken windscreen. He could, he mused, leave the car there to rust with the others. Whilst she rotted in the boot. And then he wondered how long it would take for her to decompose – he could check it out on Google - and if the confines of the boot would hold in the smell.

But then again, what if someone found the car? It was unlikely, as no one ever came to the farmhouse, but he couldn't be too certain. No, he decided, he would dump the car somewhere no one would find it. Somewhere she could disappear like his sister. Gone. Forgotten.

It had all been a lot of fucking work, he thought sullenly. Next time, it would have to be worth it.

3

St Martins Lane,
London.

Simon Porter glanced at the messages in front of him, listing them in order of preference. Who could be stalled, who needed reassurance, and who could not be ignored. As the English literary agent for the Famosa family, he was established, in his fifties, with a wife and two sons and a client list consisting of several luminaries propping up lesser talents. A dull man with skin the colour of cigarette ash and lips dry enough to strike a match on, he had a quick mind, slow digestion, and knew the symptoms of every disease, serious or trivial. As another man might become fixated with golf or sailing, Simon Porter was committed to his hypochondria.

Next to his office was a private bathroom with a capacious cabinet, readied for every illness. Throat lozenges, inhalers and camphor staved off colds, Simon's pet doctor, Ted Beckworth, called in to administer antibiotics when the phlegm landed. Bandages stood in serried rows waiting for a twisted ankle; stomach medication was on call for constipation or diarrhoea; or heartburn and numerous rubbing lotions for tennis elbow, stiff knees, or a ricked back. Clever and financially astute, Simon Porter could also be unexpectedly impulsive, leaving his wife and family for another woman. The other woman being the wife of Peter de Souza, and the mother of Thomas.

"I glad you got my message," Simon began, his voice prologued by a quick, uncertain cough. "I wondered if you'd return my call."

"I nearly didn't," Thomas replied, curtly. "Is it over?"

Puzzlement.

"Is *what* over?"

"Are you still sleeping with my mother?"

Intake of breath. "We're living together -"

"Almost respectable."

"Look, I understand that this is difficult for you." Simon blustered, "I'm sorry about what happened. We fell in love."

"Oh, for God's sake."

"I'm not" a hurried search for the right word *"excusing* what I did."

"What you **both** did." Thomas replied coldly, "I've had no call from my mother, but then I didn't expect it. You know she's never visited my father since his stroke?"

"She's been very worried about him -"

Thomas cut him off. "How old are you?"

"What? Fifty-three."

"I thought you were older."

The words upturned what was left of Simon's confidence. "Why d'you want to know my age?"

"To warn you. To prepare you for when you *do* get older. Because your turn will come. My mother left her first husband to be with my father." There was silence on the other end of the line as Thomas continued, "I see you didn't know about that. Watch your back, Porter, because she'll do the same to you."

There was a quick intake of breath. "She loves me -"

"She loves herself more than her husband or her family. But then you have that in common, don't you? I mean, you've dumped your wife and sons. I doubt it will be worth it."

Severing the connection, Simon looked up to see a tall woman walk into his office. Her expression was affectionate as she moved over to him and kissed his cheek, her lips surprisingly warm.

"Who were you talking to?"

"A client."

Anna de Souza had always listened at doors. As a child, she had been scolded for it, but the habit had stuck. Her light footedness had ensured that she was privy to many whispered conversations, and her natural suspicion filled in the blanks. She employed an armoury of skills to seduce, adept at mimicking feelings she didn't have and pretending to favour the needs of others whilst always putting her own first.

"You were talking to Thomas, weren't you?" she asked, lightly reproving, but incensed.

"I thought I should talk to him, yes."

"About what?"

"You know what, Anna."

"He's an adult," she replied, irritated to be reminded of her son's disapproval. "Thomas will come round. It's been over six months now. He wants me to be happy."

Did she really believe that? Simon wondered, taken aback. Didn't she realise that whilst her son was left to care for his father, he might grow to despise her? Was she *that* unfeeling? She couldn't be, he told himself. He couldn't have left his family for a woman like that. *Could he?*

"Don't worry, I know Thomas. He'll come round." She reached out and touched Simon's forehead, taking off his glasses and leaning towards him, "You feel warm, darling."

"I *am* a little feverish," he replied, quick to assume a temperature he didn't have. "Perhaps I'm coming down with something."

"Just relax, darling," she crooned, "let me get you a drink. You've been overworking."

As she said the words, Simon's gaze moved across the desk to where a photograph of his family had once stood. He had moved it, sliding the people he loved into the darkness of a filing cabinet. Twenty-four hours later, a new photograph had arrived.

Of Anna de Souza, glamorous, fascinating, and predatory.

4

New York

Irritated, he challenged her. “Why d’you do it?” Jimmy Famosa asked her, his sister lying back on the sofa. She was suntanned from a late holiday, her eyes coldly blue, with flecks of gold near the pupil. Rich girl eyes.

“I wanted a change.”

“She’s been worried about you.”

A shrug, shoulders barely lifted. “Our mother’s always worried about something.”

“So why add to it?” he retorted, “The auction’s important.”

“Some dead painter whose prints sell online for dollars?”

“An original Klimt is worth a fortune.”

“Yeah, but the one we’re selling is tiny.”

“Size isn’t important. It’s one of Klimt’s first studies for Salome; that’s why it matters. It’s going to break records -”

“Yeah, yeah, I know,” Kara said wearily, “There’s always some picture or statue worth a fortune. An incredible ‘find’.” She raised her eyebrows. “How come he never misses? Some might think that our father's success rate is a little *too* high."

"Meaning?"

"You know what I mean. Luis must have a crew searching worldwide for lost masterpieces in attics." She smiled archly, "It's almost like he could magic them up."

Jimmy sat down, sighing. "Ok, what is it?"

"Huh?"

"You've been dropping hints for a while now. We have enough people willing to believe rumours without one of our own adding to them."

"*One of our own*?" She parroted, "Am I 'one of our own' Jimmy? One of the famous Famosa clan? The spoilt daughter? Is that the role I've been allotted?"

"It certainly fits."

Swinging her legs over the back of the sofa, she let her head hang down over the cushions, her hair pooling on the floor. "And you, Jimmy? If I'm the spoilt daughter, who are you? The Famosa money man? Or our mother's babysitter?"

"I support the business and the family."

"She's our *mother,* for God's Sake! She's not a child." Kara replied tartly, "I hope she pays you enough to keep you tied to her apron strings."

Irritated, Jimmy went into the kitchen to make coffee, noticing that he had several messages on his phone. It would be their mother calling. The fifth call in half an hour. Nerves were unsettling Halle, Kara had picked the perfect time to disappear, just before Halle hosted the auction singlehanded whilst Luis remained in Bruges.

He was sorry that he wouldn't be there to support her, he had texted the previous night, but he knew she would be wonderful. And besides, their son would help… Jimmy made all the right noises but knew that his father's absence was deliberate, a way to unsettle his wife. What Luis *didn't* know, was that Jimmy was relieved to have a respite from his father's intimidation and a chance to gain power in the business.

Which was why Jimmy was uneasy about his sister. Kara had never expressed interest in the Famosa fortune. Instead, she had enjoyed the lifestyle and made sure not to provoke Luis, because he once had a mistress who had overstepped the mark. The woman had become greedy and threatened to tell Halle about the affair, but her defiance was soon tempered by Luis's lawyers. Jimmy had seen how the incident had jeopardised the Famosa name and wasn't going to allow Kara to cause her own schism.

Suspecting that his sister had been drinking, Jimmy made the coffee strong. Kara didn't drink like their mother once had. She only drank socially, whereas Halle had teetered on the brink of alcoholism, drying out years earlier. The threat of losing her looks and her husband had secured her sobriety, her mental instability too uncertain to risk.

"Drink it," Jimmy said, passing Kara a mug of coffee. His swarthy features, inherited from their Cuban father confirmed his heritage. And if he was a meeker version of Luis, so what? It was an advantage for people to believe he was in his father's shadow. The money man, the cleaner-upper, without the bite.

"Where were you?"

"Mexico," Kara put her head on one side, amused. "Don't try to control me, I can go where I like."

"I just asked you to stay in touch."

"You're always running everyone's life, Jimmy! Maybe it's time you paid more attention to your own. When *was* the last time you saw your son?"

He held onto his patience. "This isn't about me. I just wanted to know where you were. Halle worries."

"And we have to make sure our mother isn't worried, don't we?"

"This auction is important to her –"

"Oh, for God's Sake!" Kara snorted. "You'll be there, the family lawyers will be there, Holt, the gallery director, plus a whole bunch of paid flunkies at her beck and call -"

"But not Luis."

She sat up, suddenly interested. *"Why?* Where is he?"

"Bruges."

"Bruges?" Kara laughed, amused, "Somehow I can't see him in Bruges."

"It's about a painting –"

"And more, I bet." She interrupted slyly. "But we don't talk about the shifty side of the Famosa fortune, do we? Because art is respectable and if Luis mixed some of his other business with a smattering of Dutch interiors, who'd suspect a thing?"

Sighing, Jimmy laid down his coffee. "I didn't know you had such knowledge of business," he said quietly, "When did this sudden interest come about?"

"I thought it was about time I learned more about the Famosa fortune," she said defiantly, "In *all* areas."

"You should be careful what you say, Kara. A lot of people won't realise you're joking. Your lifestyle is only possible because of the business."

She pretended to be afraid. "I'll keep quiet, I promise! I didn't hear or see anything. I promise I'll be good."

Unsmiling, Jimmy stared at his sister. Her attitude had shifted over the last eighteen months. She had become distant, she was argumentative with him and avoiding their mother. Where once they had been inseparable, they were now remote: two beautiful bookends flanking the Famosa name.

"I don't know what the problem is" Kara continued sullenly, "I *did* call you."

"*Five days ago!*" He snapped, "For five days we heard nothing. Anything could have happened to you."

"But nothing did!"

"*This* time."

His tolerance was exhausted, and Kara's defiance irked him. As the obedient, indulged sister, she was manageable; as a mouthy, indiscreet loose cannon, she was out of control.

"Do you ever wonder *why* I go off?" she asked, "because of you! The indispensable, loyal Jimmy, who would do anything for the Famosas. Luis in particular. You even sacrificed your own family for the business."

"Don't you ever know when to shut up?"

"Don't you ever know when to butt out of my life?" She retorted, "Why should I have to report to you?"

"But that's the point, you hardly ever *do*."

"Fuck off, Jimmy! I don't need this crap, I'm leaving."

"You're not going anywhere unless you pay for the trip yourself. I'm stopping your allowance."

She was on her feet immediately. "*You can't do that*!"

"Being short of funds might keep you home."

"There are other ways of getting by," she replied, goading him. "Men like me. I wouldn't starve."

He looked at her with contempt. "If you want to act like a whore, go ahead. But from now on, you toe the line if you want your allowance. Or you could get a job, Kara. I could use some help."

"*Work in the family business?* Are you joking?"

Enraged, the siblings faced each other. Jimmy Famosa saw a reckless woman, and Kara saw a neutered version of their father.

"You should get back to your family." She said coldly. "You've been spending too much time with our mother. She'll cling to you like ivy on a brick wall."

"The business is mine, and yours. Why can't you understand that? Why don't you take pride in it?"

Incredulous, she stood up to him. "*Pride in it?* Yeah, I'm part of the Famosas, but I don't have to like it. You're in a stranglehold, Jimmy, but *I* can get out. God knows if you still can." Her voice calmed down. "It's convenient for Luis to have you locked in. Just don't let him - or our mother - manipulate you."

"Someone has to protect the future. My job is to keep our interests private."

She sighed. "Yeah, you know all the secrets, don't you?"

He nodded. "Yes. Yes, I do."

"Are you sure of that, Jimmy?" she asked. "*All* our secrets?"

"I know how to handle the money, the rumours, and the press. With *discretion*." His voice took on a harshness. "We don't want, or need, outsiders, Kara. You should remember that."

5

Hole in the Wall pub,
London
23rd November,

Despite all his planning, it had turned out to be a lousy hiding place. Who would have thought that the car would get found so quickly? The pub was decrepit, in the worst part of East London, frequented by low-rate criminals and whores. Rough as a bear's arse, his father used to say. And he would know. *The Hole in the Wall* – a dank slum inviting no strangers, a place with no CCTV inside or outside. A place even the police avoided unless they were called to a fight.

And yet, only three days after Purchass had dumped the body, his victim had been found.

It had snowed the night he left her there. Only a light covering; it was still only November after all. He abandoned the car in the darkest, remotest part of the parking lot, next to a bank of bins, a couple of other cars, and the remains of some old kitchen units. And if some of the tarts serviced their punters by the bins, so what? They wouldn't be interested in an old car. No, Purchass had thought, it was the perfect hiding place.

But then some crap driver had skidded off the road. The snow had made the road slippery, and he had lost control and plunged into the pub's car park - managing to miss every car, but the one Purchass had left there three days earlier. The driver had hit the vehicle so hard he'd bent the back wing and buckled the boot. It said in the local paper that the man had gone running into the pub hollering about a body in a trunk.

And that was it. She was found.

It was all over the *Evening Standard* by three thirty. Apparently, she had been called Ellie Chadwick, aged 25, a veterinary nurse. Funny, he'd not had her down for something like that and thought there was a kind of irony that he had practised killing her on animals first. And with the story, was a photograph of Ellie Chadwick and the line.

... appalling injuries to the body ...

Purchass thought that was an exaggeration. He'd hardly had time to do much of anything. Only some minor adjustments. He liked bright blue eyes, but hers had been light blue. So, changing the colour made sense. And injecting ink into the eyeballs should have worked, but she died on him - and despite all that rapid blinking and tears, she'd never even looked at him with her new eyes.

Pushing the cleaning trolley across the main entrance of Terminal 5, Purchass avoided staff and passengers as he headed for a staff exit, parking his trolley, and taking out some mints. He liked mints, they took away the taste of dead meat in his mouth.

He'd always suffered from bad breath, and seemed to remember that his father had too, but couldn't be sure. So, he sucked a couple of tubes of Extra Strong a day and put his hand over his mouth when he was talking to people. He tried to avoid this, but some of the passengers insisted on stopping him for directions.

Where are the toilets?
The Bureau de Change?
The departure lounge?

He had received a warning once when he had told someone to piss off. The manager said, '*Even though his work record was exemplary, he couldn't have an employee abusing a passenger. This is a warning.*'

'This is a warning.' It made him laugh to see that wax-faced little man staring up at him and warning *him.* He wouldn't dare to talk to him like that if he knew what he was capable of. Ms Ellie Chadwick. Murdered. *Even though my work record **is** exemplary.*

Still sucking on the mint, Purchass continued to read the article. The police comments were concise. Ellie Chadwick had had a boyfriend, Stuart Mills, but he had an alibi for the time of her death. Miss Chadwick had not reported being stalked or being the victim of any threats. Her colleagues at the veterinary surgery said she had been well-liked and was hoping to settle down with Stuart as she had no family of her own.

Then followed the official police statement:

The person or person responsible for this murder will be caught. Anyone with any information, please contact the police on 0800 903 3827 X7778.

The article concluded with a quote from one of the police officers who had been at the scene:

> *'One of the worst cases I've come across in seventeen years on the force. To be honest, it looked like the work of a lunatic.'*

A *lunatic*. Purchass paused, considering the word. Well, maybe so. His father had been odd, and his brother, Sean, had left school at fifteen, apparently slow-witted, aggressive, and impossible to teach. As for his sister – all Purchass could remember about her was that she had been vicious. Her features had faded from his memory, but he could remember her voice, deep pitched, almost guttural in the vowels. And her eyes, blue eyes like the scales of a fresh fish.

A thrill slid through him, confident that the police would never catch him. He had made sure he had no connection to his victim and had left no fingerprints, DNA, or fibres. For the previous two years, he had been in preparation, devouring the details of famous murders and committing to memory why the killers had been caught. He had also read volumes of true crime and watched every programme on Forensics. It had been worth paying for Sky just for that.

Purchass could remember details easily. He might look unprepossessing, tall, stooping to disguise his height, but he wasn't the stupid one in the family, which was why he had been careful, using black bin liners on the kitchen table and floor, sterilising the knives afterwards and putting them back in the block. Later, he had even cut some cheese with the same blade which had severed Ellie Chadwick's spinal cord. Then, after dumping her body in the boot, he had thrown the old, pissed-on rug onto a landfill site. The last act had been the wiping down of the car. Every handle, every surface, inside and out, voiding it of clues. The police might have found the car and the body, but they wouldn't find the killer. He was just starting.

Lanky little turd.

His sister used to call him, her eyes fixed, her voice hoarse with spite.

Fucking weird spider.

And she had spread her arms and legs out like an insect, her head jutting forward, rushing towards him, spitting.

People hate spiders, they crush them.

He wondered what she would make of him now, what his whole family would think of him. No more being bullied. No more taunting for being the ugly baby of the family. The baby had grown up and took what he wanted. And what he wanted was a new victim. He had an abundance of choice and could have any one of the plentiful passengers coming in and out of Heathrow every day. A woman with no connection to Stan Purchass. A woman picked at random, like Ellie Chadwick.

He could kill quite a few ordinary women, and no one would care that much.

Purchass's attention drifted, his gaze moving over to the British Airways arrivals, a young woman coming into view off the New York flight. Confident, tanned, wearing some kind of fake fur coat, long boots, her hair loose over her shoulders. Fascinated, he watched her as she passed him. And when she glanced fleetingly in his direction, he could see that her eyes were piercingly blue.

6

Famosa Gallery
New York

Jimmy Famosa watched the trio of attendants in their uniform brown overalls moving around the chairs. Spindly little gilded chairs set in rows like a cornfield under the overhead lights. They were facing the raised dias, the Famosa gallery having announced that they were going to hold an auction for their newly discovered Gustav Klimt painting. An auction so important that it had attracted attention from Europe to the Middle East. The image was new to the market - only previously known from sketches and a 1909 photograph - and had been the starting point for the infamous *Salome.*

The picture was smaller in scale than the fully realised *Salome*, being only 16 x 20 inches, the glisteningly forerunner of a painting that would cement Klimt's reputation. The insurance was astronomical, but as Luis said, it was worth it to pull off such a coup. The major auction houses had hoped the sale would go through them, but Luis was emphatic that the painting would be auctioned in *his* gallery. To keep it safe, he had drafted in extra security, placing men at the main entrance and at the back exit, two on the rooftop and another pair in the alleyway beyond. And, at Jimmy's suggestion, others monitored the sewer that ran below the gallery. Thieves and rats, he pointed out, didn't mind dabbling in shit.

Cameras and audio equipment were monitored consistently because Luis Famosa wanted every word and gesture recorded. An auction that had excited collectors and agents from around the globe was only a triumph if it succeeded, Luis revelling in the dealers' obsequiousness towards a man they regarded as a truculent Cuban.

He could remember their distaste for him when he had begun collecting; their barely concealed amusement at the arrival of a man known more for running Las Vegas hotels and casinos than for his ability to spot masterworks, or discover 'sleepers,' the unexpected finds that peppered the art market. How many times had he been lucky? They asked amongst themselves, Luis uncovering a Frido Karlo and a Raoul Dufy as easily as a pig finds truffles in a shady wood.

Early on, Luis had realised that art was a quick way to enter high society. A man who could wear a tuxedo and knew the difference between Correggio and Caravaggio inspired admiration. But Luis wasn't just lucky; he had instinct and had spent many years researching. Uncharacteristically fanciful, he drew similarities between the artists' buccaneering lives and his own, understanding that the value of great art never wavered. Besides, it was respectable, and the gallery was as untouchable as a shrine.

Despite his success, or perhaps because of it, the art grandees saw Luis Famosa as a chancer, his dealings suspect. There was plenty of talk, but no evidence, no bruise of hasty or hidden deals. And besides, Luis had picked the perfect wife, the daughter of an English landed gentry, with the accent to prove it. Distance had obliterated the truth, and by the time Halle was forty years of age, her past had been interred in the verdant riches of Berkshire and South Kensington. The USA adopted her, she was elegant and accomplished, and Luis had made sure that her past never impinged on their present. No one knew the reality except him, and the knowledge kept his wife on a leash.

Arriving at the gallery, Jimmy paused, watching his mother as she listened to the manager, Ivan Holt, and the Head of Security. The latter was leaning slightly towards her, his voice lowered and Halle fiddling with the belt around her waist. Nerves never showed in her face, but in her hands, the bitten nails that no amount of manicures could disguise.

Suddenly seeing her son, Halle moved over, kissing his cheek, "Jimmy, why didn't you tell me."

"Tell you what?"

"Were you going to keep it a surprise?" she looked at him, puzzled, "*That Kara's in New York.*"

He was momentarily wrong-footed. "Have you seen her?"

"About an hour ago. Haven't you seen her?"

"Yeah, briefly," Jimmy replied, nodding to the Head of Security, who was hovering with a clipboard in his hands. "So, she's staying in New York for the auction?"

"Of course she is!" Halle's voice wavered. "You've been arguing, haven't you?"

"We had words –"

"Why now? This auction is important to me," she said, her voice faltering. "I'm under pressure, and I don't need any more problems. It would be easier if Luis was here."

"But he isn't, and *I* am," Jimmy replied steadily, stemming the approaching panic. "The gallery's ready, the press are coming, the security is better than the White House, and no one's cried off."

"*Everyone we invited is coming*?" She was nervous, a childlike tone creeping into the English vowels, "All of them?"

"All of them," he confirmed, "It's your triumph, Halle, not theirs. You've organised this spectacle –"

"With you."

"With me *behind* you, but you're the star. I keep the show running, but people are coming to see *you.* The papers will be full of it, and the internet."

"But Luis isn't here."

"That's his fucking loss," Jimmy said shortly, "But don't make it yours. Come on, Halle, you don't need him. Perhaps it's time to let my father see that."

He watched her waver between excitement and terror. "I don't want to give a speech –"

"Yeah, you do," he contradicted her, "We've rehearsed it, and we'll rehearse it again. You sound good and you look amazing."

She rallied. "You think the dress works?"

"I think it's as stunning as you are," Jimmy replied, "They'll all admire you. So let them."

"I need a drink."

The words were uttered before she had chance to check them, turning to her son and smiling, *"Jesus, you should see your face!"* She said, laughing like a child. "I was teasing you, Jimmy! You know I don't drink anymore."

His face had paled. "You gave me a fright –"

"You don't trust me?"

"I didn't say that."

"Don't *ever* say it," she replied, touching her son's cheek, "There's absolute trust between us, Jimmy. I love Luis and Kara, but I *trust* you."

He wondered then if he should be honest, mention Kara's threat to leave New York, but decided against it. It was, he reasoned, merely a threat. Even Kara wouldn't be bloody minded enough to ruin her mother's big occasion. Or would she? Loyalty had cost *him* enough. By putting the Famosa fortune first he had demoted his own family, then Eva moved out and rented an apartment in Greenwich Village, taking their son with her.

Which made Jimmy Famosa a very angry man. Angry with himself. Angry with the Famosa empire. And angry with his sister who piled on the pressure relentlessly. So, at seven thirty that night, after leaving numerous texts asking Kara to get in touch, he went to his flat and re-read the plans for the auction. He read them slowly, made a couple of calls and checked that all the references for the catering staff had been cleared. At eleven thirty he stretched out on the sofa and turned off the light. Kara hadn't texted him and for once, he was relieved.

It was a feeling he would come to regret.

-o0o-

Heathrow Airport

Collecting her luggage at Arrivals, Kara Famosa made her way through Customs. The process dragged on wearily, her stomach rumbling by the time she made her way out of the airport and headed towards the taxis outside. She knew that a quick call to Jimmy would ease his mind, but she was still smarting after their argument. What her brother didn't realise was that a quick call to their mother would always ensure a money transfer should she need it. But this time, Kara wasn't going to need any funds; this time, she was going to give her brother a run for *his* money.

Kara liked London. She always had done, ever since the family had visited when she was a child. Jimmy was only a kid then, and Luis Famosa, stocky, eyes like a cannibal, charismatic, ruthless. In the sixties, Luis had come over from Cuba with his mother and an ambition, and damn near nothing else. But his persistence had paid off. At first, he thought he could make it as a singer, but that didn't last, and Luis turned to managing others. He could thrive on five hours sleep, the rest of the time hustling around Las Vegas, pressing the flesh, and doing deals to get his clients into the lounges, which paid well and publicised the acts. Then he realised that there were other businesses from which he could profit.

So, he changed tack and began managing hotels and casinos, taking care of big names that came to Vegas to party. He made friends with the hotel managers, tipped the pit bulls in the casinos, and sent customs to the call girls. He knew that, in return, they would steer their clients to him when they wanted to shop, rent an apartment, or find some art for their houses. Because

Luis Famosa had a style. He wasn't handsome, but he understood beauty, and knew that art made anyone – even a crook – respectable. Instinct drove him to buy fabrics from Italy and Iran, silver from England, and Dutch still-life paintings. He could visit a saleroom pre-auction and hone in on the dusty picture in a bad frame that needed cleaning, and it would always turn out to be a winner.

He worked Las Vegas by being smart and never encroached on anyone else's turf, or antagonising members of organised crime, gliding between the police and the criminals untouched. People liked Luis Famosa, and if he had planted a rumour about some suspicious activity in Cuba, it served him well. You didn't know with Luis, people said. It might be talk, but…

And then along came Halle Cox. She was breaking free of an upper-class English family and working part-time as a model, smoking too much weed, teetering on high heels, her long pale legs crossing the marble foyer of the casino, her dark blonde hair straight to her shoulders. God, she was beautiful, not too bright, but when she spoke, Luis heard the angels talking and was smitten. She smoked too much, drank way too much, trusted people too quickly, and Luis could have predicted her future within two days of knowing her.

Halle had left home on impulse, then realising that she had no friends abroad, found herself dithering like a sinner before a cathedral. It was the perfect day for Luis to make his approach. He became the friend she needed and never made a pass at her. Other men watched her and offered her jobs that Luis warned her not to take, just like he visited a few photographers and ordered them not to give her booze or weed, marking their card and saying – without saying it – that the pale English girl was his. Hands off. It was only a matter of weeks before Halle started to confide. Soon she was telling him about her family and how she hated modelling and really should have stayed home and got married. She would get agitated then, drumming her fingers on her knees, thick hair falling over her face.

"I don't belong here. I should go home. I can't go home, though; my parents would be so angry that I ran off." She had a joint in her hand, Luis taking it out of her fingers, having a drag, and then stubbing it out with his shoe.

"Hey. Don't do that!"

"It's bad for you. it gets you confused, Halle. Ease it back, no one thinks straight when they're taking too much of that stuff."

"But I *like* not thinking straight."

"You could get in trouble that way."

"What kind of trouble, Luis?" She asked, her pupils unfocused.

"Big trouble," he replied, "And you drink too much. That's dangerous."

She had laughed, chin tipped up at the white sky. "*Dangerous*! Why would I be in danger?"

"You never will be," he replied, then added, "if you marry me."

They married three months later. And despite their unlikely pairing, the marriage lasted. First, Jimmy was born, then Kara five years later. With enough money to tote the kids around the globe with them, a decade passed. Luis was at the top of his game, with a portfolio of properties, the Vegas casino, a country house in France, and a gallery in New York. Under the gilded umbrella of the art world, the whispers of criminality persisted but they were never proven, although an accusation of dealing in forgeries resulted in one of Luis's advisors being jailed in Rome.

As for Halle, she lost the gawkiness and learned to appreciate clever tailoring, the Valentino magic that turned a pretty woman into a beauty. Devoted to Luis and aware that her lifestyle was reimbursement for her elegance, they prospered, and by the time Jimmy was born, Halle had been weaned off the marijuana and the drinking. Her giddiness was only in private. In public, she was composed and intriguing, and as the Famosa family increased, the world smiled on them.

Another decade went by, and Luis trained his son for the future. Jimmy took to the role like a hand-me-down suit.

"You have a good brain, so use it. One day, you'll take over from me, and I'm no idiot, so listen to what I'm telling you. I learnt the hard way how to run the business and how to keep the fucking sharks at arm's length. It comes down to family; that's the bottom line. You always protect your own."

The memories stopped suddenly, like a spoke in a wheel, Kara pausing in the airport foyer. Although she had been heading for the taxi queue, she changed direction and bought a coffee instead. Thinking of Luis had made her uneasy. How would *he* react to her behaviour? Running away from New York seemed suddenly puerile. She didn't have a *reason* to run away. Well, she did have a few reasons, but were they enough? Was she really going to go through with what she had planned? *Could she?* Was it justified? Some would say yes and cheer her on; others would despise her for it. If she went ahead, there was no turning back, no begging for a forgiveness that her family would never offer.

Uncertain, Kara sipped her coffee, then reached for her cell and wrote a text to her brother.

COMING BACK HOME TOMORROW.

SORRY I'VE BEEN A BITCH.

LOVE YOU AND MOM.

She was just about to press send, but in that instant, someone bumped into her, knocking the phone out of her hand.

7

Famosa Gallery
New York

He moved down the backstairs of the main gallery, skirting the alleyway and the three guards standing there. Without even acknowledging them, Jimmy hurried up the fire escape, slamming his left palm against a barred window on the first floor. Jumping to attention, the Chief Security Officer walked over as Jimmy beckoned for him to come out onto the fire escape to talk.

"Where is it?"

The man looked at Jimmy, baffled. "What d'you mean?"

"The painting's not in the fucking vault," Jimmy said coldly, pushing the man to one side and walking past him down the fire escape knowing he would follow. When they reached the bottom, Jimmy turned. "You told me you had this place covered. So why are there only two men outside the vault? There were four here this morning."

"They've changed shifts. The new men have just come on. The others have been here since first thing.

I've checked them out myself and approved the new arrivals -"

"I want to speak to them," Jimmy cut him off, "in my office *now*."

He didn't wait for the man to answer, moving back inside and descending the inner private staircase, then taking another set of steps down into the vault.

As he walked in, the guards were jolted into action. "Can I help you, sir?"

"*You*," he pointed to the man, "and you," he said to his companion, "where were you last night?"

"On duty," the older man replied. "We were relieved around two in the morning, and we've just returned for the night session."

The Chief Security Officer and his Assistant had materialised at the doorway, watching the exchange. "Is there a problem, Mr Famosa?"

"Should there be?"

"You seem worried --"

"Where's the painting?"

The men glanced at each other dumbfounded, Jimmy brushing past them, unlocking the vault door, then moving towards the safe. There, he paused and looked at the guards, addressing the older man.

"What's the combination?"

The man shuffled his feet. "I don't know! I've never known. How would I know?"

Jimmy looked at the other guard, "What's the combination?"

He shrugged, blank-faced, "I've never had it."

"Well, somebody had it," Jimmy replied. "Turn round."

They did as they were told as Jimmy entered the combination of the safe and pulled open the steel door. Then, he gestured for the two Security officials to approach, the Chief anxious as Jimmy pointed into the safe.

"Do you see the painting?" He didn't give them time to answer, moving closer and staring into the empty safe, "I don't see it. I *did* see it last night, but it's not there now, is it?"

The older guard spoke up, "It was here last night --"

"Yes, I know that," Jimmy's voice was cold. "But now it's not here. And now I want to know who's been down here since you last saw *that* picture in *that* safe!"

The guy stammered, blustering on, "I saw it with you last night, sir! Just after eleven." He ran his tongue over his bottom lip. "After that no one else saw it, because you locked up, sir, and no one else has a key to the vault or access to the safe."

Jimmy paused; his fists clenched. "You swear that no one came in here last night after I checked?"

"No one," he replied, glancing at the other guard who nodded in agreement. "We both saw it, sir. The painting was there."

"I know, that's what I keep saying," Jimmy replied, his voice chilling as he glanced up to the camera in the corner. "So now I want to see the fucking tape from last night. I want to see it *now,* because someone came in here and took that painting and I want to know **who**, and how they got past security."

With the Chief Security guard and his assistant following, Jimmy went back into the main office, pointing to the surveillance cameras. "Show me last night's tape. I want to see it from 11:00pm."

His hands shaking, the man set it up. They watched Jimmy enter with the Chief, Jimmy unlocking the safe whilst the Security Guard was turned away. Then they both looked at the small Klimt painting. After that the tape continued to run, the Chief departing and Jimmy locking the safe again before leaving and heading up the stairs with the night guards following.

In silence, the men continued to watch, the cameras recording the empty chamber in front of the vault. Nobody entered or left. The cameras ran on, they could see the time recorded underneath. Two hours, three hours, six hours. Finally, at 5:45am, there was movement, little more than a shadow, Jimmy leaning forward to try and decipher what he was seeing.

And in that precious second, the camera faulted and stopped recording.

8

St Martin's Lane, London
25th November

Setting the alarm, Simon Porter locked up the agency for the evening and walked towards the car waiting for him by the curb. Anna was in the driving seat, waving a newspaper at him as he got in.

"Have you seen this?" She said, jabbing her index finger on the front page. "Halle Famosa's daughter is missing."

"So that's why she was calling me." Simon replied, "When I tried to get back to her this afternoon, the line was busy."

Taking the newspaper from Anna, he began reading as she pulled out into the traffic. He had been the Famosas' agent for over twenty years, organising the publication of exhibition catalogues and books Halle had written about the family's art collection. She didn't have Luis's connoisseurship, but her style ensured press coverage, and the sumptuous volumes were prized. Always keen to hire the best, Luis was willing to expend the same largesse on an image of Matisse as he was on a stylised photograph of his wife. But to Simon Porter's chagrin, the longed-for biography had not materialised. For a decade, Halle and Simon had talked about it, but it was always next year, and then Halle would stall and say she would talk to Luis about it, and the matter would be dropped.

Ever the astute businessman, Simon knew that a book about the famous and private Famosa family was worth pursuing - just as he came to realise that Halle would not be the one to write it.

"*Kara Famosa was coming to London,*" Simon read the article out loud, "No, hang on, it says that she *arrived* here. The police have tracked her on the airport security cameras."

Anna raised her eyebrows, "*And?*"

"They caught sight of her sitting down and having a coffee."

"*And?*"

He held up the paper and squinted, trying to read it. "Then she disappeared."

"How could she?" Anna replied, stopping at the traffic lights and turning to him. "If they could see her on the cameras, how could she just disappear?"

"It says that there was one area off limits. *A blind spot.*"

"So what's the bloody use of having cameras if there's a blind spot?"

"Apparently, it was just one camera that wasn't working." He tapped the back of her hand to get her attention. "Anna, the lights have changed."

Shifting gears, she drove on, continuing to talk. "Kara's always pulling some stunt. You told me how she's always going off somewhere. I doubt she's disappeared. She probably met some guy in the airport bar and went home with him instead."

Simon could feel the beginnings of a sore throat, his voice wary. "It's all over the papers. When Kara sees the drama she's caused, she'll get in touch."

"Who reads papers when they've got something more exciting to do?" Anna mocked him, "I bet they're in some flat now, with the curtains drawn and phones turned off."

Pulling up outside the house, Simon got out of the car; Anna parked and followed him inside. When she reached the study, he was already on the phone.

"... Yes, I just saw the paper just now ... Tell your mother that I rang, will you? I'll catch her later. And tell Halle not to worry too much." Simon paused, listening to the reply, "Well, you know your sister, Kara's always been a bit irresponsible; I'm sure she'll turn up. She always does." He glanced over to Anna, deadpan. "You know, I hate to say it, but everyone's been so preoccupied with the auction she probably did it to get attention." Anna could hear an indistinct reply coming over the phone line. "I've known Kara since she was a child, but she can play you up - I don't have to tell you that." Again, he listened, then finally Simon said goodbye and put down the phone. "That was Jimmy Famosa."

"I guessed."

"He said that he and Kara had a fight, and she'd stormed off forty-eight hours ago. He notified the police in London and the USA, but there's been no sighting of Kara since the one at Heathrow. She *definitely* didn't catch a flight home. No record of her going to another country either."

"I told you," Anna replied phlegmatically, "she's with a man."

"Would she be *that* thoughtless with the auction coming up? She's knows the press will be there –"

"That's exactly why she'd do it," Anna replied, "Halle is jealous of Kara, Kara is jealous of her mother. Come on, it's just a family argument, no more. I'd leave the girl to sort herself out."

Simon had moved into the bathroom, rattling about in the medicine cabinet. A moment later, he returned, sucking a throat lozenge. "You really think it would be a good idea to let her get on with it? She mixes with people her parents wouldn't approve of."

"*Approve of*?" Anna laughed, "How old-fashioned of you, darling. Kara is in her twenties, all grown up."

"She stays with Hugh Ackerman when she's in London."

Anna winced, but kept smiling, *"Hugh Ackermann*?"

"Yes," Simon nodded, "Ackerman was besotted with Halle. It was when she was first married to Luis. He wanted her to leave him."

"How d'you know all this?"

"I've known Halle a long time."

"Have *you* ever been besotted by her?"

Simon sensed the jealousy in the question and ducked it. "No, Halle's rather unstable. Never really grown up."

Placated, Anna continued, "You think Ackerman's taking revenge by sleeping with Kara?"

"I didn't say that," he replied, then thought for a moment. "Maybe there's more to it. I heard a whisper that Kara's writing a book about her family and hopes to get it made into a film."

Anna lit up like a streetlamp. "That would make a lot of money."

"Let's just hope it's an affectionate portrait."

"Better if it was a hatchet job." Anna responded deftly, "What if she brings up Halle's addictions? And all those rumours about Luis and the forgery sideline?" Her eyes were bright with malice, "And then there's Jimmy to think about. He's devoted to Luis, but his sights must be set on inheriting the Famosa throne. He won't like the Famosa secrets being aired publicly, and he certainly won't like anyone mentioning Halle's drug problem--"

Simon flinched. *"I should never have told you that!* It was years ago. Halle doesn't even drink now." He paused, rubbing the side of his nose with his index finger. "Of course, if it *did* turn out to be an expose, who would *really* be writing it? Kara? Or Hugh Ackerman?" He crunched the lozenge on his back teeth thoughtfully, "Let's hope Kara will come home for the auction and forget the whole idea of a tell-all book."

"And if not?"

Folding his dry hands together, he stared at his mistress. "If Kara doesn't return, we'll have to consider something altogether more worrying."

Anna frowned, "Like what?"

"Like, how far would someone go to stop this book from ever seeing the light of day?"

9

Maida Vale
London

For the third night in succession, Thomas de Souza wasn't sleeping; he was worrying about money instead and wondered how he could pay for his father's medical bills because he didn't have insurance. Had never thought it was necessary, he had never needed it before and had been a stranger to illness or accident. Until his wife left him for a friend and a stroke felled him.

Once, money had been easy for Thomas. He attracted it and made investments others missed. If his rise had not been so meteoric, his fall might not have been so dramatic. But the Midas touch appeared to desert him overnight when he became the scapegoat for a colleague's ineptitude. Yet revenge was no longer Thomas's first concern, a lack of money was. His Patek Philippe watch, Dunhill briefcase, Tommy Nutter suits and seven pairs of Italian handmade shoes had all been sold, at a loss. His credit card was maxed out, his overdraft at the bank close to the limit ,and the only thing left to sell was his car.

Thomas rolled over in bed, eyes open in the darkness. Foolishly, Peter de Souza had trusted his wife, and of course Anna had made sure that the impressive house was in her name. The jewellery was hers, the best furniture she had appropriated, and what remained were just the leftovers. Even keeping the professional nursing to a minimum, Thomas was desperately short of funds.

The phone rang next to him, and he answered before it could wake his father across the hall. "Hello?"

"It's Simon. Simon Porter." No response. "Did I wake you?"

"Were you trying to?"

"I couldn't sleep," Simon replied, hurrying on, "Have you seen the papers today?"

"No."

"So, you don't know that Kara Famosa's missing?"

Jolted, Thomas got out of bed. Years earlier he had dated Kara, back when she was very young, without any of the hard edges that came later. Smitten, Thomas had asked her to stay with him in England, and she had agreed. He was passionate about her, she was in love with him, and luckily, Halle had taken to Thomas from the start. She liked his ambition and the fact that he stood up to Kara. But Jimmy was not so easily won over. He saw in Thomas a threat. Attractive and urbane, de Souza highlighted his own insecurities, and Jimmy resented the speed at which he had been accepted. He warned Halle not to trust Thomas, but she teased him for being jealous. Which, of course, he was. As for Luis, he was tolerant of thc Englishman. He had gauged early on that Thomas was going places and if he wanted to take his daughter with him, they had his blessing.

And then, one protracted, wet English summer, Kara changed. She became evasive, keeping secrets, acting as all people do when they have taken a new lover or decided to leave the one they have. In the end, she crept away one night and didn't contact Thomas for a week. The love affair was over.

A while later, Thomas married, but he stayed in touch with Kara and Halle because he still loved the former and was fond of the latter. As for Luis, the Cuban seemed to keep his distance, disappointed that the relationship had floundered, but he was aware that Thomas remained in the background, visiting Halle when he came to New York. And he knew – without Halle ever having to tell him – that she wanted him back in their daughter's life.

But now it was too late. Kara Famosa was missing.

"Kara's disappeared?" Thomas repeated down the phone line, "I don't believe it."

"She was last seen in Heathrow airport forty-eight hours ago."

"She's just fooling around," Thomas replied, looking out of the window. Snow was falling on the parked cars below as he pressed his hand against the glass, "She'll turn up."

"There's something else, "Simon adopted his professional veneer, "Kara was writing a book about the family."

"Let me guess, you're her agent?"

"No!" Simon said shortly, "It's just a rumour. But *if* she's going to do an expose --"

"How could she write an expose?" Thomas asked, the glass under his hand cold. He was feeling his way through the conversation, words slippery underfoot.

"Luis is tough, but he's not a criminal, and Halle's whiter than white."

"No one's whiter than white."

"Well, you'd know all about that."

The quick jab to the gut.

"I've been wondering," Simon continued, "If there's something about Halle that no one knows e*xcept* her daughter?"

Oh, but I know, Thomas thought. The memory is clear. They had met up two years earlier, talking like familiars, and then – out of the blue - Kara had become quiet and said: "My father isn't Luis Famosa. I've only just found out."

And then, she had laughed, winking. It was a joke, the gesture said, but from then on, her relationship with Halle cooled. Weeks later, Kara turned her attention to Jimmy and the Famosa business. It was intermittent interest, but it was there.

Thomas then remembered the whispers about Luis, the rumours about his hotel and gallery, and the gossip he had always put down to malice. People envied success; they invented lies to discredit the powerful. Luis was shifting between gaudy, overheated Las Vegas and the cool cathedral calm of the Famosa gallery in New York, trying to protect both against all manner of threats. Many wanted to bring down the Famosas, Thomas knew, but how far would they go?

Simon's voice came down the line, "Thomas, are you still there?"

"Yes, go on."

"D'you think Kara has something on her family?"

"Like what?"

"Who knows?" Simon replied cautiously, "But do you think that's why she's gone missing?"

Thomas ducked the question. The agent was the last person he would confide in. "How many people know about this book?"

"It's only a rumour, so maybe only a handful in the business."

"Kara would never do the dirty on her family."

"We don't know that for sure."

"I know it. And she's only been missing for two days," Thomas insisted. "That's nothing for Kara; she's stayed away for weeks at a time before. Everyone's panicking too soon. She'll be back for the auction."

"I'm not sure about that."

Thomas caught the tone in his voice. "Why? What's going on?"

"The Klimt painting was stolen."

"What?" Thomas blew out his cheeks. "There's nothing in the papers or the internet. *When* was it stolen?"

"Two nights ago."

"When Kara went missing?"

Simon sighed, "Luis has managed to keep the theft out of the news, and Jimmy's got investigators working on it –"

"What about the police?"

"They're looking for Kara, but they don't know that the Klimt's missing."

"You think Kara stole it?"

"She had access and could move around the gallery as she wanted. No one would have questioned her –"

"Others had access too. Luis, Halle, Jimmy, or any of the staff coming and going from that place. And anyway," he said curtly, "if Kara's missing, who cares if she took the bloody painting?"

"The Klimt's worth a fortune. Many collectors and dealers would want to get their hands on it." Simon paused before continuing, "I don't mean reputable collectors; I mean the sordid end of the business. People are *hired* to steal works of art. If Kara took it for a joke, others wouldn't see it that way."

"You're saying she was taken *because* she stole the Klimt?" Thomas stood rigid at the window, trying to steady himself, "That makes no sense. A kidnapper would have already been in touch."

"What if Kara wasn't kidnapped but injured?"

Thomas could see it coming towards him. Something he couldn't avoid. Couldn't duck or dodge. It was inescapable, and he knew it would blow all their lives apart.

"What d'you mean?"

"A woman found a coat dumped on an East London street. Jimmy Famosa identified it as his sister's."

Thomas pressed his hand against the windowpane; his fingers spread out as if he was warding off something evil, *"And?"*

"It had blood all over it."

10

London
25th November

He hadn't even liked her. From the first moment he had bumped into her and knocked the phone out of her hand, she had been a fucking pain. An apology wasn't enough for her. Instead, she had insisted on seeing someone to make a complaint. His superior, she said:

"I want to see your boss," Kara had clutched the smashed cell phone in her hand, nails painted black, voice Americanised and angry. "So, what are you waiting for? Go and get him."

"It was an accident."

She hadn't been about to accept any explanation. "You walked straight into me!"

"I didn't see you!" He had snapped, then moderated his tone, checking that they were still in the camera's blind spot. Well, why not? He thought. It was risky, terribly risky, but why not? He pointed to the staff exit. "My manager's office is through there –"

"Good, we'll go and have a word with him."

It had been so easy to get her out of the staff exit into the concrete stairwell. Once there, she turned back to him, furious. Not frightened in the least.

"So, where's his office?"

He struck her with the wooden handle of his mop. Struck her so hard on the left side of her head that he felt the skull crack. Her eyes, peacock blue, had flickered like a torch about to go out. But instead of falling, she lunged towards him, hands outstretched, clawing at his face. And missing. Because then the torch *had* gone out, the eyes flat, her body falling hard onto the concrete landing.

He nearly panicked. But calmed himself and returned to the airport foyer to get his trolley. Back on the landing, he had crammed her into the metal flip-top bin. It had been easy; she hadn't weighed much, although he had nearly left one of her shoes behind, seeing it at the last minute and throwing it on top of her. He hadn't planned to seize her; he had just taken the opportunity and winged it. His original idea had been to spot his next victim and follow her. See which hotel, which flat. Watch her a little and *then* snatch her. It hadn't been meant to go like this. Not so frenzied, so reckless.

Breathing hard, Purchass reached into the metal bin and touched her head. She moaned. The relief was intense. He hadn't wanted another quick, unsatisfying death. Not like the last; this one had to give him some amusement before he killed her.

Spraying disinfectant on his bloodied hands, Purchass wiped them clean on a cloth and threw it into the bin on top of his victim. She had moaned again, prompting him to punch her twice before she fell silent. He then opened the staff exit door and pushed the trolley into the reception area.

He had had no choice. He couldn't have got the unwieldy trolley down the back stairs only to be met with locked doors at the bottom - and the lift was out of order. So instead, he was forced to push the loaded trolley through hundreds of people carrying its dreadful load. Mouth dry, Purchass avoided eye contact and headed for the side exit. As he pushed his victim along, he went over his actions. Yes, the landing had been wiped clear of blood, the mop rinsed out. Yes, he had made sure his and her fingerprints had been cleaned from the door handles. He had been careful. He had kept himself safe.

Calmly, Purchass kept pushing the trolley, *then remembered the phone.* The broken phone, the phone he had knocked out of her hand… Panicking, he looked back. Was it still on the landing? Or had it fallen down the stairs? Think, he told himself, picturing the series of events. When he had knocked into her, she had dropped the phone. Then she had picked it up back up. *But had he touched it?...* Purchass sweated, trying to remember. No, it was OK; he'd never handled the phone. Even if they found it, no one could trace it back to him.

Relieved, he began to push the trolley forwards again, just as one of the airport police had walked over to him, gesturing.

Gesturing *what?*

Purchass stopped breathing.

He was sure he could hear the girl breathing. Sure that the blood had been smearing a guilty red trail across the concourse. Sure that – if he had looked – he would see the horrified faces of the crowd staring at him.

The policeman was almost upon him, Purchass sweated as he gripped the handrail of the trolley. It *couldn't* be over, he had thought, not so soon. *It couldn't be.*

The policeman arrived at the trolley, reached out his foot, and depressed the pedal, the lid of the bin flipping up.

Purchass had stood rigid as the policeman nodded to him.

"Thanks." He said, smiling. "Don't want to leave litter lying about."

And he had *kept* smiling at Purchass without looking down as he dropped an empty sweet wrapper onto the head of the unconscious girl before the lid snapped shut again.

11

That was two days ago now, Purchass thought, only forty-eight hours but it seemed a hell of a sight longer. He was sitting at his kitchen table and staring at the outhouses where his father used to shadowbox the hay bales. She was in one of them, strung up like one of the calves his father used to secure before slitting its throat.

Getting her out of the airport hadn't been as difficult as he had imagined. He was a porter, after all. Who questioned a porter wheeling his trolley around to the bins behind the terminal? No one noticed porters. Certainly, no one had noticed him. It *had* taken some nerve leaving the trolley to get his car, and when the bloody rust heap wouldn't start the first time he'd nearly panicked. But finally, he'd driven it round to the bins and parked it as close as he dared, half in shadow. Then he'd waited until a plane was taking off - the noise loud enough to drown out anything - before tipping her from the trolley into his car boot. She had rolled into a foetal position but hadn't come round.

After locking the boot, Purchass had wiped down the bin and trolley with disinfectant and tossed the used cloth. Only then had he trundled the trolley all the way back to the staff exit, rolling it up against the others. All identical. Once back in the car, he had been surprised to find himself unnerved. Not excited, but anxious, almost tearful. The baby of the family again. The feeling had lasted the whole journey home, snow coming with the drop in temperature, his headlights snaking along the dirt track to the mouldering farmhouse. Turning off the outside lights, Purchass had dragged Kara into the largest barn and tied her hands together with rope, winching her upwards until only her toes touched the floor.

He had been annoyed to find that she didn't wake up, his gaze settling on the wound at the side of her head. Maybe he had hit her too hard. Maybe she would *never* come round… Bloody hell, he'd thought desperately, not again. Not another fucking woman going to let him down. Then, unexpectedly, she had moaned, and he hurried to gag her. Her eyes opened at his touch, her head moving from side to side as he tightened the cloth around her mouth. Blood had been oozing from the wound as she suddenly kicked out at him. Surprised, he jumped back, running his hand up the inside of her thigh and then hitting her hard. She stopped struggling, knocked unconscious, her head falling forwards limply.

He had decided that he would have sex with her later. He would have something to eat first, prepare himself. Get some lamps set up in the barn so he could bolt the door and take his time. See everything. Drink in every detail and make sure she knew exactly what was happening to her. Make sure she suffered. No severing of any spinal cord this time. Purchass had wanted her to feel his hands, to squirm against him, to try to escape the probing, callous fingers. *That* had been what he had wanted.

But she hadn't come round.

Morning came round instead as Purchass walked to the barn and looked inside. The cold was brutal, steam coming from the compost at the back of the outhouse, the blood dried on the side of her head, the peacock blue eyes closed. It was the beginning of a lousy day which dragged on relentlessly, Purchass went to work at the airport and returned to find his victim still senseless.

Gingerly, he touched her neck, feeling her pulse, reassuring himself that she hadn't died whilst he had been pushing his fucking trolley around Heathrow. To have risked so much for nothing would have been unbearable. Frustrated, he kicked out at the body, sending her swinging from the rope which held her, and then moved back into the farmhouse.

Sullen, he sat down to read the evening paper he had nicked off one of the stands and gazed at the front page, abruptly taking in his breath. There, large as life, was a photograph of the woman trussed up in his outhouse. *Kara Famosa*, the article called her. The daughter of the famous and wealthy Famosa family.

"Jesus." Shaken, Purchass threw the newspaper across the room.

He was supposed to have picked a stranger, a random woman! Miss Ordinary. Not someone *everyone* would be looking for. Enraged, he emptied his victim's bag onto the table. And there it was, her passport confirming *Ms Kara Famosa*. He read the name again and slumped into a chair. How was he supposed to know she was important? Then he remembered hearing something about Luis Famosa and his snotty English wife. They were big on charity and art, generous, well-known… Purchass raged inwardly. The bloody girl hadn't been dressed rich. In fact, he thought bitterly; she had looked like a hundred other women, only her eyes marking her out. So, of all the women who came through Heathrow every day, he had managed to pick the offspring of the powerful family.

Distrait, he wanted to cry, and he pushed his fist deep into his mouth to stifle the noise. Oh, his family would have loved this! *What a fool,* his sister would have said, what an *ugly, lanky fucking idiot* without a brain in his stinking head. And as if it wasn't bad enough that the London police were searching, Luis Famosa had got the American police involved.

He was done for, Purchass thought, glancing over to the outhouse. He'd have to kill her now. Kill her and bury her; get rid of the bitch before they traced her to him. Snatching up the newspaper again, Purchass read down the article, seeing the name *Jimmy Famosa*. Apparently, he was the brother, the family mouthpiece, who was coming to London to find his sister.

Which wasn't going to happen.

Taking a box of matches and a can of petrol, Purchass picked up a torch and headed to the barn.

12

New York

Halle wrapped herself in her coat and curled up on one of the sofas, hugging a cushion. Without makeup, she looked her age, her skin devoid of colour, her mouth compressed, holding in tears. Her gaze moved repeatedly to her watch, the phone, and back to the watch.

"Are you cold?" Blinking, she looked at her son, Jimmy, leaning towards her.

"You're wearing your coat. I can turn up the heating if you like?"

She shook her head, reaching for his hand, squeezing it, and then releasing it. Always alim, she was diminishing, a wraith in Ralph Lauren.

"Have you checked your mobile?" Her tone was light, bloodless, "Kara might be on her way home now. She wouldn't miss the auction; she was excited about it, wasn't she?"

No, she wasn't, Jimmy wanted to say. The recent interest she had shown in the business was for one reason only: to steal the Klimt. Then he wondered how he was going to tell his mother what she had done, because Halle would insist that someone else had been the thief. And then she would find hope in the situation because if Halle had the painting, it meant that she hadn't been abducted; otherwise, they would have heard from her kidnapper.

"She'll come back." Halle insisted, "Who cares about the painting. If Kara wants a Klimt, we'll buy her a dozen," she turned to her son, curious, "What were you two arguing about?"

Jimmy baulked. "Nothing important, Kara was in a mood."

"She was fine when I saw her." The reproach was coming up for air, just under the surface.

"I just asked her to stay in touch when she's travelling."

"And now she's missing," Halle replied, "She's making her point, isn't she?"

"It wasn't our argument that made her run off!" Jimmy countered, "And it wasn't the reason she stole the Klimt. She must have planned it."

Halle changed gear abruptly. "You have to ring your sister and tell her that Luis won't be angry with her."

"None of us believe that, and neither would she," Jimmy retorted.

At first, Luis had been intent on finding Kara, then incensed to discover she had stolen the painting. But when Jimmy told him about the bloodied coat, his father had ordered him not to tell Halle, issuing a public statement that the auction would be postponed. There was no need to explain - Kara Famosa was missing.

"Try your sister's mobile again," Halle said, her tone pleading.

Jimmy could see she was teetering on panic. “Her cell’s turned off.”

“Turned off...” her hand touched her face, then rested in the indentation at the base of her throat. “What about the police?”

“The British and American police are working together.”

“Should we trust them?” Halle asked timidly, “You hear about their mistakes every day. They’re always blundering,” she glanced over to the phone again. “Why hasn’t he rung?”

Jimmy frowned. “Who?”

“The kidnapper!”

“We don’t know that Kara’s been kidnapped –”

“But she might have been!” Halle replied, her voice lapsing into confusion, “You said that Kara stole the painting?”

“Yeah.”

“Are you sure?”

“Kara could have got access to the safe. And only the family know the combination –”

“What about Luis?” She asked, moving the edge of her seat, “Haven’t you noticed how strangely he’s been acting?”

“Why would my father steal his own painting?”

“I don’t know,” she said quietly, “But it wasn’t me who took it.”

Baffled, Jimmy stared at her, “I know that.”

“And *you* wouldn’t have done it,” Halle continued, “If Kara *did* take the Klimt, she knows Luis would be angry. That’s why she’s hiding for a while, waiting until things calm down.”

“*Things calm down*?’ We have to think logically --”

"You can't tell me what to think! This time, I think for *myself!"* her tone wavered, "They only found Kara's *coat*. They didn't find her body. Just her coat."

Wrong footed, he stared at his mother. "How d'you know about the coat?"

"Luis told me."

After insisting that his son keep it a secret, Luis had told Halle anyway. "Why did he tell you?"

"I'm Kara's mother!" She retorted, "And if my daughter's been abducted, you give the kidnapper whatever he wants. You hear me? I don't care about the money; I just want Kara home," she was unravelling in front of him, "If she *did* take the Klimt, he can have that too. That's fair, isn't it?"

"I'll handle everything," Jimmy reassured her. "Like I always do. You have to trust me."

She nodded dumbly. "Yes, yes… but why isn't Luis here?"

"He doing things his own way. Everyone knows my father's got a long reach. He won't let this get out of control."

Sighing, she glanced away. "It *is* out of control, Jimmy. The moment you argued with Kara, it was out of control."

-o0o-

Simon Porter walked up the London street towards his office, fully aware that someone was following him. For the previous few days, the agency had been inundated with visits from the police and requests from journalists. It was no secret that he was the London agent for the Famosa family, and the questions were endless.

Would he be prepared to comment on Kara going missing?

What had he heard?

Had he spoken to Luis or Halle?

Jimmy Famosa was coming over to London, was he coming to see Simon?

How long were they going to postpone the Klimt auction for?

Although Simon had realised he was being watched, he was irritated to be stopped by a deceptively wholesome blonde.

"Have you spoken to Halle or Luis Famosa?" she asked, her voice conspiratorial. "Does anyone have an idea where Kara might be?"

"No comment."

"What do the police think?"

"No comment," he repeated, trying to move past her.

"Of course, the Famosa family being so famous and so wealthy, it's more than likely Kara was kidnapped."

"We can't jump to that conclusion," Simon replied, his voice curt, "No one knows anything for certain yet."

"I heard a rumour that Kara Famosa's writing a book about her family."

Although he didn't show it, Simon was surprised the news had spread so quickly. "No comment."

"Rumour has it that it will be an expose."

"Nonsense," Simon replied, entering the agency, the woman following.

"I don't think it's nonsense." she persisted, "I heard that Kara Famosa was going to dig the dirt –"

"There *is* no dirt to dig!" He snapped.

" – of course, it'll be sad if they don't save Kara. But either way, it'll be a great story."

Calling for security, Simon watched as the woman was led out, Anna waiting for him as he entered the agency. Signalling that they shouldn't talk in front of the staff, she ushered him into his office.

"So what was all *that* about?"

"Don't tell me you didn't hear."

Anna ignored the remark, "The woman's right; it *is* big news. We could make a killing."

He winced at the word. "It would be immoral."

"Well, if you don't, *someone* will. You know the Famosas, you have insider knowledge."

"For God's Sake, **Kara is missing!"**

"I know!" Anna retorted, "But she'll be found. Dead or alive."

Her callousness shook him. "Haven't you got any feelings?"

"I'm not the one who abducted her! Until the kidnapper gets in touch, we don't know for sure that she *has* been taken. She could have planted that coat with blood on it. The girl's a drama queen."

"I hope you're right," Simon replied, loosening his tie.

"Whatever happened, it's an incredible story. Here and in the USA, it's front-page news. The family's famous, and the fact that the daughter might have written her own version of Chez Famosa is dynamite." She paused, staring at him, "*Don't look at me like that!* If you didn't know the family, you'd be the first to get your teeth into it --"

"But I *do* know them. And I like Halle. She's vulnerable."

"Nonsense! She has a thug for a husband and a son who babysits her --"

"*In the USA!* But I protect the Famosa interests *here,* and *here* is where Kara disappeared."

"Which gives you an advantage," Anna replied, "This could make the agency a fortune. People are talking about it non-stop. '*Kara Famosa abducted. Why? Was she really writing an expose?*"

"Jesus! Don't you have any compassion?"

"Plenty. I simply don't let it get the better of me." Knowing she had shocked him, Anna changed tack. "This an opportunity, darling. And my son could help you."

"What *are* you talking about?"

"Thomas loved Kara; he still does. His marriage failed because he never got over the Famosa girl. And Halle *adores* Thomas," Anna smiled, coaxing him. "We have to ensure that you remain in control of the situation."

"Not now, Anna!" Simon retorted, but he was listening.

"No, darling, not now. But perhaps we should think of letting Thomas write about it?"

Simon sighed. "He isn't a writer."

"He doesn't have to be Chekov to write a blog," Anna replied, "And Halle would be certain to confide in him."

"And Luis?"

"He'd work with anyone to get Kara back and stop any poisonous memoir seeing the light of day. It's rumoured Luis Famosa has plenty to hide, and as for Jimmy, I'm sure he must be sweating about his sister's book. After all, what has *he* done in the name of family?" Anna continued smoothly, "*Halle trusts my son.* By involving Thomas, we could protect the story whilst doing the right thing."

Simon looked at her blankly, "How d'you make that out?"

"You want the best for your clients. Coffee table books are all well and good, but the history of the Famosa family would be a bestseller." She perched on the side of his desk, "And besides, it would be a chance for me to help my son." Simon blinked, words failing him as Anna continued, "You're a good man, but you have to be willing to grab opportunities when they present themselves. The future's uncertain. It's only by being one step ahead that anyone can prepare for it."

13

Preoccupied, Thomas entered the supermarket. Although outwardly calm, he was numb. A visit to the bank had resulted in a humiliating refusal to extend his overdraft. Met with unyielding opposition, he had lost his temper and stormed out. Then he had walked to the nearest garage asking if they could recommend a dealer to buy his Mercedes. The car was as good as sold.

It was only a car, Thomas thought, staring at the frozen food, and beginning to drop bags of peas, carrots, and broad beans into his trolley. *It was only a car.* But his anger wasn't lifting. The fucking bank manager had been so smug, pushing around papers on his desk. *It was a shame,* he had said*, that business had been bad for Thomas when he needed money so much.* Rubbing it in, enjoying it.

Thomas paused, tempted to dump the trolley and leave. *It was only a car*. No, it wasn't. It was the last tie to his old life. To success, to status, and he was going to sell it. And with it, forfeit the last of his assets. When the car had gone; there was nothing else to sell. How long before the sacrifice got swallowed up in lint and cotton wool? Tossing a frozen chicken into the trolley, Thomas paused, thinking. Every attempt to make contact with his old colleagues had been ignored, there had been no way back into the financial world. The apartment in Maida Vale was big for just him and his father, but they couldn't sell it as it was in Anna de Souza's name. As for the flat Thomas had shared with his estranged wife, that had been rented.

Thomas's gaze rested on the low fat ice cream on the freezer shelf in front of him, so preoccupied that he flinched when someone touched him on the shoulder.

"*Thomas?* I thought it was you," Simon Porter smiled awkwardly, holding a basket with three under-ripe avocados. "Do you shop here?"

There was a moment's pause, Simon realising at once that Thomas knew their encounter was no accident. "Waitrose is round the corner," he said, his tone sarcastic.

"Is everything alright?"

"Blissful," Thomas replied, picking up the ice cream and putting it in his basket. As he walked away, he could hear the agent falling into step behind him. The supermarket was virtually empty: a bored man stacking shelves by the door, a middle-aged woman on the checkout fiddling with Lottery scratch cards, and a couple hovering by the Off License counter.

"I'm glad I bumped into you," Simon began, his long, thin legs striding down the narrow aisle, "I wanted a word."

"Well, I don't."

He could see the hostility and faltered, "Hear me out –"

"I don't want to hear you out! You broke up my parents' marriage. No, that's not right. My mother would have done the running, but you went along with it. You put my father into a wheelchair, and you were supposed to be his friend."

"I'm not proud of what happened. Let me explain -"

Thomas put up his hands, "Don't you see how ridiculous this is? We're in the middle of a supermarket, and you're pretending to shop." He glanced at the agent's basket, "Your wife used to do the shopping, didn't she?"

"Leave my wife out of this."

"Why? You didn't leave my father out of it," Thomas replied icily, "What do you want, Porter? Because you do *want* something, don't you?" He glanced at the avocadoes, amused, "Incidentally, those won't be ready for a week."

Embarrassed, the agent abandoned his basket, his voice low to avoid being overheard. "Look, I know you're not working at the moment, and I know money's tight."

Keep walking, Thomas told himself. *It doesn't matter that you need the money. This is fucking Simon Porter. Keep walking, or you might hit him.*

"I've got a proposition for you."

"I don't want your help."

"You need it. You need the money."

Thomas wondered how he knew. Was it simply a guess, or had Simon found out just how little cash was left? Or was he guilty, knowing Anna de Souza had stripped her husband like a hyena stripping a lion kill?

"I said no."

"Take the offer," Simon repeated, his tone almost pleading, "Let me do something --"

"Oh, for Christ's Sake, grow up! You're only doing this because my mother told you to. I don't want your help." Thomas repeated, but at the same time, he was

wondering if he should let the bastard off the hook. The agent was feeling guilty; why not ease that torment if it suited him and his father? Why turn away a chance to make money because of pride? "I know my mother put you up to this. She can always spot an advantage," Thomas continued, smiling wryly, "So tell me, what does she want from me? What are you offering?"

Simon Porter cleared his throat. "Remember when we talked about Kara Famosa the other night?"

"Yeah. I spoke to Halle this morning."

"She took your call?" Simon said cheerfully, "You see?"

"*See what*?"

"Halle's fond of you. She trusts you," his grey eyes in the grey face looked unusually animated, "and she needs people around her she can trust."

"She has a husband and a son."

"Luis is preoccupied with finding Kara; he's got numerous leads and investigators –"

"In the USA?"

"Yes. And Jimmy is coming to London to talk to the police here. What's happened to Kara has made the whole family vulnerable."

"And you too," Thomas interrupted him, "You wouldn't want to miss out on Kara's book, would you?"

He ignored the barb. "I've got the press on my back constantly about the Famosas. I'm inundated at the agency, and I could use some help –"

"Are you off your bloody mind?"

Simon shrugged his shoulders meekly, "Hear me out. I'll pay you well. I've spoken to Hallc; she'd like you to go to New York and stay with her. She needs someone to confide in --"

"You want me to spy for you?" Thomas stared at his mother's lover, "What about my father, you cringing bastard? Remember him? *He* needs me more than Halle Famosa."

"I can arrange for someone to look after Peter whilst you're away."

"And I'm supposed to be *grateful?"* Thomas retorted, "How stupid d'you think I am? You just want to plant me with Halle to keep an eye on things for you."

"You had a relationship with Kara Famosa. You know her --"

"Yeah, I do. I know her enough to realise that she could just turn up, large as life, and laugh at us for being so gullible."

Simon nodded, "She could. But it could be worse."

"You mean she could be dead?" Thomas's voice flat-lined, "Why jump to that conclusion? You *want* that ending?"

"Thomas –"

"I mean, if Kara was killed, that would stop any embarrassing expose being published. The Famosas would be relieved."

Stunned, Simon stared at him. "Are you suggesting--"

"I'm suggesting nothing. I'm the one that still thinks Kara's fooling around. Or, at worst, she's been the victim of a hit and run."

"The police considered that. They searched the area where they found the coat and then checked all the hospitals. But they found nothing."

"What if she was killed outright and her body was dumped?"

"They would have found it."

"In the whole of London?"

"I don't know --"

"That's right, you don't fucking know!" Thomas snapped.

"You should control your temper," Simon said, flushing, "Anna says you're always angry –"

"My mother is no judge of character, or she wouldn't be with you," Thomas replied, ignoring the stare from the shop assistant. "You want me to help you? You want me visit Halle? Report how the Famosa family is taking the news when they hear that Kara's dead?" his voice hardened, "You want to make money from misery?"

"Well, if not me, *someone* will."

"I can hear my mother's voice in those words."

"Look," Simon continued, almost shamefaced, "I'm the agent for the Famosas -"

"And you want your pound of flesh."

"It's my job!"

"Did my mother tell you to say that too? It's the kind of excuse she'd use." Thomas regarded the agent with contempt, "If I were you, I'd watch for holes cut into the back of your suits. She's aiming to make you into a ventriloquist dummy."

Simon floundered. "Whatever you say, it's the truth. *Someone* will profit from this situation, yes. But how much better if it's someone who cares about the Famosas? Have you never thought that we could *help* Kara?"

"Help her? *How*?"

"Use the internet. Sct up a blog."

"I know nothing about a blog!"

"It's easy! I'll show you how to do it," Simon hurried on, "You can keep Kara in the public eye and just write about anything that could jog peoples' memories," he could sense that he was on the right track. Thomas de Souza was angry but emotional. "Think of the good it might do. Someone might remember seeing Kara. Or hearing something. You can let the world know what's going on in real-time. You can be the public face of a private tragedy." He was moulding the truth to make it acceptable to both Thomas and himself. "Halle needs you. She thinks the blog is a good idea."

"What about Luis?"

"He's convinced that it might help Kara."

"And Jimmy?" Thomas asked, "He runs the Famosa business privately, without outside intervention. I can't see him agreeing to it."

"He will if he's persuaded. They *all* want Kara back and will agree to anything to bring that about."

Narrowing his eyes, Thomas studied the agent, "The Famosas must be worried about Kara's expose."

"They're good people --"

"I'll take your word for it," Thomas said, unconvinced. "But if Kara *has* been abducted, won't it piss off the kidnapper to see a blog popping up?"

"We'll have to gauge it carefully," Simon replied, hurrying on, "Look, I don't like this any more than you do, but someone will report what's going on - and it should be you."

Thomas moved towards the till, thinking. Was Kara *really* planning an expose? He had always dismissed the innuendoes as malice, but what if there *were* forgeries and double-dealings organised by the Famosa father and son? How big a threat would an expose be to that?

Kara's words came back to him: *'Luis isn't my father.'*

Had Luis found out that he'd been cuckolded? If he had, and felt threatened by Kara's book, how much easier would it be to bear the loss of *another* man's child? Or even organise it?

"Are you moving, or what?"

Startled, Thomas stared at the cashier's irritated face, then pushed his produce along the conveyor belt.

Completely unaware of what he was thinking, Simon talked on, "This could make a fortune for you *and* your father. Money would give you options."

"And ease your conscience."

"I know what I did."

"Which is exactly the point. Would you have offered me this 'chance' if you hadn't been shacked up with my mother?"

Simon flinched. "Think what you like. But I'm trying to help."

Paying the cashier, Thomas walked out of the shop. He had already decided to take the agent up on the offer but would be careful in his dealings with the Famosas. His role in the drama was to be the ex-lover, family friend, and confidante. A sympathetic face card in his mother's stacked deck. And that was *exactly* what Thomas was going to let them believe.

"I can pay you well," the agent went on, "You'll have money to get Peter the best treatment. You can think what you like of me, but I'm giving you a chance." He paused, adding the words Anna had drilled into him earlier, "If you won't think about yourself, Thomas, think of your father."

14

The snow was getting thicker, covering the uneven path and the cluster of trees which circled the farm-house. Holding a sack over his head, Purchass hurried through the snowstorm and kicked open the door of the barn. It fell back with a clattering echo as he shone his torch inside.

She was awake, hanging from one of the beams like a dead carcass, her peacock eyes watching him. She had almost managed to remove the gag, her eyes widening as she saw the petrol can. Putting it down on the floor, Purchass walked over to her, gesturing towards the petrol.

"See that?"

She nodded, terrified.

"That's for you. You know why?" He pulled up a bale of straw and sat down on it, just out of reach of her legs should she kick out, "Because you're a liability. *You're fucking famous.* Or rather, your family is." She was trying to speak, Purchass's head going to one side, his expression questioning, "*What?* I can't make out what you're saying."

Jumping to his feet, he startled her, Kara jerking backwards as he ripped off the gag. Her skin was raw, and her lips dry and swollen. "Don't…"

"Don't what?"

"… burn me," she said, pleading, her eyes fixed on him, her arms dead, the pain in the side of her head a drowning sensation. "Don't burn me."

"Why not?"

"Think about it …"

"I have done. You were supposed to be a nobody, like the other one. But you turned out to be a rich girl that everyone's looking for." He glanced over to the petrol can, "I'm not going to jail for you."

"Listen to me--"

"Why? Are you going to beg?" Purchass asked, trying to get excited as he looked at her body.

But there was nothing stimulating about her, and disappointed, he felt frustration instead. She was just a problem. A chance he could get caught. A lump of meat hanging in his barn, just waiting to be found.

"You're no good to me."

He reached for the petrol can, Kara shouting at him hysterically.

"NO! My family's rich! Ask for money." She could feel her toes brushing the floor of the barn and ached to plant her feet on solid ground. "You can get a lot of money for me. Ask Luis Famosa; he'll pay. My family will pay you anything you want."

"But I'm not a kidnapper," Purchass replied, circling her with the petrol can in his hand, jiggling it, the liquid sloshing inside. "It's much easier to kill you now and burn the evidence."

"You could be rich."

"Yeah, but I could also get caught. How many kidnappers get away with it?"

"How many kidnapper's victims *help* them?" Kara replied, turning her head to look at him as he circled her. She was fighting, trying to bargain. "I can arrange everything. Let me talk to Luis or my brother. When you've got the money, you can let me go."

Purchass hesitated. Luis Famosa *was* famous and rich. Perhaps he hadn't been so stupid and unlucky after all. Perhaps he *could* use the bitch to barter with.

"You've seen my face," he said, "You could identify me."

"I want to live!" She hurled back, "Why lose the chance of getting all that money? You could do anything, go anywhere. Start afresh with a fortune. And it *would* be a fortune," she was trying to gauge his reaction, if she was getting through to him, "I'll get you the money. The money - in return for me."

"And what about the police?"

"What police?" She countered, glancing at the petrol can in his hand. "We can keep them out of it. You don't know Luis Famosa. He won't risk losing me. If I tell him not to involve the police, he won't –"

"The police are **already** involved!" Purchass snapped, his voice dropping as he approached her, "You're all over the papers, luv. Here, and in America. You're fucking famous, and everyone's looking for you."

She was momentarily fazed, then rallied. "But they haven't found me. They don't know what's happened to me, do they?" Her mind was working fast, "If you haven't asked for a ransom, who knows I've been kidnapped? I could have just gone off somewhere."

He was listening, head on one side, "Go on."

"You got me out of the airport without anyone seeing. You must have, or they'd have found you by now."

He nudged her with his elbow, sending her swinging, her arms straining. "You're right, no one saw me."

"Because you were clever." Kara continued, "Clever enough to snatch me when there were hundreds of people around. So how easy is it going to be to swap me now? No police. Just me, you, and-- "

"You think Luis Famosa would go along with that?"

"**He will!"** She assured him, "He'll never see your face. *I* can arrange it all. Let me talk to him. Let *me* do it."

Purchass paused, jiggling the petrol can in his hand, then shook his head, "Nah, too risky-- "

"There's no risk! I won't *let* there be a risk." She stared at him desperately, "If you kill me that won't be the end of it. If no one asks for a ransom they'll just think I'm missing. And then they'll *never* stop looking for me. My family's worth a fortune. However long it takes, however much money it costs, they won't stop."

"Go on, this is great news," Purchass said sarcastically. But he was listening.

"You said I wasn't the first," she could see his eyes flicker as he realised, he had let something slip. "So, if there *were* other women they'll catch you. You'll have made a mistake somewhere --"

He slapped her hard across the face, sending her swinging, "You bitch!"

"Take the money!" She shouted. "You don't have a choice. You can use me or get caught."

In silence, he watched her and waited until she had stopped swinging, her toes just brushing the floor of the barn. He could see, with some satisfaction, that she was in pain. "How much?"

"What?"

"How much could you get me?"

"A million."

"How soon?"

She struggled to work out the timing. "My father and brother are in America --"

"Your brother's coming to England," Purchass replied, "Should be here soon."

"Then I can get the money quickly!"

He walked around her, studying her, considering what she had said. Then he picked up the petrol can and unscrewed the cap.

"No!" She screamed, jerking on the rope, **"Please don't."**

"I'd never get away with it. The police or your fucking family would see to that. You think I'd risk dying in prison for money? No, you're not worth it."

"I might not be," she countered, "but the painting is."

He blinked slowly, "*Painting?* What the fuck are you talking about?"

"Have you still got my things, my flight bag?"

"Yeah, but I'm going to burn them –"

"No!" Kara shouted, "No, look in the flight bag. There's a red jumper, and wrapped inside it is a small painting."

"Fuck off!"

"*It's true!* It's by Gustav Klimt, and his pictures are worth millions," she said, holding his gaze, "If my family doesn't want me, Luis Famosa will do *anything* to get that picture back."

"Why's that?" Purchass asked, jiggling the petrol in the can, "Well, come on, speak up! Why's a bloody painting so important?"

"It's one of a kind." Her voice was dry, rasping. "It was to be auctioned in New York, and it's set to break records."

Purchass jiggled the petrol can in his hand, smiling, "What's to stop me from getting rid of you and selling it myself?"

"You don't have the contacts," she replied, hurrying on, "Listen, please. My father and brother want that picture back. They'll do a deal with you."

"If you're lying to me –"

She sighed, "*Why would I?*"

"OK. You can call them; I'll get you a mobile." Purchass moved away, then turned back, "And I want *two* million *pounds*, not bloody dollars. When I get the money, Luis Famosa can get his painting back *and* his daughter."

She nodded weakly. "I'll tell him."

"Two million pounds. Or I burn you alive."

15

New York

"It's me."

Pressing the phone to his ear, Jimmy took in a breath. *"Kara!* Are you OK?"

"Yeah, yeah." She was breathing rapidly down the line, her brother looking through the door into the sitting room. On the sofa, Halle was dozing, still wrapped in her coat, her feet tucked under her. "Where are you?"

"I can't say."

Then he remembered where she had last been seen. "You're in England?"

"Yes…"

"Are you hurt?"

"No," she lied, "But I need help. The man that took me wants two million dollars. No! Not dollars, *pounds.* He wants it in pounds."

Jimmy sensed she was not alone, that someone was listening in on the call. "OK. OK," he agreed, "but I want to talk to him."

"You can't," she said flatly, "Talk to me. Only me --"

"Kara!"

"Listen to me! Talk to *me*," she sobbed, then pulled herself together at the other end of the line. "Get the money. I'll call you…" a pause, a man's voice in the background, "… late tomorrow. Then I'll tell you when and where to bring the money. Aren't you in England now?"

"I will be tomorrow."

"Thank God."

He caught the fear in her voice. "Kara, hold on."

"I want to come home!" She said desperately. "You'll come for me, won't you?"

"Yeah, I promise I'll come for you."

"Just **don't tell the police.** Don't let the police know --"

He interrupted her. "But they already do."

"No! They know I'm missing, but not that I've been kidnapped. You **mustn't** tell them, Jimmy." Her voice dropped. "I took the Klimt."

"I know."

"I've told him it's worth a fortune," she was breathing rapidly, "And I want you to tell Luis I've got the painting."

"The picture's not important --"

"Come on, Jimmy! Don't lie, not now," she hurried on, "You *have* to do what I say. And you have to keep the police out of it. If you don't, he'll kill me."

"OK, OK. Just tell me why you took the painting."

"For collateral. I was going to use it as leverage."

"I don't understand."

"Yes, you do," she retorted. "And if you really don't know, ask Simon Porter or Hugh Ackermann about the book."

He was shaken. "So, you *did* write a book. Why?"

"I had my reasons, Jimmy," she hurried on, "You have to pay this man. Pay him and get me home," she hesitated, then whispered under her breath. *"I'm not the first."*

And in that instant, the connection was cut.

Still holding the phone, Jimmy replayed the words, '*I wasn't the first.*' What had she meant? That there was another woman being held with her, or that there had been another victim?

"Was that Kara?" He turned, Halle walking into the room, her expression accusing, "**Was it Kara**!"

"She's OK –"

"So why didn't you let me talk to her!" she screamed, lunging at him. "You bastard, why didn't you let me talk to my baby!"

"Kara was only the line for a minute," he said, trying to calm her, "But she's OK. She's alive --"

"Where is she? Who took her?"

"She's in England. I heard a man's voice in the background. He wants two million pounds."

"So, she *was* kidnapped!" Angrily, Halle pushed her son away, "We need the police –"

"No police!" Jimmy snapped**,** "Kara was clear about that. No police."

"Are you mad? We need them."

"No, we don't! Kara's arranging everything with me."

Halle paused, doubtful, "You're talking to the kidnapper?"

"No, just Kara."

"But you have to talk to *him!"* She wailed, distraught, "You have to find out who he is! Kara can't bargain for herself."

"She wants me to negotiate --"

"*You're not capable!* I want Luis to sort it out."

"But my father's not here, is he?" Jimmy countered, stung, "*I'm* here. And I can handle it."

She turned away. Angry, strained. "I don't care what you say, we need the police. I'm not risking Kara. Or you. We need professionals –"

"**No** police."

Defiant, she crossed her arms, surprising him by her sudden show of strength. "If the police *were* handling this, the phone would already be tapped. They could have traced the call."

"The house phone **is** tapped!" Jimmy replied angrily, "Kara was calling my mobile–"

Confused, Halle stared at him. "But why didn't she call Luis?"

"Probably because she stole the Klimt."

Her eyes widened, her confidence waned, and her gaze fixed on her son. "Kara admitted it?"

"Yes."

"Why did she take it?"

"She said it gave her leverage."

Halle shook her head, bemused. *"Leverage*? I don't understand."

"She told me to tell Luis that she had it," Jimmy said, moving on quickly, "We have to do what my sister says."

"But she's in *danger!"*

"I know! But if Kara says no police, then it's no police. If she wants to talk to me, and me alone, that's what we'll do."

Shaking, Halle began to pace up and down the room. "What if we don't get her back? Jesus, what if she panics?"

"She won't panic. And we can't either."

"But we could lose her! How many kidnappings succeed? How many times do they manage to get the hostage back?"

"I'll get Kara back."

"We need Luis! He should have taken the call," she paused, her tone wavering, "Did Kara sound OK?"

"She sounded in control."

"But she's on her own, she's alone."

Is she? Jimmy wondered. Was she with someone else? Or was the other woman already dead?

"Kara's tough," he said calmly, "Always has been. She'll have worked out the odds and kept her nerve. We just have to do what she says."

Halle was pacing the floor again, chewing at her thumbnail. "I should be *doing* something. *We* should be doing something --"

"We can't. This time, Kara takes the lead."

16

New York
26th November

They crossed mid-Atlantic; Thomas flying to New York as Jimmy was heading for London. Met at the airport by Halle's chauffeur, Thomas was driven to the familiar brownstone house and shown into the drawing room. The drapes were half drawn to keep out the lens of the paparazzi, a mock fire burning in an ebonised grate.

"Thomas," Halle said, walking in and kissing him on both cheeks, "I'm so glad you're here."

She had made an effort, but her makeup wasn't blended properly, and her hair was flat at the crown. Taking a seat on the sofa, she continued, her voice thin, without substance.

"I can't believe all this is happening. Kara missing…" Thomas took a seat next to her, Halle gripping his hand, "I want to go back to when you were living with Kara, and both of you used to come and visit - remember that time we went to Japan?" She paused as though talking was a physical effort. "You and Kara got drunk on sake."

Laughing, Thomas nodded. "Jesus, was I *so* sick."

"You were one of the family then."

"I doubt Jimmy would agree with that."

She smiled faintly, "Jimmy's bark is worse than his bite."

"Maybe. But he likes to think his teeth can do some real damage."

"Like yours?"

He smiled at her. "Everyone has to fight sometimes."

She fell silent, her voice subdued when she spoke again. "You know how fond I am of you, Thomas. I keep thinking that if Kara had stayed with you, she wouldn't be missing now. You'd have kept her safe. I know how much you loved her."

"I've always loved Kara," saying her name with more feeling than either of them expected, "Have you heard anything?"

Halle hesitated, wondering how much to say. Jimmy had insisted that no police were involved, but Thomas wasn't police, he was a friend. And Kara's ex-boyfriend. Not the young man who had taken Kara swimming, nor the same man who had driven through the night to take her daughter to the airport for an early flight. Now, he was changed, hardened.

"Why didn't you stay with Kara?"

Thomas shrugged, "It just fizzled out."

Halle nodded.

"You've not had it easy lately, have you?" She asked, "I talked to Simon. I was shocked when he left his family for your mother. I'm sorry, I've never liked her…" Halle played with the fringe on the edge of her jacket, curling it around her fingers. "Of course, Simon doesn't tell me everything that went on, but I know it affected your father badly."

"He had a stroke."

"And you?"

"No stroke," Thomas smiled, "Well, not yet anyway."

Affection passed between them. "I have to talk to someone. Jimmy's a rock, but he's gone to England now. Apparently, Kara won't deal with anyone else, and Luis is hustling, chasing his contacts…" she trailed off.

"I thought he'd be with you."

"*I* thought he'd be with me," Halle agreed, her tone listless, "He's distant, in shock, I suppose. Kara's missing, and he's worried about so many other things ..."

"Like what?"

"… Kara stole the Klimt painting."

Thomas leaned back in his seat, blowing out his cheeks. "I hadn't heard. Was that why the auction was postponed?"

She nodded. "I only just found out myself. Jimmy told me. To be honest, I can't believe Kara took it. Luis is so angry."

"Surely he's not bothered about a bloody painting?"

"But he is," she said, bewildered, "He's *very* worked up and afraid the news will get out. He's always been fanatical about keeping business private."

"So, no one knows the painting's missing?"

"I don't know. They don't tell me what's going on. Jimmy's a carbon copy of his father, just as controlling. We've always been a very close unit. Or is that *closed* unit?" She was somewhere between irritation and despair, "Can I trust you, Thomas?"

"You trusted me with your daughter."

"But can I trust you now?"

"I'm here, aren't I?"

"I know, I know... " Halle took in a breath. "Kara phoned yesterday and talked to Jimmy."

"So, she's alive. Thank God for that."

"And we know she was kidnapped. But Kara was adamant that we don't tell the police." Having begun confiding, Halle couldn't stop. "The man who took her wants two million pounds. Kara's organising it with Jimmy."

"She didn't ask for Luis?"

Halle shrugged. "No, just said that she would deal with Jimmy."

"Did she say where she was?"

"No, only that she's in England."

"You haven't called the police, have you?"

"No!" Halle snapped, "Jimmy's going to the UK to sort it all out."

Thomas was wondering if Jimmy Famosa was the right man for the job. As the money man for the Famosa fortune, he was formidable, but as a negotiator?

"Kara called her brother on his mobile?"

"Yes. The police have tapped the phones here."

"So, the police *are* involved –"

"Luis insisted! I couldn't stop him. You know how he is."

"Yes," Thomas agreed, "I know how he is."

His attention was caught by Kara's photograph on a side table, and he paused, thinking about the rumoured expose. Was that why Kara had visited London? To see Simon Porter?

Curious, he turned back to Halle, "Why did Kara decide to leave New York?"

"She'd had a fight with Jimmy and went off in a strop. They're always fighting, but Jimmy would die for her. Like you," her gaze fixed on him, "You loved Kara, didn't you?"

"She was easy to love."

Halle stared at him. "I didn't always find her so."

"Didn't?"

"What?"

"You used the past tense," Thomas replied, watching her.

"What d'you mean?"

"You said 'I *didn't* find her so' instead of I *don't* find her so."

A moment passed before Halle spoke again. "I can't just sit around doing nothing! There must be something I can do."

"Did you tell Luis that Kara had been in touch?"

"Jimmy told him before I got a chance." Her tone was mild but resentful. "They're shutting me out like they always do. Usually, it's business, but this time is different, it's Kara, and I *should* be involved. I'm her mother. If anything happens to her, it will destroy me." She got up from her seat, then sat down again, agitated, "I don't care about the money or the business. My husband just wheels me out so I can be the elegant face of the Famosa fortune. In reality, he thinks I'm still the girl he married, still the silly pothead who drank too much and forgot things…" Surprised by the unexpected outpouring, Thomas let her continue. "Luis loves me, but he doesn't respect me. And that's alright, usually, but not this time. I want my daughter back, and I don't care what has to be done - *or who has to be hurt* - in order to make that happen."

"I understand," Thomas said calmly, "She comes first."

"Kara *always* comes first! My daughter is *always* first with me," Halle replied, then changed tack, "So what happens now?"

"We don't tell the police Kara's been kidnapped. Let them think she's just missing."

"*Just missing…*"

Thomas sighed. "I detest Simon Porter, but he's right. We *have* to keep Kara in the news," he paused, and when he saw there was no response, continued, "We have to make people care about her."

"By writing that blog, Simon was talking about?"

"Yes."

"… but what if the kidnapper sees it? Won't it make things worse?"

"We'll have to be careful. Don't do anything to antagonise him, just enough to keep Kara in the public's eye, in their pity."

"*In their pity…*" Halle repeated the words, "Yes, we must make her matter. Tell them about the Kara you love," she gripped Thomas's hands. "I've got so many photographs of her. Get her face out there. Get her familiar and easy to spot. I want everyone to know her."

"Are you sure about that?" Thomas asked. "The Famosas usually don't like people prying –"

"*Luis* doesn't like people prying. *Jimmy* doesn't like people prying, but I don't care if it brings my daughter home!" She gripped his hands tighter, "*Make my daughter matter.* Make the public love her. Like I do. Like *you* do."

"The press digs deep, Halle, and they *keep* digging. Especially if it's about someone well-known. There's always a chance too much might get uncovered. If you want to use the media, fine; just realise that the media will also use you. If you have any secrets, Halle, tell me now. Because once we start this, we can't stop it –"

"Kara's writing a book."

Wrong footed, Thomas stared at her, "*You knew about it?*"

"Yes, Simon Porter told me. He had to, didn't he? Because if I'd found out any other way, I wouldn't have trusted him ever again, and besides, he'll want to handle it."

"Did Porter say what kind of book Kara's going to write?"

"What *kind* of book?" She repeated. "Why? You think Kara wants to do an expose?"

"She's your daughter, what d'you think?"

"I don't know," Halle admitted, "We're not as close as we used to be, and Kara can be secretive. But everyone in this family can be secretive. I can't treat her like a child."

"Is Luis her father?"

The question seemed to crackle in the air. There was an agonised pause before Halle began laughing, Thomas staring at her incredulously.

"She confided in me years ago –"

"*She lied to you,* Thomas!" Halle chided him, tapping the back of his hand. "Kara loves drama, and she makes up all kinds of stories. You know what she's like." Her smile faded, disappointment in her face. "She told you she wasn't Luis's child?"

"Yes. Then she denied it, said it was a joke."

"Because it was! Kara needs attention; she wants Luis to take notice of her. He spends so much time with Jimmy that she feels left out." Halle sighed, "I encouraged her to get involved in the business, but she wasn't interested until lately."

"Was she interested in the auction?"

"She said not," Halle glanced down, thinking, "but she was spending a lot of time in the gallery. The manager, Ivan Holt, said that Kara was asking him about the Famosa collection and how much she liked the Klimt painting."

"She never had an interest before."

"No," Halle agreed, "and Kara was also asking about Luis's artists."

Thomas's eyebrows rose. "*Artists?* Who d'you mean?"

"Modern artists, whose work Luis collects –"

"He usually collects traditional art."

"He's discovered contemporary paintings as well," she replied, unimpressed, "I don't like their work, but Luis does, and, of course, they have other talents."

"Like forgery?"

"I didn't say that."

"Yes, you did," Thomas replied, "So the rumours are true about Luis trading in fakes?"

She glanced away. "There are always rumours. Let's just say that my husband is not averse to expanding his interests."

"Is the Klimt a fake?"

"No!" Halle replied, shaking her head. "Luis wouldn't do that. Selling privately is one thing; holding an auction in the middle of New York that has attracted global interest is another. The Klimt was authenticated in London by specialists from Vienna, and the provenance is right." She paused, adding, "I checked because I wanted to know for my own peace of mind. The painting's a genuine Klimt."

“And Luis is angry that Kara’s pissed off with it? After all, a daughter is one thing; a multi-million dollar Klimt is another.”

“You’ve changed,” Halle replied, shocked, “You’d never have said that before.”

“But I don’t lie. If you want me here just so I can hold your hand, I understand, but what good will it do, Kara? I *had* to know about the Klimt.”

“You’re right,” Halle nodded. “Kara must have known it was genuine, too. Jimmy said she took it because *it gave her leverage* – that’s what she told him.”

Leverage. The word resounded in Thomas’s head and reignited all the doubts he had earlier about Kara and how much she knew about the Famosa business, and how vulnerable that knowledge might make her.

“If I write a blog,” Thomas said suddenly, “I need to go over everything that happened since Kara went missing at Heathrow Airport. It was the evening of the 26th of November?” Halle nodded, Thomas continued, “and she was snatched in amongst hundreds of people. She just vanished… No one does that.”

“Someone must have seen something.”

“Yes, they must have,” Thomas agreed, “So they are either keeping quiet or need reminding.”

17

England
27th November

The pain had changed. It was no longer a raw ache but a buzzing in her head. Her hands and ankles bound, Kara felt the shards of hay pricking through her clothes, but she was grateful to be lying on some hay bales instead of being suspended from the rope. Tied up several yards away from her was a massive pig, snorting and shuffling; Kara at the chain that held it to a metal ring in the wall. Apart from the fact that it stank, hadn't she read somewhere that pigs were used to dispose of human bodies? Or was that just some film she'd seen? Either way, she watched the shadowed outline of the beast, wondering if it would come for her, snapping the chain that held it and attacking.

Stay calm, Kara told herself, stay calm and think. The barn was in virtual darkness, but if she stretched up, she could see through a gap in the wooden slats across to the farmhouse beyond. The bastard was in there. He might come back out and rape her again, or not. It didn't matter anymore; all that mattered was getting away.

She was learning fast. Devising ways to manipulate her captor. How to avoid his unexpected, random violence, or his acts of degradation. Kara had realised early on that her eyes fascinated him and feigned sleep when she heard his footsteps approach. She knew her head wound fascinated him, too. The way he looked at it, curious and revolted in the same instance.

Flinching, she heard the farmhouse door open. A moment later, the barn door was kicked in and a man's shadow fell across the floor.

"Phone your brother," Purchass said, tossing a mobile onto the hay next to her.

"You have to untie my hands first."

He sighed wearily, "I don't think so. Give me the number."

Punching it out, he listened, then held the phone to Kara's ear when Jimmy answered.

"Hello?"

"Jimmy, it's me. Have you got the money?"

Purchass leaned down to hear Jimmy's answer: *"Yeah. All of it."*

He then put the phone back to Kara's mouth as she continued, "It's an old quarry. Fifty miles from London, on the outskirts of Dorking," She repeated the directions as they had been told to her earlier, Purchass watching for any sign that she was trying to tip her brother off. "Be there at six o'clock tomorrow morning. Can you do that?" A murmur of ascent. "Good. But no police, Jimmy. You hear me? *No police.* Come alone."

"I'll be alone."

Purchass was listening, then unexpectedly chipped in, "You better be. Or your sister's as good as dead."

18

New York

Thomas had moved into the brownstone, given his own suite of rooms and a private back entrance to avoid running the daily gauntlet of the press and TV cameras. Although flattered by Halle's trust, Thomas wondered what she *really* thought of him, coming, as he had, via Simon Porter. Did she think that he was there to help? Or to spy?

Having quickly set up the blog, Thomas was now staring at his first entry, re-reading what he had written. His hand hesitated over the word publish, before he pressed enter, knowing that in seconds, a plea for Kara Famosa would be circling the world.

As Simon Porter pointed out, Thomas should be prepared for the endless queries, suggestions, and conspiracy theories; people will have their own take on what had happened to Kara Famosa, and as he thought of the agent, his mobile rang, Simon's upper-class English voice coming, long distance, over the Atlantic.

"How are you doing?"

Thomas ignored the platitude, "How's my father? It's too late to ring him now."

"I spoke to Peter's nurse about an hour ago. Don't worry, he's doing well. He'd be proud of you..."

Thomas doubted that.

"…I've just seen your first posting. Very moving. People will start following you."

"And the publicity won't hurt your agency either."

Simon pressed on. "Good idea to put up those photographs of Kara when she was a little girl. Makes her vulnerable."

"She *is* vulnerable."

"I know, I know…" Simon blustered, discomforted, "So, what's happening in New York? Has Halle been talking about Kara or said anything about the book?"

"No, nothing."

He enjoyed lying to his mother's lover. Withholding information which would have made Simon Porter salivate. How the agent would have rejoiced to hear about Kara's *kidnapping.* What twists of divided loyalties would be employed to get her stricken phone calls reported? What subtle reminders of paid medical bills and nursing care? You believe you're in charge here, Thomas thought, but you're not. *I* am.

"How's Halle coping?"

"How d'you think?"

"I'll call her later," Simon replied, ignoring the hostility. "I'm trying to contact Luis, and I've advised Jimmy to avoid giving interviews whilst he's in the UK. The same goes for Halle in New York."

"You think she's interested in giving interviews?" Thomas replied, "You don't know her that well, do you?"

"I've been the agent for the Famosa family for over twenty years. What makes you think that you know her any better than I do?"

Because I do, Thomas thought. You might be her London mouthpiece, but your client's keeping secrets from you. Secrets relevant to Kara's disappearance. *And you don't know, you smug bastard.*

Simon had caught the shift in Thomas's voice and reacted carefully, "We *are* working on this together, aren't we?"

"Of course."

"I wouldn't want there to be any divided loyalties."

Thomas's response was silken, "I know where my loyalty lies."

"Excellent. Rest assured that your father's being well looked after whilst you're away. I know you're worried about him, but he's having the best of everything." Simon paused, unable to resist a jab, "As I always say, money can be a great help."

"What for? A guilty conscience?"

19

Dorking, Surrey, UK
28^h November, 5.45am

He'd be glad when the whole thing was over. As if all the media attention wasn't enough, some arsehole had set up a blog, blathering on about Kara Famosa, putting up her photographs and asking if anyone had seen her. But no mention of any kidnapping, and no further police involvement. To the world at large, Kara Famosa was simply missing.

It had amused Purchass no end, goading his victim about her online admirer.

"Poor fucking sap's got the hots for you," he had said the previous night, "Wouldn't fancy you so much if he could see you now." He had nudged her with his foot, "You're going to become the Hostage Madonna. Maybe they'll set up a shrine where future victims can worship." He laughed at his own joke, clasping his hands together in a mock prayer.

Kara said nothing.

"So," Purchass had taunted her, "Who is he anyway? The mug writing the blog?"

She had mumbled something behind the gag, Purchass pulling the cloth aside.

"What?"

"He's called Thomas de Souza," she ran her tongue over her dry lips, "Someone I used to know."

"Thomas de Souza? Jesus, how do people get these fucking names?" Purchass mocked, putting the gag back in place. "Well, make sure you thank him when you're released, won't you? The poor bastard's earned a blow job, at least."

But that had been the previous night, and now Purchass was silent and concentrated on the matter at hand. Glancing across to the van's passenger seat, he could see the wound on Kara's head, the blood caked and darkening against the fair hair. It was crispy now. Crispy blood, only occasionally oozing pus. Infected.

That had put him off her even more. No man could fancy a woman who looked like that. He could smell the infection from the driver's seat. But soon he'd be rid of her and be two million pounds richer. Purchass felt a stirring in his groin. Two million quid, he could *buy* a lot of women for that. He could do what he liked with them for that. Bitches put up with a lot for money. He wouldn't be a fucking loser with two million quid. Even his family would have been impressed, his sister the most.

He tried to recall her face, but nothing came. Only the blue eyes. And then, finally, her name – Kathleen. *Kathleen Purchass*. Yeah, that was it! Kathleen, ***Kat***.

Still driving, Purchass struck a pothole hidden under the gathering snowfall. Kara winced but stayed silent. Good thing, Purchass thought, he'd become irritated by her voice as well as that bloody smell. He had given her a bucket to use but not much water to clean herself up, and her clothes were rank. In fact, she was messing up his van, and he wanted her out of it.

It was pitch black. No stars, no curious moon. Blackness, too early for birds or for any speck of morning. The snow was falling hard, making a morgue out of the countryside. the trees white as dry bones. When he had the money, Purchass promised himself he would buy a car. A good car. And give up his porter's job at Heathrow. He would travel. Yeah, travel, and see what women were like in other countries. See if the police were as stupid abroad as they were in the UK. Weeks had passed, and no one had connected the death of Ellie Chadwick with the abduction of Kara Famosa.

And they never would.

The posting for Dorking caught his eye, and he took it. A little further on, he left the main road and began a meandering route between rural villages and smug country houses. Finally, at 5.45am, he found the disused quarry. The spot was carefully chosen so that from his vantage point, Purchass could see anyone approaching and whether they were alone. If Jimmy Famosa had been stupid enough to bring the police, Purchass would know, and the meet would be off.

Parking, he turned off the headlights and checked Kara's gag, tying her bound hands to the door handle of the van. She didn't struggle, but he could feel how tense she was. Not frightened. Expectant.

He moved towards the quarry; the snow crushed under his feet.

Then he stood at the edge.

And waited.

20

Jimmy quickly drove up the narrow lane, rounding the bend, turning a sharp right, and parking. In the glare of his headlights he could see the quarry, an old sign partially covered by snow, a pair of iron security gates pushed back. But as he stared ahead, he could only see the falling snow, no car. No van. No lights. Just blackness.

Reaching for the bag holding the money, Jimmy glanced at his watch, 5.45am. Perhaps the kidnapper hadn't arrived yet, he thought, looking around. He had the right place. He had carefully followed the directions Kara had given him. He had the money. He was ready. It would soon be over… He glanced at his watch again, thinking of the last time he had seen Kara. Sulky, bickering with him, and he remembered how he had reassured his mother:

'I can do this, trust me.'

and then he thought of his sister's comment about the Klimt:

'I was going to use it as leverage.'

Jimmy stared ahead, hands gripping the steering wheel. Come on, you bastard, he murmured. Come on.

His parents had been arguing on the phone earlier, Luis blaming his son for causing the fight that had made Kara bolt, Jimmy wondering why his father hadn't made it back to New York to console Halle. Or maybe there was something more pressing in Bruges. More important than an abducted daughter.

Whatever it was, he didn't know, and Jimmy didn't like that. There were suddenly a few things he didn't know, and that irked him.

Focused, unblinking, Jimmy waited for a movement, a speck of oncoming light. But there was nothing.

And the snow kept falling.

21

Standing at the edge of the quarry, Purchass glanced at his watch. Jimmy Famosa was early, good. Must be keen. And he was alone; Purchass was sure of that. There had been only one set of headlights and no movement elsewhere.

Carefully, he adjusted the night goggles he was wearing, the ones he had bought for poaching but had since turned out to be incredibly useful. In the green light, he could see the snow-covered trees, the black banks of hedges, and Jimmy Famosa's car. His palms itched, longing to get the money in his hands, as he walked towards the far side of the quarry.

Purchass knew he had the advantage because he was a countryman. Famosa was an American city boy, he wouldn't hear him coming until he was on top of him. No chance to play the hero. If he was quick, he could knock Famosa out and get the money without a struggle.

And then back to the van, and home.

Purchass kept his gaze fixed on the headlights of Jimmy's car, his night vision glasses catching the movement of a fox. Excited, he ran his tongue over his bottom lip, his hands sweating as he walked. Only thirty feet to go, Purchass thought. It was easy. Easy money. Thirty feet to a fortune.

And then, out of nowhere, came the sound of a police siren.

22

Startled, Jimmy turned, seeing the outline of a man only yards away, across the quarry.

"**Stop!**" he shouted. "**I didn't call the police! I DIDN'T CALL THEM!**"

Desperate, he began to run, slipping in leather shoes, the deep snow slowing his progress as he scrabbled around the side of the quarry trying to take a shortcut. His eyes were fixed, staring ahead, but Jimmy couldn't see the kidnapper any longer. He could only hear the scream of the siren, the gunning engine of the police car, and see the headlights coming ever closer.

The same headlights that illuminated - for one brief second - a van disappearing into the night.

BOOK TWO

23

It was a hell of a bloody price to send a small package, Purchass thought indignantly. Not that he would have minded if he'd got his two million. But without the ransom, the forty quid he had had to pay out seemed like fucking robbery. Banging the snow off his boots, he walked up the back steps to the kitchen door, raging with frustration. *To bring the police!* Bloody Jimmy Famosa! Did the Yank take him for a fucking idiot?

All that noise, the drama. Why not bring along a bloody band as well? Purchass thought, remembering the sudden, confusing glare of headlights and the screaming insistence of the siren. He would have been caught if he hadn't known his whereabouts. But he was too smart for them. He had kept his headlights turned off until he was onto the B road, so no one could track him. He knew that with luck, the police would take one of the dead ends by mistake, giving him time to get away. And they had done just that, the sound of the sirens quickly fading into the distance.

Purchass snorted, remembering Famosa shouting about not having called the police when they had come blaring up behind him!

Why would they have been there if he hadn't called them?

Obviously, he didn't care enough about his sister.

Or cared too much for his money.

Or maybe he just didn't want her back.

The cow was nothing but a bloody nuisance to everyone.

The temperature had dropped overnight, and the farmhouse was echoing with cold. Cheap draft excluders that his father had fixed years earlier were peeling off, mottled with the damp, the boiler rattled as the pilot light puked into life. Thoughtful, Purchass glanced over to the barn. He should have had more sense, he thought; kidnapping was a fool's game. But he'd been tempted by the money - and where it had got him? Almost caught.

He wouldn't make a mistake like that again. No, he'd stick with what he knew. After all, he could get a woman easily. Hadn't he proved that with Ellie Chadwick? And she had been forgotten quickly enough. No fanfare for her, not like the fuss about the Famosa girl. As for Jimmy Famosa - who the hell did he think he was trying to trick *him*? Trying to catch *him?* Oh no, Mr Famosa, Purchass thought, I've not done with your family. Or you, just yet.

Safe in the grim farmhouse, Purchass daydreamed about what he would do after Kara Famosa was gone. If he didn't pick a woman off the street, there were plenty coming through Heathrow every day. Women who needed help, which was duly offered by some kind member of the airport staff. Because he *could* be kind when it suited him. Purchass knew how dopey he looked, how unthreatening. His technique had been refined over the years until he could always spot a vulnerable woman. A woman travelling alone, with no one to meet her.

Kidnapping wasn't *really* for him. After all, he didn't need much money to live. It wasn't the money he was doing it for. It was the killing, pure and simple. The picking out of the victim. The watching, waiting, then striking. Finally, the kill. *That* was what he knew. *That's* what he wanted. He had just been sidetracked by the bitch in the barn and the lure of money.

Throwing two teabags into a mug, Purchass poured in the boiling water, his eyes fixed on the outhouse. It would be freezing in there. The door didn't close properly, and although the windows were patched up, they were only partially boarded. Another long night, so cold that even the piss in the bucket would freeze… Purchass stirred his tea, leaning forward and clearing a peephole in the window grime.

The barn was squat, almost defiant in the winter morning.

The wind blowing snow feathers around the silent yard.

24

London

Who had called the police? The question kept going round and round inside Jimmy Famosa's head as he stared at his cell phone.

Just ring, he willed it, *just fucking ring.*

He couldn't think clearly, couldn't stop reliving the chaos. Who had called the police? Who else knew about the meet? *His mother?* No, Jimmy thought; Halle didn't know the details because Kara had talked to him on his cell phone. She couldn't have overheard. But she *could* have got the police to follow him. She knew he was arranging a meeting with the kidnapper.

No, Jimmy told himself, Halle would never risk her daughter. It was *his* fault. He had failed, and he would have to admit it. But then he wondered if Halle had told Thomas de Souza about the meeting. Immediately, Jimmy tensed. Surely, she wouldn't have confided in him? Or maybe she would. She liked Thomas. Even in his early twenties, he had been smart and quick-witted - it was obvious he would become successful on his own merit, as Luis often reminded Jimmy. No handouts, no family backing for de Souza; he had made his own glittering way in the world.

When it came, Jimmy had enjoyed Thomas's fall, believing it would be the last of the Englishman. But he was wrong. He was always just a phone call away.

And now Kara was missing.

And de Souza was back.

So, was he involved?

Jimmy frowned. De Souza was certainly well-placed. Ensconced in New York, his blog was well-received, his feelings about Kara as lyrical as they were contrived. Jimmy's jealousy uncurled. Instead of rescuing his sister, he had bundled it. And now he had to tell his mother, who would tell Thomas de Souza, who would probably write it up in his fucking blog...

De Souza was getting famous.

Milking a tragedy.

But was he involved?

Jimmy reached for his coffee and drained the cup, recalling everything Kara had said to him since she had been taken. And then he remembered:

"I'm not the first."

Her words came back to him. Whispered, furtive. Desperate words. There was another woman. Another victim. But who? And why was no one looking for her? Was she kidnapped or dead? His mind replayed the moment when the police arrived and spooked the kidnapper, reliving the agonising seconds as the van disappeared into the night with Kara in it.

Then he paused.

Had she been in it?

He didn't know.

He should have asked to see her! Proof of life, they called it. *Proof of life*... He burned with frustration; an organised man thrown into havoc. He had been only yards from his sister, and now where was she? After missing out on the ransom, the kidnapper might have rid himself of his hostage. He would have known how close he had come to being caught. Why risk his safety by keeping the woman who could identify him?

Unless he was going to try again.

Desperate, Jimmy grabbed at the thought. The kidnapper would *have* to keep Kara alive. He needed her to make another attempt. And this time, Jimmy would bring his sister home. Yes, he thought, steadying himself, he *would* sort it out. Prove himself to Halle and, more importantly, his father.

He would bring Kara back.

Together with the painting.

25

New York
29th November

He was awoken by the sound of screaming and someone hammering on the bedroom door so hard that the wall vibrated.

Quickly, Thomas snatched the door open to find a police officer standing there. "Can you come downstairs, sir?"

"What's happened?" Thomas asked, trying to see over the man's shoulder as he pulled on some clothes, "Is Halle OK?"

"Just come with me, please."

She was sitting rigid, not screaming any longer, just fixed, as though someone had driven a pole down her back and into the sofa beneath her. Her hands were lying flat on her thighs, her eyes unfocused.

"Halle?" Thomas looked back to the officer, "Call a doctor, for Christ's Sake!"

"The housekeeper's sent for one --"

"What happened?"

"What's your name, sir?"

"Thomas de Souza."

"Oh," he said, recognising him. "You're the guy writing that blog about Kara Famosa's kidnapping."

Thomas cut him short, "She's *missing*. We don't know it's a kidnapping."

"We do now," The officer replied dryly.

Thomas looked through the door towards Halle, "What's going on in there? Why was she screaming?"

"A parcel was just delivered. We've been intercepting the mail for days, but this one was marked *Private and Confidential,* so I gave it to Mrs Famosa to open. She was expecting a package, she said. It looked like a jewellery box," he paused, talking too much, trying to excuse his actions. "You know the kind of thing? I gave it to her myself. Watched her open it…"

"And?"

"...There was an object in it."

Thomas could hear Halle crying and moved to the door, but the officer stopped him. "I need to ask you some questions, sir --"

"Questions? You want to ask me questions!" Thomas shook his head in disbelief. "What the hell for?"

"You seem to know a lot about the family and Kara Famosa. We just want to talk to you, that's all," he placed himself between Thomas and the door, "We need all the help we can get about the kidnapping --"

"Did her brother get her back?"

The words were out before Thomas had time to think. The officer frowned. "*Was he supposed to?"*

"You've just told me that Kara was kidnapped," Thomas replied, recovering fast, "and Jimmy Famosa would want to get his sister back."

"I think you know more than you're saying."

At that moment, the door opened behind them. “Mr de Souza isn’t going anywhere, officer,” Halle said, taking Thomas’s arm, “I need him here.”

“But –“

“No buts! If you want to ask him questions, ask them here. Or I’ll talk to your superior.” She was cold, immovable, “Mr de Souza will answer anything you need to know. But not today.”

Composed, she steered Thomas into the drawing room, leaving the housekeeper to show the officer out. They both heard the front door close, Halle sat down, silently. The fire was sending cold licks of flame into the chimney, a piece of string, cut from a small package, lying on the floor.

Thomas looked at it, Halle following his gaze. “It was in a parcel. I thought it was a piece of jewellery I’d commissioned. Special Delivery, *Private and Confidential.* I took it from the police officer; I didn’t want him to open the box. He had such big hands. Did you notice how big his hands were?” She carried on without waiting for an answer. “It was in tissue paper. Like a piece of jewellery...” Thomas waited “I pulled back the paper. There was cotton wool underneath. I thought it was jewellery…” She stopped, then started again. “And then I saw the blood…but I still didn’t understand...” She was reliving it. “He cut off her finger. *Jesus!”* She screamed, *“Why did he do that? She’s my baby!”* Then her voice dropped, falling into a whisper. “Kara’s still alive, isn’t she? *Isn’t she*?”

“Missing a finger won’t kill her.”

Stunned, she stared at him, “*Don’t you care*!”

“It’s just a finger, Halle. Losing it won’t kill her,” he was being deliberately blunt, shocking her back from panic. "She's alive; that's all you have to concentrate on. *She's alive.*"

"How can you be so sure of that?"

"The kidnapper still wants his money. If he'd dropped the idea, he'd never have bothered to send that," Thomas pointed to the bloodied parcel, "Instead, we'd have found Kara's body."

Halle nodded, her face waxen, "You're *sure* she's still alive?"

"Yes," he said firmly, "I'd stake my life on it."

26

1st December

Two days passed. Kara hadn't called her brother. Instead, Halle called Jimmy, still reeling from the package she had received, her anguish directed unfairly at her son.

"What did you do? What went wrong?" she asked repeatedly, making him go over the events time and time again; Jimmy was embarrassed by his failure, and Halle was distracted.

"You should have got Kara home. You *promised* me," she said, her voice shrill over the phone, "You let me down --"

"Someone called the police! They scared the kidnapper off!"

"Or maybe you did," Halle replied, her voice faltering.

Her words were like a slap. But he kept control. "I'm not giving up. I'll get Kara back. I don't believe she's dead."

"Thomas said the same."

Thomas said the same… Jimmy flinched at the thought of Thomas de Souza's involvement.

"I'm coming back to New York –"

"You can't return without Kara! *You promised*! And besides, Luis will be back tonight," Halle's voice became childlike. "You don't know what it's like here; the press are everywhere. TV people, journalists, the phones. They want to know everything about Kara's kidnapping --"

He reacted sharply. *"How do they know she was kidnapped?"*

"It got out! How could it not? And they know he mutilated Kara. There was even some sick cartoon on the internet --"

"Who told them she was kidnapped?"

"*I don't know!"* Halle answered, distracted.

"De Souza shouldn't be writing that blog. It's looking for trouble."

"You can't blame Thomas! He didn't reveal the kidnapping. It was leaked some other way."

Unconvinced, Jimmy persisted, "I'll come back to New York."

"No, stay in England! Your father will be with me tonight," Halle replied, "I want Luis here. He needs to sort this out.

"I would have sorted it out if someone hadn't tipped off the police."

"But someone did!" Halle remonstrated, "and we couldn't stop it. The American police are liaising with the British now. They'll find her. They have the experience and the manpower. I know you're trying to help, Jimmy, but I think you should back off," she paused, her voice low, "Hand it over to Luis --"

"Are you joking!"

"He wants to take control."

"And you're letting him? Even though he hasn't put in an appearance until it was convenient for him to show up?"

"We have to work together as a family–"

"That's what I was trying to do!" Jimmy replied, enraged. "But now you're letting Luis take over."

"I have to! He wants Thomas to keep writing the blog, keep Kara's story out there –"

"So, Luis and de Souza have been promoted. This is my punishment, is it?" Jimmy replied, his voice rising. "*What happened wasn't my fault!* I didn't call the police –"

"I'm not punishing you," Halle said, trying to soothe him. "You have to let your father take control now, and let Thomas continue to help."

"Because de Souza's an expert on kidnapping, isn't he?"

She flinched. "Don't take it the wrong way."

"There is no right way," Jimmy replied, his voice petulant. "You've always liked him. De Souza could never do any wrong. But he doesn't run the business and prop up the Famosa image, does he? Remember, I know everything, and I've sacrificed a hell of a lot."

"I never asked you to," Halle replied, intimidated, "It was your choice."

"Yeah, to keep everything *in the family*. But you've broken ranks now. You've let de Souza in. Has it ever occurred to you that he might be involved in the kidnapping?"

"Thomas?" The thought shook her, "What are you talking about?"

"Perhaps he and Kara plotted this together."

"Are you out of your mind? She's been hurt."

"Has she? Maybe the loss of a finger was worth it," Jimmy countered, "After all, why *was* she kid-napped? For money? Or something else? Maybe it was to stop her expose, letting all our mucky secrets out. And how odd that Kara ran off with the Klimt. Don't you think that's strange, mother?"

Halle paused, confused, "I don't understand."

"My father keeps the business in the family in order to control it and protect it. If I were you, I'd watch who you invite in." His voice was calm again, but it had an edge to it, "You think you know him? Do you think Thomas de Souza is like another son to you? Well, be careful. He's lost everything. He's in disgrace and short of money. Don't let him play you."

"Why not?" She replied helplessly, "You and your father have been doing that for decades."

27

Purchass tucked his mobile into his pocket and left the farmhouse, checking that the doors to the barn were locked and chained. The snow had been a good friend to him, covering all traces of tyre tracks and footprints, wiping the courtyard clean. He knew the roads outside Dorking would be the same, especially the winding, uneven B roads which lead to the disused quarry. Any trace of his tyres would be long gone. Not that it would matter if the police *had* found them: Purchass wasn't a fool; the van he had used two days previously was dumped back in one of the disused outhouses, washed down, and covered with a tarpaulin. It was all sorted. Neat and tidy.

Thoughtful, Purchass walked to the battered old Escort he used for work and headed for Heathrow. The papers had made good reading. His gruesome present for Halle Famosa had been reported across the media, TV news, the papers, and the internet. Even on TikTok, someone making a crude joke about a severed digit. But most people had been shocked.

The outrage surprised him. What a fuss for one finger, Purchass thought. People lost fingers every day and didn't have them reported across the world. It was ridiculous, out of proportion, and all because the Famosas were famous. Yet despite all the time and effort the police were putting in, they were no further to catching him. They had no leads, no clues. The kidnapper of Kara Famosa remained unknown. Which was all well and good, but what was the point of victory if it was unseen? His thoughts shifted to Thomas de Souza's blog. Quite a revelation. As for Jimmy Famosa, what a loser. He wasn't going to like being demoted now that Daddy was muscling in.

Pulling over to the side of the road, Purchass thought, for one uneasy moment, that he could hear his sister's voice, Kat's peculiar timbre coming through the falling snow. Unnerved, he turned off the engine and got out of the car. Dozing villages and sullen, snow-packed fields were empty of people, not even a scarecrow pretending to be humanity. But he could still hear her. Confused, he climbed onto a nearby stile and looked around him. In the distance an early winter sun sneered through a covering of trees, Purchass tilting his head to one side. His eyes narrowed, trying to focus, remembering.

It had been her seventeenth birthday. A hot day - and Kat could never take the heat. She was sweating between her breasts; he could see that when she bent over, and her face was red, her left cheek swollen from a wasp sting.

What the fuck are you looking at, freak?

He had jumped, but for once, he hadn't stepped back. He was bigger now. Taller than her.

You're looking down my front, you bloody pervert!

The wasp sting had looked painful, puffing up the skin under her eye, forcing a wink out of her. And he had laughed because she wasn't frightening anymore. Because she looked like a boil in a summer dress. And she, the bitch of his life, had been suddenly afraid of *him*.

An angry cawing of rooks brought Purchass back to the present, his sister gone with the cackling of the birds, his confidence soaring as he took out his mobile. For several moments, Purchass's fingers wriggled over the keys, then he pressed the entry he had marked **Jimmy Famosa.**

28

He picked it up on the second ring. “Hello?”

Silence.

“Hello?” Jimmy knew who it was without even hearing his voice. “I didn’t call the police! I want you to know that. I didn’t call them.”

Silence.

“We can still do this. I can bring the money to another place. Just tell me when and where.” Jimmy paused, hand sweating as he gripped the cell phone. Keep him on the line. “Is my sister alright?”

Silence.

“I want to talk to Kara. Put her on the phone. Please.”

Still nothing.

“I just want my sister back. Nothing else. Tell me what to do, and I’ll do it.”

There was a muffled noise at the other end, a voice amused, disguised. “You’ve been fired. Was that your mother’s idea?” Purchass laughed softly, “Fuck me, did she smack your little bottie because you didn’t catch the bad man?”

Jimmy took in a breath. "Why did you injure my sister?"

"… And now I have to deal with Thomas bloody de Souza. Who sounds like a fucking ponce. I just wonder why they think he'll be a better negotiator than you." Purchass continued, baiting him, "Your sister's ex-boyfriend --"

"How d'you know that?"

"I read his blog. Nothing like doing some research," Purchass replied, moving on, "Just thought I'd call, Jimmy. Wanted to say that there were no hard feelings."

"Why did you hurt my sister?"

"To make a point."

The words were chilling.

"Is she alright?"

"She's alive."

"In pain?"

Silence.

"Look, I've got the money," Jimmy said urgently, "I can get it to you as soon as you want."

"With the police in tow?"

"No, no police! I told you it wasn't me. I didn't tell them --"

"They just turned up by coincidence?"

"I didn't bring them!"

"You wanted to catch me --"I don't care if you're caught!"

"Yeah, right. Well, I'm not negotiating with you anymore. Not since you've been demoted." Purchass continued, sounding bored, "I should go.|"

"Don't do that!"

Jimmy knew he was on a hook, humiliated, and being played. Purchass could ring off and never contact him again. Never contact Thomas de Souza, either. Which meant that no one would get Kara back. Or the Klimt. He also knew that every thought that had occurred to him had already occurred to the kidnapper.

"Are you still there?"

Silence.

"*Are you still there?* Answer me!"

"I'm here. But like I said, from now on, I talk to de Souza."

Reluctant, Jimmy nodded. "OK, OK, but give me something. There has to be *something* I can do."

"Sweat." Purchass said simply.

And then the line went dead.

29

St Martin's Lane,
London

Staring at the internet report, Anna de Souza glanced over as Simon walked into the agency, blowing his nose loudly. In silence, he moved over to his desk and sat down. After blowing his nose again, he reached for the newspapers in front of him. The Famosa name was the banner headline, along with the grisly details of Kara Famosa's mutilation.

It had caused a stir. News readers and celebrities were talking about it on TV and in blogs. Mainly because Kara Famosa was good-looking and young, but also because her family were glamorous, with a shifty undertone of scandal, and no one could resist watching the rich suffer. Private citizens put up their condolences and thoughts on the internet and on Thomas's blog. The response, from whatever quarter, was always the same. How could anyone injure a woman like that? Physically scarred, if not mentally destroyed. Her kidnapper was a sadist, a madman. No sane man could do such a thing and then send the proof of his sadism to the mother of his victim.

People wanted blood. And, as ever, they forgot their own troubles in hatred. In loathing the kidnapper, they diluted their own worries; their lives became more tolerable in the face of such deviancy. If it could happen to someone as talented and successful as the Famosas, no one was safe. Yet despite efforts on both sides of the Atlantic, the police made no progress. Everyone was looking for the kidnapper. Everyone wanted him caught. He was the ghoul who had abducted the daughter of a celebrated family - and it seemed that he might get away with it.

"You see," Anna said, pointing to her son's latest posting, "I told you Thomas would come good. Halle's relying on him more and more. She's demoted her own son in favour of Thomas. *He's* negotiating with the kidnapper now."

Anna was slick with pride. Thomas had made Kara into a martyr figure. Each post making her more human:

This woman is worth loving, worth caring about, worth saving. I know.

It made poignant, irresistible reading.

Thomas was even talking to his mother again. Not from choice but because they were, indirectly, working together and forced to communicate.

"My son's doing us proud," Anna crowed, "I just hope it doesn't end soon."

The words were brutal and made Simon wince. As ever, when he was under pressure, his hypochondria increased. He was running a temperature, his grey hair sweaty, his throat swollen, taut with tension.

"There's been no mention of Jimmy for a couple of days," he murmured, scanning the computer screen over Anna's shoulder.

"Who cares? Thomas said that Luis wasn't even taking his calls."

Simon raised his eyebrows, *"Seriously*? Jimmy's done everything for the business. He even put his own family second."

"No one gets to the top and stays there without having a ruthless streak," Anna replied coolly. "Luis is punishing his son. In time, Jimmy will be welcomed back in the fold – Halle will make certain of it – but first, he has to be made to suffer for his failure." She turned back to the computer, reading the new posting on her son's blog: "Good God! It says here that Halle's collapsed," she looked at Simon, "Did you know about that?"

"I do now." He said wryly, "Seems that Thomas is first with all the news."

Anna continued to read the post out loud. "Apparently, Halle's been put on bed rest,"

"Bed rest?" Simon frowned. "That's not good."

" And they've cancelled the Klimt auction! All that build-up for nothing."

"I suppose they'll hold it when Kara comes home."

"They should have gone ahead," Anna said curtly, "They had people salivating over that damn painting."

"Klimt's very collectable."

"For millionaires. I suppose it's under heavy guard in New York. Can you imagine what the insurance costs?" She caught a fleeting expression on Simon's face and pounced, "What is it?"

"Nothing."

"There's something you're not telling me! Don't you trust me?" She looked wounded, "Come on, darling, you can't keep secrets from me."

"I don't know anything."

"You know *everything,"* she crooned.

"Really, I don't,"

"What is it?"

He capitulated. "You have to say nothing to anyone, Anna."

"I promise."

"Not one word --"

"About *what?"*

"The painting."

Her eyebrows rose. "*What about the painting?*"

"Kara stole it. She had the Klimt with her when she was abducted."

"Oh, shit." Anna laughed, "She pinched a painting worth millions?"

"That's what I heard –"

"How did you hear?"

"I know Ivan Holt, the manager at the Famosa gallery." Simon admitted, "Look, no one knows –"

"Well, that's not true, is it? The Famosas know, *you* know, and the gallery manager knows - which means that the men who were guarding it know too –"

"Luis will have come down hard to keep it quiet."

"But for how long?" Anna replied, "I wonder why Thomas didn't tell me about the Klimt? I hope he's not siding with the Famosas."

"You put him there," Simon countered meekly.

She ignored the comment. "That explains why Luis has finally come home. Have you spoken to him yet?"

"I'm talking to him later."

"Staying away like that was odd, wasn't it? Just when his wife needed him the most," she paused, thoughtful, "I wonder what Luis thinks about Kara stealing the Klimt."

"It won't matter to him."

"*Don't be a fool, Simon*! That picture's worth a fortune," she started pacing the office, her high heels making indentations in the carpet pile, "No wonder Jimmy Famosa was so keen to meet up with the kidnapper – he was after his sister *and* the Klimt." Her tone was light, but she was piecing it all together, "Good thing Luis is back to sort it all out. Jimmy's bound to resent his father taking over --"

"And your son being Halle's confidante," Simon gestured to the phone, "Ring Thomas and ask if Jimmy's been in touch, will you? We need to keep the family together, make them look united."

"Even if they aren't?"

"We can't afford to lose public sympathy now."

She nodded. "Maybe Thomas could have a little chat with Halle about them all *'pulling together'*? Even if there are difficulties."

"We don't know if there *are* any difficulties."

"With Jimmy being ousted?" She raised her eyebrows, "Come on, Simon, you can hear the ructions in court from here. A shift in power, the theft of a painting worth millions. Oh dear, such a lot of things to hide, so many reputations on the line."

Simon studied her in silence. He was changing, and knew it. He felt uncomfortable. Anna's closeness – once arousing – was now claustrophobic.

"You know how the business works," she continued, "From the moment the Famosa story broke, this agency has thrived. And Thomas's blog is *keeping* it in the news. As for Jimmy Famosa - he's finished. Which is lucky for us, because" she kissed the top of Simon's head, "we don't want anyone knocking *our* cuckoo out of the nest."

30

New York

Silent, Luis Famosa came out of the bathroom, wrapping himself in a towelling robe and combing his damp hair. In the mirror, he could see Halle reflected, sitting on the bed with her knees drawn up and her arms wrapped around her calves. She had been crying for a long time, begging Luis to hold her, to make love to her, to comfort her. And when he had resisted, she had cried again.

"Why don't you have a drink, Halle?"

She glanced up, baffled, "*What?*"

"A brandy would do you good."

"I… I don't drink, Luis, you know that," she said, her voice uncertain.

"One brandy won't harm you. It might steady your nerves," he replied, walking into his dressing room, and returning half-clothed.

"Are you going out?" Halle asked, "I thought we could talk."

"We talk all the time," Luis replied, moving over to the mirror and checking his reflection. Burly, in a sombre suit and white shirt. Nothing flashy, nothing too Cuban. "Was there something you wanted to talk about in particular?"

Reverting to a lifelong habit, Halle chewed her thumbnail, watching as Luis poured some brandy and handed her the glass. There was always booze around the house, but it had never interested her, not since her younger days. Alcohol confused her and muffled her thoughts, Halle's gaze resting on the glass as her husband held it in front of her.

"Drink up."

She shook her head. "I don't want it."

"You're overwrought; you need to relax. The brandy will do you good. Then we can talk about anything you like." He jiggled the glass in front of her face. "Don't I always know what's best for you?" When she wouldn't take the glass, Luis continued, "I've been hearing some interesting things. Jimmy said that Kara would only talk to him. Why's that? Because she stole the Klimt?"

"I don't know…" Halle replied, still staring at the glass in front of her.

"What father would care about the theft of a painting when his daughter is in danger?"

"No father would."

He nodded. "That's right. No father would." He took her hand and closed her fingers around the glass, "Now, drink up."

She had begun to cry. "Why are you doing this?"

"Doing what?" Luis asked, his tone gentle.

"I don't understand. What's wrong?"

"I'm worried, Halle. Which father *wouldn't* be worried about his missing daughter?" He lifted her chin, looking into her face, "Drink the brandy."

Not daring to refuse, she sipped at it, the spirit burning her throat, Luis sitting down beside her on the bed. "You used to like to drink and smoke weed. A lot of it."

"I was young then –"

"Yes, but you went back to it, didn't you? When we'd been married for a couple of years, you slid back into your old ways," he paused, dark eyes fixed on her. He needed a shave, Halle thought, he always needed to shave twice every day; otherwise, he had a five o'clock shadow. Her father had teased her about that, saying that whatever he did, Luis Famosa would always look like a Cuban.

"Drink it up, Halle."

"I don't want to."

"I've been drinking," he admitted, "a lot lately, in fact. Stress in business, then Kara going missing. So many things seemed to happen at once, and that made me anxious. I never expected Kara to show any interest in the business - but to steal the Klimt? That came out of the blue. Why d'you think she did that?" He tipped the bottom of the glass to Halle's lips as he continued to talk, "And then to hear that she was writing a book. Did you know about that, Halle?"

"She didn't mean it --"

"What didn't she mean?"

"To write a book about us... She didn't mean it." Halle stammered. "Kara was always telling stories, making up things, you know that. She did it for attention –"

"But you knew she was thinking about it?"

"She was just acting up."

"Why would she *want* to write a book about our family?" He asked, his tone even, "Was she writing an expose?"

"I don't know, Luis, I just –"

"I mean, why would my daughter do that? Why would *any* daughter turn on their father?" Suddenly, he knocked the glass upwards, the brandy spilling over Halle's face. "But then again, she's *not* my kid, is she?"

"What?" Halle was trembling, backing away from him.

"I had her DNA tested," he explained, refilling Halle's glass and handing it to her. "Drink up, darling, you're going to need it. You see, I noticed that Kara's attitude had changed. She was distant from the family, on the defensive, and it made me wonder why." He pointed to the full glass, "You *are* going to drink that, aren't you?" he asked, watching as Halle reluctantly sipped at the brandy. "And her sudden interest in the business - pumping Jimmy for information, chatting to the gallery manager – it all seemed out of character. As for me, Kara could barely look at me. She was remote, almost hostile. Then, when I caught wind of the book, I realised that all her snooping was information gathering because how much did she *really* know about the business? How much could she expose? How much could she *sell*?"

"Luis, listen –"

He cut her off, gesturing to the glass in her hand. "*Drink it!* It was then I understood what was going on. Kara wanted revenge, particularly on you, Halle. And on me, too, because discovering that she wasn't an offspring of the Famosas must have come as a hell of a shock. But what a story it would make. It could set her up for life."

"She was lying –"

"**Like her mother**!" Luis snapped. "You lied too, Halle. You let me think Kara was my child. *You lied to me!"*

"And you lied to me…" she replied desperately. "You had a mistress, and you thought I'd never find out, but I did. You had a daughter with her, a whole life that you kept secret –"

"So, you got your revenge by getting yourself knocked up and palming someone else's kid on me?"

Halle rose to her feet, Luis lunging forward and gripping her wrist. "Who is he?"

The brandy had already had an effect; Halle was dizzy, her voice timid when she answered. "I don't know!"

"Liar!"

"I don't know!" she shouted, confronting him. "I'd been drinking for days, smoking pot, out of my mind. You don't understand, do you? You were my *world,* Luis. You rescued me, and then you betrayed me."

"The woman meant nothing to me --"

"But it meant *everything* to me!" Halle retorted, her voice wavering, "You said I'd be safe when I married you, but you were lying."

He tightened his grip on her wrist. "*Who's Kara's father*!"

"Stop asking me! I don't know!" She repeated. "I'd gone to Las Vegas to look for you, but I couldn't find you, so I stayed on. I didn't know where else to go. And I kept drinking. Some of the people there were friends; I stayed with them… I was hurt, lost, drifting. I don't remember what I did, it's all a blur, I can't remember what happened –"

"Or who you slept with?"

“That’s right,” she admitted, “I don’t remember who I slept with --”

“Bitch!” Luis snapped, putting his hands around her throat and shaking her. “I could kill you for what you’ve done to me.”

She didn’t even try to break free. “Then do it, Luis, because if anything happens to my daughter, I won’t want to live anyway.”

31

New York

The cell phone was lying on the step next to him, unanswered. Having just returned from London, Jimmy had only spoken briefly to his father. Luis had been coldly polite but dismissive of his son's excuses, informing Jimmy that he was now taking over. It would have been pointless to attempt any argument, and instead, Jimmy walked out into the garden at the back of the brownstone, struggling to keep control of himself.

Lighting a cigarette, he tensed when he heard footsteps behind him.

"We have to talk."

He turned, looking Thomas up and down, his expression hostile, "You've been clever. But you always were, weren't you? Always panting around this family."

"It was Halle's decision --"

"To humiliate me publicly? To get some snotty Brit to show me how it's done?" Jimmy snapped, rising to his feet and facing Thomas on the steps. "Kara's not your flesh and blood."

Thomas sighed. "I never said she was."

"But you were on that fucking plane as soon as the news broke --"

"Your mother asked me to come."

"And you wasted no time, did you?" Jimmy countered. "But then you've got time on your hands now, haven't you? Since you've been fired --"

"That's something we've got in common."

" – but *you're* broke." Jimmy shot back. "No work, no wage. Lucky that the Famosas are loaded, isn't it? And lucky that Simon Porter happens to be fucking your mother."

"Cut it out," Thomas said warningly.

"I don't like you. I never have. You're too involved with my family."

"And you think you can do something about it?" His voice was mocking, "You can't bully me, Jimmy, so don't even try it. For Kara's sake, we have to work together."

"No, we don't. You shouldn't have stayed in touch with my sister after you married, but you couldn't let go, could you?"

Thomas laughed. "Piss off! You're hardly one to offer relationship advice."

"Why *are* you still around? What are you after?"

"You're paranoid," Thomas replied dismissively. "I'm a friend, no more."

But he was lying. He *did* know secrets. Like Luis not being Kara's father, because even though she insisted it had been a joke, he knew it was true. Did Jimmy know? And if he did, just how would that upset the balance of power amongst the Famosas? A half-sister didn't have the same status as a full sibling. A *kidnapped* half-sister planning an expose might be considered collateral damage. And there was the painting to consider. Kara believed it gave her *leverage* – for what? No normal daughter or sister would have said that. But who *was* normal within the Famosas? Halle, Jimmy, and Luis all hiding something. And was it something Kara had threatened to use against them?

How many people wanted Kara's return?

How many wanted to make sure she never did?

"You should leave now," Jimmy said, cutting into his thoughts. "My father's taking over, he doesn't need you."

"You're wrong," Thomas corrected him "Luis wants me to negotiate with the kidnapper –"

"*You*?" Jimmy said, jumping to his feet, the ash falling off his cigarette onto the stone steps. "You're not even family!"

Thomas put out his hand. "Let me have your phone, Jimmy. I need it for when Kara calls –"

Enraged, Jimmy knocked his hand away. *"You're not taking my fucking phone!* You think you know the type of man who's taken Kara? You think you can deal with him? He's been cheated out of his money, but you think *you* can handle it? You shouldn't even be here!"

He lurched forward, throwing a punch as Thomas ducked out of the way. Almost losing his footing on the steps, he struck back and caught Jimmy under the chin, watching as he staggered and then fell.

"You fucking clown!" Thomas shouted, snatching the phone out of Jimmy's hand and towering over him. "I'm not the man you should be fighting."

32

Returning to London, Thomas had decided that he was going to retrace every step Kara had taken from the time she left New York to her arrival at Heathrow. It had been easy to get the details from Kennedy Airport, the flight number, and the estimated arrival time, but what happened to Kara after she arrived at Heathrow was unknown.

With Jimmy Famosa's cell phone in his pocket, Thomas made his way to the airport and Kara's last sighting. Walking across the foyer, he noticed the cameras and surreptitiously photographed their positions. No one was exactly sure where Kara had been snatched, only that it was out of camera range. Having discovered that Heathrow had over 6,500 CCTV cameras in operation, Thomas began his search in Arrivals, knowing Kara would have passed through there when she came in from New York. As he moved, the red light of the nearest camera traced him, and as he walked on, the cameras continued to watch, their red blinks tracking him as he searched for the camera that didn't light up. The 'blind spot' mentioned in the police report. Time passed. He kept looking. Left Arrivals and moved into the foyer, his progress captured by another lens.

At one point, Thomas thought he had found the dead camera and stepped back, almost knocking a woman off her feet just as the machine flicked back on. He could hear people behind him, the usual cacophony of airport noises, voices, music, and a dim siren sounding on a motorised trolley. A sense of dread overwhelmed him as he looked around, seeing what Kara had seen moments before she had been taken, sharing her last instants before everything changed. For another hour, Thomas searched, then paused, looking up to find himself staring into a blank CCTV lens. It was supposed to cover an area of about twenty feet, but the camera had no sensor and no red light. Thomas raised his arm and waved it around, but there was no response. The lens was dead. He had found the blind spot.

The space was sandwiched between a hoarding advertising Gucci perfume and a Costa Coffee shop. Thomas could feel the hairs go up on the back of his neck: Kara could easily have been snatched there. Someone who had been hiding behind the hoarding or someone in the coffee shop could have taken her. Perhaps they had faked an accident? Spilt coffee over her coat, and Kara, being Kara, would have been angry. They could have taken her into the back of the shop to clean up - then overpowered her.

"Can I help you?"

Thomas glanced at a young man watching him, wearing a label, **MICKY, Costa Coffee**.

"D'you work here?"

Micky nodded, "Yeah, d'you want something?"

"Did the police talk to you after Kara Famosa was kidnapped?"

Discomforted, Micky shifted his feet, "Are you a journalist?"

"No, I'm a close friend of the family." Thomas glanced round again, "Did you know about the blind spot?"

"Only when I read the papers afterwards."

"Doesn't it seem strange that Kara disappeared in that particular space? Unless someone took her *knowing* they wouldn't be seen? A regular traveller. Or someone who works at Heathrow -"

"I didn't do anything! I didn't even see her!" Micky said, panicked. "I was off sick that day."

Thomas put up his hands. "I wasn't accusing you. I'm just asking questions and trying to get some answers. You must have talked about Kara Famosa's disappearance," he continued, "Did anyone see anything suspicious that day? Anyone hanging around?"

"Look, I've got to go," Micky replied, eager to leave.

"What about the airport staff? Did the police question them?"

"I dunno! You'd have to talk to Personnel. They'd know."

Nodding, Thomas turned away, spotting an unmarked passageway behind the hoarding. "What's down there?"

"Staff exit."

He headed for it, Micky running after him. "Hey! You can't go there! It's for members of staff only."

"But someone could take a wrong turn?" Thomas suggested. "Or go here on purpose? Who'd stop them? No one's stopped me, have they?"

He paused at the doors marked staff exit and pushed them open, walking out onto a concrete landing. On his right was a lift labelled Service Only. Was this the place? He wondered. Did the man who had snatched Kara bring her here? He studied the floor: no skid marks, no sign of a struggle. Had Kara come here willingly? Or had she followed someone out?

"Did the police check this place?" he asked, Micky still hovering behind him.

"They went everywhere, checked everything. But they found nothing. I overheard them saying that she'd disappeared into thin air."

Thomas tried to imagine what had happened. If Kara had been overpowered, where would the kidnapper have taken her? She might have been unconscious, a dead weight, difficult to move… He glanced to his right, looking at the lift, then pressed the button. An instant later, the doors slid open: the lift empty, scrubbed clean.

"Who uses this?"

"Hundreds of people. They bring goods up in it and take the rubbish down in it." Micky paused, curious. "What are you looking for?"

"I'm not sure," Thomas said, moving to the stairs and beginning to descend. On the fourth step, he found some cigarette butts. "People come here to smoke?"

There was a pause before Micky replied. "Look, we're supposed to go outside. But when it's wet, we have a fag in the stairwell." He shrugged, then followed Thomas as he moved further down the steps. "It's cleaned every day. You won't find anything."

"How many flights?"

"What?"

"How many flights of stairs are there?"

"Five. No, six." Micky replied, curious. "Why?"

"Because he could have taken her up. People would think he would take her down to get her out of the building, but what if he took her *up?*"

"Then what? There's only the roof at the top."

Thomas's mind was racing. How *did* the kidnapper get Kara out of the building? Did he leave her on the roof and go back for her later? No, he couldn't have got her off the roof without someone noticing. So, he must have taken her *down* and out through the basement.

Turning back, Thomas descended, taking the steps two at a time, Micky still following him. At the bottom were two bolted Exit doors.

"Are these always locked?"

Micky nodded. "Yeah, always."

"So how d'you get outside for a smoke?"

"We take the lift. It stops in the basement." He paused, his expression changing, *"The lift was out of order!"*

Thomas stared at him, "What d'you mean?"

"When the girl went missing, the lift was out of order," Micky repeated. "No one could use it for two days."

Leaving the landing, Thomas walked back through the short passageway which led to the airport. At the blind spot between the hoarding and the Costa Coffee shop, he paused, looking out onto the melee of people in the foyer beyond.

The kidnapper had had no choice. He couldn't go upwards with Kara's body. And he couldn't go down because the lift was broken. Instead, *he had had to cross the foyer*. But how could a man move a woman's body through hundreds of people without being seen?

In the middle of the airport crowds, as Departures displayed its messages and the Christmas carols trilled on, Thomas de Souza stood within feet of where his ex-lover had been abducted.

And on the balcony above, Purchass leant on his trolley and watched him.

33

Chelsea Wharf,
London

No one looking at Hugh Ackerman would have realised how powerful he was. His weighty, shabby appearance and monotonous voice were more suited to an archivist than a connoisseur specialising in Japanese ceramics and 19th-Century European art. In a world where rivalry and excess were commonplace, he seemed sombre and old-fashioned. Yet, his dullness hid a ruthlessness few could match, his memory prodigiously long and famously unforgiving.

But now he was crying.

The sobs were coming from low inside his chest, a string of snot running unnoticed from his nose. Alone in his office, he sat with the drapes drawn, his phone unplugged, and mobile turned off.

Outside, Ackerman's secretary listened at the door but didn't dare enter.

"He's still in there," she whispered, gesturing to the company lawyer who had just arrived. "I told you on the phone; he's been crying for over an hour."

David Gates stared at her incredulously, "What the hell happened?"

"I don't know. He was already in his office when I arrived."

"So why don't you knock on the door?"

"*You* knock!" she snapped, backing away, "I'm not disturbing him."

David stared at the door, thinking of Stalin. The Russian dictator who had so terrorised his staff that he had lain unattended for 24 hours after having a stroke. But this was different, David thought, Ackermann was obviously very much alive. But *crying?* God, who would have believed that? He thought of their meeting the previous day. Ackermann had been as unemotional as ever but perhaps a little preoccupied? Perhaps the eyes behind the thick glasses had been a little more distant when he had called the meeting to a close so hurriedly?

"Is there trouble at home?"

The secretary stared at David blankly, "How would I know?"

"You've been his secretary for fifteen years."

"And I know as much about him now as I did when I started," she replied, staring at the locked door. "Mr Ackermann doesn't confide. And no one asks him personal questions. You should know that by now - your predecessor learnt the hard way," There was a certain smugness in her tone as she moved behind her desk. "Mr Ackermann doesn't do small talk."

Mr Ackermann wasn't doing any talk. He was still crying. Still sitting at his office desk, unable to stop. And in his hand was a copy of *The Times* with a photograph of Kara Famosa on the front page.

34

2nd December

At first, Purchass was alarmed to see someone snooping around, making notes and taking discreet shots of where the cameras were placed. But then he had recognised Thomas de Souza from his photograph on the internet.

A very different man to Jimmy Famosa, Purchass thought. Where the American had been stiff-backed, de Souza was quick and tall, his hair long at the neck, his face alert. As soon as he had seen him, Purchass's attention had been caught, moving over to the side of the mezzanine to watch him unobserved. Of course, he had nothing to worry about. If Thomas *had* looked up, he wouldn't have recognised him. Just one of the cleaning staff. Some poor anonymous sod with a trolley.

Intrigued, Purchass had watched de Souza as he moved around, then disappeared, walking out of his eyeline. But Purchass wasn't worried. The police had examined the area before and found nothing. Why should de Souza be any different? Oh, but it was fun, Purchass thought. More fun that it had been with

Famosa because de Souza was a nob, fallen on hard times. The internet had described his elevation in the financial world and then his sudden descent. How did that happen? Purchass wondered. How did a man go from being a powerhouse to a nanny overnight?

... Mr Thomas de Souza is at present taking care of his father,
the retired London surgeon, Mr Peter de Souza...

Retired London surgeon, Purchass thought. A butcher with a brass plaque. So why didn't Tommy boy go in for medicine? He thought of the fallen hero. Handsome without trying, someone you could hate on sight. Which was why it was going to be such a pleasure to have de Souza on the ropes, and he was going to make it last. There was no reason to rush. Let de Souza – and the police – think he was after a ransom.

It suited him to wrong-foot them. Purchass had read enough books on criminal psychology to know how everyone liked to label criminals and had decided that he would let everyone think he was after money - when what he wanted cost *nothing.* He chuckled to himself, thinking that the police would bring in someone used to dealing with kidnappers. A negotiator in waiting. He wasn't going to negotiate with anyone. Except for de Souza.

Dialling the number, Purchass waited.

It was picked up on the second ring. "Thomas de Souza?"

"Yes."

"Hell of a name, that," Purchass sniffed, "You up for this?"

If he was expecting a nervous reaction, he didn't get it.

"How's Kara?" Thomas asked, composed.

"She wants to leave. She wants to get back home."

"Everyone wants her home," Thomas replied. "Where d'you want to meet?"

"I want three million quid."

"It was two before."

"Jimmy Famosa fucked me about," Purchass replied, "so the price has gone up. Three million."

Thomas agreed, "Alright."

"Maybe I should have asked for four?"

"I can get you three million, that'll have to do."

"It's not your fucking money!" Purchass snorted, "You're a bit glib with someone else's cash."

"I'm authorised to pay you. Where d'you want to meet up?"

"I'll call you tomorrow --"

"Can't we do this now?" There was a pulsing silence down the line. "Are you still there?"

"I'm running this show," Purchass's voice was threatening, "Remember that. What I say goes. Otherwise, I could ring off and never get back in contact. Then what? You'd never see the bitch again."

"You're right, you're in charge. I'm sorry."

"You should be."

"You're calling the shots."

"Yeah, I am."

"When d'you want to meet up?"

"Like I said, I'll call you tomorrow," Purchass replied, cutting the connection.

Left with the phone humming in his ear, Thomas slumped into a chair, taking a deep breath. He would give the mobile number to the police, but he knew it would be pointless. The kidnapper was using burner phones. Untraceable. Thomas had tried to sound calm, but his hands were sweating. He didn't know what he had expected, but the man's voice had surprised him; benign, faintly Northern, the tone almost amused. No obvious aggression, yet frightening. He knew that all he could do was wait for the next phone call. His life suspended on the whim of a lunatic.

As he had been instructed, Thomas phoned the police and asked for Detective Jameson, the man in charge of Kara's kidnapping.

"My name's Thomas de Souza, I've returned to London, and I'm taking over from Jimmy Famosa --"

"We were told all about it." the detective interrupted impatiently. "And I checked you out with Luis Famosa in New York. He said to help you any way we could."

"Is there any news?"

"No news, sorry."

"I want to ask you something," Thomas began. "The other night, when Jimmy Famosa went to meet up with the kidnapper, who told the police?"

"It was a tip-off. Anonymous." Jameson's voice quickened, "And frankly, Mr Famosa should have told what he intended to do."

"He wanted to get his sister back --"

"Really?" Jameson bristled. "Did Mr Famosa know that his sister was even in that van? Did he know that the kidnapper would have swapped her for the money? D'you think he'd had given Kara back to her brother and let them drive off?"

"I don't suppose he thought of any of any of that --"

"He should have done."

"Believe me, he's suffering now," Thomas replied, surprised to find himself coming to Jimmy's defence.

"Kara has seen her kidnapper," the detective continued. "She can identify him. She could put him away for years. Mr Famosa might have thought he was doing the right thing, but he could have signed his sister's death warrant… Don't make the same mistake, Mr de Souza. Work with us, not against us."

"I will." Thomas lied. He had considered passing on the information he had worked out at the airport but resisted.

"Kidnappings are never simple."

"You've handled others?"

"Only one."

"And what happened?"

There was a long pause. Long enough to tell Thomas everything he wanted to know.

35

Snow was falling again, drifting onto the old farmhouse and landing noiselessly on the roofs of the outbuildings. Fine snow, thin snow, white as a bride's veil. Or a corpse's shroud. Snow that came like dust from a sky shaken clean. Snow throwing navy shadows and oyster highlights. Snow solemn and snow sly.

She could barely see him, just hear him, and knew he was watching her. The pain from where he had severed her finger was increasing, the blood staunched by a wedge of cotton wool held with masking tape. He had come at her so suddenly she hadn't had time to react, pulling her arm over his knee and then sawing, hacking away at her hand… Her stomach jolted with the memory. The pain and shock had made her pass out. When she came round later on, she wept, hysterical, panicking in the darkness. No one heard her. No one came. So finally, Kara stopped crying and stayed still, in the cold, in pain, motionless. As she was now.

She could sense him watching her. Only this time, Purchass hadn't brought a torch, this time he was using the light from the snow to guide him. Snow and moonlight illuminated the broken windows of the barns and made an early Advent calendar of that rotten little plot. His feet paused by her head. She waited for the kick, but nothing came. Instead, she heard him breathing through his mouth. Noisily, like he had a cold.

It hadn't been Jimmy's fault. She could tell from her brother's panic that he hadn't known the police would turn up. Or had he been acting? No, she told herself, Jimmy *had* wanted to save her. He might even have pulled it off if someone hadn't sent the police. So, *who* had contacted them? Who else knew about the meet? Luis and her mother - because her brother would have told their parents. But no one else. Unless Halle had told Thomas, but if he had known he would never have betrayed her.

Someone had, though.

Had someone deliberately set out to murder her? Had they *wanted* the meet to fail? Had someone hired the kidnapper to abduct her? Kara shuffled towards the wall, leaning back against a stack of hay bales. She felt safer when she could see who was coming. Like now, when she could see the kidnapper's silhouette, his form too big for the milking stool where he had sat down, lighting a roll-up.

Her thoughts moved on. Who would *want* to see her dead? Because of the book? The expose she had mentioned to friends, joking that no one knew the real Famosa family but her. The same book she had discussed with Hugh Ackermann. The distant figure who had always been kind to her, even though her mother had rejected him long ago, choosing to marry Luis Famosa instead.

Kara knew that people gossiped about her relationship with Ackermann, but so what? Let them think she was sleeping with him, even if he *was* decades older than her. At first, she suspected that he was being nice to pump her for information about Halle, but she was wrong. There was nothing Machiavellian about his interest. He was just lonely… She thought of the book again. No, Hugh Ackermann wouldn't harm her to get revenge on her mother. It was madness to even think it. But she *had* confided in him, hadn't she?

The temperature was dropping, a chill moved through her body. It settled on her skin like the snow outside, and she thought of Luis Famosa. Her father. But not her father. Her parents were seen as a blessed couple, their brief estrangement kept a secret. It had only lasted for a few months, but long enough for Halle to seek comfort elsewhere, and the result had been Kara. She thought of the day she had found out, and the resentment which had followed. To be raised as offspring of the Famosa dynasty, only to discover she was another man's bastard, had been devastating.

The core of herself - of who she had believed she was - had gone. And with it, the person she had believed her mother to be. If Halle had told her the truth, it wouldn't have been so shocking, but the secrecy had made Kara resent her mother, and when she found out Luis wasn't her father, she became vengeful, willing to consider all the gossip she had heard for so long. All those shabby, sticky rumours that could tar and feather a reputation.

Cautiously, Kara tried to move, watching the kidnapper smoking, her body tense, waiting to see if he would attack her again. And then she remembered a vague story about her father's early years in Las Vegas. When she repeated it, Ackermann looked shocked then laughed, his eyes tearing up with amusement. But when

Ackermann had stopped laughing, he admonished her, warning her never to mention it again because:

'*People get things mixed up. And besides, it's just bullshit.*'

With an effort, Kara raised her bloodied hand and rested it against her shoulder, trying to ease the pain. Ackermann had been infatuated with her mother, so obsessed that he had never loved anyone else. When he spoke of the young Halle - how silly she had been, how vulnerable - his deadpan voice became soft. He said she had been beautiful but lost, always needing someone to protect her. He would have done it willingly; he had told Kara:

'If she had let me, I would have given my life for her.'

But she had chosen Luis Famosa instead, and Hugh Ackermann had chosen to live in London in a house chockful of Oriental antiques and 18th-century European paintings. His admiration of Gustave Klimt was no secret; the artist's female portraits reminded him of Halle.

Furtively, Kara glanced over to the kidnapper, still smoking, the smell pungent, strong tobacco mixing with the steaming hay. Had he found the painting yet? Did he believe that it was worth a fortune? Maybe even her life? She was glad she hadn't told Ackermann she was going to steal the Klimt. He would have wanted it and gone to any lengths to get it. But he would never have harmed her for it, Kara told herself, even for a Gustav Klimt that resembled her mother. Then again, Ackermann *was* a fanatical, ruthless collector known to employ runners to steal pieces he craved. And Ackermann *had* encouraged her to write the book. She had thought he was just showing an interest, but what better revenge than to use her to expose Luis's criminal activities and punish Halle for rejecting him?

Restless, Kara tried to stretch her bound legs, her thoughts incessant. What if her abduction had just been random? Fate offering an opportunity to blame her death on a kidnapping? No one would suspect anyone of organising that, would they? She rested her head back against the straw, flinching as it caught in her hair. Who would be damaged by her threatened expose? Her mother's infidelity would be of fleeting interest. So, what would *really* matter? The answer was obvious - the Famosa name and business. Adultery was accepted by the rich, but fraud was another matter. All the gossip about Luis's businesses had been overcome, but if she exposed his trading in forgeries, he would face ruin. The grandees of the art world, the uber-rich collectors and the duped auction houses would come after Luis. And *he* knew it. And *Jimmy* knew it. And *Halle* knew it. They all knew that Kara could topple them, and they *all* had a reason to want her out of the way. But how far would they go? Would they kill her to prevent the book from being published?

Suddenly, the kidnapper rose to his feet, dropping the cigarette stub and grinding it out with his boot. He ground it for far longer than he needed to, working it into the dirt of the barn floor. The horror of the situation suddenly hit her. She might never escape, and here she would die. Outside, it was snowing. She could see it through the gap in the wooden boards and remembered that it was late December, the run down to Christmas. Memories of past Christmases came back. Christmas with her family, with Halle, with Luis, with Jimmy. Christmas in Las Vegas, New York, or Hampshire. It could be Christmas anywhere for the Famosas, but this time she wouldn't live to see it. Instead, she was going to die in a sordid barn and then buried in a field. Lost. Forgotten. Unless she fought to live.

"I can help you sell the painting."

Her voice made Purchass jump, turning to look at her. "*Painting?* That daub's worth fuck all."

"You're wrong," Kara insisted, "It's worth millions –"

"Give it a rest!"

"It's true, everyone wants it."

"Why don't you just shut up!" Purchass snapped, lunging forward and kicking her left leg. "You're a bloody nuisance, a bloody aggravation."

Wincing from the pain, Kara persisted. "Thomas will help you sell it. Talk to him," she pleaded, flinching as Purchass leaned down and grabbed hold of her chin, jerking her head up.

"Shut it!" Purchass shouted, "I don't like you. I don't *want* you," he said, leaning so close that his breath was in her face. "And I don't need all this fucking messing about. I need to think. And I need you to keep quiet."

He let go of her and stood up, angry and impatient, his feet heavy on the floor as he paced. Kara could see he was agitated, his head moving from side to side as he massaged the back of his neck. She could imagine what he was thinking - *Why hadn't he killed her? The police were looking for him. He was going to get caught.*

Warily, she broke into his panic. "Let me help you –"

"**Just let me think!**" He shouted, "**For Christ's Sake, let me think**!"

She pushed on, desperate to save herself. "You'll get a fortune for the Klimt, and for me. Then you could leave the country. Go wherever you want," she pleaded, "I won't tell anyone about you."

"**Stupid bitch,"** Purchass said, turning back to her, "Don't you get it? No one's going to save you."

"Listen," she begged, crying, "please, listen to me."

"Shut up!"

"Please," she whimpered again, "*Please*, listen –"

And then he reacted. Bending down, he lifted up the anvil beside the door, moving back to Kara and raising it high above his head.

Then he howled. Once, before letting it fall.

36

3rd December

"I want to talk to her."

Exasperated, Purchass stumbled back to the farmhouse, mobile in hand. He had slipped up. He should have dumped the burner phone after he had used it, like he always did before. Everyone knew what you did to avoid getting caught. But he hadn't, and now de Souza was calling him like they were bloody mates. Christ, he *had* to be more careful.

"De Souza," he said, rubbing his forehead, "What the fuck d'you want?"

"I want proof of life. I want to talk to Kara."

Purchass raised his eyebrows, drinking a glass of tap water before answering. "You want her back or not?"

"I want to talk to her."

"You're not making the fucking rules here!" Purchass snapped, "I want my money."

"Tell me when and where."

"Seven o'clock tomorrow night. Peasbold Place, Leatherhead –"

"Where's that?"

"Use a bleeding map!" Purchass replied shortly, "Seven o'clock tomorrow. Bring me the three million quid, and you'll get her back."

"Peasbold Place? Is that a residential area?"

"Not now. The houses are all boarded up, ready for redevelopment. The place is cordoned off by the builders. There's only one way in, through an iron gate. You can't miss it. Oh, and no police. Come alone."

"I'll be alone."

"Oh, I know you will," Purchass retorted sarcastically, "When you park, flash your headlights on and off four times. Hear me? On and off. Four times."

Then he rang off, without waiting for a reply.

37

Maida Vale
London

On the sofa, Peter de Souza was sleeping, a rug over his legs. He was ageing, Thomas thought, staring at the concave cheeks and the thin line of his father's mouth. His pleasure at seeing his son's return from New York had been fevered, strange - until Thomas realised that Peter de Souza had thought he would never see him again.

Turning back to the computer, Thomas re-read his next blog entry. The days were passing, and there was still no breakthrough. After the first frenzy of Kara's disappearance, the number of people reading his blog had dropped. Posting comments from the New York Police Department and the Famosa family did not help, Thomas realised that even the horrific was only potent for so long. Though Kara's mutilation had made her tormentor a hate figure, the stream of outrage and sympathy was dwindling, and despite Thomas's best efforts, people had started to forget.

He had believed that his intervention *might* bring Kara home. That amongst all the trivial messages and lunatic theories, a clue would surface. But although he examined everything that was sent to him, there was no flicker of hope. The bandwagon was stalling. In desperation, Thomas had even considered announcing the new meeting with the kidnapper. Tell everyone that he was about to barter three million for Kara Famosa. But as soon as he thought it, he dismissed it. A gamble was just that, a gamble. Reckless if it concerned money: treacherous if it risked a life.

So, he decided that he would write nothing more until after the meet.

Then he would write and tell everyone that he had saved Kara Famosa.

Or maybe he would never write anything again.

Because he had lost her.

38

It was a stupid mistake because the blood had gone everywhere with the force of the anvil hitting the pig's skull. It had splattered the walls, the hay bales, even the fucking rafters. But he'd lost it because she'd driven him mad with her gibbering. On and on, the fucking woman never shut up.

She was quiet now. Shocked, yeah, she looked shocked, rigid, and just to make sure she *stayed* silent, he had put tape over her mouth. She hadn't struggled, her eyes moving over to the dead pig with its head flattened. He knew what she was thinking, that it could have been her. And she was right, it could.

Purchass shone his torch on the blood, then glanced back to the body at his feet. The pig looked odd with no head. It looked like its body stopped at the neck. He was angry that he'd killed it and now had a mess to clean up. The girl had been a nuisance from the bloody start, Purchass thought, reaching for a tarpaulin. Cursing, he pushed the anvil off the pig's skull, then pulled the body onto the tarpaulin and rolled it up, folding in the ends to avoid any seepage and tying the package with farm twine. When he had finished, he stepped back to study his handiwork.

It looked like a Christmas tree bound up. Only someone would have a hell of a fucking surprise if they opened this on Christmas Eve. Heaving the parcel onto his shoulder, Purchass began walking. The day hadn't finished, but there was a heavy mist, barely giving him enough light to see his way across the field into the rough pasture leading to the pond. In the past, his father had buried the dead livestock here. *Dead* livestock, Purchass thought, grimly amused. How could you have dead *live*stock?

Picking up the shovel, he began to dig. But the ground was iron hard, the ice making progress impossible. Groaning as his back ached, Purchass leaned on the shovel, defeated. He had wanted to bury the pig where so many other carcasses had been dumped. He couldn't even guess how many dead sheep and pigs had been buried there before.

He had even imagined putting Kara bloody Famosa there, where she would wake up surrounded by the skeletons of farm animals - and a couple of other skeletons. Not farm animals. Not those. Human skeletons. Very old. Purchass sighed to himself, remembering his sister's voice. Funny how much he was thinking about Kat now. What a bitch she'd been, but tough. He had admired that about her, her barbarity.

Looking at the rigid earth, Purchass rubbed his stiff back with his left hand, realising that he wasn't going to be able to dig a grave in the ice-hard ground. He was stuck with a dead pig that would soon stink, even in winter.

Unless he could get rid of it another way.

39

London

"Why isn't he posting more often?" Anna snapped, turning to Simon accusingly. "Why don't you chivvy him?"

"You're his mother. You're the one who wanted to get Thomas involved," he paused, hunched over his desk, "You said he had a 'special relationship' with Halle."

"He has! But he can't report news when there isn't any."

Simon avoided her gaze, fighting a phantom cold - and his conscience. "I should have kept in touch with Jimmy Famosa –"

"Changing sides?"

"Jimmy is Kara's brother."

"But Thomas is in charge now. He's the one who knows what's going on."

"Does he?" Simon retorted, "No one knows anything. I rang the police this morning. No news, they said. *We'll keep you posted.*" He blew his nose noisily, "I should have stayed in touch with Jimmy."

"Oh, stop saying that!" Anna threw up her hands, exasperated. "You don't even get on. What makes you think Jimmy Famosa would confide in you? You always said it was difficult doing business with him; he's hardly likely to share personal matters. Thomas is our best bet."

Simon's eyes widened, "And you think your son tells you *everything?"*

"What's that supposed to mean? He loves Kara."

"So does Jimmy," Simon replied, getting to his feet and closing the office door so that they wouldn't be overheard. "Look, I can't get in touch with Halle. She's not taking any calls."

"She talking to Thomas."

"**This isn't a competition!"** Simon retorted, uncharacteristically sharp.

"Everything's a competition. Life's a competition to *anyone* who wants to succeed."

"Oh, spare me the pot psychology."

Although shocked, Anna refused to show it. Instead, she walked over to Simon and sat on the edge of his desk, smiling sympathetically.

"I know how stressed you are, darling. It's difficult fending off the press and all their questions."

She stroked the top of his head, but to her surprise, he jerked away. "I'm not a bloody child, Anna! Don't treat me like one. I need to talk to Jimmy Famosa."

"But why bother with Jimmy when we have Thomas?

"*This is my agency! My clients!*" He was irritated and wasn't prepared to hide it. "Anna, I appreciate all your help, believe me, I do. But it was *Jimmy* who tried to meet up with the kidnapper."

"And failed."

"Yes, but only Jimmy has contact with the man."

She raised her eyebrows. "Not anymore, he doesn't. Don't you know? Thomas has taken over. He's in contact with the kidnapper now."

Wrong-footed, Simon faltered, "How d'you know that?"

"Luis and Halle want it that way."

"They told you that?" He responded weakly.

"Thomas told me," Anna replied smugly. "You see, my son *does* tell me everything."

She had felt the shift between them and wanted to mend it fast. Having walked out of her marriage to throw in her lot with Simon Porter, it was discouraging to see that after being so blindly besotted, he was beginning to cool.

"If you don't mind my suggesting it," Anna soothed him, "Perhaps you should go over to New York and visit Halle yourself?"

"I've already thought about that," he admitted, dabbing at his nose with a handkerchief, "Heavy cold or not, I should go."

"Yes, you should. Get Dr Beckworth to give you some antibiotics, you don't want to have a bad flight." Secretly, she hoped he would have a miserable trip. "Halle will be so pleased to see you. She needs you, Simon. *Your* advice is what she needs now."

He hesitated, He would think about it. Yes, he would definitely think about it.

40

Peasbold Place,
Leatherhead

Jimmy Famosa's failure had taught Thomas a lesson. If the police had been tipped off once, they might be again.

No one knew the arrangements he had made. He hadn't confided in anyone, and to make doubly sure, he had taken extra precautions. Aware that the police might have him under surveillance, Thomas had left his flat that afternoon and hired a rental car. He then drove for a while along the motorway, getting off a various exits to see if anyone was following him. No one was.

There were to be no mistakes this time. Nothing was to be overlooked because he couldn't fail. There would be no third chance. And so, he had carried out his plan meticulously, even making sure that the money provided by Jimmy Famosa had been entered into one account, then sent it into another account in another bank, before it had been withdrawn again. Untraceable. After all, Thomas knew all about money.

And now he was sitting in a rented Ford, staring at the traffic lights and checking his rearview mirror. The mist had hardened into fog, the snow increasing, making driving difficult and visibility down to fifteen yards, but that hadn't worried him. In fact, Thomas had decided that it was an advantage. If anyone *had* still been following him, the weather would defeat them.

There were very few cars on the road to Leatherhead that night. The fresh snowfall, which had seemed picturesque in the city streets, had turned ugly. The snow slashed into nothingness on the motorway lanes. Steadily, Thomas drove along, finally arriving at Peasbold Place, its exact location not marked on his sat nav but on a local map.

Parking, he turned off the engine and prepared to wait. He was focused, but his mind still wandered back to the past, and to Kara. He could feel her skin, remembered the mole by her left elbow and the way she insisted that they made love with the lights on. But later, when she wanted to talk, she talked in the dark. Where are you? Thomas thought. Who took you, and why?

Don't ask her, he told himself. When you get her back, don't ask. Don't make her tell you until she wants to. Wait until she's ready.

And what if she doesn't come back?

No, he told himself, *don't think that. She's coming home.*

He continued to stare ahead, thinking of the Famosas - Luis, Halle, Jimmy - and wondering again if any of them had been involved in Kara's kidnapping. Nothing will make me back off, he told himself. If I have to turn the Famosa family inside out, I will because I don't *really* know who any of you are. I know what you've allowed me to see, but the truth? I don't know that. Luis is defensive and guarded, Jimmy is committed to the Famosa name, and Halle is doggy paddling, afraid to drown. All of you are desperate to conceal the truth. But would any of you sacrifice Kara to keep it hidden?

Thomas's heart rate speeded up, the dashboard clock reading 6.45pm. The building contractors had encircled the derelict houses on Peasbold Place with steel fencing, topped with barbed wire and signs warning off any interlopers.

DO NOT ENTER.
HARD HATS TO BE WORN
DOGS ON PATROL

Thomas could see no dogs, and there was no light coming from the Portakabin on site. The visibility at Peasbold Place was worse than on the motorway; he could only make out thirty feet ahead, the furthest houses on the row furred by fog.

There were two streetlamps, but the one by the iron gates was broken and Thomas had skirted the second to avoid announcing his presence. Glancing at the clock again, he read the time, 6.47pm. The temperature dropped. He wondered if he could turn on the car heater but resisted, not knowing if the kidnapper had already arrived and spotted him. Instead, Thomas pushed his cold hands into the pockets of his coat and hunkered down in the car seat, his gaze fixed ahead.

Silence descended.

Complete, absolute.

All enveloping.

Eerie.

After another few minutes, he let down the window and listened for sounds, *any* sounds. But there were none. It seemed that the snow and the darkness had swallowed all noise. Again, Thomas glanced at the clock, 6.48pm. Had he got the right place? Of course he had; there were no other Peasbold Places in Leatherhead. Anxious, he looked around him. But there were no headlights, no cars. No police. And somehow, that was worse. To know that no one was watching him. Or watching out for him. He was alone in a desolate place.

Waiting.

Leaning back against the headrest, Thomas thought of Kara again. He closed his eyes to her memory, then reopened them, fixing his gaze ahead. The clock read 6.52pm. Come on, he willed, come on. His eyes ached to see headlights, a car which would bring Kara back. But no car came.

The strain was unbearable.

Time seemed to be stalling.

And the snow kept falling.

41

Purchass was sweating with excitement, his van hidden under an overhang of trees, although the fog was the best cover he could have hoped for. Having read the last emotional outpouring on Thomas de Souza's blog, Purchass felt it would almost be sad when it was all over. When he had finished manipulating de Souza and playing the police for the fools they were. But the feeling didn't last. After this was sorted, there would be another woman. This time an *anonymous* one. He would make certain of that. Keep to the ones no one missed.

First, he had to solve the problem of the Famosa girl, because Purchass could tell that Thomas de Souza was never going to give up on her. The family might be fucking about, but de Souza wasn't going to stop. And besides, there was the painting to think of. Purchass had gone online to look up Gustav Klimt. It had taken him a few attempts to spell it, but finally, he had found the artist. He didn't know much about painting, but the images online *did* look like the small picture he had found in Kara Famosa's luggage. Some black-haired woman surrounded by gold paint and patterns, like a cheap sundress. His sister had had a dress like that once, thin material that creased and bunched up around the waist. Purchass thought about what the Famosa girl had said, that the picture was worth millions. He shook his head. Who paid a fortune for crap like that?

It was a pity that he would never get a chance to see the coroner's face when he got to examine a pig instead of an heiress. The police, the Met psychiatrist, Jimmy Famosa and Luis Famosa - the world, in fact - had been after a *kidnapper.* A man who wanted money above everything. Three million quid, Purchass thought. Did they *really* think he'd be stupid enough to take it? Mind you, he could buy a lot of first-class draft excluders with money like that.

Purchass's moment of greed had gone. The money might have been tempting, but he had bigger plans. Plans that relied on the bargaining chip of Kara Famosa. It was one thing to be a killer, another to be a kidnapper, but why not go for the triumvirate and be a blackmailer, too?

Three million pounds was *nothing* to the mayhem he could cause. Three million pounds wasn't flesh and blood. Wasn't torture. Wasn't darkness. Wasn't cries from the outhouse. The knowing you had a victim, and they were going to die. How and when was your choosing. Three million pounds was nothing to that. Certainly nothing to a family who had a fortune - and secrets to keep.

Purchass glanced at his watch, then saw it – the signal. The headlights turning on and off four times.

Getting out of the van, he pulled the balaclava over his face and moved along the bank of trees, staring into the snow and fog. He could just make out the figure of de Souza and then heard him call out:

"ARE YOU THERE?"

Purchass said nothing, just bit his lip, aching to speak but resisting. Instead, he inched along further, under the bare branches, knowing every morsel of the familiar ground.

"It's seven o'clock!" Thomas shouted. **"I'm here."**

"Go to the gates."

Purchass could feel de Souza's flinch rebound in the fog. He hadn't known he was so close behind him.

"Don't turn round!" Purchass snapped, pushing him forward. "Go inside."

"I've got the money."

"GO INSIDE!"

He did as he was told, moving into the compound in front of the derelict houses. The visibility was poor, Thomas strained to see ahead of him, holding out the bag he was carrying.

"I've got the money…"

He could hear someone laugh and felt the hairs rise on the back of his neck.

"… give me Kara."

"Kick the bag over here," Purchass said, coming through the gates, an indistinct figure in the snowy fog.

"I want to see her."

"No, money first."

"Kara," Thomas repeated.

"You either kick that fucking bag over to me, or you'll never see her again."

"How do I know you'll keep your word?"

"You don't," Purchass replied, "But you've no choice, have you?"

There was a pause before Thomas kicked the bag towards Purchass's feet. For a moment, he looked down at it, and then, to Thomas's astonishment, he kicked it *away,* running out of the compound and locking the gates behind him.

"What the hell!" Thomas shouted, "**Where's Kara? Where is she?"**

Desperately trying to wrench open the gates, he watched the figure run back towards the trees, and a second later, floodlights came on. Temporarily blinded, Thomas covered his eyes before noticing a figure propped up against the door of the nearest house. Calling Kara's name, he ran towards it - then stopped short. The hunched shape was distorted, the head pulped, caved in. His hands shaking, Thomas lifted the sack and saw the pig's bloodied carcass, Purchass's muffled laughter echoing as he disappeared back into the snow.

42

27th December

News of Kara Famosa's fake death flooded the media. And with it came, piece by piece, the events surrounding it. The second botched meeting. After Jimmy Famosa, it had been Thomas de Souza's time to fail. The kidnapper had outsmarted him, and rejected the ransom.

The opinion voiced on both sides of the Atlantic was that there was more to this than anyone understood. *Why* had a kidnapper rejected the money? Why abduct Kara Famosa for no apparent reason? Within forty-eight hours conspiracy theories abounded. Sites appeared on the internet, all asking questions for which there were no answers. And then someone posted:

> ***Kara Famosa was writing an expose of the Famosa family. Was this the reason she was kidnapped? Or maybe murdered?***

It was a question that Thomas had already asked himself. It haunted him like the image of the dead pig illuminated in the floodlights. He had stared at it, not understanding at first, wondering if it was Kara's butchered body, but when he had heard Purchass laugh he kicked it, and the carcass toppled onto the bloodied ground.

The police were called, Detective Jameson short-tempered with his questions. An officer handing Thomas the bag holding the ransom money. He had thrown it onto the back seat of his car, not remembering anything of the drive home. He didn't remember talking to Luis either. Halle was too distressed to take his call, the Cuban monosyllabic as he passed the phone over to Jimmy.

"Feels like shit, doesn't it? Knowing you've been made to look a fool."

"You think that matters?" Thomas had countered, "He still has Kara. Or have you given up on her?"

The remainder of the night dragged on. Sleep avoided Thomas, and reflected on every surface was an image of Kara. She was laughing, then pulling a face, opening presents at Christmas. She was reaching up to him, planting a kiss on his forehead.

He believed he was going to rescue her, but it had been a trick, and now Kara Famosa was gone. Back into the past, the dark corpse of the present drowning her out. She was everywhere and nowhere. Images of the missing Kara Famosa on the phone, the television, the internet, even the steel surface of the fridge door.

And everywhere the damning posting on the internet, for all the world to read:

Kara Famosa was writing an expose of the Famosa family.

Was this the reason she was kidnapped?

Or was she murdered?

Just after dawn, Thomas's mobile rang, the number unknown to him.

"Hello?"

"It's me, Halle."

"Halle, I'm so sorry –"

"No, no," she said hurriedly, "It's alright, it's not bad, because it *wasn't* Kara. It was a sick joke, but it wasn't her, so it means she's still alive," her voice was childlike, "I want to see you, Thomas, *I need you.*"

"I'll come back to New York –"

"You don't have to; I'm in England now, in the country house. I need to be close to Kara and be near my baby. I had to get away from Luis, too."

"What's happened?"

She ignored the question. "Did you see what they put on the internet? About the expose?"

"Yeah, I saw it."

"Do you think... do you think" she breathed in sharply, "It *can't* be true that she was killed because of it. It would mean that someone arranged all this."

Thomas was quick to soothe her. "People put up all types of malicious posts on the internet. You can't let it affect you, Halle. I warned you about this –"

"But I didn't really think that Kara *was* writing a book."

"Neither did I. I thought she was just fooling around."

"I suppose someone encouraged her to write it."

Thomas raised his eyebrows. "Who'd do that?"

"Simon Porter. Or maybe someone else."

"Like who?"

"Hugh Ackermann," Halle replied, her voice low, "He hates me for choosing Luis over him."

"And Simon Porter?"

"He'd encourage Kara to get the deal for the agency. Think of the money it would bring whilst he could ensure that the book told the version he wanted."

Thomas sighed. "Look, I detest Porter, but he's fond of you."

"Affection counts for nothing in the end. Like love, it's all … *flexible.* And your mother will urge him on." She changed the subject, "I trust you, Thomas. Can you come and see me?"

"Of course I can."

"It's urgent," she added solemnly, "I have to explain why I lied to you."

-o0o-

Only minutes after his conversation with Halle ended, Thomas's mobile rang again. This time, it was Simon Porter. "I've been thinking about the whole situation," he began, "and wondering if Kara really *was* writing a book, not just threatening to do it."

Thomas thought of what Halle had just been saying. "Don't tell me you believe what's on the internet."

"But what if Halle…" he paused, Thomas could imagine the agent rising from his desk and closing the office door before continuing "is actually hiding something? Something Kara knew. Something about the family."

"And, of course, you'd have no vested interest in an expose, would you?"

Simon's tone stiffened, "I'm Halle's agent and, by extension, Kara's."

"Oh really? I didn't know you'd signed her up. That's odd because only last week you were telling me that you thought the whole book idea was merely a rumour."

"I didn't say I'd signed her up!"

"But you wouldn't be averse to it, would you? An expose would be reason enough to dump your principles for money. No doubt my mother approves –"

"This has nothing to do with your mother!"

"You're such a liar."

"How dare you talk to me like that!" Simon replied heatedly, "Remember, you work for me --"

"No, I don't. I've resigned. I'm not on your payroll anymore."

"You're not on *anyone's* payroll."

"You're going to be feeling the chill too, before long."

Uneasy, Simon paused, "What's that supposed to mean?"

"Halle's leaving your agency."

"What!"

"She told me yesterday. Halle doesn't want to write anymore. She wants to find her daughter – we all want that."

"Halle wouldn't leave me!" Simon's tone was wounded, "We've had a long and successful working relationship."

Thomas twisted the knife, "Losing Halle *would* be a body blow for your agency."

"I'd lose a dear friend --"

"Who also happens to be a cash cow."

"Money's not everything!"

"Since when?" Thomas snapped, "You live for money and what it brings you. You think my mother would give you the time of day if you weren't rich? Believe me, she won't stay around when she hears about this –"

"You're a bastard!"

"You're right there, and I've had more than enough of you."

"You were keen to take the money I paid you to write the blog --"

"You paid me to spy for you!" Thomas snapped, "And I'm ashamed I agreed to it. But I won't do it anymore. You don't own me, Porter. Neither does my mother. You both thought you had me over a barrel, but you're wrong. I'm not working for anyone but myself."

"Quite a speech," Simon replied unsteadily, "So what are you planning?"

"An expose of my own."

"What the hell!"

"I'm going to find Kara and find out *why* she was taken - if you know anything, you should tell me now."

Simon's voice wavered, "You might have been important before, Thomas, but you're a nobody in my world. Best to stay out of it."

"Are you threatening me?"

"Giving you some advice."

"What if I ignore it?"

"You might regret that."

Thomas caught the edge in the agent's voice. It was unexpected and ignited his curiosity. "Are you afraid of something?"

"No. But you should be."

Thomas took a shot in the dark. "What are you hiding?"

"Everything and nothing," Simon replied enigmatically, "Like everyone else. We all have something we want to suppress. Things we did, things we're ashamed of. Petty lies, big betrayals. No one's immune. Not even you, playing the hero." He paused, his voice warning, "If you force people to face what they've done, they can react badly."

"Who are you talking about?"

"I'm trying to warn you, Thomas, back off. Look after your father; he needs you more than anyone."

But Thomas wasn't about to be diverted. "Did someone want to stop the book from being written? Come on, Porter, it's all over the internet that Kara was kidnapped to keep her quiet."

"She was kidnapped by a lunatic!"

"Was she?" Thomas persisted, "Or did someone organise the abduction? Was *that* why the ransom wasn't taken?"

"You're talking rubbish!"

Thomas pressed on, "Of course, if the killer was professional, he'd be wary of taking money that could be traced. Or maybe he's going to be paid for *killing* Kara."

"Jesus!" Simon replied, his tone strident, "You're losing your mind. You're unstable --"

"Did my mother tell you that? It's her favourite ploy: my father was unstable, I'm unstable." He changed tack, "I'm angry, not crazy, and I don't understand what's going on. The kidnapper didn't take the ransom; he set up a stunt with a dead pig and kept Kara. *Why?* She said something about the painting being 'leverage' – is that it? He can't kill Kara until the Klimt's recovered?"

The agent shook his head, incredulous. "You really *are* insane."

"I'm getting closer to the truth, aren't I? Was Kara's book going to reveal Luis's art dealings? Let's face it, one of his associates served a prison sentence in Italy for trading in fakes –"

"He was a criminal! Luis dismissed the man –"

"With a big payoff, no doubt," Thomas said dryly, "Luis's casino has got a clean bill of health, and his hotel's pristine, but there's still that lingering stink about fakes, isn't there?"

"I don't know what you're talking about!" Simon replied, his voice grandiose. "Luis Famosa hardly needs to deal in fake pictures. He has a gallery and a private collection that museums envy –"

"But what a thrill it would be for Famosa to dupe all those uppity dealers who've always looked down on him." Thomas interrupted, "The perfect con for a gambling man. Famosa likes to gamble, doesn't he?"

"You should stay out of his business –"

"Why? For the good of my health? Or for the good of yours? You've been doing business with the Famosas for a long time," Thomas continued, "and I'm guessing that you *really* want to agent Kara's book. That way, you could control it, show it to Luis and tip him off. But she outsmarted you, didn't she?" Simon Porter had fallen silent, Thomas continuing, "Kara wasn't going to give *you* control, she was going to handle the expose herself."

"Really?"

"Yes, really. She knew it wouldn't be enough to make accusations, she needed *proof*."

Seconds passed before Simon Porter spoke again. "You don't know what you're getting yourself into, de Souza."

"No, I don't," he agreed, "but I'm not backing off. Whether the kidnap was planned or simply random, I think Kara has evidence that no one wants to come out. *No one.*"

There was silence down the phone line. Thomas waited for the agent to speak again, but he didn't. Instead, Simon Porter put down the phone without saying another word.

43

England
December 10th

For three days, Purchass had followed the news, uselessly banging the top of his television to get a better picture, the aerial outside hanging off-centre on the chimney stack. He only got a signal on some channels, and Sky had lousy reception, but he was hardly likely to call in a repairman. No one was ever invited to the farmhouse. It was concealed by the trees and, if there was heavy and persistent rain, the lane would flood and leave Purchass stranded. It wasn't a problem; a brick lean-to acted as a pantry for tinned food, together with a chest freezer for meat. A freezer that ran endlessly, with its slabs of pork and tough mutton, well past their sell by date.

Purchass's attention moved back to the television. He thought he would buy himself a better set, but what was the point? He hardly ever watched it - unless it was news about him. And there had been a lot about him recently. But nothing about Sam Purchass. No one knew who *he* was, even though the press and the media were all baying for the skin of Kara Famosa's kidnapper.

He found it amusing how angry people had become at his stunt with the pig. Wouldn't you think they might have been relieved that it *wasn't* the bloody girl? Purchass couldn't understand that but he enjoyed the way he had outsmarted everyone. What kind of a kidnapper didn't take a ransom? They were asking. But he *wasn't* a kidnapper, was he? No one would ever find him because no one had any leads. He hadn't taken the ransom. And he hadn't left any evidence behind.

Only one person had seen his face, and she was in the barn, tied up. Silent. Purchass yawned, turning from the television, and walking over to the kitchen table. He looked longingly at the cardboard box sitting there and then tipped out its contents. Kara Famosa's flight bag fell out next to one of her boots, the heel broken. Curious, Purchass picked it up but felt no thrill and turned his attention to an object he hadn't seen for a while. A black evening dress. Small size, short, lace at the hem.

He liked the dress. Liked it a lot. Had even slept with it, rubbing himself against Ellie Chadwick's dress. He had never fucked the woman, but he had fucked the dress… Purchass shook his head, then dropped a few of the items back into the box and walked into the yard. Once there, he tossed the box and its contents onto a pile of wood, threw on some petrol, and set it alight. For one instant, he almost snatched the dress out of the flames but resisted. It had been a risk, a tie to Ellie Chadwick. He had also considered throwing Kara Famosa's handbag and boots onto the flames to watch them burn but changed his mind, picking up the

Klimt painting and propping it up against a bottle of HP sauce.

Purchass tilted his head to one side. It was a crappy picture. Too much gold on it for a start. Worth millions? Not even if the gold had been 24 carat. But then again, how did he know? And *why* had the girl stolen it? That was pretty shifty, Purchass thought, stealing from your family and your big-shot father. He wondered fleetingly how the Cuban had taken the news and whether he'd been so pissed off that he didn't want her back. The painting, yes. The daughter, maybe not.

But Kara Famosa wasn't going to die. She was hanging on like the bitch she was.

It was deliberate, fucking up his plans.

If he had killed her, he would have been free to go back to Heathrow, push his trolley around and dream about his next victim. Certainly, he wouldn't pick up anyone at the airport again; that would be stupid. He wouldn't shit on his own doorstep twice. Next time, the abduction will take place a long way from Heathrow.

Sam?

He turned, surprised by the voice coming from one of the outhouses.

Sam?

Moving away from the fire, Purchass frowned, walking towards a far barn. Snow had snuggled it, banked up at the windows and the battered, bowed doors. Warily, he moved around the building, feeling into his pocket and flicking open the hunting knife he always carried.

"Who's there?"

Nothing.

"This is private property," he threatened, "You're trespassing."

Snow crunched underfoot as he moved closer, the knife in one hand, his other hand pushing open the door.

She was sitting on a hay bale, her legs crossed, swinging her left foot in his direction. The dress she was wearing, a cheap summer dress, was stiff with blood, her face swollen under a mess of bruises. But her eyes were alert and bright with malice.

In one easy movement, she jumped down from the hay bale and moved towards him, Purchass stepping back.

I taught you how to do it... Remember?

He couldn't speak, the baby of the family again, his sister coming closer towards him as he stood, immobilised with shock.

In the yard behind him, the fire suddenly crackled; Purchass startled, stumbling, and then running away. Leaving the barn behind him, he only glanced back when he reached the safety of the house. The doors were standing open, but the building was empty. No ghosts. No Kat. Not even a pig shuffling the dust inside. It was empty, and the only things moving were the startled flames of the fire, leaping upwards into the gurning sky.

44

Berlin

Sente Fleishman was wondering which city to visit first, Paris, Rome, or London. For the last two years, she had been saving money for her trip. Money that had been difficult to hoard away on a nurse's salary. But after two years, Sente had *finally* garnered enough cash to explore other parts of Europe. But which city first? London sprang to mind, but then again, she had always wanted to visit the English capital, so maybe she should save London until last. Treasure it. Savour it. Make it all the more special.

She was looking good and knew it; her blue eyes her more arresting feature. An affair with a German architect had fizzled out, and her promised promotion to Nursing Sister never materialised. What better time to leave Berlin and all its disappointments? Sente wasn't a woman to brood on failure. Appealing to men, she was confident that she would have plenty of company on her travels. It was time for an adventure, she decided, buying her plane ticket to Rome. Paris would follow, then London. She smiled to herself. Yes, London would be special, she knew it. She could feel it.

It would be a place she would never forget.

45

Hampshire

Halle removed herself from the world, retreating to the country house in England, with a housekeeper, personal assistant, maid and bodyguard accompanying her. Since Kara had been kidnapped, Halle had deteriorated, becoming fretful and desperate for her own safety, overreacting to any unexpected noises, Luis's phone calls unsettling her further. Their argument had been ignored as though merely dreamt, and when Halle spoke about Kara, he was distant, feigning sympathy.

"I've got people with contacts in the English police. I've been thinking of coming over to England –"

"No," Halle replied quickly, "I'm better alone. There are people looking after me, and I talk to Jimmy every day."

"What about Thomas de Souza?"

The question was loaded, and the answer was meek. "He knows I'm in England."

"He'll visit you."

"Yes, when he has time."

"He's got no job; he's got plenty of time! I see he's still writing the posts about Kara. Not doing much good, are they?" His interest waned, "I've got to go. I'll call you tomorrow, sweetheart."

Sweetheart. The word sounded like a criticism.

Three weeks had passed since the kidnapping, and Thomas's blog was losing impact. How could it not, when every twenty hours there was another tragedy to feed the masses? As for Halle, her everyday needs were attended to by the staff, particularly the housekeeper, Miss Reid, who had been with the family for decades. Few others were allowed into the closed world. Only Thomas had free access and arrived during a rainstorm, running in from the car, his hair and clothes wet, the heat of the interior making his jacket steam. He had not been to the house for over a decade but remembered the incised carving in the hall and the overlarge mantel flanking the grate below, the fire as warming as the housekeeper's welcome.

"Mrs Famosa will be so happy to see you." Miss Reid said, handing Thomas a towel to dry his hair. "She has been talking about you all morning."

"How is she?"

"Not good. She asked for you to go upstairs."

Moments later, Thomas walked into Halle's bedroom, taken aback by the lack of daylight. It took several moments for his eyes to adjust to the dimness, surprised to catch sight of Halle lying on her bed in her towelling robe, unwashed, an empty pizza carton beside her.

"Halle?"

She sat up, pulled her dressing gown around her, and pushed away the carton. "I was hungry."

Thomas looked at the floor beside her bed, where there were two other empty cartons, his expression wry. "You even don't like pizza."

"I do," she stammered, "it tastes good and stops me thinking."

She didn't confess that piling down the soggy pastry filled her up and made her stomach bloat, momentarily taking her mind off Kara. She didn't admit that she ate like someone who had been starved; sauce dribbling down her face, her lips closing over the warm soft comfort of the cheap food. Sometimes, she even threw it back up, hanging over the toilet. But after a couple of hours, she ordered more.

"I'm not drinking."

"Good," Thomas said, sitting at the foot of the bed, "but you don't have to apologise to me, Halle. Do whatever makes you feel better."

"I can't risk drinking…" She smoothed her hair back from her face. He could see grease marks down her robe. "I can't because alcohol punched holes in my memory, pieces are still missing. At times, I was so drunk I did things I daren't think about." Her blue eyes glanced at him, then glanced away. "I smoked a lot of weed, too…"

"People did. People do." Thomas replied, surprised by her ramblings.

"… they said that it messes up your memory, and that's true. I don't remember a lot of things from when I young, particularly in Las Vegas, until now. I'm beginning to remember things. Or perhaps I'm remembering what I've been *told*."

"You're under a lot of stress, Halle, the mind plays tricks on all of us –"

"But what if it was my fault?"

"What if *what* was your fault?"

"Kara," she wrapped a blanket around her. "Is it very cold?"

"It's raining. England's always damp," he smiled, "You want the heating turned up?"

"She's very kind."

"Who?"

"Miss Reid. She was so happy when I said you were coming to see me. She thinks you're wonderful. And she's read every post you've written…" Halle stopped talking, face crumpling, "Kara isn't coming home, is she?"

"Yes, she is."

Halle shook her head frantically, "No, she isn't, and it's my fault! It's my fault because Kara isn't Luis's child." She lowered her head as she continued to talk, avoiding his gaze. "You're not surprised, are you?"

"No, I suspected it. Kara said she was joking when she told me, but she wasn't. Does Luis know?"

"Oh yes, he knows."

Thomas chose his next words carefully. "Is that why you left New York?"

"He was so angry. *He frightened me*! He told me he'd had Kara's DNA checked, and that's how he found out. He said he'd become suspicious that her attitude had changed, and then he discovered she'd taken the Klimt… I could see it in his eyes."

"See what?"

"I think he suspects her."

"Of what?"

"*Betraying him!"* Halle replied frantically, "Kara was asking questions about the business. She kept trying to find out about the Famosa collection and the gallery. She wanted to know about the finances -- "

"Jimmy wouldn't have given her the time of day–"

"No, *he* wouldn't, but Ivan Holt would."

"So, you think Holt would have confided in Kara?"

"If she told him that *I* wanted him to, yes."

"How long has Ivan Holt been working for the gallery?"

"Ten years, but since he's been promoted, he's become more vocal, challenging Jimmy in particular."

Thomas raised his eyebrows. "But not Luis?"

"No one challenges Luis," she paused, her gaze still turned away, "Why haven't you asked me who Kara's father is?"

He answered with another question. "Did you tell Luis who it was?"

"I couldn't."

"Couldn't?"

"Because I don't know the answer! And I told Luis that, but he didn't believe me." Finally, she looked at Thomas, embarrassed. "I'd never cheated on my husband before, but I found out that Luis was having an affair, and I lost my mind. *I was heartbroken.* I got drunk and smoked too much pot. God knows there was always enough around there –"

Thomas was struggling to follow her, "*You were in Vegas?*"

"Yes," she nodded. "Luis had a mistress there. He didn't even deny it when I found out! He said that she meant nothing but that he'd known her for a long time, and they were old friends."

"That's one way of putting it," Thomas said wryly, "Who is she?"

"I don't know!" She shook her head. "I don't want to know! But when I challenged Luis about it, he said they had a daughter."

Thomas took in a breath. "How old would she be now?"

"Why? What does it matter? I don't care –"

"You should, Halle, if only for legal reasons. The woman could claim that her daughter is entitled to a chunk of the Famosa fortune should anything happen to Luis. As it is, she's a half-sister to your son. Does Jimmy know?"

"**No one knows!**" Halle cried, "Luis apologised and begged me not to leave him. I didn't. Instead, I sobered up and forgot about it. Buried it. It was a long time ago, and time moved on; *we* moved on. I became his perfect consort, but when Luis discovered he wasn't Kara's father, I couldn't lie any longer. He knew that I'd cheated on him –"

"You had reason to."

"Reason? Or excuse?" She queried, "I don't know who Kara's father is. So, what does that make me, Thomas?"

"A pissed-off wife," he said sympathetically, "What you did was understandable –"

"*Was it?* Was it really? I was drunk for weeks. I knew everyone in Vegas and leant on people who wanted to protect me, who took my side. This was decades ago. Luis was doing really well, but he wasn't the big shot he is now. I was still young, silly, and stumbling around, staying with people. All kinds of people, artists, musicians, croupiers from the casino, they were all friends. I didn't care what Luis thought – maybe I *wanted* him to hear about it, I was just so hurt." She shrugged, barely moving her shoulders, "He said he'd always protect me, that I'd be safe. And he'd lied."

"You never thought of going home to your parents?"

"My mother would have said that men were like that, and my father had always hated Luis. I couldn't go home, and besides, I *loved* Luis. I just wanted to hurt him." She pulled the blanket up to her chin, her voice dropping, "I've been so angry with Kara for sleeping around, but I was no better - she just didn't know about it. I should have been a good mother and tried to understand –"

"Kara isn't easy to understand."

" – I'm so afraid she's gone forever."

"We'll find her."

"Will we?" Halle hesitated, "She's still missing - and it's my fault."

"Not it's not your fault. What makes you think that?"

"I can't remember, you see." Halle's voice dwindled to a whisper. "Not all of it. It's blurry. But suddenly, I'm remembering things… Luis manipulated me. It wasn't my fault. Besides, it might not even be true."

Thomas leaned towards her: "*What* might not be true?"

"What I'm trying to remember!" Halle replied frantically, "I should have asked him, demanded to know - but I couldn't risk knowing if it *was* true. I can't piece it together. I can't work out what's real and what's fantasy –"

"Just a minute, Halle," Thomas said, putting up his hands. "Explain what you mean, I don't understand. What are you talking about?"

"*The past.* In Vegas. When I was first there. When I met Luis."

"You met Luis, what then?"

"I was still partying, and Luis didn't like it, so I stopped drinking and doing drugs. But then later --"

"How much later?"

"Years, well, not that many, Luis was doing really well by then. He had the gallery and was challenging the dealers in London and New York. I'd stayed sober, a credit to him, and then he suddenly started encouraging me to drink again. To drink *with* him. But I didn't want to because he can drink a lot, and it doesn't affect him, but I can't handle it."

"Did you refuse?"

"You can't refuse Luis! I was on medication, and drinking with it was too much," she paused, Thomas remembering how Kara had said her mother had been diagnosed as bipolar. "I told Luis that I didn't want to drink because I'd hallucinated in the past when I'd mixed sleeping pills with uppers and downers. Amphetamines don't mix well with pot or booze --"

"What are you taking now?"

"Anti-depressants, sometimes sleeping tablets, but nothing else. That's why I *daren't* drink. I can't afford to be muddled." She paused, embarrassed. "That was the old me when I wasn't in control. I thought she'd gone. But for some reason I keep thinking about her – *me* - and what Luis was like. When we argued last week, I could see him as he had been then."

"When are you talking about?"

"I can't remember!"

"Think, Halle."

"I've tried, believe me, and I *keep* trying, but I can't remember!" She cried helplessly, "Now I'm wondering all sorts of strange things. Nonsense."

"What kind of nonsense?"

"Bad thoughts, dark thoughts," she hurried on, "and so many weird questions keep going around in my head."

Concerned, he leaned towards her. "What kind of questions?"

"Would a man…" she struggled to finish the sentence "kill a child he had once believed his own?"

46

14th December
London

Unnerved by Halle's confusion, Thomas returned home and scrolled through the biographies of Luis Famosa and Halle (nee Forrester) on the internet. Skipping what he knew, he went back to the beginning, the early days in Las Vegas, irritated when his mobile rang, interrupting him.

"Why haven't you called me back?" Anna demanded. Imperious, ready for war. "Why is Halle in England, and why won't she see Simon?"

"She's grieving; she wants to be on her own."

"She sees *you*," Anna responded curtly. "What about the blog? You haven't put up a post for two days."

Thomas leaned back in his seat. He had noticed a slight tremor in his mother's voice and wondered why she was nervous. "Halle doesn't want me to post so often."

"She's a fool! They haven't found Kara and won't do at this rate. Doesn't she give a damn about her daughter?"

"The police are doing everything they can –"

"They might *never* find her! The story's slipping off the front pages. Every day it is moved further back in the papers. If you don't keep it going, it will be forgotten." Anna paused, her tone threatening. "There's a lot riding on this, Thomas. You can't afford to be sentimental."

"Sentimentality isn't something that troubles you, is it?"

His irritation was due in part to guilt. He loathed the fact that he had colluded with his mother and agreed to use an old love affair for money. Thomas might fool himself into thinking that his motives had been sincere, that he had believed he might help Kara. But in reality, his behaviour had been shabby. He might even use the excuse of his father's illness and medical needs to assuage his guilt, but the reality was different. He had temporarily sold out.

"Simon said you'd been rude to him –"

"Simon Porter is a prick," Thomas retorted, "And you should know. I'd watch out for him, Mother, he doesn't like to lose face."

Her tone froze. "Are you giving me advice on my love life?"

"If I was, I'd tell you to keep away from my father when it doesn't work out with Porter," Thomas replied, changing tack, "Halle's close to a nervous breakdown."

"She isn't the only one! Look, the woman trusts you. She chose to confide in you over her son, for Christ's Sake! You have to go back to posting. People were reading your blog; surely that means something?"

And then Thomas realised that his mother was panicking. She had been riding high, planting her son into Jimmy Famosa's absented slot. Making sure

Thomas was crying out from the nub of a tragedy to a greedy, gaping world. But Thomas wasn't playing ball any longer.

"You have to do something!"

"You're really het up, aren't you? The thought of Kara's expose slipping from your fingers is really burning. Makes my heart ache to think of the commission Porter will lose. I mean, it's not just the book, is it? There would be interest for a film too, and that's big money."

Stung, she struck back. "We can't keep paying you when you're not working! You had a wonderful opportunity. You've only yourself to blame for ruining it."

"Funny, that's exactly what I was thinking about you."

Incensed, Thomas put down the phone and turned back to the computer screen. The entries listed everything he had already known about the Famosa family, only one detail was new to him. During the early eighties, Halle Famosa was once engaged to Hugh Ackermann. Thomas entered his name into Google Search and watched as the information came up. Ackermann was a Northerner, a wealthy, highly respected dealer in Oriental ceramics and 18th-century European art. Luis Famosa's entry was more expansive, depicting his origins in Cuba and the impressive success that had followed in casinos, hotels, properties, and art dealing – all of which had made him an estimated fortune. There was no figure put on that largesse, Thomas turning to the images on Google; a photograph of a younger Luis in Las Vegas, mixing with the likes of Judy Garland and Tom Jones, and later Celine Dion. Then, one sentence caught his attention.

In his early life, Luis Famosa lived hard and fast, his early rumoured

excesses curtailed by his happy marriage and the births of his children.

At once, Halle's voice came back to him.

'Kara isn't Luis's child.'

and Kara's words from years earlier:

'My father isn't Luis Famosa. I've only just found out.'

She had laughed, claiming it as a joke. When they both knew it wasn't.

Thomas stared at the computer screen and the old photograph of Luis Famosa, stocky, in a dinner jacket, smiling. So, who *was* Kara's father? And how badly had Luis taken the news he had been duped? A Cuban cuckold. Hard to swallow for a man like that. Had it provoked some action? Set in motion some tragedy? Then Thomas thought of an old rumour he had heard. One of the many that circled Famosa, it was something he had not taken seriously at the time. It was not an innuendo about forgery, nor even the casino manager being jailed, it was something more subtle - the intimation of an old crime which had involved four people who had known each other in Las Vegas decades earlier.

His instinct was to dismiss the rumour. Simon Porter might season his clients' pasts with a frisson of the noir, but with Luis Famosa, it could be true. The incident Halle had skirted over was supposed to have happened in the nineties. Who had been in the Famosa circle then? Luis, Halle, Simon Porter and possibly Hugh Ackermann. Ackermann had lost to Famosa, Halle had sobered up, and Luis had gone from up-and-coming to all-encompassing. And yet, somehow, Halle had forgotten it all - until Luis discovered that Kara was not his child, and the old memories had started to emerge.

"I can't remember, you see. Not all of it. It's blurry... Luis

manipulated me, it wasn't my fault. Besides, it might not even

be true... I should have asked before, demanded to know...

I can't work out what's real and what's fantasy..."

Startled by a loud noise from outside, Thomas turned off the desk lamp and looked out of the window into the street below. There was a row of parked cars and a woman struggling with a baby's pushchair, nothing out of the ordinary. Except... He leaned forward just in time to see a man ducking out of sight and dipping into the alleyway across the road. Something had altered. There was a threat in the air. Still at the window, Thomas watched, but it was quiet outside. He thought of his father and wondered if he had inadvertently put Peter de Souza in danger. Then he thought of Jimmy Famosa, of his accusations when they had fought:

"*What d'you know, de Souza?"* he had asked, *"what have you got on my family?"*

Did Jimmy Famosa suspect that Kara had confided in him about the expose? Or why she had stolen the Klimt? Both Simon Porter and Jimmy Famosa were spooked, was that because they feared what Thomas knew? Certainly, the agent had become unusually aggressive, his public school veneer evaporating. Why? Were all the secrets the Famosas had hidden for decades, all the workings of their empire, now threatened with exposure?

Thomas then realised that, as Halle's confidante and Kara's ex-lover, he might be in danger. If Kara had been kidnapped to keep her quiet, what might happen to him? Another thought followed. What if Kara had been forced to confide in her kidnapper? Was *that* why he hadn't taken the money? If he knew something the Famosas wanted to suppress, he could milk them for decades... Motionless, Thomas stood at the window, looking out. Someone was watching him; he could sense it. He thought of what Kara had told Jimmy, Halle repeating the words to him:

I wasn't the first.

There had been another victim. An unknown murder that needed to be exposed. Because Anna had been right. Despite the outcry about Kara's faked death, the story was fading. It needed fresh blood to keep it alive. It needed the kidnapper to be found. But how likely was that? He was clever and wouldn't be caught unless he committed another crime. So, what would make him do that? Provocation, Thomas realised. He needed to be taunted into action, into giving himself away.

Turning from the window, Thomas drew the blinds, troubled. Was he wishing for another kidnapping? Another murder? Was he hoping for another woman's death? The thought lodged in his mind. If there *was* another crime, they might catch the kidnapper - and Kara would be propelled back into the public gaze.

It was cold-bloodied, but it would work. The kidnapper had to be forced to act again. He couldn't go to ground, or it was over. There *had* to be another kidnapping or another murder.

But how? Thomas asked himself.

How?

47

Maida Vale
London

The following morning, Thomas gave his father breakfast and waited for the nurse to arrive when the bell rang, and Jimmy Famosa stood at the door. Nodding a curt greeting, Thomas stepped back as the American entered, ushering him into the study. The sofa was covered with crumpled newspapers. At once Thomas closed the lid on his laptop as he gestured for his visitor to sit down. "D'you want some coffee?"

"Yeah, thanks."

Moments later, he returned with fresh coffee, Jimmy watching him. "My mother told me that you visit her."

"Now you're back in England, you can," Thomas replied. "Incidentally, why *are* you back?"

"You mean - who needs me when you're handling everything?"

"I didn't say that –"

Jimmy interrupted him. "I'm going back to New York today, but I wanted to talk to you first. Were you involved?"

"What?"

"In Kara's kidnapping. *Were you involved?"*

Thomas put down his mug and folded his arms. "Are you bloody crazy?"

"If it turns out that you *were*, you'll suffer for it."

"I wasn't involved. Were you?"

"She was my sister!"

"That hasn't stopped other men from killing their relatives." Thomas countered, wondering if Jimmy Famosa really didn't know that Kara was his half-sister.

"Then again, you wouldn't have gone to the meet if you'd been involved" Jimmy replied, intent on his own line of thought. "You put yourself deliberately in danger."

"You did the same."

Jimmy nodded. "Yeah, and we both failed." He sighed, changing the subject. "I have to go back to New York; I can't leave the business too long. My father needs my support."

Thomas said nothing.

"... I don't really know if I can trust you, but I have to."

"With what?"

"There was another victim before Kara."

"I know."

Surprised, Jimmy's expression hardened. "My mother told you what Kara said to me?" He was struggling to contain his irritation, "So you must also know that Kara stole the Klimt?"

"Yes."

"What else?" Jimmy asked, needling, "I've always wondered how much you know about our family."

Thomas could sense the growing hostility, "If you don't trust me, why are you here?"

"This other victim, I don't think anyone else knows about her."

"You didn't tell the police?"

Jimmy shook his head, "No, not the police in the UK police or in New York. Tell me, did you know about the book Kara was supposed to be writing?"

Thomas feigned surprise, "*A book?*"

"You must know about it! Simon Porter or your mother will have told you –"

"Oh, you mean that expose she was 'threatening?'" Thomas picked up his coffee and took a drink, "It was all nonsense, she was just fooling around."

They were shadowboxing, both trying to assess how much the other knew.

"You think she was kidding? I'm not sure. Perhaps she was really going to do it."

"What for?"

"Money. A name," Jimmy answered. "Exposing her family and our wealth would be irresistible to the media, make her a star overnight. Finally, Kara would come out from the long shadow of the Famosas."

"You think the payoff would be enough to betray her family?"

Ignoring the comment, Jimmy looked around the room. "I was sorry to hear about your father having a stroke and your mother going off with Simon Porter. Seems like you've had a rough time of it." When Thomas didn't respond, he continued, "Halle's very fond of you, and Kara loved you. Seems like you're

Father Confessor to both. Might even know something I don't." His eyes were flinty, "What is it?"

"You're wasting your time; I don't know anything." Thomas replied, finishing his coffee, "I'm sorry if there's bad blood between us –"

"Why would you say that?" Jimmy replied sarcastically. "You usurped me and turned my mother away from me. God knows what you could have managed with my sister if she hadn't dumped you – but bad blood? No, there's *no* blood between us."

"You think I've got something on your family? You're wrong. All I'm concerned about is getting Kara back." He stared at Jimmy. "My father had another stroke whilst I was in New York. He's recovering in hospital."

"I'm sorry."

"D'you know what it costs to be treated in the London Clinic? A hell of a lot. But not enough for me to work for Simon Porter again. And before you ask, Halle is helping with the finances because I'm helping her. That's the way it works when people pull together." His tone hardened. "I want you to stop asking me stupid fucking questions about 'secrets.' I don't know any! And I don't *want* to know any." Thomas studied his visitor. "Did you hire someone to watch me?"

"What?"

"Someone's been watching the house. I wondered if that was down to you."

"No."

"Maybe it's Simon Porter. Or maybe it's *Halle?"*

"What the hell are you talking about?"

"Well, who *can* I trust?" Thomas retorted. "After all, I've nailed my colours to the mast. I've been asking questions, sniffing around, looking into your family."

He could see the flicker in Jimmy Famosa's eyes. "Why would you do that?"

"Your father's an important man in New York and Vegas. But Vegas is where he started, wasn't it?"

"What are you getting at?"

"There are rumours about Luis Famosa."

"There are rumours about every famous successful man."

Thomas nodded. "True, and usually, I dismiss gossip as envy. But there was one old rumour that I came across about an incident in Vegas that involved four people."

The air chilled between them. Thomas could see that he had hit a nerve.

"I don't know what you're talking about," Jimmy said after a pause.

"You've never heard the rumour?"

"No, and I'm sure I would have done if there had been anything to it. I'm Luis Famosa's son, remember?"

Oh yes, Thomas thought, I remember. And you're trying hard to hold onto your temper. Or is it something else? Are you spooked? He could see Jimmy run his tongue over his bottom lip, his expression hostile.

"What was this rumour anyway?"

"I don't know any details, just that there was a scandal involving a quartet of people. Your mother was one, as was your father." *Didn't* he know? Thomas wondered. Or was he trying to find out how much *he* knew? "As I say, I don't know any details."

"Some quartet if you can only name two of them. Did Kara know about it?"

Thomas shrugged. "We never discussed it. I just remembered the rumour myself the other day."

"Convenient."

"What's that supposed to mean?"

"Did you remember *before* or *after* my sister was kidnapped?"

Thomas shook his head, his expression weary. "I thought we were working together, sharing information."

"I can't share what I don't know. Did you talk to my mother about this?"

"No."

"But you feel fine talking about it behind her back?"

Thomas didn't rise to the bait. "I haven't said anything against Halle."

"You suggested she had something to hide."

"But you said she hasn't, and you would know, wouldn't you? You asked me what I knew, Jimmy. That's *all* I know, and apparently, it amounts to nothing." Thomas concluded, changing the subject. "If the kidnapper has murdered another woman, he could kill again. Before too much longer, he'll start feeling confident --"

"You think he'll kill Kara?"

"No, he needs her. And as long as he does, she's safe."

"The police have nothing to go on."

"Neither have I," Thomas admitted, "but I want to find out about the first victim. It might lead me to the kidnapper."

Jimmy smiled bitterly. "I wonder if you'd have been so keen a while ago."

"Meaning?"

"Professionally, you're fucked. Broke, on your uppers. You've nothing to lose. That's why you're going after the kidnapper. Otherwise, it makes no sense. Kara isn't a member of your family."

"I love her."

"We *all* love her!" Jimmy snapped. "I'm not giving up on her. I've hired investigators in the UK, so you don't have to risk yourself any longer."

"You want me to walk away?" Thomas shook his head. "No chance. Like you said, I'm fucked with nothing to lose."

"Kara's not on the front pages anymore." Jimmy pointed to the discarded newspapers. "You're right; before long, the kidnapper will feel confident, and then he might act again."

Thomas was watching him, trying to interpret what he was saying. *Are you thinking aloud or warning me? Are we allies or enemies?*

"So, you think he'll kill again?"

"I want him to," Jimmy replied, standing up to leave, "and you want the same because that's the only way you'll catch him. Let's just hope he doesn't come after you first."

BOOK THREE

48

Bowing his head, Hugh Ackermann crossed himself and then slid into an empty front pew in the Brompton Oratory. His father had been Jewish, but his mother had been a rabid Catholic, devout to the point of fanaticism, instilling in her children the tenets of the faith. Ackermann might be ruthless in business but in private he was under the Catholic cosh.

His wife had been a Catholic, too. They had even agreed that their children would be brought up in the faith, but a stillborn son was the only fleeting grab at fatherhood Ackermann ever experienced. After his wife died, he had a few half-hearted, chilly affairs, but none lasted long. Besides, no one matched Halle. So, he turned his attention to his business, making a fortune in Oriental ceramics and travelling all over the Far East. He returned with unique items that he offered – discreetly – to clients who chose to think they were special. Ackermann knew that whether he was selling Japanese Imari ware or Ming China, he had a market, and when he grew bored and expanded into 19th-Century European painting, his market followed him. Egon Schiele fascinated Ackermann, as did the more intimate drawings by Degas, but he idolised Gustav Klimt and like every great salesman, he wanted to share his passion, which came down to marketing, marketing, marketing. His success led to vanity. Hubris, too. But that was the way of humanity.

Those whom the gods wish to destroy,
They first make mad.

He thought of the quotation as his eyes fixed on the statue of the Crucified Christ above the altar. How many modern men would die for a faith? December had started its countdown to Christmas; Ackermann was already resenting the holidays as it would mean a suspension of business. He might celebrate the birth of Christ - but it would cost him.

Slipping into the pew next to him, David Gates coughed, Ackermann ignoring his lawyer and pretending to pray. He stayed in the same position for another five minutes before finally getting off his knees and sitting back in the pew.

"What?"

"I need to talk to you, sir," David replied.

As an atheist, he was awkward amongst the incense and gilding, his pinched face bearing the look of a man needing a holiday. At first surprised to be hired by Ackermann, after the harried departure of the last lawyer, David Gates had soon realised that his legal expertise was all that was required. No personal comments or banter. Hugh Ackermann wasn't interested in his employee as a person, merely as an animated law book.

"Get on with it."

Flustered, David continued, his voice barely above a whisper, "I'm sorry, but I didn't understand your note."

Ackermann turned to look at him. His eyes were magnified behind thick lenses, his chin jutting out like a gable end. "I want to know who kidnapped Kara Famosa."

David had the sense not to look surprised. "I see. But how do I do that?" he asked, bewildered, "Should I talk to the police?"

"Hire someone."

"From the police?"

Ackermann stood up, crossing himself, and made for the door.

For a moment, David hesitated, then hurried after him. Out on Brompton Road, he ran to catch up with his employer. "I'm not sure I know what you want, sir. If you could just clarify it a bit."

Ackermann stopped walking, staring over the top of David's head. "You have no contacts?"

"Well, no. Not like that."

Ackermann considered the answer for a moment, then gave a weary sigh before walking off.

It left David with the feeling that he had failed a test he had not even realised he was sitting. And in the fifteen minutes it took him to get back to the office, David Gates kept wondering *what* Ackermann had actually expected of him. In fact, he was still thinking about it when he entered reception to find Ackermann's secretary in a tense exchange with a dark-haired man.

"You can't see him, sir," she insisted, "Mr Ackermann has just returned to his office and is busy for the rest of the day with meetings. He's not seeing anyone."

"He'll see me," the visitor retorted. "Tell him it's Thomas de Souza."

49

St Martin's Lane
London

Sente Fleishman's trip hadn't turned out at all as she had expected. London was hellishly expensive, and she needed to work to bring in some cash. Luckily, it was the run-up to Christmas, and St Thomas's needed another A&E nurse to deal with the increase in accidents and attacks. After checking Sente's impressive work record in Germany, she was hired for a month, with the proviso that she could extend in the New Year if she wanted to.

She didn't, but she wasn't going to tell them that. Sente was just grateful for the work, rapidly fitting in at St Thomas's. An Amazonian woman, competent, and quick-witted. She was popular with the men, patients, and staff alike, which put a few of the other nurses' noses out of joint. Sente did what she always did; she pretended not to notice and earned her wage. Big enough to hold her own - and experienced enough to cope with the heavy traffic of the A&E department - Sente was reliable, and if she did like a drink and a smoke, so what? Who cared what she got up to off duty? If she had a one-nighter with a lab technician again, so what? She was uncomplicated and street-smart. And she was terrific at handling the drunks.

No one messed with Sente Fleishman. Or so everyone thought. But that was because no one had noticed a tall, stooped man watching her. Always furtive, the unseen Purchass had followed her journeys to and from the hospital, and her visits to a local pub. Of course, her blue eyes had caught his attention first, and then he had considered the rest. Her height and weight could have been daunting, but although her physique was impressive, she was careless. Off duty, she drank too much and walked home when it was dark. And late. Too late for a single woman to be out alone. Too late for safety. Too late for other people to be out and about. Too late for anyone to intervene and help her.

But it was the perfect time for Purchass.

50

Glancing briefly at his mistress, Simon Porter decided that Anna de Souza was bad luck. Before he had met her, he had been a happy man with a wife and family. He had a sound business, with the Famosa empire providing his income and pension fund. But now everything was changing. Anna, together with her son, had become too involved in his agency, *his* business. How could he ever have thought he loved her? It was sex, that was all, sex. Sex that had made him leave his family. Sex that had inflamed him and damped down his conscience. Sex that had turned a dull, judicious man into an overheated teenager. It was mortifying.

Simon took the thermometer out of his mouth and stared at the reading. Normal. How could it be normal? Irritated, he tossed the instrument to the back of the cabinet and moved into his office. Halle hadn't returned any of his calls for a week, and Kara Famosa had slipped off the front pages, overtaken by a banking scandal. In another twenty-four hours, she would be forgotten. Of course, if they found her kidnapper, then it would be news again. But what was the likelihood of that? The man hadn't even taken the ransom money

– and that made no sense. Unless Kara Famosa was dead, and then the expose would die with her.

His conscience nudged him. He had known from the beginning that she was serious, but it had been better to pretend otherwise and keep his eye on what she was doing. See if Kara would really expose the Famosa fortune, with all the deals, the rumours, and the sleazy Vegas days brought into the sunlight. Besides, he needed to know what she was doing, and he needed to know first. If Kara *did* dare to seek revenge in print, she would put herself at risk because Luis Famosa had a coterie of lawyers who ensured that his business ran smoothly. The Cuban wasn't going to allow anyone to upturn his fortune or freedom. As for Jimmy Famosa… Simon paused. Since Thomas had usurped Jimmy, their bond had been severed. When he called the New York offices, Simon was told that Jimmy Famosa was busy and that his messages would be passed on. But direct communication? Nothing.

Thoughtful, Simon stared at the internet headlines. The Financial crisis was all over the news, Kara's kidnapping had been obliterated. If only Anna hadn't fanned his expectations and made him believe his agency would make a fortune from the abduction. Instead, the opposite had happened. Kara's disappearance had faded, and with it any chance of a best-selling expose.

Rather than being promoted to the top of the midden, Simon Porter was now staring at his mistress and wondering how the hell it had all gone so wrong.

51

Hampshire

Wandering around the country house, Halle dismissed her assistant and sent Miss Reid for some provisions in the village. The bodyguard was talking to the gardener in the garden beyond, and as she drifted, her mobile rang in her pocket. She knew without looking that it would be Luis and ignored it. Her defiance amazed her, looking at the bodyguard again and reassuring herself that he was still there, keeping her safe. Even from Luis. Because now she was afraid of her husband, her mind struggling with a past that was always just beyond her reach. The hazy memory of an event she knew was damning and might prove dangerous.

Having avoided her daughter's bedroom since Kara's abduction, Halle pushed open the door and walked in. The fading winter light was closing down the afternoon as she moved towards the mirror, staring at the postcards stuck into a wooden frame. They were old, she thought, people sent texts or emails now. She had never dared to ask who the senders were. And if she *had* asked, Kara would have been evasive, making a mystery out of a message from a friend.

It had been different when Kara was a child. Then, she had been affectionate, almost clingy, enjoying family holidays, Luis arranging everything, the secretaries, the staff, and the nanny in tow…Reaching for one of the half-hidden postcards, Halle glanced at the image of a city at Christmas time. Bruges, where Luis had bid for a Frans Hals at auction and got it, beating dealers from around the globe. It hadn't made him popular, but Luis never cared about popularity, only winning.

Dizzy from the tablets she had taken on an empty stomach, Halle sat down on the side of the bed, turning over the postcard. The message was short, the words sharp, black shards of ice on white paper.

Luis Famosa isn't your father.
I'm sorry.

She read the words three times, barely understanding, her breathing rapid, her hands shaking as she gripped the postcard.

Finally, she understood what had caused the coldness between her and her daughter. Kara had discovered the secret her mother had hidden for decades, the truth sent by *postcard*. Two lines, one a malignant apology after destroying a person's life. Clutching the card, Halle realised how betrayed her daughter would have felt, her animosity fair punishment for her mother's adultery and lies. Her rage had been slow, finally leading Kara to write the expose as a means to castigate her mother and destroy the family to which she didn't truly belong. Having hero worshipped Luis all her life, Kara would have suddenly seen him as others did; flawed, ruthless, and perhaps, worse.

Surely, she *had* suspected she wasn't his child? After all, Halle thought, she had confided in Thomas, even if she had then denied it. But deep down, hadn't she guessed? Letting the postcard drop from her hand, Halle looked into the mirror, startled by the change. She had become a hag, the tide marks of fear and guilt eating into her features.

A sudden noise jolted her out of her thoughts. The sound of footsteps coming from below - but not those of the bodyguard. These were different, unfamiliar. Cautious, she rose to her feet, pausing at the door, wondering why there were no noises coming from the sitting room or the garden. The daylight was failing, shadows tree-tall across bare boards as she listened.

Outside, the bodyguard was still talking with the gardener. Halle heard them in the distance as she looked down the stairwell and into the hallway beneath. Someone *was* in the house. The footsteps were not loud, but not disguised, the person unafraid of being heard. Unnerved, she froze, not knowing whether to call out or run. Her thoughts were confused by the medication, and she tried to calm herself. Maybe it was just a delivery man.

Call out, she told herself.

But she didn't.

The footsteps continued moving around downstairs, walking into the kitchen and returning to the hallway, only yards beneath her. Covering her mouth with her hand, Halle held her breath. The footsteps stopped. A moment later, they started again, this time stepping onto the stairs as a shadow began to move up the wall.

Someone *was* coming for her.

Terrified, she moved back into the bedroom, stumbling towards the window and lifting the glass pane. It moved noiselessly, her focus blurring as she felt the frigid air enter her lungs. She could escape, she told herself; there was a flat roof below, only a few yards away. She *could* jump. But what if she fell? She was unsteady from the pills. She could fall.

In the instant she wavered, the footsteps speeded up, mounting the stairs and running along the top corridor towards Kara's bedroom. Whimpering in panic, Halle clambered out of the window, her dizziness increasing, her legs giving way as she closed her eyes and jumped.

And from the bedroom above, someone watched her go.

52

Chelsea Wharf, London
16th December

"You recognise my name?" Thomas asked, walking in and facing Hugh Ackermann.

He was hunched over his desk, his eyes unreadable as he gestured for his visitor to sit down. "I recognise your *mother's* name. She left your father for Simon Porter. How's that working out?"

Thomas avoided the question. "I need to talk to you."

Ackermann sighed. "Make it quick."

"I know about you."

The eyes remained steady behind the dense lenses. "So does everyone that's been on Google."

"But I know something intimate about you," Thomas continued. "I know your secret."

To his surprise, Ackermann shook his head, "No, you bloody don't. You don't know anything." His voice was a low monotone, "I read your blog about Kara Famosa. You had a relationship with her, and her mother used to be a girlfriend of mine before Luis

Famosa poached her." He scratched his lantern jaw. "So much for history. But I'm interested to know what *you* know about Kara Famosa's kidnapping."

"You read the papers; you know as much as I do."

He had some balls, Ackermann thought. Just walking in and throwing his weight around. Impressive. Stupid, but impressive.

"I hate the word secret," Ackermann continued, "Sounds melodramatic. Sounds vaguely threatening too. Like you think I might be coerced into your keeping this 'secret' quiet. In fact, it sounds a bit like blackmail --"

"I'm not asking for money."

"I hear you could use it."

Thomas smiled grimly, "I'm not rich anymore, and that's a fact."

"So, you want a job?"

"Amazing how many people want to hire me lately. Simon Porter and now you. But I've gone freelance. I'm going to find out who kidnapped Kara Famosa."

"And why did the kidnapper not take the ransom money?" There was a flicker of interest in Ackermann's gaze as he studied Thomas. "I want to know that myself. And I want to see Kara back safe --"

"Because you're her father."

The words shuffled in the air between them. For several moments, Ackermann stared at Thomas and then finally spoke, "Was that your big secret? Sorry to disappoint you, but I'm not Kara's father."

"She told me --"

"That I was her father?"

"No," Thomas conceded, "that Luis wasn't."

"And you thought it was me?" Ackermann shook his head. "No, we're not related. I just like Kara; we're friends."

"Even though her mother dumped you?"

Ackermann took off his glasses, a massive Gustavian clock ticking sonorously in the background. Outside the office windows, the London skyline let in the winter afternoon, clouds morose on a sullen wind.

"So, who was Kara's father if it wasn't you?"

"Search me," Ackermann replied. "How many people know that she *wasn't* Luis Famosa's kid?"

"Only me."

"And Kara told you herself?" Ackermann asked, having sensed the lie before Thomas uttered it.

"Yes, then backtracked and tried to make a joke out of it."

"So, what if it *is* true? People don't get kidnapped to cover up adultery." Ackermann said drily, "Who cares if someone exposes Halle for cheating on her husband? It's a non-story. Might have been a scandal once, but not now."

"Kara's writing an expose –"

"Kara's doing nothing at the moment," Ackermann replied, his tone and appearance threatening.

" -- you were encouraging her to write it."

"Was I? Why?"

"For revenge."

Ackermann put his glasses back on, the lens magnifying the expressionless grey eyes. "Come on now, Mr de Souza, let's not fuck about anymore. You've been thinking about the book Kara was writing and trying to piece it together with the kidnapping. And wondering w*hy* the kidnapper didn't take the money."

"Have I?"

"Everyone has. But you must have *brooded* on it. You went to the meet, you thought you'd rescue Kara - and found a dead pig instead." He wheezed with laughter, then became serious again. "You loved her, you probably still do. So that nasty trick must have made you mad," Ackermann paused, reverting to the old monotone. "What about the Gustav Klimt?" He saw Thomas's expression flicker and nodded, "Oh yes, I know Kara stole it. And now you're wondering *how* I know. Or perhaps she took it for *me*? Would that tie into your revenge theory?"

"Don't say you wouldn't want to get your hands on the Klimt."

"If I had, there are other ways I would have got it," he replied, deadpan. "But returning to the subject of the expose - what if Kara had *already* written it?"

"Has she?"

Ackermann was enjoying himself and leaned back in his seat. "How would I know?"

"You seem to know a lot about Kara. You seem very interested in her."

"Like I said, I like her."

"But you didn't like Halle?"

"Don't put words in my mouth, Mr de Souza," he said warningly. "Halle left me to go to some smarmy Cuban. Old news, but the sting's long gone."

Ackermann would have had anyone else thrown out of his office, but although irked by Thomas's questioning, he was wondering how to play this unexpected interrogator.

"Did you stay in touch with Halle after she married Luis?"

"We were friends," Ackermann replied, relaxing and letting out a little of his fishing line, "Besides,

I knew Luis Famosa from a long time back. Common little crook, but clever."

"He was a crook?"

"Luis is very successful. All highfliers bend the rules."

"But he bends them more than most?"

Ackermann sighed, twitching the line. "What are you *really* after?"

"I want to know what was in Kara's book. Whether it was the reason for her abduction," Thomas replied. "Did you read it?"

"Did you?"

"I've never seen it. I don't even know if it exists. Although you're implying it does. Does it?"

There was a long pause before Ackermann spoke again, reeling in his catch. "I'll make a deal with you. I'll pay you for information about Kara Famosa's kidnapping."

"I don't know any more than the police do."

"*You must do!* You're close to Halle, so you'll know what Jimmy Famosa's up to, and I'd like to know that, too. I have my own investigators - but no one with your advantage. You can find out things the police never will. If you apply yourself." Ackermann leaned back in his seat, putting some distance between them. "Like you said, you're not rich anymore, and your father's a sick man, so here's the deal. I'll pay all his medical expenses if you'll tell me *everything* about the kidnapping and what's going on with Halle. I hear she's in England now, left Luis in New York. I'll pay you for everything you find out. What you know first, I want to know second. Are we in agreement, Mr de Souza?"

Thomas rose to his feet. "No."

To Ackermann's surprise the line snapped, the fish off the hook. "You're going to regret ever walking into my office."

"No," Thomas replied, "The only thing I'll regret is not walking out sooner."

53

Purchass had always enjoyed his hobby of watching. But now he was enjoying watching not only a woman, Sente Fleishman, but a man as well. Thomas de Souza. He alternated between the two of them. He might begin the evening watching Sente, then travel across London to Maida Vale and stake out the de Souza house instead.

At first, Purchass had been dismissive of his rival. After all, he had outsmarted de Souza easily enough, but he didn't look like a cowed man. He looked purposeful, with a classiness Purchass envied. Jealously caught him by surprise and increased his dislike of Thomas. Of course, Kat would have drooled over him; the rich boy with his flashy name. Even fired from his job - regulated to his father's carer and Purchass's puppet - de Souza wasn't broken. That festered inside Purchass, making him wonder how he *could* be broken. As he stared at the door of the de Souza house, a plan began to form. What would it take to reduce a privileged man, possessed of good looks and charm, to nothingness? How could he belittle de Souza and strip him of his virtues? How could he make him an equal? Or better. *Less* than an equal. There had to be a way to keep a man alive and murder his spirit at the same time.

Leaning against the wall, Purchass jiggled the change in his pocket. He remembered the meet and how he had tricked de Souza and driven off triumphantly. But he couldn't stay away. Instead, he had returned a while later, camouflaged by fog, enjoying his victory. The joke he had played on everyone. Watching Thomas de Souza, covered in blood from where he had cradled a dead pig.

There had been a lot of police involvement afterwards. So many police, Purchass thought. But that was life, wasn't it? If she had been some woman off a sink estate, there would have been no fanfare, no blog, and no front-page news. Just another dead woman, like Ellie Chadwick. From his vantage point, Purchass had watched a van take the dead pig away and then saw the police arrive, with Thomas de Souza following them out of Peasbold Way.

That was where it should have ended. But Purchass couldn't resist. He had liked watching Jimmy Famosa, but the American had been a blunderer, and de Souza was altogether more fascinating. So, he *kept* watching him. After he finished work at the airport, he spent his evenings in the dented old Ford, stalking him because he wanted to see where de Souza went and what he did.

And he *was* busy. It had amused Purchass to observe him visiting the police station, then walking into the Underground - never releasing that Kara Famosa's kidnapper had been in the same carriage. Never knowing that the man he had brushed into when he made for the exit had been the same man who had tricked him in the snow.

So, on Purchass's next day off, he spent it watching the man he'd made a fool of, following Thomas de Souza across London. As the days ticked by, something ignited inside Purchass, a black malice. He had enjoyed killing Ellie Chadwick and kidnapping the Famosa girl but was undecided about what to do with the latter. Alive, she meant money; dead, she meant the threat of being caught. Then there was the painting to think about. Was it *really* valuable? Purchass didn't know, but he wasn't about to get rid of something he could use as a bargaining tool.

"Why don't you let me talk to Thomas?" Kara had asked him the previous night.

Purchass had ignored the question because her whining voice grated on him. But she was tough, he'd give her that. The wound in her head had healed, and having decided not to kill her, he was giving her more food and an old blanket to keep her warm. Keeping her alive, for now. What he was going to do in the long run, he hadn't decided, but he was enjoying having the Famosas on the end of a line - and jerking around Thomas de Souza at the same time.

Purchass's imagination was expanding. His sense of humour, too. The stunt with the pig had been inspired. Ducking into the shadows, he continued to watch the de Souza house, his hands twitching, his breathing rapid. An hour passed, and he sucked two mints as he waited. Smoked a roll up, and waited longer. When Thomas finally materialised, he hesitated for only a second before following him.

It was a decision that would destroy them both.

54

17th December

Having discovered what he could on the internet, Thomas visited the library to see their newspaper records, going back over the previous twelve months. He was looking for a death, a murder, or a victim. But he didn't know where, or how and when, she had been killed. All he knew were Kara's words:

I wasn't the first.

He started his search in London because that was where Kara had been abducted: trawling slowly through the computer newspaper images and articles, many of which would not have been listed in such detail on the internet. Over the previous year, there had been one hundred and three murders in the capital. 60% were killings of women; 45% of those were victims killed as a result of domestic violence with the remaining 15% murdered by unknown persons. Thomas concentrated on the last, narrowing his search down to the previous two months, knowing he could go back further if necessary.

The first murder had been committed in Lambeth; the murderer was caught in October. The second had been in Lincoln's Inn Field, the woman in her seventies. Thomas made a note of the details. She had been strangled but not beaten nor tortured. Two further murders were due to arson. He dismissed those too, looking for killings which involved torture, finally coming across the killing of a young woman who had been battered and thrown in the Thames during mid-November. But her body had not been specifically mutilated.

Thomas kept searching, day by day, until finally he came across a newspaper article from the 19th of November, only days before Kara went missing. The girl's name meant nothing to him, but she had been around the same age and had a similar colouring to Kara, and when he glanced at her photograph, her eyes were blue. Brightly, boldly, blue. Ellie Chadwick was the woman's name. She had been tortured, and her eyes had been mutilated and injected with dye.

Thomas stared at the article. Why hadn't the police been looking into the case? Or maybe they had and were unwilling to give him any information he might use for his own ends. After all, Thomas thought, they must have noticed the similarities. Then he realised that there *weren't* any. Ellie Chadwick had been working in London, her body left in the boot of a car outside a slum pub. A random killing. Whereas Kara Famosa had been the victim of a kidnapping. An American from a rich family. A woman whose fate was being followed by millions. The two women had nothing in common. Or did they?

Thoughtful, Thomas continued to read. The murderer had not been caught, and the police were offering no information except the bare bones of the case.

Apparently, Ellie Chadwick had had no enemies and had been due to marry her fiancé, Stuart Mills, who had an alibi for the time of her death. That was it. Yet there was something about her eyes, Thomas thought. She had had unusual eyes, like Kara's. Eyes that attracted attention. He paused, uncertain. He could be wrong. After all, it was just a feeling. He wasn't an investigator. Did he *really* believe that he could find the kidnapper, succeeding where the police had failed? Yes, he did because the police didn't know Kara Famosa. Detective Jameson wasn't grieving for an ex-lover. Kara's abduction was simply a case. Important, but not personal. Her kidnapping would not haunt him as it haunted Thomas.

He *would* find Kara, Thomas promised himself.

And he would expose her kidnapper.

Then, finally, he would know *why* she had been taken.

55

Hampshire, UK

Shouting for the bodyguard, Miss Reid climbed up the step ladder, staring with disbelief at Halle's body lying on the flat roof.

"Mrs Famosa!" she cried, reaching out for her hand. "Mrs Famosa, are you alright?"

The guard had chosen easier access, climbing through the bedroom window, picking up an unconscious Halle, and returning her to her master suite, the housekeeper following.

"What happened?"

Miss Reid shook her head. "I don't know. I just heard a thud and found her there. Where were you?"

He ignored the question. "Get Mrs Famosa's doctor, and hurry –"

As he said the words, Halle opened her eyes, flinching and touching her forehead. "What... on earth…" She gazed at the guard and then the housekeeper, embarrassed but still frightened. "I jumped because there was someone in the house. Someone was coming for me –"

“There’s no one in the house, madam,” the guard reassured her.

“You were in the garden; how would you know!” Her voice wavered, her head throbbing as she laid back against the pillows. There *had* been someone in the house; she knew it. They had been coming for her.

“Mrs Famosa,” the guard insisted “no one’s broken in –”

“You’re wrong,” Halle mumbled, glancing at Miss Reid imploringly. “I heard them. I heard their footsteps…”

“Rest now,” the housekeeper soothed her, “you need to rest and wait for the doctor –”

“I don’t want a doctor! I know what I heard. I *know* there was someone here.” Halle rose to her feet, unsteady. Miss Reid glanced at the bodyguard as she moved into the corridor and pointed down into the hall. “They were there at first, then they came up to Kara’s room. I was in there - and they knew it, that’s why they came.” She glanced down the passageway, her body shaking. “He was walking quietly at first, then running, and I jumped. I jumped out of the window to get away.” She looked at the bodyguard, defiant. *“Where were you?* You should have been here --”

“I’ll call the police, madam –”

“Yes! *No*!” Halle contradicted herself immediately. “No police. You **don’t** call the police!” Her head ached, blood seeping from the cut on her forehead, Miss Reid putting a supporting arm around her.

“Come back to bed and wait for the doctor. You have to be careful, Mrs Famosa, you could have a concussion. Why didn’t you call for me?”

"He would have heard me!" Halle said helplessly. "I was scared, so I stayed quiet. I thought it *was* you at first..."

She paused, dizzy, faltering as the housekeeper helped her back into her room. There were to be no police, Halle repeated. No report of a break-in, and the bodyguard was not to tell Luis. *Or did Luis already know*? Had Luis sent someone? Her thoughts were scattered. Maybe she should call Jimmy instead? No, he would tell his father. So, who *could* she call? Simon Porter? No, he wasn't family, and she didn't trust him. Thomas? Of course, *Thomas.* She would call Thomas.

Shivering and feeling the blood running down her forehead, Halle reached into her pocket for a tissue, her right hand closing over the postcard she had taken from her daughter's mirror earlier.

56

Clapham, London

"Mr Mills?"

He turned when his name was called. A slight, sandy haired man in his twenties, holding a sandwich from the local shop. "Yes. Who are you?"

"Thomas de Souza." He gestured to a nearby bench. "Can I have a word? I think we might have something in common." Curious but wary, Stuart sat down, London buses passing them only yards away. "You lost your fiancé, didn't you?" Thomas went on, "She was murdered, wasn't she?"

Stuart nodded, looking away across the street. Hanging onto his feelings. "She was killed. Her name was *Ellie*. I don't mind talking about what happened - no one else wants to talk about her in case it upsets me. The thing is, I can't be any more upset, because she's dead and she's not coming back." He kept staring across the road. "I only came to London because of Ellie. I suppose I'll go home now."

"Where's home?"

"Manchester. The police will probably close the case soon. They don't know who the killer is and have no clues. None they're telling me anyway." He gave a sideways glance at Thomas. "You said we had something in common; what was it?"

"I've been looking for someone I care about. She was kidnapped. Kara Famosa."

Stuart jerked upright. "I read about that in the papers! God Almighty, it's everywhere you look. The kidnapper didn't take the money; why was that?"

Thomas shrugged, "I don't know."

"Leaving that dead pig for you to find, that was bloody sick."

"Yes, it was."

"You think the murders are connected?" Stuart asked. He was blunt and straight to the point.

"They might be," Thomas replied, changing tack. "What was Ellie like?"

"Sweet. Good fun, pretty. I thought so anyway."

"Anything different about her?"

"Her eyes. She had the most beautiful bright blue eyes. The bastard who killed her ruined them." Stuart paused and swallowed. "He tortured your friend too, cut off one of her fingers, didn't he?"

"Yes, and sent it to her mother."

"Christ." Stuart stopped short, staring at Thomas. "You think it's the same man?"

"Maybe."

"Why?"

"Ellie and Kara look a little alike, both had – *have* – unusual eyes."

"But the police haven't connected them. Their lives couldn't have been more different. Ellie didn't have money, she wasn't famous. She was ordinary. Not to me, but to everyone else she was just a nice girl."

They were both finding the conversation difficult, Thomas careful with his words. "Did Ellie ever talk about someone she was afraid of? Someone she didn't like?"

"Nah. She got on with everyone. She was a veterinary nurse, and all the patients liked her. The two-footed ones *and* the four-footed ones," he tried to smile, but it didn't come off.

"Maybe she rejected some man, and he took it badly?"

Stuart shook his head. "Nah, Ellie wasn't the type. I loved her. She was beautiful to me but she wasn't the kind of girl men hit on. You know what I mean? Some girls are always looking for attention…"

Thomas thought that the description might not suit Ellie Chadwick but matched Kara perfectly.

"… Ellie had been lonely for a long time, and she was happy at last. We were getting married. Then she was killed. The police asked me all sorts of questions; I think they even suspected me until they checked my alibi." He glanced at Thomas. "Shouldn't you talk to them? See if they've come to the same conclusion?"

Why tip them off? Thomas thought, changing the subject. "Are the police still working on Ellie's case?"

"I dunno. I don't think they had any other suspects," he looked back to Thomas. "What if it *was* the same man?"

"I'll let you know."

Stuart nodded. "I keep thinking about how Ellie died. How scared she must have been," he paused, tugged out the words. "You see, Ellie had no family, she was alone in the world. I hate it that she died the same way."

57

18th December

Throwing back the blanket on his bed, Purchass got to his feet and walked into the kitchen. He was restless, walking from room to room, trying to calm his mind. But it didn't work. Neither did the coffee or the beer. Instead, everything seemed to inflame him further, all because of a fucking dream.

Purchass never had trouble sleeping. In fact, he was such a heavy sleeper that it became a family joke that he was too stupid to wake up. His mother used to rouse him, then after she died, the duty fell to his brother. But Steve punched him awake, leaving marks on his arms and legs, always in places that were hidden by clothes. He even bit him once, leaving the imprint of his crocked teeth on his little brother's arm. Much smaller, much younger, Purchass was bullied constantly. Having once wet the bed, he was stripped naked and made to stand in the yard until Steve let him into the house again ten hours later.

After that, Purchass slept with his penis wrapped in a plastic bag. After a week or so, he got a rash, but it didn't stop him. He just filled the bag with newspaper to prevent the chafing. No one ever knew. His room was at the top of the farmhouse, riddled with damp and wood rot, the stairs were so steep Steve stopped trying to climb them as he got fat. And he *did* get fat. Wheezy too, even so young, neglecting the small holding, leaving animal shit about, turning into acrid pools when it rained, the cattle's hooves sucked into the putrid stench.

Purchass did the cleaning up. Steve would sit, watching and talking about the thing he always talked about: their father, Declan. How tough he had been, how he had been a bare-knuckle fighter and had killed people over in Ireland and Liverpool before coming down South.

'You're lucky he's dead. He hated you. Would have done for you if he'd lived.'

Kat would come over and sit next to Steve, and they would both watch their little brother as he shovelled up the shit. When Purchass got blisters on his palms he went to school in mittens. He was cold. It was winter, said he said…

Breathing noisily through his mouth, Purchass slumped into the kitchen chair. It was covered in a faded plaid, mottled with grease marks where the men of the family had rested their heads. Decades of shiny black hair oiled up, looking like the cattle should have looked as if they'd been well-fed. First, it was Declan sitting there, then Steve. Only Steve got fat, and the chair didn't get any bigger. Kat started sitting on the arm next to her brother, her legs crossed, swinging her bloody foot...

Unsettled, Purchass tried to think of something else, but he couldn't because he remembered the dream he had just had. Only it wasn't a dream; it was a sleeping memory.

It had been sticky hot that June, the last few wasted cattle stinking in the outhouses, flies settling in their droves. The fields had become parched without rain, the yellow acres turning to early brown, birds too hot to sing. He had come home from school, leaving his books at the back of one of the outhouses so Steve wouldn't spoil them, and then walked into the kitchen.

She was sitting with her knees wide open, fanning herself. Sweating in a print dress, old yellow stain marks under the arms. Her eyes, burning blue, had fixed on him. He was fourteen years old. She was sixteen, blousy already, her tongue hot, angry as she kissed him. Kissed her little brother and sniggered as she felt inside his pants, Purchass trying to wriggle free, Kat finally pushing him away.

Freak. Fucking freak.

It went on all that boiling summer. The next time, she had come to his bedroom. Steve was too fat to waddle upstairs. Her eyes had glinted in the semi dark; weird and terrifying. She had given him an erection whilst he sobbed with guilt, climbing on top of him and riding her little brother like a night terror.

Freak, fucking freak...

It was summer. That hideous summer. Without water, without shade. With only a burning sky, as blue as her eyes...

Purchass got to his feet, walking over to the window, and looking over to the outbuildings. Remembering Kara Famosa. Remembering Ellie Chadwick. Remembering his *sister*... and then Purchass knew what he had to do. The only thing that would calm him down and stop the dreams. He had to find a new victim. Someone with blue eyes. Someone who would fear him and look at him the way his sister had. With hatred. Because he *had* hated her.

Almost as much as he'd loved her.

58

Hugh Ackermann was sitting in First Class, thinking, and as the train moved through the landscape, his thoughts turned to Kara Famosa. How she used to stay with him in London. How she used to talk to him and occasionally confide in him. Kara wasn't a woman who would trust easily, but sometimes she would let down her guard because she liked to provoke her mother by being friendly with her ex-fiancé. Never realising that it afforded Ackermann a handy way of keeping tabs on Halle.

That morning, he had trailed through his investigators' reports and discovered nothing. All that money spent, for nought. No news, no insights, not even some inspired guesswork. The kidnapper had been clever and eluded everyone. Ackermann didn't want that. He wanted him caught. Not just because he had abducted Kara but because of what he might know. Because a kidnap victim might confess *anything* to save their life, they might share information that Ackermann would have preferred to remain hidden.

Agitated, he pressed his hand against the carriage window, his fingers stretched out on the glass. Was her kidnapping random, as he hoped? Or had it been planned? Had Kara been targeted and then, to stay alive, confided in her killer? Had she told him about the expose? About the criminal sleight of hand, Luis Famosa's infatuation with forgery? The Cuban might cover his tracks – allowing a well-compensated acolyte to serve a prison term for a fake Famosa had sold from his New York gallery – but Luis found the world of forgery as enticing as gambling. The same risk, the same adrenalin rush.

Ackermann's thoughts slid to the Gustav Klimt and how agonised Luis Famosa would be feeling. To have such a valuable artwork stolen was bad enough, but for Kara to be the thief? Ackermann chuckled to himself. She had really meant business by stealing a work that had been trumpeted globally, snatching it away from an auction that was temporarily *postponed*. But what had she *really* intended? Ackermann wondered. To sell it elsewhere? Or merely to humiliate Luis? His forays into the art world were still sneered at by some; how it would sting if people discovered that the Klimt had been stolen by a member of the Famosa family.

Clicking his tongue, Ackermann thought of the bullish Thomas de Souza. The nerve, asking him outright if he was Kara's real father! The man was arrogant, but Ackermann admired his balls. He was better than Jimmy Famosa, who was too much the company spook to stand up to his father. Too careful of the family fortune to alienate his parent. By contrast, Kara had often challenged Luis - but then again, she wasn't his daughter, was she? Kara the cuckoo wrongfully occupying a place in the Famosa nest for many years. So how would Luis react to the threat of an expose from a child that wasn't even his?

Taking his hand away from the train window, Ackermann straightened the sleeves of his heavy worsted jacket. His poker player's face served him well, but inside, he was struggling to control himself. Because what he and others had believed buried and forgotten, might finally be seeping out. It had been over twenty years earlier, Simon Porter was in Las Vegas visiting the Famosa family and staying longer than he should have been, bleating about missing London. It was then that Ackermann and Luis struck the deal to effectively silence Halle. In case one day she remembered. In case somewhere down the line, her alcoholic amnesia lifted. It had seemed unlikely because she had always been highly strung with a drug habit. A pretty woman who drank too much and had blackouts, but there was always a chance she would remember.

"We have to act," Luis had said that boiling hot night in Las Vegas, as they stood outside under a Van Gogh sky. "We have to do something –"

"Like what?" Ackermann had replied, hefty even then, bi-spectacled, stolid.

"There's only one thing we can do," Luis had continued. He was smoking, the tip of the cigarette a red blood spot beneath the white stars. "It's best for everyone."

No one had known the truth. Oh, there had been a rumour, but it was too far-fetched to be believed and was laughed off. No one suspected Ackermann of being involved. After all, weren't Luis and he love rivals? Bitter enemies? Which was exactly what they wanted everyone to believe. Competitors aren't allies. So, for a while, they were home free, Simon Porter returning tight-lipped to London. Three guilty men - one befuddled young woman - locked into silence.

Until they realised there was a *fifth*. That the quartet was, in fact, a quintet and someone else knew what they had done.

They had approached Luis first anonymously, then Simon Porter, then Ackermann. Finally, Halle, who reacted with confusion, denying everything. It was true, she *couldn't* remember anything, because she was still trying to come to terms with Luis's adultery and consoling herself by drinking too much. Using his cronies, Luis Famosa had set out to find out who was threatening them. However, although he had a backing singer run out of his Las Vegas hotel, they were never sure if he was the right man. An ugly altercation with the garage manager did nothing but provoke further questions, so Luis pulled his horns in. All through that sweating summer, they rode it out. Famosa in the USA, and Ackermann and Porter in the UK.

Unsure of Halle, Luis watched over his wife. When once he had discouraged her drinking, he now encouraged it. Her instability and unhappiness made her pliable; he swore that he had ended his relationship with his mistress and their daughter and Halle pretended to believe him. They had sex and drank more, and Luis bought Halle expensive clothes that she would try on in the hotel suite before slumping into a chair, too dizzy to go out. She didn't want to be seen, she said, as Luis watched her reflection in the mirror. He seemed to want her too much, but she didn't really want him. Not for sex, anyway. Instead, she let him do what he wanted and lay back until he fell asleep beside her. Then she would find herself thinking - and Halle couldn't face thinking. Just like she couldn't face leaving Luis. Because where would she go?

They were all trapped, all afraid. Fear bought nothing but silence and everything *did* go silent. Stayed silent for decades.

Until Kara decided to write a book.

A train passed suddenly, Ackermann flinching as it crossed by the window and his carriage entered a tunnel. The lights flickered, the newspaper on his lap coming in and out of focus, the rhythm on the track sounding in his ears.

Now's the time.

Now's the time.

Now's the time.

He had to find Kara's kidnapper. He had to know if he was safe or not. And if not, he had to deal with it - before someone dealt with him.

Again, his mind returned to that summer. Heat. Desert. Miles of it burnt dry for centuries. Thick with dust and cacti, some as tall as a horse. Freak plants coated with flick knives.

Now's the time.

Now's the time.

Now's the time.

Still in the tunnel, the train's interior lights suddenly went out, Ackerman looking around blindly as the door to his compartment opened.

59

Hampshire
England

Outside, the sun was dodging clouds, the winter cold sapping the leaves from the trees, and a listless brook fighting the impulse to freeze. Christmas was coming, only this time, Halle would be alone because Luis was working with Jimmy in New York; both men concentrated on finding Kara from a distance. Or so they said. On their instructions, Halle was told to stay calm and wait for news, with the bodyguard and housekeeper for company. At one time, Halle would have turned to her husband for protection, but she had changed, her suspicions keeping her quiet. Mistrustful, only allowing Miss Reid to keep her company, Halle struggled with her thoughts. Within days the bodyguard was joined by another guard as the house and grounds were monitored constantly.

That was a good sign, wasn't it? Halle told herself, because if Luis was going to hurt her, he wouldn't have her protected. *But why was he going to hurt her?* Had she *really* thought that? Was he watching her instead of guarding her? Were the cameras tracking her movements, sending back reports to New York? But if she *was* being filmed, he would see nothing. Only Thomas visiting and Miss Reid sleeping in the bedroom next to Halle.

But there *was* something to see, wasn't there? Because Halle was drinking heavily, very heavily. Particularly at night. Unplugging the phone and giving the housekeeper instructions not to disturb her. She didn't enjoy the taste, but by the time Halle had finished the first bottle and was onto her second bottle of vodka, she was crying for her missing daughter and for her absent husband. Her mind blurred, booze and guilt unbalancing her. She dozed, woke abruptly, and then dozed again. Yet, through the alcoholic daze, she started to remember.

'Shut the fucking door. Hurry up! Jesus, hurry!'

Luis turned her around to face him.

'You didn't see anything. Nothing.'

He ran his finger along her bottom lip.

'Don't let me down.'

Don't let me down…

It had been Christmas. She had visited Las Vegas from New York, Luis eager to show her the church statues he had acquired. Art as hard cash. Not as he ran the gallery in New York, but how he hustled in Vegas. Paintings traded to pay off a loan, a Virgin Mary and St John the Baptist settling a gambling loss, their purity absolving the smut of an art dealers over-enthusiastic weekend jaunt. At the time, Simon Porter was in London having cardiac tests, but Hugh Ackermann had been in Vegas on business and had called on the Famosas, keeping their dodgy friendship going, each of them watching for the other to show weakness.

Later, Luis encouraged Halle to meet up with Ackermann and report back to him.

'Find out if there's a problem. We have to stay allies,' Luis told her. *'You know why.'*

She didn't, but she agreed and met up with Ackermann. He was just as imposing as always, a bison in glasses, although surprised by her drinking. Halle had been relying on alcohol to control her panic attacks, her fear that Luis might find out that she had been unfaithful. Imbibing enough to cause memory lapses, she slipped back to her single lifestyle of booze, marijuana and blackouts. So many that she had told herself that what she *thought* she remembered was just another blurred, confused recall.

Docile, she had listened to Hugh Ackermann, his heavy jawed face flushed, his hand gripping hers tightly, both of them drinking. Halle was wounded from the discovery of Luis's adultery and ready to be consoled.

She had woken up in a hotel room in the early hours.

Six weeks later she had discovered she was pregnant.

Was it Ackermann? He had never, by a look or a word, intimated that anything had taken place between them. Yet Halle could never be sure.

That night she returned home to find Luis waiting for her outside. Sat by the swimming pool, smoking.

"You're late."

"Ackermann wouldn't stop talking."

"All day? He must have had a lot to say." Luis had glanced up at her. "Anything interesting?"

"He was talking about the old days." She was dizzy, her stomach queasy, as Luis rose to his feet and kissed her.

"You're drunk."

"I just had a few drinks."

"You're drunk," Luis repeated, pushing her into the pool, the cold water slapping her sober.

Halle never knew who had fathered her daughter. Was it Ackermann? It could have been, but she had been drunk for weeks. It could, within reason, be a number of the people she mixed with in Vegas. When the crisis was over, Halle gave up the booze and made sure that Luis and Kara never discovered the truth. Or so she had thought – until she found the postcard sent to Kara two Christmases ago, her daughter's animosity tallying with the date stamp. In the eighteen months that followed, Kara had said nothing; she had just planned her revenge. An expose to ruin the Famosas, to expose Luis as a crook, her brother as a weakling, her mother as a whore, and the whole intricate workings of Luis's businesses and forgery empire.

Her hand trembling, Halle lifted the glass and drank again, feeling the punch of the vodka hit her stomach. Before long, she would fall asleep. She wanted that because she was only safe asleep, dead in a world that would keep turning with or without her. Drunk, Halle didn't have to think about what was coming. Because something *was* coming, she knew that. Yet, although she kept drinking, she wasn't getting drunk. She was wired instead, remembering the intruder who had spooked her, panic making her jump out of an upper-floor window.

The bodyguard might deny it, but there *had* been someone in the house. Maybe someone hired to scare her. But who? *Who?* She could hardly claim to be an innocent. She deserved her punishment because it was *her* fault, all of it. Her mind went back to Kara's kidnapping. She banished Jimmy because he was more eager to please his father than to protect his mother…

Halle stopped short; she was lying. She had banished Jimmy because she was terrified he would find out that *she* was the one who called the police.

She had been responsible for panicking the kidnapper.

Her interference had threatened her daughter's life.

So how could she look at her son and *not* confess? And with that confession, how many others might follow?

Halle's mouth dried as she thought of Jimmy, wondering if he knew what Kara was going to put in the expose. Had it been Jimmy who had sent someone to scare her? Using the same tactics her husband would have done. Had Luis - humiliated by his wife's betrayal – sought an ally in his own son? Everyone knew that Jimmy was the willing keeper of secrets and heir to the Famosa fortune. A fortune he would not want to share with a half-sister.

The room was full of shadows. Trees outside the window shifted in the wind, a light moving under the door. Footsteps were all around. Was that the housekeeper's tread or a stranger's? Or maybe Luis's footsteps. Or those of a man who had been with them all those years ago. A man sitting next to Luis in the back seat of a car which Hugh Ackermann had been driving…Terrified, Halle moaned to herself. The secrets were finally snaking out. As fast as she had tried to crush one, another reared up in its place. She was back in Las Vegas on a hot night standing bare foot watching a car drive into the darkness.

Was it all in the book? Kara had been digging into the business, quizzing Jimmy about the finances - why would she do that except for revenge? Or had someone manipulated her into doing another's dirty work?

Halle looked at the postcard again, struggling to recall. There had been four of them that night: Simon Porter, Luis, herself, and Ackermann; but someone else had been there.

Someone who had been silent since the 1990s.

60

Surprised by the startled expression on Ackermann's face, David Gates sat down in the train seat opposite his boss.

"Are you OK, sir?"

Curtly, Ackermann nodded, then stared out of the window as they left the tunnel. Jesus, he was coming unstuck. He couldn't have that. Couldn't lose his nerve now. His face was putty-coloured in the unflattering daylight as he ignored his lawyer, thinking of Thomas de Souza and of the man he had hired to watch him. Because one man was never enough, you hire one to work for you, and another to watch *him*.

Almost apologetically, David Gates passed him some papers, "You need to sign these, sir."

"Not now!" Ackermann barked.

Taking off his glasses, he rubbed his eyes, staring out of the window at what was now a murky blur. He imagined – unusually fanciful – that that was how emotional people saw the world. Blurry, indistinct. Putting his glasses back on, Ackermann relaxed as the carriage came back into focus and snatched the papers from his lawyer's outstretched hand but he wasn't concentrating. Instead, he was thinking of his beginnings. The family had been poor then, properly poor. Hugh was always the promising pupil who had won a scholarship to grammar school, climbing up to a summit only he could see. But by Christ, he was going to get there. He closed off, because emotion got in the way, and besides, he didn't want parents or friends slowing him down.

He went up.

He went high up.

And he went up alone.

He moved away, too. He moved to London and wrote home occasionally but he rarely visited. His father died followed shortly by his mother, ending the family. Ackermann continued to stare at the papers, his lantern jaw clenched… It was at that point in his life he discovered somcthing vital: First, money was muscle Second, always set people against each other. Make them rivals. An individual man might become careless; a secure man relaxes. A threatened man will betray anyone to protect himself. So, by dint of his methods and spies, Ackermann controlled himself and his burgeoning empire through fear. He was afraid of exposure, and everyone else was afraid of him.

Brusquely, he handed the papers back to David Gates. "Anything new on Kara Famosa's abduction?"

David shook his head. "Nothing."

"You find out what else I wanted?"

He nodded, rummaging in his case for the notes, then passed them to Ackermann, "I looked back at other murder cases --"

"Stop blathering!" Ackermann snapped, reading. He had to admit the Gates had done a good job, managing to scratch out every bit of information like a bird scratching out corn from grit. His gaze moved down the printout, then paused on the third page. "November 22nd."

"Oh yes, that was --"

"I can read!" Ackermann interrupted him, "A woman called Ellie Chadwick was murdered, her blue eyes injected with dye. Where?"

"London."

"Has she got family?"

David swallowed. "Just a fiancé."

"Did he do it?"

"What?"

"Did he kill her?"

"No… no, the police spoke to him, but he had an alibi at the time of her murder. He was cleared."

Ackermann continued to read. Only a week before Kara had been kidnapped, Ellie Chadwick had been tortured and killed. He made a low sound in his throat. It *could* be the same man; the women were of similar age, and both had intensely blue eyes. It was a long shot. But it was possible.

"I want to know everything about Ellie Chadwick."

David nodded. "Right --"

"But don't tell anyone what you're doing," Ackermann warned him. "I don't want anyone to know. Especially the police."

Oh no, he didn't want that. The police would open their own investigation and exclude him. And that wasn't going to happen.

He was going to find Kara's kidnapper.

And the book.

61

Over the weeks, Kara had learned how to survive. She knew how to keep quiet; to avoid looking at Purchass; to eat the repugnant food he gave her and to drink the stale water. That was how she was going to live. If no one came to save her, she would save herself. She watched her kidnapper, grateful for any titbits of news he shared, but never once asking questions. Questions made him violent and sent him into rages where he would become volatile, as he had done when he killed the pig.

Kara knew only too well that it could have been her head smashed into the barn floor, and she didn't want that; she didn't want him to win. Instead, she studied his behaviour, noting his agitation and the almost catatonic slump that followed, hearing him talking to himself or the sound of the television turning on from evening until light.

He thought she was beaten and cowed, and Kara let him think that relieved that he no longer abused her. Instead, he seemed to be planning something else; there had been a definite heightening of tension since his meeting with Thomas. At times, he mocked him, sneered at his name as he came into the barn, staring down at her and kicking her backside to wake her up.

"That boyfriend of yours – how much does he care about you?" She didn't answer. He wasn't expecting her to. "Full of himself, isn't he? Not like your brother, not like little Jimmy at all. Nah, de Souza thinks he's going to outsmart me, even though he doesn't know why I didn't take the money," he laughed, making a roll-up and then flicking the match onto the floor. "That hay could go up like a firework! Whoosh!" He said, amused, "and you'd burn with it. All tied up, you'd be helpless, burning like a leg of lamb."

Purchass stopped talking and glanced around before inhaling on his smoke. Kara had noticed the nervous reaction before, as though he had heard something. But she had heard nothing, and she was listening constantly. There was no traffic, no road nearby, the farm obviously remote, the place so dilapidated that if anyone did come across it, they would assume it was abandoned.

"I'm going meet your boyfriend," Purchass said, Kara was still listening but remained silent. "Have a chat with him about you and that crap painting you nicked."

He paused again, his good mood dampened as he moved quickly to the door of the barn and looked out. Alert, Kara listened, hoping for some sign of rescue, but there was none. Instead, Purchass walked into the yard and glanced over towards the house. Staring through the crack in the timber, Kara watched him as he paused beside the outer steps, his voice harsh but uncertain.

"Fuck off! You can't come here, fuck off."

Straining to see what he was looking at, Kara realised that the steps were empty and Purchass was talking to someone who wasn't there.

"Yeah? Well, I'll show you, bitch. You wait and see." He stomped towards the steps, laughing, acting as though he was shooing someone away. "That's it, fuck off, Kat! I'm not afraid of you. Never was." Laughing louder, he mounted the staircase, standing at the top and putting his hands on his hips. "I'm the boss here now, king of the midden. Cock of the walk."

Still watching, Kara saw him enter the kitchen door and slam it closed. Silence followed. No noises came from inside. Whoever he had seen wasn't there any longer. Whoever he had been talking to had disappeared.

And for the first time in weeks Kara Famosa felt a sliver of hope.

62

"Mr de Souza, how d'you douza?"

Thomas recognised the voice at once. "Why didn't you take the money?"

"Sorry about the pig, but at least it wasn't your girlfriend," Purchass said blithely. He had been tracking Thomas for days, ready to put his plan into action. "How did it make you feel when you saw it?"

"How did you want me to feel?"

"You should have been grateful, you wanker! You could have got enough bacon off that pig to keep you for a year."

"I don't eat pork –"

"You Jewish?"

"No."

"Not a fucking vegetarian!"

"No, I just don't like pork… Where's Kara Famosa?"

Silence on the line.

"Is she alive?" Thomas persisted. "Just let me know – *is she alive*?"

"If I told you that I'd be giving the game away, wouldn't I?" Purchass replied. "And that wouldn't be any fun –"

"You'll get caught."

"Police didn't catch me."

"I will."

Purchass liked that. He could tell that de Souza was rattled. "I don't think so, unless I let you, and why would I do that?"

"Why are you calling me?"

Good point, Purchass thought, definitely a good point. "I want to know more about you."

"What?"

"I'm interested. You and me, we've got history now." Purchass continued. He could tell he'd got de Souza on the back foot and pushed further. "I read your blog, and I have to say that it's pretty good for an amateur. Unless your mother helps you write it."

"What d'you want?"

"I could give you a 'scoop,' like the Americans say. Like that clumsy oaf, Jimmy Famosa would say. I could give you a real inside story," Purchass went on, sucking his front tooth. He'd have to get to a dentist before long, he had a hole the size of a cave. Had to be what caused his persistent halitosis, something Kat had always taken pains to point out. "So, de Souza, what d'you say about this crappy painting?"

"Have you got it?"

"I burnt it."

"Good for you."

Purchass raised his eyebrows. "*Good for me*? I thought it was worth a bloody fortune."

"Who told you that?"

"Your girlfriend. She thought it would work in her favour and that her family might value a daub more than her. That's pretty sad, I'd say. Wouldn't you say that?" There was a pause on the line. "Hey, de Souza! You still there?"

"I'm here."

"She told me another secret."

"What?"

"That's the 'scoop'," Purchass paused. "You want to talk now?"

"Go on."

"Tell me about yourself first, then I'll tell you about what she said."

Thomas paused, his tone contemptuous when he replied, "I don't think Kara told you anything."

"Oh, but she did. We have some chats, me and her," Purchass continued. Come on, you snotty bastard, take the bait. "I'll tell you everything in return for what you tell me. Let's start with what your childhood was like."

"Are you out of your mind?"

"Are you?" Purchass countered. "Think about it: you want your girl back, and you want to catch me. Well, I'm giving you an opportunity. I might slip up and give you a clue. Then WHAM! You'd have me. Not tempted? You should be, because if I ring off now, you'll never hear from me again. And you wouldn't like that, would you? You'd spend the rest of your days wondering if you should have talked to me. Wondering what I could have told you, wondering what it was your girlfriend said –"

"I was born in London."

"There now," Purchass coaxed him, "that wasn't so hard, was it?"

"I'm an only child. My father was --"

"A surgeon, yeah, I read that."

"And my mother's dead."

"Now that's just fucking cheeky," Purchass said, his tone warning. "She's not dead at all. What's the matter with you, de Souza? You think I'll go after her? I like young women, she's way too old for me. Don't lie to me again." He paused, "Did you have a happy childhood?"

"We had money, a nice house."

"Same one you're in now?"

"Have you been watching me?"

"*Have you been watching me?*" Purchass parrot-ed. "Nice accent. Sort women go for. Were you a hap-py child?"

"Yes."

"Liar," Purchass replied. "You had a fucking lousy childhood. I can tell. I know some things, and I know that. How's your father doing?"

"He's fine."

"No, he's not. You're nursing him because your mother – the one you tried to tell me was dead – pissed off and left him. In fact, it's been a bad year for you, hasn't it?" Purchass paused, but when Thomas didn't answer, he carried on. "Lost your job. Oh, that must have hurt. You see, having fuck all means you can't lose anything. Being rich and powerful and then being fired…" he whistled down the phone, "Not good."

"What did Kara tell you?"

"I haven't finished my questions yet!" Pur-chass snapped. "You have to give me more. How tall are you?"

"Six foot. You?"

Purchass laughed, dodging the question. "You keep yourself fit, don't you? Suppose you go to a gym. But they cost a lot, don't they?" He leaned forward, wiping the condensation off the kitchen window and staring into the barren yard outside. "I've never had money."

"So why didn't you take the ransom?"

"I didn't want it."

"What *did* you want?"

Purchass ducked the query. "What's it like to have women fancy you? I saw a photograph of your wife, or should I say *estranged* wife, on the internet. Good looking woman--"

"Leave her out of this!"

"Don't panic, I'm not after her either." Purchass shook his head, "Jesus, you're paranoid. Anyway, you don't owe her anything, she left you,"

"You don't know that."

"I know you're back at your parents' home looking after your father, with no sign of a wife around," Purchass replied deftly. "You're better off without her. I mean, you were just a 'trophy husband'." He laughed, wiping the back of his mouth with his sleeve. He was goading the man on the other end of the line and enjoying himself more than he had hoped. "I just want to know what it's like having women fancy you. How does it feel?"

"Don't women like you?"

Purchass rolled his eyes, "Fuck me, de Souza, you're not trying to psychoanalyse me, are you?"

"They'll do that when they catch you."

"They won't catch me."

"They will," Thomas insisted, "*I* will. And then you'll be locked up. And then you'll find out what it's like to have women's attention. So many women will be looking at you, fascinated by you, because you're a freak."

The word drummed over the phone line, Purchass falling silent. He didn't say a word, just breathed slowly, evenly, down the line. The malice was palpable, moments passed before he finally spoke again.

"You shouldn't provoke me. She provokes me, too. Even when hog tied, she still has a try. But she's quiet now." Purchass went on, his tone deadly, knowing he was making Thomas nervous.

"Let her go. I'll do whatever you want," Thomas said urgently, "just let her go."

"Maybe I already have."

"She's dead?"

"She's got one less finger - but not dead. Yet." Purchass said, adding, "I could kill you, de Souza. I mean, you don't know who I am or what I look like. I know you; I watch you, but you wouldn't know if I was standing bchind you." He paused. "You still want to know what Kara Famosa told me?"

Thomas's voice was barely a whisper, "Yes."

"I bet you do."

The line went dead.

63

Smiling, Anna de Souza was shown into Hugh Ackermann's office. She had already been told that he would be delayed and was quite prepared for the wait. The time would be useful to perfect her speech. Crossing her legs, Anna glanced around the office, grimacing at the Japanese paintings in their heavy walnut frames and the print of an English shooting party. Pretentious, she thought, the nearest Ackermann had ever got to a shooting party was working the fairground when they were kids.

Her cousin had been a lout then, but big enough and dour enough to scare the shit out of everyone. Not that they had ever been close; Hugh had abandoned his hometown as soon as he was able, and Anna's family had left long before that, moving upwards into the middle class when her father made a killing in the building trade. She hadn't seen Hugh Ackermann for decades, but had read the occasional article about him and looked him up on Google. She was wondering how he would greet her.

She didn't have to wait long. He came lumbering in, moving behind his desk, and sitting down. Age and weight had added to his gigantic frame, his bovine jaw jutting forward as he looked at her.

"What d'you want?"

"It's good to see you too," Anna replied dryly.

There was no point using her looks. Instead, she had to use her intellect, the same intellect which had proved so productive over the years. But not lately, because Simon Porter was losing interest. She had even caught him staring at the old photograph of his family, and at times, his tone was more than a little sarcastic.

As if it was *her* fault that Halle had turned into a recluse. Or that Kara Famosa's abduction had dropped from the public interest. Of course, it was irritating, but other news had taken over. If the killer kidnapped or murdered again, the story would be resurrected, but nothing had happened. And the interest in a book and film had dried up. How could that be *her* fault? Simon seemed to think so. All her reassurances had been brushed aside; her lover even spotted having lunch with some unknown woman.

He was using her, was he? Anna thought, amazed. Simon Porter wasn't even handsome, and yet now – because he had left his family and was regarded as a late-blooming roue – women were flocking around him. Well, she thought, two could play at that game, and having abandoned her own husband for Simon Porter, she wasn't going to lose face now.

"Well?" Ackermann was staring at her, "What d'you want?"

"I heard that Kara Famosa lived with you when she was visiting London," Anna began. "I also heard that she was writing an expose, which made me wonder about her kidnapping. What if someone abducted her to silence her?"

Ackermann's face was expressionless, "Go on."

"I mean, if the Famosas had something serious to hide, they might go to any lengths to protect their reputation and finances."

"Go on."

"Halle dumped you for Luis. Perhaps you were having an affair with Kara to get revenge?"

"Go on."

"Or," Anna continued, "Kara told you about the book, and you encouraged her to write it. Again, to get revenge on Halle."

Ackermann glanced at his watch. "Is that it?"

Is that it?" Anna replied, taken aback. "It wouldn't look good for you if it became public knowledge."

"What interest would any of this be to anyone?"

"Quite a lot - if it led to Kara Famosa's kidnapping. Or murder," she stared at him fixedly. "After all, we don't know if she's still alive. We can't just let things roll on like this."

To her amazement, he smiled. It was fleeting, hardly noticeable, but there. "I see where your son gets it from."

She flinched. *"Thomas?* What about him?"

"He tried to pressurise me too."

"Thomas was here?" She sat upright, " You didn't tell him anything, did you?"

"About us being related? Why would I? What advantage would that give me? No, Anna, relax. Your son has no idea we're family. You lied about your past to snare Peter de Souza, I understand that. No woman likes to have her roots showing." he smiled at his own joke, "and I like to keep secrets, just like you do. Mind you, I was a bit taken aback when you shacked up with Simon Porter."

"We're in love."

"*Really?* Does he know?"

She sighed. "I don't want to blackmail you, Hugh. I want to make a business deal. Jimmy Famosa's gone back to New York to team up with his father, who's got people working on the case here and in the States --"

"So?"

"Jimmy fought with Kara before she was abducted. He *has* to find the kidnapper to absolve his guilt -- "

"Fifty quid says your son will beat him to it."

Anna was thrown. "Is that what Thomas said?"

"That he wanted to find Kara's kidnapper? Yes."

Anna shook her head. "Then we'll have to put him off the idea!"

"You think you can? Your son didn't look like a pushover to me."

"Thomas has a heart. I can appeal to that." She said, her tone brusque. "As for Jimmy Famosa, he can be kept to the sidelines –"

"And Luis?"

"Does he *want* to find his daughter?" She asked, "I mean, is Kara *really* his daughter?"

"Now you've lost me."

She snorted dismissively, "I doubt that."

"You're saying that the Cuban would get rid of Kara because she's not his kid?" Ackermann asked, his face expressionless, although he was surprised that Anna knew, or had guessed, so much. "Where did that idea come from?"

"People talk –"

"People talk bullshit," he interrupted her, "and even for your lurid imagination it would be a little extreme."

"Not if the expose was going to ruin Luis Famosa, rip open his reputation and destroy his fortune."

Ackermann put up his hands to stop her. "You're missing something. If there **is** a tell-all book, then *anyone* threatened would want it suppressed. Perhaps you should spread the net a little wider, Anna? Don't just concentrate on Luis; what about Halle? She can be very unbalanced, the type to panic. Or Jimmy – what would he do to protect the Famosa name? He runs the money side; he must have plenty of secrets." Ackermann raised his eyebrows. "You follow me? That's three people already who might go to any lengths to protect themselves –"

"People don't murder members of their own family."

He sighed, "I'm not saying they do, I'm just expanding your theory, making you think a bit."

"I've been thinking! If Kara has dug up the dirt about Luis, he'll want the book stopped. He must be enraged that she pinched that Klimt painting. He *must* want to find her." She glanced around the office at the opulent porcelain and paintings. "Luis is very successful in the art world, isn't he? I mean, so are you, but you're not in his league. That must be galling. Must make you wonder if he cheated you –"

"Like how?"

"—sold you a pup. A fake. I heard you bought some pieces from the Famosa gallery," she went in for the kill, "How hard would that be to know that the man who stole your woman also played you for a fool?"

"What are you getting at, Anna?"

"*You* have to find the kidnapper."

Ackermann sighed portentously, "*Me?*"

"When he's caught, the story will be front page news again --"

"Which will benefit your lover's agency, and you."

"Precisely. The person who finds the kidnapper, gets the glory."

"So why don't you find him?"

"I don't have your connections! The victory has to be yours. It might even make Halle see you differently." She leaned back in her seat, triumphant. "I mean, come on, Hugh, I know you from way back. You *aren't* Kara's lover, are you? And if you *did* put her up to writing the expose, you can always deny it." She hesitated, "*did* she write a book?"

"How would I know?"

"OK, have it your own way," Anna replied, "but think about my proposition. You'll be a hero when you find Kara Famosa's kidnapper. It will bring attention to your business and you'll get Halle's undying gratitude."

He could hardly believe his luck. Like everyone else, Anna de Souza thought that Ackermann wanted revenge on Halle and Luis, never realising that he wanted to find the kidnapper for his own, more pressing, reasons. What Ackermann wanted was not glory but the book. And here was Anna de Souza, daft cow, willing him on.

"Luis wants to find his daughter's kidnapper," Ackermann said calmly, "but you're suggesting he wants Kara gone. That's quite a thing to say. What proof have you got?"

"He's ruthless."

"He's a businessman. Like me." Ackermann strung her along, "and I don't believe Halle was ever unfaithful to him–"

"You're a romantic! *Everyone* is unfaithful, given the opportunity." Anna snorted. "When you find the kidnapper, that will be sweet revenge on Luis Famosa. Simon will get you a book deal and make you into a hero. He has contacts everywhere."

Ackermann smiled to himself. Anna was clever but low on facts, unaware that he had known Simon Porter for decades.

"... The people who were clamouring for news about Kara Famosa will be keen to sign on the dotted line as soon as her kidnapper is caught."

"What if," Ackermann suggested, "her kidnapper turns out to be her murderer?"

Anna paused. "Well, that would be sad, but it would make a bigger story." She studied her doughty cousin. "Of course, this is between us..."

Ackermann nodded, laughing inside.

"... no one has to know that we're working together. Especially not Simon. He might not understand."

"Losing interest, is he?"

She shrugged. "Not for long. When the story's big again, he won't care how I did it. Only that I did." She stood up, offering her hand, "Have we got a deal?"

64

She would do, Purchass thought, watching Sente Fleishman. Tall, athletic, blue eyes. Nice. He studied her from his vantage point, watching as she left Tesco with a bag of groceries. She looked strong, like a blow on the head would just faze her, not kill her outright. He had killed Ellie Chadwick too fast, and Kara Famosa, well, that had been a bloody fiasco. But this woman was going to be perfect.

She wasn't famous or related to anyone famous. She was German, too. A foreigner. Even better. The police would be screwed with this one. What possible connection could Sente Fleishman have with the other victims? They all had different jobs, different nationalities, and different appearances. Apart from the eyes, of course. But why would a German nurse be connected to Kara Famosa? Or why would the timid Ellie Chadwick know the promiscuous Sente Fleishman? They had nothing in common, he thought, which was precisely why the police weren't going to connect them. Or catch him.

Sniffing, Purchass pulled off his boots, his socks rank as he padded across the kitchen and made himself some tea. Strong, the colour of creosote. He was really on form, he thought, getting better all the time. Impressive. Because despite what his fucking family had thought, he wasn't stupid. Not academic, but cunning. And that's what mattered in the end, not the crimes, but the plotting. Anyone could kill, but only a few got away with it. And Purchass was going to be one of them. In fact, he was inspired. Let some soft sod paint a picture or compose some music, he was working with humans.

And now he going to destroy someone by default. He had never seen it done before, which was why it was so thrilling. In time, he would be written about. Books about him alongside those of Ted Bundy and Dennis Neilson. But he would better them all. He would show the world what a real freak could do. He had read the phrase a while back in some crime book:

'Transferred Malice' *A legal doctrine that holds that, when the intention to harm one individual inadvertently causes a second person to be hurt instead, the perpetrator is still held responsible*

There were only two things left to do:

Plan one: pick the victim.

Plan two: pick the killer.

-o0o-

London wasn't what Sente Fleishman had expected, and she was already regretting her decision to spend Christmas in the British capital. The landmarks, the iconic buildings, and even the River Thames weren't what she had imagined. It was bitterly cold for a start, and everything smelt damp. It might snow intermittently, but the glamorous white didn't settle, it just turned to slop on the roads. Splashed by passing cars and ignored by taxis, Sente made her way back to the Bayswater Hotel. In the lobby, she took her key and asked for any messages. There were none. Not even a reply from her mother. Slowly, she made her way to her first-floor room, opening the window and leaning out to smoke.

Maybe she had to give it time. Perhaps London was just one of those cities that grew on you. Perhaps she had expected too much. Perhaps she should have travelled with a friend. But Sente hadn't wanted that; she liked her freedom, and she didn't want to be judged. Besides, who wanted the competition?

Inhaling, she glanced down into the street, watching a man pass. Flicking her cigarette out of the window, she grinned as it fell downwards, missing him by inches. That was what she needed. A man. Some sex, some fun to make the city come alive. What good was a holiday without a romance? Fuck Nelson's Column, she wanted a living, breathing column of her own.

Turning off the light, Sente left her room. Five minutes later, she was entering a pub off Sussex Gardens. The place was unremarkable but full of men.

Maybe it wasn't going to be such a bad Christmas after all.

65

19th December

When the nurse arrived to take care of his father, Thomas headed for the front door, keys in hand. "I'm just going out for a couple of hours. Wait until I get home, will you?"

She could see the obvious signs of stress. The poor soul needed a break, she thought, nothing but trouble for Thomas de Souza. It was difficult for a man to be a carer, and his father needed a *lot* of caring, which was why she was more than willing to fill in for a couple of evenings a week to let Thomas off the hook. But tonight, he looked as though he had already had a drink, maybe a few, and she wondered if it might have been better if he stayed home.

But who did you meet if you stayed home? Sheila thought. What Thomas de Souza really needed was to meet a woman, but he wasn't thinking about that. He was thinking about Kara Famosa; still hooked up to her tragedy like his father to a drip. Still writing his blog, raging with anger when he read the 'theories' on the internet and ducking the occasional journalist who tried to corner him. Anyone could see that he wasn't sleeping, only inches away from a breakdown, taking early morning runs to try and work off his frustration. A man on the edge, spending too much time with his sick father, too much time thinking about his missing ex-lover, and too much time trying to find sleep that didn't come.

"I'll wait until you get back. Going anywhere nice?"

He took the innocent inquiry as prying. "I said I'd be back soon. Around midnight."

"Fine, I'll stay as long as you like," Sheila hurried to reassure him. "No problem."

"It'll be midnight. I can't afford to pay you for any longer."

"It's OK, you don't have to be back on the dot."

He took her kindness the wrong way. "You're right. Part of an hour costs the same as the hour --"

"*Thomas, I didn't mean that*! I was just trying to make things easier for you."

He apologised, shame-faced. "Sorry. That was a lousy thing to say --"

"Sssh," she tapped him on the shoulder sympathetically. "Go on, give yourself a break. You need it."

As he left, he could hear her slide the bolt on the door and stood outside until he saw a light come on in the living room. Upstairs, Peter de Souza was already asleep in his bedroom. He would never know that his son had been out because, come morning, Thomas would be opening the curtains on another day, like so many others. Days full of hope. Days full of disappointment. Days that might bring news. Days that didn't.

Turning up the collar of his coat, Thomas began to walk, jumping on a bus marked Bayswater and almost missing the step. God, he had drunk more than he thought. His tongue felt furred, his breath stale, and he needed a shave - but he needed a drink more. Getting off the bus at Bayswater Road, he walked towards Sussex Gardens, to a pub he had frequented a while back, but it was under new management, its shiny metal entrance uninviting.

Disappointed, Thomas walked on, finally picking a nondescript pub, The Goat's Inn. The bar was badly lit, which suited him, and it was crowded. Pound Store Christmas decorations dangled from old-fashioned wall lights and the carpet was sticky underfoot. Sliding into a seat by the window, Thomas sipped his drink. The day had offered nothing. He had made an enemy out of Hugh Ackermann - which was stupid - and he was still under Purchass's thumb, his mind shuffling between optimism and despair. But Kara was still alive, and that was all that mattered. He just had to find her.

To find her. How? He had expected the kidnapper to set up another meeting, but obviously, he had something else in mind. Thomas wondered if he should have brought up the subject of Ellie Chapman when they spoke, asked the kidnapper outright if he had killed her. But then what? Would that have scared him off? Scuppered any chance of saving Kara?

Sighing, he ordered another beer and glanced across the bar, catching the eye of a striking blonde sitting a couple of tables away. Immediately, Thomas looked down. He wasn't interested, he just wanted to drink. In peace. Alone.

"Can I join you?" The woman had come over to his table and was gesturing to the chair next to his. "I'd really like some company," her smile was welcoming. "I'm Sente Fleishman."

Smiling stiffly, he nodded. “Thomas de Souza.”

“You look thoughtful, bad day?”

“Yes, bad day,” he agreed, without enthusiasm, his eyes fixed on the beer.

“I came to London to spend Christmas here,” she said, obviously lonely in a strange city. Not flirting, just wanting company. “It’s not like I thought it would be. London, I mean.”

“Where d’you come from?”

“Berlin.”

They both fiddled with their glasses, almost in unison, Sente the first to speak again. “London’s a pretty lonely place.”

Downing his beer, Thomas nodded, “Most big cities are,” he said, hesitating and then finally ordering more drinks. The beer was relaxing him, rubbing off the rough edges of the day, Purchass’s taunting voice beginning to fade. She was attractive, with amazing eyes, he thought, and imagined, to his surprise, kissing her, then felt disloyal as though he was cheating. Not on his estranged wife but on his ex-lover, Kara Famosa. A woman he hadn’t seen in two years.

Thomas gestured towards their empty glasses, “You want another?”

She smiled warmly. “Why not?”

One hour and three rounds later, they were both animated and talkative; Thomas relaxed and put his hand on Sente’s arm. She didn’t reject him and instead responded to his touch. All the time she was talking, Thomas was watching her mouth, imagining how it would feel to kiss it. It had been a while since he had kissed a woman. Months since he had made love, and he missed it. Longed for it. Maudlin from its absence.

Drink was making them both flushed, leaning back in their seats, then leaning forwards to talk to each other, heads almost touching. Thomas forgot the time. He forgot his father. He forgot everything but the young woman who was welcoming him, attracted to him, *wanting* him.

"I think it's amazing that you look after your Dad."

"I *am* amazing," he replied, flirting.

"I mean, I'm a nurse, but I don't know if I could care for a relative day in, day out. Most men wouldn't do it," she said. "Isn't it hard work? I mean, it'd be like being on call 24/7."

"You get used to it."

She seemed unconvinced. "Maybe…"

Feeling the alcoholic euphoria slipping away, Thomas changed the subject. "Are you spending Christmas with your family?"

"I don't have any. Just a brother, and he's married and living in Holland."

"No boyfriend?"

She gave him a shy smile. "No boyfriend. What about you, no girlfriend?"

"No, no girlfriend. Separated from my wife - but that was a while ago."

"I bet she was sorry to lose you," Sente replied, Thomas warming to the obvious show of interest.

"What can I tell you? She was insane."

They both laughed, Thomas curious. "So, you're staying in London for Christmas?"

"Yep."

"Where?"

She drained her glass. "At a hotel nearby. It's not much, but it'll do. You won't believe it, but if you're going out, you have to ask for a key! They lock up at midnight."

The words cut like a machete. **Midnight.** He had to be home by midnight. Back to being a carer at midnight. On watch at midnight. And after midnight came tomorrow. And after tomorrow came the day after, and the blog, and the hanging around waiting. Waiting for the phone to ring. Even if it was the kidnapper, that was better than nothing, it might just make *something* happen.

Recklessly, Thomas ordered more drinks, Sente refusing then relenting as he pressed her. Get drunk, he willed himself. Forget. Kiss her. She likes you, kiss her. But despite how much he drank, instead of increasing the tipsiness, it *lifted.* In its place came disorientation and nausea.

"I'm so glad wc met..." Sente murmured, her words swallowed up by the noise in the pub.

What had already been busy was now jammed with customers, all jostling for their few inches of space, bodies pressing up against each other, voices pumping like an organ bellows to the strains of potted music. Dizzy, Thomas stared at Sente, like a man spotting land moments before drowning.

Her mouth was still working, but the words were out of sync, furred. "I didn't ask you," she said, leaning closer towards him, "if you live in London?"

He frowned, deafened, music blaring. *"What?"*

"I said," she repeated more loudly, **"Do you live in London?"**

"Oh, yes, yeah."

"Nearby?"

The noise was making Thomas's head throb as he tried to hold onto the euphoria he had felt, the promise of affection and closeness. But it had shattered, and he merely felt drunk, ill at ease, and almost angry. The bar was still filling up, businessmen mixing with dozens of office girls in Father Christmas hats, all of them over animated, frenetic, singing together when someone turned on the carols. The music was so loud that the floor was vibrating under Thomas's feet, the red tinsel shuddering overhead. By the fireplace, a Christmas tree trembled, dozens of tiny reflections blurring to the background of carols and the stink of spilled beer.

"Are you alright?"

Surprised, Thomas looked at the woman sitting opposite him. For a moment he had almost forgotten Sente was there.

"Yes…I'm OK…"

"You just looked a bit --"

He challenged her. *"What?"*

"A bit drunk?" She asked, smiling.

But the smile suddenly seemed like criticism and made him bristle. "You're right, I'm drunk. But you're drunk, too."

"Because you keep buying me drinks!"

"I do, don't I?" Thomas said, leaning back from her, putting distance between them.

He wanted to get out because he was kidding himself. They weren't going to make love, and he wasn't going to forget. How could he even think of it? He was too tired, too drunk, too fucked up to think clearly. It was half past eleven. Half an hour of freedom left before he had to go home. Pay the night nurse, see to his father, and wait for tomorrow.

Despondent, he stared at the clock. "Only a little time left."

She frowned, not understanding. *"What?"*

"Half an hour to midnight."

"Who are you, Cinderella?" she asked, laughing, "what happens if you don't get home in time?"

"The world ends. It all ends…" Thomas said drunkenly, Sente frowning.

"Are you in trouble?"

He baulked at the question. Why did she want to know? He thought, staring at her. And why was she so willing to talk to him? Drink with him? She could have chosen anyone in the pub, so why him? His confidence splintered, fear encroaching. *Had Ackermann sent her?* Was he spying on him?... Jesus, Thomas thought, he refused to work for Ackermann and pissed him off, so he is now being watched.

Unsettled, he shifted in his seat, Sente frowning.

"What's the matter?"

"Nothing. Nothing." Her face was coming in and out of focus. "Who are you?"

"*Who am I?*" she said, laughing.

"Yes, who are you?" he repeated, his tone hostile.

"I'm Sente, Sente Fleishman," she repeated, laughing. "You're *really* drunk, aren't you?" She said, leaning forwards and touching his arm.

He reacted as if he had been knifed, jumping to his feet, and stumbling past the drinkers. But when he reached the door, it was blocked, Thomas doubling back as he headed for the exit.

And escape.

66

Hearing voices, Purchass ducked into a doorway, looking towards the alleyway at the back exit of the pub in Sussex Gardens. He had followed Thomas there, but had lost interest and was about to leave when he saw de Souza stumbling out with a woman following him.

Curious, Purchass watched them.

"You crazy bastard!" she shouted, drunk but good-natured. "What's the matter? I thought we were getting on."

The fresh air hit Thomas full force, increasing the alcohol's effect. "We *were* getting on. *We were.* I like you," he was weaving on his feet. "But I have to go –"

"So, take me with you!" Sente said, tossing her bag over her shoulder. "We could have a good time."

Purchass stared at them, intrigued. The light was dim, but he could see enough to realise that he *knew* the woman, that she was the nurse he had been following for days. What a coincidence, he thought. Who would have laid a bet on his next victim being acquainted with Thomas de Souza? You couldn't make it up, Purchass thought, continuing to watch them. They were both pretty drunk, too. You shouldn't be picking up women in bars, he thought to himself, amused. Not unless you know what to do with them.

Thomas had paused at the mouth of the alley, turning back to Sente, his voice weary. "I'm sorry."

"*What*?"

"I'm really sorry," he was agonised, confused and drunk. "But I have to go –"

She was also confused but for different reasons. "*Why* d'you have to go?"

"I just have to --"

"I don't understand!" She wailed, putting her hands on her hips, tipsy and angry. "What's your fucking problem?"

"It's not you --"

"So why run off!"

Thomas hesitated. He didn't trust her. Didn't know who she was and suspected her. But if she *was* innocent. He had no right to involve her in his troubles. Go home, he told himself, sober up. Home was the only safe place.

"I made a mistake --"

She was almost screaming. "*I* was the one who made the bloody mistake!"

"Sssh!"

"You gay or something?"

Exasperated, Thomas sighed. "No, I'm not gay –"

"You act like a gay!" She retorted, mean-mouthed, jabbing his shoulder with her forefinger. "I thought you were up for it."

"Well, I'm not!"

"But you bought me all those drinks --"

"LET IT GO!" Thomas snapped, turning away.

But she was having none of it.

"I want another drink! Oh, come on, let's go somewhere." She was persistent, strident, shivering in the cold. "Please..."

Then she lunged towards him and he reacted without thinking. Because he was drunk, tired, and suspicious, he reacted by throwing his arm out and catching her off balance. It was a fluke. Another foot, another six inches, and she would have missed it. But she didn't miss it. Instead, Sente Fleishman fell backwards, striking the bollard with such force that it cracked her skull.

Thomas de Souza had wanted another victim.

But never suspected it would be his own.

Panicking, he knelt down and felt for a pulse. The blood was seeping out from under her head, creeping across the pavement, her blonde hair already matted. It had been an accident, that was all. It hadn't been deliberate, just a random accident. But who would believe that? Thomas thought desperately. He was obviously drunk, and they had been fighting, people would have seen them arguing. It was clear what would follow. The police would arrest him, and then what? What would happen to his father? Or Kara? Panicked, Thomas looked around him, trying to work out what to do. He was trapped by an accident. A freak accident that could ruin his life.

Hesitating, he stared down at the nurse, then lifted her under her arms and slowly dragged Sente Fleishman back into the darkness of the alleyway.

A minute passed before Thomas re-emerged, looking around to check that the street was empty. Then he ran.

Hidden in the doorway beyond, Purchass watched him go.

67

After counting to ten, Purchass crossed the empty street, moving into the alleyway. He could hear the noises coming from The Goat's Inn, but there was no one outside. The cold was keeping people indoors. Moving over to the slumped figure of Sente Fleishman, Purchass flicked on the pocket torch he always carried and studied her.

Blood had made a sticky halo around her head, her legs neatly placed together, her arms by her sides, as Thomas had left her. Tidy bugger, Purchass thought. But *so* unlucky. He crouched beside the body. It had been an accident, of course, but for who? Certainly not for him. Purchass smiled in the semi-dark. It wasn't what he would have chosen, but then again, why pass up on an opportunity? Poor blog boy. Who would have believed that he would turn out to be a murderer? But there it was. Proof. A body. A victim that would serve Purchass well.

All he had to do was to make this woman *look* like one of his victims. The police would be certain to connect the women then. Ellie Chadwick, the missing Kara Famosa, and now this girl. All mutilated in some way. All killed by the same man. Purchass knew he had been lucky not to be caught, but a scapegoat would *ensure* that he never was. When the body was found, and the police questioned the customers, someone in the pub would remember Thomas de Souza. They would remember the woman, too. Both drunk. They would remember that they had sat together, drank together, left together.

Then the police would know who had killed Sente Fleishman.

At first, they *wouldn't* know that her murderer had already killed Ellie Chadwick and abducted Kara Famosa. That he was the man police had been looking for on both sides of the Atlantic. The man who had made a fool out of them and caught the curiosity of the world… Purchass smiled, relishing his plan, knowing that it would only work if *she looked like the other victims.*

Taking a penknife out of his pocket, Purchass knelt over Sente Fleishman, staring at her right hand. Sever a finger or two? He sighed, glancing at her feet. Cut off a toe, perhaps? Or a foot? Nah, that would be hard work, too difficult to do quickly and besides, the idea didn't excite him. Holding the torch in his left hand, he shone the light onto the white face and then, with all his force, plunged the blade into the woman's left eye. Her head rocked with the impact, Purchass jerking the blade out and then looking at the right eye. It was open, staring at him. Blue as a delphinium.

Gently, he ran the knife blade along the upper and lower lids. He could see the eyelashes ruffled by the touch, the tear duct bleeding a little moisture. Intrigued, he touched the open eye, felt the slippery smoothness, and then wiped his finger on his jeans. Her perfect eye fascinated him, blood was still oozing from her head and the mutilated left eye - but the right was intact.

Leaning forwards, Purchass shone the torchlight directly into her pupil. It was wildly, madly blue, and for one instant, it still seemed to have life in it. Unsettled, Purchass flinched, then - with all his force - plunged his fingers into the socket, tearing out the eye and leaving it, mangled and bloody, on her right cheek.

It had taken him only a couple of minutes.

One hundred and twenty seconds to turn Thomas de Souza from a caring son into a killer.

68

20th December

It was all over the morning newspaper –

> **GERMAN NURSE MURDERED AND MUTILATED IN CENTRAL LONDON**

How a young nurse, Sente Fleishman, had visited The Goat's Inn pub and met up with a man ,who had killed her in the alleyway outside. Mutilating her. No details, but Luis Famosa didn't need them. He had come to London only hours earlier, ostensibly to chase the police and later visit his wife, but instead he had been greeted by the newspaper headlines and immediately rung Detective Jameson. His message was curt, asking Jameson to call him back. It was urgent, Luis insisted. Really urgent.

He left his hotel in Park Lane and headed for The Goat's Inn, arriving in time to see the alleyway cordoned off with tape, police officers keeping people back, and a mess of journalists and photographers gathered around the entrance of the pub, which was closed.

Joining the melee, Luis glanced at the man next to him. "Anyone talking?"

He grimaced. "No one's come out the pub, and the police aren't saying any more." The photographer glanced at Luis. "Serial killer with any luck."

"I read that he'd mutilated the victim." The Cuban replied, expressionless. "You know how?"

"If I did, would I tell you?"

Luis shrugged. "It looks like the other ones, doesn't it? I mean, there have been two women killed within a month, one woman abducted, and all of them mutilated. Must be the same man." He took out a cigarette and offered the photographer one, which he took willingly, Luis lighting up the smoke as he continued to feel his way along. "They were similar –"

"Kara Famosa's an American. Like you."

Luis nodded. "Yeah, we're interested in the story over there. People want to find out who kidnapped her --"

"And killed the other women."

"So, you think it's the same man?"

"I didn't say that. But I'm hoping it is. Serial killers make good copy." He paused, altering the camera strap around his neck, his collar bunching up. "I got paid well for the shots of the Ellie Chadwick murder scene."

Luis's black eyes remained steady. "Did you see this woman's corpse?"

The photographer gave him a slow look. "Which paper you with?"

"American Globe."

"Never heard of it."

"It's an internet site."

The journalist looked unimpressed. "Not proper journalism."

"I'm out on the street like you. Following the story the hard way."

The photographer turned away, staring at the pub door, willing it to open. "I'd have thought America had enough of its own serial killers without poaching ours."

"Like I said, Kara Famosa is big news back home," Luis replied evenly. "I'm surprised the police have shared news about this victim."

"There's a reason for that." The photographer was happy to talk, almost to brag about the UK's better policing. "That's because the landlord discovered the body first thing this morning and recognised her."

"So, she'd been at the pub before?"

"Couple of times, yeah." The photographer looked Luis up and down, middle-aged hack in a well-cut suit with manicured hands. "What did you say your name was? You look familiar to me."

Luis was quick to throw him off track. "We've probably covered the same stories."

"Yeah." The man shrugged, his thoughts moving on. "Wonder why he picked a German after picking a Yank."

"What?"

"Kara Famosa was American –"

"Was?"

"Hey?"

"You said Kara Famosa *was* American."

"Well, she's not likely to still be alive, is she?"

"A kidnapper can't claim a ransom if there's no hostage."

“But he wasn’t interested in the money, was he? I tell you, that girl’s dead.” They were jostled as the pub door opened a crack and then slammed closed again. Sighing, the photographer lowered his camera. “Fucking hell, I’ve been here two hours already and not one photograph worth a light.”

“Did you see the body?”

“Nah.”

“No idea what she looked like?”

“I heard she was young, tall and blonde.” The photographer said wearily. “What a waste.”

A moment slumped between them, Luis the first to speak. “Did she have blue eyes?”

“No eyes,” he responded, “blue or otherwise.”

69

Maida Vale,
London

Cramming his clothes into a black bin liner, Thomas threw in his shoes and coat, tying up the bag and taking it out of the house. The previous night, he had returned home, removing the light bulb in the hallway and calling out to the nurse in the semi-dark. He had pretended he was drunk, her figure reproachful at the top of the stairs.

"You're lucky your father's asleep for the night," she had said coldly. "I'll let myself out."

Muttering something indecipherable, Thomas had waited until she had left, then headed into his room, taking care not to make any noise. His father had been asleep, snoring, his bedroom door open, Thomas pulling it closed as he passed. He had felt the cool handle in against his palm and wondered why he had been able to feel that and not feel his arms or legs. His extremities were numb.

But he wasn't drunk anymore. He had been sick instead, shaking, his hands clenching and unclenching as he had stood in the bathroom. Panic had overwhelmed him, but he hadn't given way to it. Instead, he had seen the blood on his clothes and stripped, standing naked in the moonlight surrounded by his father's medicine, inhalers, and a hot water bottle. Madness, he had thought, it was all madness.

For ten minutes, he stood there, battling with his thoughts. Why had he spoken to the woman in the pub? Because he had been lonely? Wanting to make love to her? A German nurse. Jesus, a *nurse.* He had *pushed* her. Fuck. *Why* had he pushed her? *Why?...* At the memory, his legs gave way and Thomas slumped to the floor. What should he do? He asked himself. What *could* he do? His watch read 1.30 am. It was morning already. Silent, he turned onto his side, curling his legs up into his chest, shivering in the chilled bathroom. And then – he would never believe it when he looked back – he fell asleep.

But now Thomas was fully awake, dressed, slipping down the back stairs by five in the morning. It wasn't dawn yet and was still thickly dark as he hurried along the street. He passed no one and walked for several minutes until he reached a communal bank of refuge bins. Glancing around him, Thomas dropped the full black bag into the nearest bin - and then took it out again. Lifting the other bags out, he then threw his into the bottom and loaded the others on top. Then he began to retrace his steps home.

With luck, his father wouldn't wake until eight. Peter de Souza was a heavy sleeper, which gave Thomas a few hours to work out a plan. How many people had seen him at The Goat's Inn? There had been a crowd, but they had seemed to be on a work outing, and most of them had been pretty drunk. Did they notice the couple talking at a table on their own? A dark-haired man and a blonde woman? Did they see him overreact and leave the pub suddenly? Did they see her follow him out?

Oh God, he'd been drunk, he'd been so drunk…

What had happened then? He struggled to remember the series of events. It had been late, and he had wanted to get home, his father's nurse waiting for him to relieve her… Thomas jumped as a car passed, turning away from the headlights. Did that look suspicious? Would someone later say that they'd seen a man out very early in the morning, acting oddly? Looking guilty?

He *was* guilty.

He had killed a woman.

Crouching in a doorway, Thomas pushed back against the wooden panel. His breathing accelerated, his lips moving silently, his hands ice cold.

I killed her.

A woman I met in a pub.

Killed her.

Trembling, he felt sweat trickle down his back.

I didn't mean it.

It was an accident.

I just pushed her.

I didn't want to hurt her.

But no one would believe that, would they? Especially not the police. They would go to The Goat's Inn and talk to people, and they would describe Thomas, and then they would come looking for him… He tried to steady his breathing. But *how* would they find him? Who knew him there? He had never been to The Goat's Inn before. The only conversation he had had with the barmaid was to order drinks, and she had been preoccupied with the partygoers. It was Christmas, the busiest time of the year, who would remember one face in amongst so many?

Then another thought struck him - had he left traces of his DNA? Thomas strained to remember. No, there was no DNA because he hadn't had sex with her, but he *had* pushed her, for Christ's Sake! Sssh, be quiet, be quiet, he willed himself. Think. He had never been arrested, never had his fingerprints taken, or given a DNA sample. How could anyone isolate one piece of evidence in the middle of a sleazy pub? Besides, no one had seen them outside in the alleyway. Thomas was sure of that. No one had seen Sente Fleishman fall and hit her head.

His stomach turned as he remembered the crunch as her skull struck the bollard. She had been kind, and he had liked her, and now she was dead. He had wished for another murder and got his wish, only it was a devil's wish, and he was the killer. And now they would arrest him, and his life would be over. Peter de Souza would be put in a home, and Thomas would be put in prison. Incarcerated for years for a mistimed, careless reaction. For pushing a woman in a drunken haze.

The world spun around him, shimmering like hot tar. Sente's face mingled with the faces of the pub drinkers, her blood mingling with the moonlight. And then Thomas's clothes loomed up before him in a hallucination, shaking their limp arms at him. *But how could they?* Thomas thought madly. He'd got rid of them. No one could track the clothes back to him. No one could track *anything* back to him. It had been an accident, no more. An unlucky accident, nothing willfully wicked. He was a good man, Thomas assured himself. He had never harmed anyone; it had just been a fluke. He could live with it. His conscience could live with it because it wasn't deliberate malice. He was a good man, a good son.

No one would ever know otherwise.

70

Detective Jameson's return call to Luis was polite but evasive. He hadn't expected the Cuban to arrive in the UK and was cautious, knowing about Famosa's intimidating reputation - and his legal backup.

"We're looking into a connection between the death of Sente Fleishman and your daughter, Mr Famosa --"

"Two women dead in a month. One woman abducted," Luis's voice was emotionless," all disfigured."

"But we haven't yet released details about Sente Fleishman's body."

"You're behind the times, Detective. You didn't have to reveal it, it's plastered all over the internet. Her eyes were put out. Mutilated. Like Ellie Chadwick. You *do* know about Ellie Chadwick, don't you?"

Jameson prickled with irritation. "Of course I do –"

"Well, it's obvious that it's the same man," Luis persisted. "It's his signature, he wants us to know it's him. He goes for women with blue eyes. It's always the same type. You have to warn people --"

Jameson snorted down the phone. "And tell every woman with blue eyes that her life is in danger? What would that do, apart from cause panic?"

It was the wrong attitude to take.

"*What would that do*? It could save lives," Luis retorted. "What the killer does to his victims is in the public domain for anyone to read. But if the police made a statement that certain women should be extra vigilant, it would be taken more seriously."

"And what if the killer changes his pattern? What if he starts targeting women with brown eyes?"

Luis's voice hardened. "What harm can it do to warn people?"

"It can cause panic!" Detective Jameson retorted, "You get lunatics confessing. Worse, copying what he's done. There's a reason we keep information to ourselves --"

"Listen to me," Luis interrupted, "Ellie Chadwick was killed, Kara was abducted, and now a nurse has been murdered. He's speeding up."

"Believe me, I know how much you want him caught, Mr Famosa. I understand how personal all this is for you --"

Luis cut him off. "You have *no* idea how personal this is for me, and it's going to get very personal for you if you don't catch him. This man is confident, ready to kill again, and Kara had better not be his next victim."

The detective's voice was no longer polite. "Don't tell me how to do my job."

"Why not?" Luis retorted, "Someone has to."

71

The Goat's Inn
London
20th December

The barmaid wasn't having any of it. "I don't remember anyone unusual last night," she said, putting down a pair of empty beer bottles, her acrylic nails clinking against the glass. "It was busy, we had parties in from six thirty until we closed. It was a crush in here."

"The victim was blonde," Detective Jameson persisted, showing her a photograph of the dead nurse.

She looked at it blankly. "Don't remember her. A blonde, you say? That hardly narrows it down."

"And you didn't see a couple sitting on their own? Talking? Arguing?"

"No," she said flatly, "like I say, it was busy, I could hardly keep up with the orders, and" she paused, dropping her voice, "I'd left home wearing my glasses and forgotten to put my lens in my bag."

"So?"

She smiled, embarrassed. "Look, no guy tips a barmaid in glasses. So, I had to manage without them," she spelt it out for him. “Last night I wasn’t wearing my contact lens, and I’m really short-sighted.”

He could feel his hope sinking. “So, every face was a blur?”

“’Fraid so. To be honest, I could have served a moose and not noticed.”

There was little joy elsewhere. Most of the customers had been out on office parties, everyone concentrating on getting pissed or getting laid. No one taking much notice of anyone outside their group. Except for a couple of women who mentioned seeing a man talking to a blonde woman.

Hopeful, Jameson pushed them, “Was this the woman you saw?” He asked, showing them the photograph of Sente Fleishman.

“Yeah, I think so,” one woman said.

The other, thinner and younger, shrugged. “Maybe.”

“Was there a man with her?”

“Yeah,” they both agreed.

“What did he look like?”

“Dark --”

“No, he wasn’t!” The first woman snapped, “he was mid-colours.”

The first woman folded her arms, her tone emphatic. “He was dark, with a beard.”

“He had no beard!” The second woman replied indignantly. “He was sitting by the Christmas tree --”

“Oh, I’m not talking about a man by the tree,” the first woman replied, “I’m talking about the man wearing a coat, sitting near to the door.”

Detective Jameson cut in, showing her the photograph of Senta Fleishman again. “Was he talking to this woman?”

"I think he was," the woman replied, smiling apologetically, "I don't remember much about the woman. But I remembered him."

"Why?"

"He was nice looking, posh for this dump."

Jameson leaned towards her. "Were the two of them talking?"

"Yeah."

"Did they look like they were familiar, like they knew each other?"

"Maybe… yeah, I'd say so."

"Were they arguing?"

"No," she said firmly, "they weren't arguing. I'd have remembered that. Look, I just noticed the guy for a second, that was all." Her eyes fixed on the policeman, curious, "Did he do it? Did he kill that woman in the alleyway?"

Jameson ignored the question: "Would you recognise him again?"

She thought for a long, drawn-out moment, then nodded. "Yeah, I think I would."

"You sure of that?" he pressed her, "why?"

"There was something about him," she said, nodding. "Something different from the men that usually come in here. So yeah, I'd know him. I'd know him again."

72

Breathing in deeply, Purchass rubbed his face against Sente Fleishman's scarf. It carried the odour of skin and oil, some inkling of sweat mixed with perfume. He could imagine her wrapping it around her neck and wearing it on the way to work. Running for a bus or the Tube, pushed in amongst the commuters, sweating – just a little – in the heated crush. He inhaled again and took a little of her into his lungs, excited. He would have liked to have known Sente Fleishman longer. Liked to have brought her back to the farm and played with her for a while. As victims went, she was just his type, it was a pity he had been cheated out of a kill.

His mood changing, Purchass threw the scarf onto a chair and thought about Thomas de Souza. His face had been a study when he realised he'd killed the nurse. Shock, disbelief, and regret flickering past like a Victorian peep show. Some people were just born unlucky, Purchass thought, smiling at the ready-made scapegoat who had dropped into his lap. Someone to take the heat off him, trick the police and the bloody Famosas into looking the wrong way.

It was like it was all meant to be.

Purchass didn't believe in luck, but he believed in evil. His gaze travelled upwards to the cold, narrow bedroom above. He didn't sleep there anymore; he hadn't done for a long time. Because it was the only place that still frightened him. The memory of beetles scuttering, mucus smells on their backs, making slimy trails around the bed, and Kat. Kat, with her blue eyes. The sound of her moaning humming like a mess of flies around a dung heap.

In the barn outside, Kara was peering through a gap in the wooden slats. The lights were on in the farmhouse and Purchass was inside, talking to someone. Now and again, she would hear him speaking, then shouting, his voice aggressive, then mewling. Kara had never caught sight of the woman, but had heard him call her name, Kat. After she visited Purchass would change, veering between overconfidence and unease. Like he was now, playing music in the kitchen, probably preparing something to eat, something he would put on the barn floor and then push over to Kara with his foot. He never handed her anything. He never touched her, either. His interest had gone. He just left a pail of water in which she could wash herself and a bucket for a lavatory. That was the only time Purchass unfastened her hands, watching as Kara relieved herself, grimacing as he emptied the bucket afterwards. Every day he gave her jug of water to drink, and three times a day some stinking concoction Kara would eat because she didn't want to die. For the rest of the time, she was left alone, thinking. Just like she was now.

The terror of her kidnap, of believing she would die, had dimmed and when the sexual abuse ended, she began to hope, to plan an escape. Because there *had* to be a way out, she just hadn't found it yet. The ropes

Purchass used to tie her up were becoming worn with her sweat, a few threads had broken from where she had rubbed them against the side of the pig pen. If she could get one hand free, she could release the other hand and then untie her ankles. But she would have to be careful because Purchass was quick to notice any changes.

There were quite a lot of changes in the way he was taking care of her. Showing her little acts of mercy, such as giving her an old pillow stained with hair oil. His mood had lightened, too. Jazz music played late at night; the television tuned to a shopping channel. Why the difference? Kara asked herself, realising that he had decided to keep her alive. He wasn't going to kill her. Not now, anyway. Perhaps he had talked to Thomas because Kara knew he would never give up on her. She couldn't say the same about Luis or Jimmy. Perhaps the latter was even relieved by her absence, especially if he knew she was only his half-sister. Jimmy wouldn't fight to save a half-sibling, the author of an expose that would ruin them all. Perhaps Luis and Jimmy had decided that the Famosa empire would be best served without her…

Still watching through the slats, Kara saw the barn door open, a shuffle of wind following Purchass's silhouette. She could tell he was agitated and hyper.

"You want to know something?" Purchass said, continuing without giving her time to respond. "Your boyfriend has just killed a woman."

She shook her head. "No!"

"I'm telling you the truth," Purchass crouched down on his haunches, facing her. "It was an accident - but not for me. For me, it was a lucky break. Know why? I framed him, and now the police are looking for Thomas de Souza."

"He's not a murderer --"

"Oh, but he is, and he put out the woman's eyes."

Kara was staring at Purchass in the semi-dark, his face shadowed, unreadable.

"He wouldn't do that –"

"He *did*," Purchass said, nodding, "and he's in real fucking trouble now. Not like me; no one's ever going to catch me."

"No, no one *will* catch you," she said urgently, agreeing with him, "if you have enough money to get away. Did you talk to Thomas about the painting?"

Purchass laughed. "He's got other things on his mind."

"But he'll help you. Get you more money than you can imagine."

"You're so stupid!" Purchass shook his head, irritated. "Still banging on about a ransom, when it's more fun watching de Souza fall apart."

"I don't understand --"

He cut her off. "No, you don't, do you? You don't understand anything. Just some rich girl that never had to worry because she came from money. Being poor is no joke."

"I can make you rich –"

"*I can make you dead!*" Purchass laughed, amused by his own joke. "The Famosas are powerful, so what? I don't give a shit. I'm not scared of anyone."

"But *I'm* afraid." Kara said, her voice wavering "I'm afraid of you - and the woman who comes here."

He flinched. "*What* woman?"

"She comes at night. She has done for the last few days…" Kara lied. She knew she had his full attention, his breathing speeding up as he listened. “She told me her name began with a K, like mine.”

Kat, Kat…

She could see the lie take root, Purchass wiping his mouth with the back of his hand. “Fucking liar.”

“What? No! I’m not lying!”

“Kat wouldn’t talk to you,” Purchass said, rising to his feet and standing in front of her. “Why would she talk to *you*? She’s not here anymore, she’s long gone.”

“I’m sorry…” Kara mumbled, “but I’m not lying. She *does* come here. I’ve heard you talking to her –”

“You nosey bitch!” he snapped, backhanding her, Kara’s head jerking to one side. “You want to keep your mouth shut! My sister’s gone.” He emphasised the words. “MY SISTER’S GONE. You heard nothing, you saw nothing. She doesn’t live here anymore. She’ll never come back. You hear me? **You hear me**?” Moving to the door, he paused, then asked over his shoulder. “What did she say to you?”

And in that instant, the power shifted.

73

Chelsea Wharf

Ackermann read all the newspaper reports, then turned to his computer, scanning every detail about the Sente Fleishman murder. Another victim. Same killer, it had to be. Even though the police were denying it, the words *serial killer* were making their presence felt in the tabloid and viral lexicon. Thoughtful, Ackermann leaned back in his seat, eyes fixed on the grainy photograph of the dead nurse alongside the images of Ellie Chadwick and the kidnapped Kara Famosa. All pretty women. All pretty dead.

When the phone rang, he didn't need to be told who was calling. "Anna."

Her voice was light, like a girl excited about a summer party. "Have you heard the news?"

"Another murder. It wasn't you, was it?"

"Don't be ridiculous!" She snapped, missing the joke. "I read that there are *three* victims. Some other woman was killed before Kara Famosa –"

"But Kara isn't dead."

"Yet." She replied, her callousness repelling him as she hurried on. "You'll have to move fast to catch him. I told you, people are ready to make deals; it's in the bag if you find him." Her voice dropped. Was she ringing from the agency? Ackermann wondered. Trying to avoid her little conspiracy being uncovered by the dour Simon Porter. "It shouldn't be that difficult for you, there's a witness. A woman saw the killer. No one's printed her name, but you could find out. Don't let Luis Famosa steal the glory."

"I heard he was in London. Have you got him under contract yet?"

She wasn't sure if her cousin was joking or not. "Luis won't take Simon's calls."

"And you're surprised?"

"Simon is the literary agent for all the Famosa clan," Anna retorted. "That Cuban is just trying to muscle in, but you have to stop him. *You're* going to be the big hero."

Ackermann smiled, wondering how someone so cunning could be so impressively stupid. His reasons for finding the killer were not based on old grievances but on getting hold of the expose - and enacting revenge for the death of his sister, Miriam. The long-forgotten victim that Anna de Souza didn't even know about. So, whilst she tried to buy his loyalty, Ackerman kept spinning Anna along to keep himself informed of what she and Simon Porter knew.

"You'll have to be quick to beat Famosa. I'd guess he's got plenty to lose if Kara's book comes out, and I imagine he could fight dirty if pushed." Anna's voice sped up, "Throw everything at it. Money, time, effort. You've got contacts, I know you have. You always know the right people for the job." She was cajoling her cousin without realising that he was immune to her manipulation. “Find the killer and you’re made.”

Without answering, Ackermann put down the phone.

Then he did something he hadn’t done for years; he started laughing.

74

Maida Vale,
London

Motionless, Thomas stared at the internet, reading about the latest on the murder of Sente Fleishman. But it wasn't *his* murder they were talking about. When he had left the nurse, she was lying on the alley floor with an injury to the head. Dead, but not mutilated. He hadn't mutilated anyone. He hadn't attacked her. Hadn't cut out her eyes. Someone else had done that. Someone else had disfigured her. The injuries weren't done by him. He **hadn't** done it. But who had? Who would defile a corpse? For what purpose? And then he remembered that Ellie Chadwick's eyes had been mutilated. In exactly the same way as Sente Fleishman's.

"Oh, Jesus..."

He could see the full danger of his situation and held his head in his hands. The police would make the connection, too, and then link the murders with Kara Famosa's abduction and her mutilation. All done by the man seen inside The Goat's Inn pub sitting with the nurse. Arguing with the nurse. Killing the nurse...

In one night, he *had become Purchass's scapegoat,* Thomas realised, suspicion turned away from the killer and onto him. What better way to avoid capture than by framing someone else? The drunk man who was seen arguing with a woman in a pub…

Pacing the floor, Thomas went over the events of the previous night. No one had seen him in the alley and there had been no one out on the street.

Then he stopped short as a news flash came up on the laptop.

…. witness able to identify the man last seen. with murder victim Sente Fleishman…

The words were tic-a-taping across the bottom of the BBC website. *A witness.* Nothing else, no mention if it was a man or a woman. Just that a witness had seen a man.

Thomas began pacing again, pausing as another thought came to him. They had seen someone but was it *him* they had seen? Maybe they had seen the man who had mutilated Sente Fleishman's body? Maybe he, Thomas de Souza, *was* in the clear… He started pacing again, this time more urgently. Perhaps the witness might be his salvation.

He turned as he heard his father wheel himself out into the hallway and kicked aside the newly delivered paper so his father wouldn't see the headlines. "You want to go out? We could go to the park and have a walk. Well, I could walk, and you could ride in the wheelchair."

Peter smiled, nodding jerkily. "It would be nice… later."

"Then we'll go out later. I'll make some tea now." Thomas said, picking up the discarded newspaper and going into the kitchen to scan the front page for news.

But there was nothing new. Just a recent photograph of Sente Fleishman. No description of the man the witness had seen. Just that they '*would know him again.*' Leaning against the sink, Thomas thought of his father. If his son was accused of murder, it would kill him.

But he *was* a murderer, wasn't he?

But not deliberately.

It was an accident.

He never tortured anyone.

Momentarily, Thomas thought of confessing but quickly dismissed the idea. He was panicking. He had to stay cool and not overreact. Maybe he could still get away with it. The witness could have seen the *other* man. Kara's kidnapper, the man he knew, the man who had taunted him, the man who had managed to back him into a corner. If they had seen *him,* he might still come out of this intact.

Then the doorbell rang. Thomas startled, staring at the front door and the blurred outlines he could see through the glass. The police *couldn't* have found him, he thought. Not so soon.

Peter de Souza also glanced at the door, then looked over to his son. "Can you answer that?"

But he couldn't move. He was rigid, immobilised.

"Thomas! Get the door." Peter de Souza repeated.

"Leave it!"

Startled, he stared at his son. "But the door --"

"Leave it!"

For an instant, they faced each other.

Then the bell rang again.

75

St Martin's Lane, London
21st December

Despite her anger, Anna wasn't about to give herself away. Instead, she kissed Simon Porter on the top of his head and leaned against the desk, smiling regretfully.

"Another murder."

He glanced at her, expressionless. "That was what you wanted, wasn't it?"

"I never wanted someone to be killed!" she retorted, "I merely implied that it would bring the matter back into the public eye. Which it has," she said, dropping five newspaper editions onto the desk in front of him. "It's on the front page of all of them, apart from the Telegraph, but they never go big on murder. The police think it's the same man who kidnapped Kara Famosa because of the others being mutilated --"

"I can read," Simon said coldly, picking up a newspaper and scanning the article.

He had to admit that Anna was right, the story *was* big news again. Good for the agency, good for a book and the promise of a film deal… at any other time but now. Not since his conversation with Luis Famosa the previous evening, when the Cuban had intimated how damaging Kara's expose might prove to people who had a shared history.

Eager to allay his fears, Simon had said that by being their agent he would have first sight of the expose, and the chance to destroy it. The words had seemed to soothe Luis, but Simon wasn't sure he could stick to his promise. Ambition nibbled away at his loyalty as he thought of the unfinished book Kara had given him, about a hundred pages - with the promise of more to follow. It had been a clever move on her part, Simon thought. It kept him dangling, wondering if any of it was about the hidden events in Las Vegas. There had been plenty about the Famosa business and the forging, but what else? A gambler would have held out, waiting to see what more she delivered and what could serve him best. But a frightened man would go to Luis with what he already had. Curry favour? Or wait?

Simon Porter decided to wait.

"So, what d'you think?" Anna asked.

"I doubt," he said carefully, "the police will catch him. Luis Famosa suspected that there would be more killings."

She frowned, wrong-footed. "When did he say that?"

"The other day, when he called."

"You never said –"

"I don't have to tell you every detail of my life, do I?"

"It's just that the other day you were pissed off that Jimmy wasn't responding to your calls - yet now Luis Famosa's getting in touch. A bit unexpected."

"Why? He's a client."

"I know that," Anna replied patiently, "I was just surprised that you hadn't mentioned it.

"As I said - I don't have to report to you," Simon stuck in the knife and was happy to twist it. "After all, we're not partners in business."

"No, only in bed, darling."

Oh, he would regret his attitude when Ackermann found the killer and *she* got the story for the agency. Simon Porter might have become temporarily bored with her, but the coup would soon reignite his flagging interest. And then he would be grateful to her, so beholden. Just like her cousin would be, Hugh Ackermann manipulated perfectly into her pocket with the promise of hero status.

"What else did Luis say?"

"That neither he nor his son would rest until they caught Kara's kidnapper."

"Poor souls."

Simon looked at her suspiciously: "Who are you pitying?"

"I feel sorry for both of them," Anna replied, her tone sympathetic. "I mean, Jimmy tried to be a hero but failed --"

"As did your son."

Ignoring the interruption, she continued. "And Luis – for all his muscle – seems to be floundering. I doubt any family member will catch the kidnapper, however much they want to." She moved away, pausing at the door. "If only you hadn't fallen out with my son. Thomas is the one who cares about Kara the most. Even more than her own family. And he was there – on the spot, right in the middle of the story - and you had to ruin it."

"Thomas walked out –"

"Indeed, he did."

"All right," Simon said impatiently. "What are you up to?"

"*Me?* Nothing." Anna replied. "I just think it's a pity that we don't have Thomas working for us anymore. We could do with someone close to home."

76

Maida Vale
London

Thomas and Peter de Souza remained motionless, facing each other.

Peter was staring at his son and wondering what was going on. Why all the colour had left Thomas's face and his hands were shaking. He was terrified, he could see that. He had never seen his son afraid before. Angry? Yes. Exhausted? Yes. Afraid? Never.

And that frightened him.

The doorbell rang again.

Thomas stared at his father, Peter staring back in the dim hallway.

Then someone knocked on the door again.

Once, twice.

Loudly.

Grim-faced, Thomas gestured to his father to stay quiet.

Silence followed.

Then, there was a sudden, violent thumping on the door; Peter startled when a voice shouted. “**It’s me, Luis Famosa.**”

Taken aback, Thomas opened the door, Luis glancing at Peter in his wheelchair, his surprise evident. “Sorry,” he said curtly. “I didn’t mean to scare anyone.”

Without replying, Thomas wheeled his father into his bedroom, reassuring him that everything was under control - something Peter didn’t believe. When he returned to the sitting room, he could see Luis holding a newspaper. He had rolled it up tightly into a baton and was tapping it against his left thigh.

“I want to talk to you.”

“Are you following up on your son’s visit? Last time we spoke, he told me to piss off.” Thomas said belligerently.

“There’s been another murder.”

“Yes.”

“You don’t look surprised.”

“I read the papers,” Thomas replied, wondering why the head of the Famosa clan had suddenly come to London, holding a newspaper announcing the murder of Sente Fleishman. The atmosphere was static, wired.

“It’s the same man who kidnapped Kara and killed Ellie Chapman.”

Thomas nodded awkwardly, his whole body seemed disjointed and out of sync. Was that what a guilty conscience did to you? he wondered. Or was that fear?

“It could be the same man.”

“But he slipped up. This time, there’s a witness.”

“Really?” Thomas folded his arms so that Luis didn’t see his hands shaking.

“You working for Hugh Ackermann?”

"D'you see my father running the Marathon?" Thomas countered.

"So, you're working for Ackermann to pay for your father's care?"

Thomas hesitated; in fact, Halle was paying for it, but he could hardly tell Luis that. And as for Ackermann, he had tried to walk away, but he had got him over a barrel, forcing Thomas to work for him or he would report him to the police for attempted blackmail. Blindsided, Thomas had agreed; police intervention would be fatal for a man who had just committed murder.

"What the hell are you smiling at?" Luis asked, bemused.

Thomas shrugged. "I'm not sure."

"I'll pay you to tell me what's going on with Hugh Ackermann."

"Going on?"

"I want to know why he's so interested in Kara's kidnapping and if he's involved with this so-called expose."

Thomas was still smiling, Luis non-plussed. "Are you on something?"

"Just high on life," Thomas replied sarcastically, hearing his father's radio playing in the next room. He jerked his head towards the sound. "If anything happened to me, he'd be helpless."

Luis stared at him, confused. "You're not suicidal, are you?"

"Not yet," Thomas replied, moving on. "He won't tell me anything. Ackermann, I mean. He's too wary to confide, and he thinks I'm just an errand boy." His attention was fixed on the newspaper, still tapping against Luis's leg. Jesus, was he doing it deliberately?

"I want to know if Ackermann gets close to the kidnapper."

"Why?"

"Because I want to get to him first." Luis replied, "I think Hugh Ackermann knows a lot. Just like you."

"Me?" Thomas said, surprised. "I don't know anything."

"Yeah, you do. You know Kara. And I guess you know a lot of her secrets. Maybe she confided in you. Did she do that, Thomas?" He was still tapping the newspaper against his leg. "Do you know why she was kidnapped? Or why she stole the Klimt?"

"How would I? We haven't been in touch for months –"

Luis cut him off. "Hugh Ackermann's involved somehow. I need to find the book Kara wrote. This expose."

"I told you before, I don't know anything about it."

"No? Well, Ackermann might. My wife rejected him to marry me. Ackermann might want revenge for that." Jimmy stopped tapping the paper against his leg and dropped it onto the coffee table. It fell open on the front page, the photograph of Sente Fleishman exposed. Unnerved, Thomas could see her out of the corner of his eye as Luis continued to talk.

"If Ackermann **is** involved, I want you to find out." He misinterpreted Thomas's discomfort as reluctance. "I'll pay you –"

"I can't do it."

"Why not?"

"I just can't," Thomas repeated.

"Are you in trouble?"

Am I in trouble? Thomas thought, incredulously. Yes, I'm in trouble. I killed a woman - and working for

Luis Famosa, spying on Hugh Ackermann isn't going to help.

"I can't work for you -- "

"Think again," Luis replied, hearing the sound of Peter de Souza's radio playing next door. "I need your help. So, I'm prepared to make a deal."

"That might not be a good idea."

Curious, Luis studied Thomas's ashen face. He wasn't drunk, but he looked near to collapse. "I don't know what the fuck's wrong with you, but you *will* work with me. In return, I'll make you a promise. Should anything happen to you, I'll make sure your father's taken care of."

The words got through, Thomas thinking fast. "I don't want him put in a nursing home."

"No nursing home."

"Or in some geriatric hospital ward. You hear me?"

"No nursing home, no hospital. I promise," Luis replied emphatically, "So, do we have a deal?"

BOOK FOUR

77

Hampshire,
England

Halle paused, then clicked off her mobile. How could she ring him? What would she say? Better to keep quiet. Yes, she told herself, keep quiet, no point trying to plead with Luis. He was angry, and she knew what he was like when he was humiliated. Leave him be, let him come to her when he was ready… Then she thought of the intruder and wondered if Luis hadn't *already* decided on her future.

Lying on the bed, staring upwards, Halle remembered the postcard and its toxic message:

> ***Luis Famosa isn't your father.***
> ***I'm sorry.***

Jesus, she thought, no wonder Kara had hated her. If only she had confessed to her daughter and shared her secret. But no, she had continued to let Kara think that Luis Famosa was her father, even when she knew better. Not once had Kara asked her mother who her real father was; instead, she had avoided the question, and Halle was relieved. How could she tell her daughter that it might be Simon Porter or Hugh Ackermann - the man Kara stayed with in London? Halle flinched, remembering the rumour that her daughter and Ackermann were lovers. No, she thought, Ackermann was ruthless but not deviant. As for Simon Porter, Halle wasn't certain if they had been lovers. He had comforted her at times, but had they slept together? She didn't know.

So, who *was* Kara's father?

She didn't know.

But the person who had written the postcard knew.

The handwriting was unfamiliar, so Halle was unable to identify the person who had unpicked Kara's world, but knew it had to be someone close to the family or the business. Many people had entered and left the Famosa stronghold, but only a few had become close... Halle thought back. It *had* to be someone from a long time ago when she and Luis were estranged, and she had been looking for comfort and sex. Not with the kind of men she knew now - not the ones who attended the New York gallery and Private Views, not those - but the ones she had leaned on in Vegas, confided in, trusted, never realising that words spoken in the dark would one day come back to haunt her.

She tried again, but *couldn't* identify the handwriting, and couldn't fill in the missing pieces in those sordid months when she had drifted. She *wanted* to remember, but the images were merely painted backdrops, constantly moving between scenes. And then her mind shifted back to Kara. Who had kidnapped her child? The person who had written the postcard? Had

Kara been abducted to expose the truth? Yes, Halle thought desperately, *that* was why Kara had been taken.

Another thought followed, reminding her of her guilty stupidity. She had wanted to help, but what had been the result? She had called the police to the meeting with the kidnapper. *She* had done that. Kara's own mother drove the kidnapper away… But her mind couldn't cope and immediately shifted responsibility. No, she told herself, Kara's abduction wasn't because of *her*. She wasn't responsible. *It was him!* The man who had written the postcard. He had taken her child.

She wasn't really a bad person, just silly, that was all.

78

Heathrow Airport

Stubbing out his roll-up, Purchass got to his feet, looking around the airport car park. It was too warm for December, the sun winking its way between the bare trees and ugly steel lamplights. He didn't like the heat, but he *did* like plotting, and that was what he had been doing during his tea break. Plotting.

A group of women came out suddenly, walking past him without even glancing in his direction. Employees from one of the airport's numerous coffee shops, in their cheap uniforms and crumpled paper hats. Stuck up bitches, not even giving him the time of day. Purchass's gaze followed them, his interest settling on a slim redhead. Slipping a peppermint into his mouth, he rolled it around his tongue, but he knew he couldn't go after her, she wasn't alone, and it was broad daylight. But the thought stimulated him. Made him long for a woman again.

His scapegoat ploy had gone even better than he had expected. People linking Sente Fleishman's murder with Ellie Chapman and the kidnapping of Kara

Famosa, creating a bona fide serial killer. Purchass continued to suck on the mint. He had been clever - but he was feeling melancholic. If no one knew *how* he had framed Thomas de Souza, what was the joy in it? It might have taken police attention off him, but Purchass wanted more. He imagined de Souza following the news online; his accidental murder turned into a madman's mutilation and killing. And to cap it all off, there was a witness.

Purchass paused, having the same thought that had struck Thomas earlier. *Which man had the witness seen?* Fuck, Purchass muttered under his breath, had they seen *him*? If they had, it was a problem, his tall, stooped form was easy to recognise. Far more memorable than Thomas de Souza. If the witness had seen de Souza, he was in the clear. But if the witness had seen *him*, he was in real trouble.

Enough trouble to make him find the witness and stop them from seeing anything else ever again.

79

Chelsea Wharf
London

Pressure was something Hugh Ackermann knew all about. He could endure it and apply it. He could gauge it like a pharmacist gauges a dose of medicine that's perfectly compatible with the patient. Judged with precision to keep the pressure intense but not enough to buckle the victim, which was why he was worried about Thomas de Souza, wondering why he was coming unravelled. He *had* pressurised him, that was true, but not enough to affect the deterioration he could see now.

Thomas stood by the door, his shirt open at the neck, wearing jeans and a heavy coat. One that looked curiously old-fashioned.

"You wearing your father's clothes now?" Ackermann asked.

"I left my coat on a bus."

"Lucky it wasn't your wallet," Ackermann replied, gesturing for Thomas to sit down. "Luis Famosa came to see you today. What did he want?"

Thomas had suspected he was being watched and had prepared himself. "He was talking about the latest victim..." A pause, he sounded steady. Could he keep it up? "…about how people thought she'd been killed by the same man who killed the others."

"What did Famosa think?"

"That it was the same man." Thomas paused and swallowed drily.

"What's the matter with you?"

"I didn't sleep."

"You hungover?"

"Yeah," Thomas agreed, "I'm hungover."

"Moron," Ackermann replied simply, "Your mother came to see me."

"My mother? She really does get around. Is she having an affair with you, too?"

Ackermann ignored the question. "She's very keen for me to find the killer and beat Famosa to the punch. Did Famosa mention the witness?"

"No. Yes, Thomas nodded, "yes, he did."

"It's a woman."

The words winded him. "A *woman*," Thomas said at last. "How d'you find out?"

"I find everything out, sooner or later. Remember that. She's an office worker, Mrs Carol Humber." He was staring at Thomas from behind his thick glasses. "Says she'd know the killer again."

"Did she describe him?"

Ackermann leaned across the desk. "You look sick. You should sober up, pull yourself together. You're no good to me like this. I should never have hired you --"

"Why does Kara Famosa mean so much to you?" Thomas dived in, "I don't get it."

He thought he had gone too far and hesitated whilst Ackermann wondered how much to confide. He needed Thomas on his side, but he also needed to keep him guessing. No point confiding anything that might get back to Anna de Souza. Or worse, Luis Famosa. Unless, of course, he *wanted* it to get back.

"There was *another* victim in the past. One no one knows anything about."

That was the last thing Thomas had expected to hear. "Who?"

"Can't tell you that."

"Because they were close to you?"

"Yes."

He nodded, "A member of your family?"

Not as stupid as he looks, Ackermann thought. "It was my sister and when I catch the man responsible for her murder, *all these murders,* I'll make him sure he never hurts anyone again."

"When was she killed?"

"A long time ago."

"How long?"

Ackermann was feeding out the information like breadcrumbs to a greedy starling. "Don't ask me anything else."

"If it was a long time ago, surely it couldn't be the same man?"

"I didn't say *how* long ago it was."

"But if it had been recent, it would have been in the papers. And if the murder had been similar to the latest ones, the police would have connected them."

"Very good," Ackermann said dryly, "do go on."

"So, when *did* it happen?"

He ignored the question. "It seems that Luis Famosa and I are looking for the same killer."

"Does Famosa know that?"

"No. And I trust you not to pass on the information." Ackermann replied, hoping for the opposite. He gestured to the computer screen which showed a photograph of Sente Fleishman. "The bastard's still killing after all these years. He tore out her eyes. You read that? She was a nurse, and he tore out her eyes. People like that should be put down..." Thomas was silent, rigid "... but only after they've ripped him limb from limb and made an example of him. Of course, the witness will be the deciding factor. When Mrs Humber identifies the killer, it's over for the bastard. The mob can do what they like then."

Thomas was sweating in his father's overcoat. The mob would come for *him.* They would think it was him.

"What if she was wrong?"

"What?"

"What if the witness *can't* identify the man?" Thomas continued, "It was dark, how much could she have seen?"

Ackerman paused for a long moment, then said simply, "Enough."

It was only after Thomas had left that he considered what he had heard, remembering the words with blinding clarity:

'... it was dark, how much could she have seen?'

How much indeed, Ackermann thought. The witness had supposedly spotted the suspect *inside the pub.* In a pub bar, just before Christmas that was lit up with lamps and blazing with Christmas decorations. She had seen him *inside,* where it wasn't dark, not dark at all.

So, what the hell was Thomas de Souza talking about?

80

Purchass stood in the doorway, watching Thomas de Souza's house from across the road. A light was on in an upstairs window, a shadow moving across the blind as he checked his watch, 11.15pm. He hadn't been watching de Souza long enough to know his routine, but when the carer arrived, he guessed that she was going to be babysitting the old man again. Which meant that blog boy was going out. Which was just what he wanted.

He liked tracking Thomas de Souza, it amused him, but his momentary good humour didn't last. Instead, he thought back to what Kara Famosa had told him.

"...She comes at night. Has done for the last few days... She told me her name began with a K, like mine."

Jolted, he felt sick, his palms sweating. His sister could always do that, could always terrify him, make him feel less than the yard animals, more loathsome than the pigs. She could look at him with those penetrating eyes and shrivel him into dust... So, he *hadn't* been imagining her after all, Purchass thought. If the Yank had seen Kat, that meant she *was* around. That bitch in the barn said she was, said they'd talked, but what had his sister said about him? Had she talked about the bed wetting? Jesus, *what had she said?*

His panic spiralled, then just as quickly, it dipped. Kat **wasn't** around, he told himself. When he thought he saw her it was just his imagination playing tricks on him.

But how could it be *if the girl saw her too*?

Shaken, Purchass slid another mint into his mouth, letting the peppermint sting his tongue. He would think about it later. Yeah, that's what he'd do. Think about it later. For now, he would enjoy watching Thomas de Souza. One thing at a time. Slow and steady, one thing at a time.

-o0o-

Thomas couldn't look at his father, he couldn't risk catching the expression in his eyes. The look which said – *What have you done?* Instead, he made their dinner, and they talked in stilted sentences about nothing important. And his father didn't hear a word of it because he was scared for his son and for himself. Something terrible had happened. He didn't know what, only that a slick dread had come over him. The same sensation he had had when his wife left him. The same feeling he had experienced when the stroke straight jacketed his body.

This is bad.

His eyes followed Thomas's every move, fixed on him, the son who nursed him. Something a man shouldn't have to do. Something *no one* should have to do. He should have said something before, telling

Thomas how grateful he was. Thanking him for the hours and days and months forfeited. But he never had, and now he wondered if it was too late.

Slowly, Peter's glance moved over to the newspaper Luis Famosa had left on the table earlier, Thomas noticing and reacting immediately. "I've got to go out."

"It's past eleven. Why?"

"I need some air," Thomas replied, ringing the nurse, and asking her to come over.

She was curt over the phone, still angry with him, but sympathetic. Hurriedly, Thomas made the arrangements then stood by the front door, leaving as soon as the nurse came round the corner.

"I got here as fast as I could --" Surprised, she turned, watching as he hurried past without saying a word.

Out of the house, Thomas could finally think. He was sober, truly sober. Which was worse, because now he could see just how much trouble he was in. A name of the witness hummed in his head, Mrs Humber, Mrs Humber, then he remembered what Ackermann had said.

'... they should rip him limb from limb... make an example of him.

The mob could do what they like ... and no one would care...'

It was dark, the street emptied of people, and there was only one man out with his sullen dog. Without realising it, Thomas had walked into an unfamiliar area, not recognising the road sign, Mountbatten Avenue. Where the hell was that? He wondered, looking around him at the suburban street, lined with houses, and families, with the kind of lives Thomas de Souza could never have. Normal lives, with schools and jobs,

MOTs, bills. All so boring, all so blessed. And all off limits to him now. Because he had killed a woman.

The thought stopped him dead, but he knew he couldn't go to the police. If he did, he would have to admit that he *had* pushed the woman.

'*I didn't mutilate her, officer. Didn't tear our Sente Fleishman's eyes.*

... I just killed her, that was all. I just killed her...'

The real killer had him over a barrel, but Thomas had no way to prove it. A sudden car horn made him jump, turning to stare down the street. Across the road, a lighted Christmas tree twinkled from a bay window, a dog barked at a back door. A friendly street, and yet... Was he being followed? It felt like it. He could sense it, feel it, the hairs standing up on the back of his neck.

And then he heard him.

"Hey, blog boy."

He turned in the direction of the voice. "Who's there?"

"I saw you kill the nurse."

The voice was so low that Thomas couldn't work out where it was coming from. "Who's that?"

"It was an accident. Anyone could see that."

And then Thomas recognised the voice and the muffled laugh.

"I didn't mutilate her! *You* did that."

Purchass had moved and was now standing behind Thomas, taunting him. "Perhaps I did, but you killed her --"

"It was an accident!"

"I'll give you that, but you were pissed. It was unlucky," Purchass continued, "but now everyone thinks that *you* killed Ellie Chadwick and Sente Fleishman and kidnapped Kara Famosa --"

"Is Kara still alive?"

"No. Yes." Purchass mocked him. "I mean, if she's alive, it means that she's just been abducted. But if she's dead, it's one more victim. Another of *your* murders."

"I'm going to the police --"

"Don't be fucking stupid!" Purchass snapped, "You can't shop me without giving yourself away. Besides, you don't know anything about me, got nothing to make it sound real. They'd think you made it up –"

"I can prove it," Thomas challenged him, "I've got alibis for where I was when you murdered those women."

"So, risk it and go to the police." Purchass replied, "but you won't. Face it, you're fucked. Thanks for taking the blame --"

"I can't do that! I won't!"

"Oh, but you can, and you *will.* Only two people know the truth, and neither of us is talking. And if you feel tempted, remember that one word from me and the police will come for you --"

"I could tell them about you."

"You said that before, but it's bullshit. What *can* you tell them about me? You don't even know who I am," Purchass said from the shadows. "You don't know what I look like or where I live. You go telling the police about me, and they'll think it's just a pathetic attempt to cover up your crimes."

Thomas's voice rose. *"They aren't my crimes!"*

"No, but they'll *think* they are. And imagine what Luis Famosa will do when he finds out you killed his daughter."

Thomas was becoming desperate. "I would never hurt Kara --"

"I believe you, blog boy," Purchass said sympathetically, "I read what you wrote about her - but frankly, it sounded like she dumped you and that would count as a motive, especially if her body turns up." He could see Thomas move and warned him. *"Don't look round!"*

"I want to see your face."

"I bet you do," Purchass said dismissively, "but you don't want to draw attention to yourself by throwing a punch and startling the neighbours, do you? If you give yourself away, there'll be no one to look after Daddy. You ever been to prison, blog boy?" He clutched his arm. "You wouldn't like it. Do what I say, and I can keep you free. You and me, we've got a secret. We're safe --"

"There's a witness."

"I heard."

Thomas was thinking quickly. "You know who it is?"

"No, do you?"

"No," Thomas lied. "Maybe it's not true. Maybe there is no witness. Maybe no one saw you --

"Maybe no one saw *you,"* Purchass corrected him, "We'll find out soon enough. In the meantime, keep your fucking mouth shut, or I'll do your girlfriend, remember that. Now piss off."

Reluctantly, Thomas backed away.

And Purchass followed him.

81

St Martin's Lane
London

Pleased to see Luis Famosa walk into the agency, Simon hustled his secretary out of the office and motioned for his visitor to take a seat. "I thought you might have gone back to the States."

"Not yet. Unfinished business."

Simon nodded, pleased at the thawing of hostilities, and there was the added bonus of knowing that it would infuriate Anna. Her hopes of promoting Thomas had backfired and Luis Famosa was now the front-runner.

"How's Halle?" Simon asked, "I'm worried about her, and she won't take my calls."

"She won't talk to anyone until Kara's found."

"Is there any news?"

"Police are no nearer to catching him." Luis was being cautious, feeling his way around. "They have a witness. That's something."

"Witnesses can be notoriously unreliable, but let's hope." Simon smiled awkwardly, wondering where the conversation was headed.

He didn't have long to wait.

"I've been thinking," Luis began, "about Kara's expose. I know you said you had nothing to do with it, but Kara wouldn't have just started writing a book. She wasn't disciplined, she'd have needed someone to advise her."

Simon met his gaze without flinching, but his hands were clammy. "It wasn't me."

"Perhaps it was someone else in the business? Or someone she knew well. Like Thomas de Souza."

"What about him?"

Luis could see the agent was getting nervous. "They were close. Maybe he helped her write the book."

"You'd have to ask him."

"My son did, and so did I. He denies knowing anything about an expose."

The door of the office opened suddenly, Anna walking in and glancing at Simon and then Luis. Putting down her parcels, she smiled brightly at both men.

"How good to see you again," she told Luis, turning to Simon. "I didn't know we had a visitor coming in."

"Neither did I."

"We must have lunch --"

"Maybe another time," Luis said shortly.

Realising that Anna's arrival might free him from the awkward meeting, Simon welcomed the suggestion. "Lunch is a good idea, we'll go --"

"I was asking about Thomas," Luis interrupted, looking at Anna. "Did your son help Kara write a book?"

She was caught off guard but landed on the balls of her feet like a cat. "Thomas never said anything, and we were very close when he was with Kara." She sighed regretfully. "It's no secret that we've had our differences, but in the past, my son confided in me."

"What if Kara wrote the book *recently*?"

"If Thomas knew about it, he'd have given it to me and I'd have passed it onto Simon," she was all elegant plausibility. "That would make sense, Simon would make the deal for any book Kara wrote. He's the agent for your family."

"But if it was a hatchet job --"

Anna laughed. "How could it be?" She could sense the unease coming from Simon and pretended to think, "What *could* Kara expose about your family?"

"I don't know," Luis replied, turning to Simon, "Do you?"

"The whole talk of an expose is nonsense!"

Luis wasn't convinced. "But if people *believed* there was a scandalous book, they'd go to any lengths to make sure it was never published."

"You think someone kidnapped Kara to stop it?" Feigning shock, Simon reacted, "*That's ridiculous!* This is a tight business; any talk like that would spread."

"Unless Kara went to another agent," Luis replied, "or someone with a grudge against the family. Like Hugh Ackermann."

The name ping-ponged between them, Simon unsettled, Anna nervous. *"Hugh Ackermann?"* She smiled at Luis. "Is he still stinging from your wife's rejection?"

"All the more reason for Kara to turn to him if she wanted to take revenge with an expose --"

Impatiently, Anna interrupted, "There *is* no expose! If there was, we'd know about it." Her tone faltered, with a catch to it, pretending emotion. "I don't want to upset you, Luis, but if your daughter was killed because of a book, why did the *other* women have to die?"

Oh, she was smart, Simon thought, impressed as he watched Luis process the question. "Maybe Kara was the *real* victim, and the others were meant to throw everyone off track?"

"Two women murdered!" Anna shook her head, "you can't believe that."

"People can be ruthless when they want something," Luis replied, rising to his feet. "I'll talk to your son again."

That was *not* what Anna wanted. "*Thomas?* I thought there was some bad feeling. Especially between our sons."

"There was, but Thomas has been kind to my wife."

Anna shrugged. "Nevertheless, Jimmy must have resented his interference."

"I don't think of it as interference."

"He usurped your son."

The shot was accurate and found its target.

"Jimmy's reign was very brief," Luis shrugged. "That happens."

She was pure ice. "What does?"

"When people think they're indispensable," he replied, "that's always when the axe falls."

82

Carol Humber was tired of the police and bored with repeating what she had seen on the night of Sente Fleishman's death. Asking her the same questions endlessly wasn't going to magic up a memory, and when she was brought into the police station to do an Identikit, she was beginning to feel sorry that she had opened her mouth.

"Perhaps," Detective Jameson said hopefully, "it might jog your memory." He turned to the policeman who was preparing the computer programme on screen. "Take all the time you need. We just want a clear image, that's all."

Smiling half-heartedly, Clare Humber looked at the screen and the first images that appeared. A hundred face shapes flirted up like blank masks.

When she didn't respond the policeman glanced over to her. "What shape face did he have?"

Who knew? Carol thought. Bloody hell, she'd only looked at him once, and that hadn't been to take measurements.

If she was honest, she couldn't remember anything much, and her husband was giving her a hard time about getting involved with the police. *But I'm a witness,* she had told him, and he'd reminded her about his conviction for fraud ten years earlier and how he didn't want it coming out. How, if she had had a thought in her fucking head, she would have kept her mouth shut and never mentioned anything about some man in a pub. Besides, what had she been doing in a pub anyway when she said she'd been going to see her mother?

He had been pissed off, truculent in a vest. "And what if you do recognise him?"

"I'd tell them."

"And if he's a killer, he could come after you."

Her face had paled.

"I always said you were stupid," Terry had gone on. "Who volunteers anything to the police? Anyway, how many men were in the pub?"

She had been nervous, trying to stay focused. "A lot."

"A lot? So why d'you notice him?" He had put his face close to his wife's, intimidating her. "Did he have SERIAL KILLER stamped on his fucking forehead? Or perhaps he was hitting the woman with a bat whilst you watched?" Exasperated, he had pushed her out of his way. "Stupid cow! You tell them you were wrong; you don't remember anything –"

"I can't do that!"

"If you don't, you know where all this will lead, don't you? A court case, a trial, and publicity. And the papers will write about you - and *me*. You silly bitch!" He had moved to the door. "Either say you were wrong or pick out some other man, but don't get any more involved."

He had stayed out all night to punish her, and now Carol was sitting in a cramped room next to a young policeman who smelt of cigarettes, staring at a computer screen. All because she had mentioned seeing some man. A man who might be a killer, and might come for her. Or then again, he might have been some innocent drinker who had had nothing to do with the death of Sente Fleishman.

Carol had been married for nearly fifteen years. Terry Humber had been her first boyfriend and the father of their two children. He had also been a bastard at times, teetering on the wrong side of the law, but she had loved him. She *still* loved him. So, the threat of losing him made up her mind. After all, she could have been wrong. The man in the pub probably hadn't been the killer. He hadn't looked like a bad man. The nurse was dead, nothing could bring her back or the other victims. It was sad, but she had to think of the living now.

"The man had a long face," Carol said finally.

"OK," the officer nodded, putting up an image on the screen. "What else?"

Over the next twenty minutes Carol Humber picked out a pair of eyes, a nose, a mouth, and a head of wavy hair. The finished image was convincing, believable. It was the face of a man you could have seen anywhere. On any train, in any pub. It was everyone and no one.

And it didn't have the slightest resemblance to Thomas de Souza.

83

Maida Vale,
London

He was almost laughing as he stared at the small TV screen, making sure the kitchen door was closed. The news was on, a breaking headline showing the Identikit of the suspect the police wanted to question regarding the murder of Sente Fleishman.

And it wasn't him.

Thomas stared at the image, scanning every feature. But nothing resembled him. After all the worrying, the witness hadn't seen him after all, which meant that the face he was looking at could belong to the kidnapper. Thoughtful, Thomas stared at the man's image but couldn't marry this face with the voice he had heard. The Identikit image seemed relatively young. There was nothing intimidating about it, and the man who had been following him was terrifying.

Relieved, Thomas let out a breath, the Identikit wasn't *him.* He could walk into a shop and not worry if his face might appear on the newspapers or if a policeman would tap him on the shoulder and arrest him and so would begin the long trail to the court. To conviction. To incarceration. But not now. Now, Thomas de Souza was just another face in a crowd. Mr. Anyone. Now no one would be able to point a finger and say, *'That was the man.'*

He was safe.

Telling his father he was going out, Thomas hurried down the back steps into the street. The morning air felt gentle, almost loving to him. He was out of danger from the police.

Now, he had only the killer to worry about.

-o0o-

As soon as he heard the front door close, Peter wheeled his way into the kitchen knowing that Thomas wouldn't be back for a while. Now was his chance. The newspaper was lying by the sink, dirty breakfast plates next to it, the morning television chuntering in the background. Suddenly, there was a news announcement and an image flashed up.

> *This is the Identikit image of a man last seen with Sente Fleishman in The Goat's Inn, just before she was killed on the night of 19th December.*
> *If anyone recognises this man, or has any information, please contact…*

19th December had been three days earlier, Peter thought. That was the night Thomas had gone out and returned home late, drunk. He could remember waking up to hear the nurse exchange words with his son: their voices had been hushed, but he could tell she was angry. Feigning sleep, Peter heard Thomas pass by his room, then retrace his steps and close his father's bedroom door. Strange, Peter had thought at the time. Usually, he left it slightly open so he could hear if his father called out to him. But that night the door had been closed.

Anxiously, Peter thought of what had followed the next day; Thomas had been different, both of them strained, the atmosphere uneasy. Then he thought of the incident in the hallway, Thomas startled by the doorbell, Luis Famosa arriving unexpectedly. *Luis Famosa*, the father of Thomas's ex-girlfriend, who had been kidnapped, mutilated, and possibly murdered. Like the nurse who had been killed on 19th December, on the night Thomas had come home late…

No, Peter thought, it had nothing to do with his son. Not Thomas. He had a temper, but he was a good man. He knew his son. Thomas loved Kara Famosa and was looking for her whilst supporting Halle and caring for his father without complaint. He was a good man… *But he had lost his coat.* He had lost his coat on the night of the 19th December. Or so he had told Peter, borrowing his father's the following day. Lost his coat? Or did he destroy his coat? Perhaps to rid himself of evidence which could give him away?

It *couldn't* be Thomas, Peter told himself again. His son couldn't be a killer. But if he was, if anyone found out, he would be arrested. And then what? Prison? And Peter would be left to fend for himself… Troubled, he turned his wheelchair around and headed for his bedroom. He would wait until Thomas came back and then they would talk. And whatever he had done, he would protect his son as Thomas had always protected him.

Struggling to steer the wheelchair, Peter could feel his heart pumping, his head firing with the threat of another stroke as he struggled to the bedroom and wheeled himself inside.

And as he did so Sam Purchass came out from behind the door.

84

Luis read the text message. Then he tried to ring Thomas, but his mobile was on voicemail and instead he read the text again.

Ackermann's sister was murdered. He thinks
it was the same man who killed Kara.
No dates.

Despite all his prolonged and intense investigations Luis hadn't known about Ackermann having a sister. The secret didn't surprise him, Hugh Ackermann had all but obliterated his past, leaving no history to hold him back or trip him up. But no one could hide a *murder* forever, however hard they tried. Looking out of his hotel window, Luis studied the London landscape, his mobile interrupting his thoughts.

It was Thomas. "You got my text?"

"Yeah. Ackermann thinks it's the same killer, does he?" Luis's gaze fixed on the bulbous outline of the gherkin building. "I didn't know he had a sister."

"He told me to keep it quiet, but I think he wanted me to tell you."

"You've no idea when his sister was killed?"

"Perhaps I can find out --"

“No. Leave that to me.”

Thomas changed tack. “Did you get anything from Simon Porter?”

“He denies there’s an expose.”

“You think he’s lying?”

“Probably. Your mother was there. She’s a piece of work.”

“She is indeed.”

If Luis thought Thomas was going to say more on the subject, he was disappointed.

“I have to go now --”

“What about Ackermann?”

There was a long pause before Luis replied, “Tell him I’m going to the country to see my wife.”

With that, he severed the connection, Thomas walking home carrying a full carrier bag and a large container of milk. Struggling with his key, he finally unlocked the door and just about to walk in when he caught a faint, unmistakable smell of peppermint.

85

Purchass was sitting on the end of the bed, Thomas walking in and then glancing over to his father. Peter de Souza had slumped sideways in his wheelchair, his eyes pleading as Thomas straightened him up in his seat. Automatically, he felt for the pulse at the side of his father's neck.

"I have to hand it to you, I couldn't do that," Purchass said, crunching a mint on his back teeth, "It's women's work."

Thomas turned on him. "Who the hell are you?"

Purchass sighed. "Oh, come on! You can do better than that. You said the other night you wanted to see my face, well now you can." Purchass replied, tossing the newspaper over to him. "I ask you," he said, pointing to the Identikit "Who the fuck does that look like?"

With what little strength he had, Peter gripped his son's jacket, Thomas calming him. "It's OK, I'm going to sort it out. I'll just put you in the other room –"

"No, leave him here!" Purchass snapped, standing up. He was over six feet, stooped but menacing and surprisingly fast. "From now on, you do what I want, blog boy. Leave Daddy here." Turning to Peter, he bent down towards the man in the wheelchair. "You don't want putting out of the room like a dog, do you?"

"Don't talk to him like that!" Thomas snapped. "He's sick --"

"But he's not dead. Which is something he's got on the nurse."

The words were out. Thomas could see his father react, his body flinching as their meaning struck home. Slowly, he looked towards his son, Purchass studying the two men.

"Would you say you were like your Dad?" He asked, jerking his head towards the old man. "I mean, apart from the wheelchair… Can his piss on his own?"

"What?"

"Can he piss on his own? What about shitting?" Purchass asked, staring at Thomas, "Can he shit on his own?"

"He's had a stroke."

"So, if anything happens to you, Daddy will just sit there and piss and shit himself forever and ever." Purchass blew out his cheeks. "It would stink after a while. Bodies do. Stink, I mean." He looked back at Peter de Souza. "Were you in the war?" he asked, tapping his shoulder, Thomas moving between them.

"Leave him alone! This has nothing to do with him. What d'you want?"

"I just want to know if he was in the fucking war!" Purchass repeated, his eyes malevolent. "Well*,"* Purchass repeated again, "*was* he in the fucking war*?"*

"No, he was too young."

He turned back to Peter, disappointed. "That's a shame. So, he never killed anyone?"

"No, he never killed anyone!" Thomas snapped.

"So where did *you* get it from?" Purchass asked, taking out a roll of mints and offering one to Peter.

"He doesn't want it –"

"Let him tell me that!" Purchass shouted, staring at Peter de Souza. His mouth was hanging down at one side, his eyes fixed helplessly on his son. "You know something? I think I shocked your Dad," Purchass continued sucking the mint and staring at Peter with his head tipped on one side, curious. Then he lost interest and turned back to Thomas. "I just wanted to call by and introduce myself. Celebrate with you – because *we're* in the fucking clear. That witness was an idiot. She couldn't identify either of us. People are so bleeding unreliable," he paused. "Just tell me one thing. Did you like it?"

Thomas ignored the question.

"Oh, come on, you can tell me. Did you feel good when you killed her?"

"It was an accident! And you bloody know it." Thomas replied, trying to keep calm for his father's sake. "Like you said, it's over now. No one identified you. You're in the clear and I won't say anything. I can't, and you know that too. So why are you here? What d'you want?"

"I want to worry you," Purchass replied, "I want you to remember that your girlfriend's life depends on what you do. And I also want you to know that I'm going to be around for the rest of your life." He tapped the top of Peter de Souza's head, like patting a dog. "Don't go to the police, or act the martyr. Or…" his hand rested on the top of Peter's head, the fingers enclosing his skull. "I'll break your father's back. And then I'll make you watch him piss and shit himself until he dies." He walked to the door then stopped, sniffed the air, and frowned. "You know something? I think he might have crapped himself already."

86

22nd December
Hampshire

Nighttime was creeping and curling around the bolted windows, sliding, slick and malicious, down unlit chimneys. Shutters that should have kept out the light, allowed slivers of moonbeams through mean little cracks, the painted floor of Halle's bedroom a white, water world. Unsteady from a mixture of booze and sleeping tablets, she woke to the sound of the phone ringing; the bedside clock reading 5.45am as she reached out to answer it:

Her voice was tentative, almost afraid. "Hello?"

"It's Luis."

Was that good or bad?

"Where are you?"

"In London."

She sat up in bed, groggy. "Is there news?"

"No."

"Are you OK?"

"Yeah. You?"

"I… I miss you." She said uncertainly, reaching for the wine bottle beside the bed and drinking from it directly. The alcohol jolted her into focus. "I said I missed you."

Immediately, Luis changed the subject. "I want to talk about Hugh Ackermann."

It was still dark, but the moonbeams were creaking through the edges of the shutters, making light ladders across the bedspread, Halle was cautious when she answered.

"You know about Ackermann. I left him for you --"

"Is he close to Simon Porter?"

"No, he knows him from the past – we all do - but they're not friends," Halle replied, but she was unnerved. God, why now? Why was he talking about Ackermann now? And Simon Porter, why bring him up?

"You remember Ackermann coming to Las Vegas?"

Halle took another drink. "Yes, he visited –"

"When we were estranged?"

"Luis, I can't remember," she said, her mouth drying. "He might have been around then."

"Were you close?"

She flinched. "Not in the way you mean –"

"What way is that?"

"Hugh Ackermann was coming to see a few paintings that you'd recommended. Some landscapes. It was when he wanted you to organise a commission, to hire the artist that could fake -"

"Your memory's improving."

His tone unsettled her. "Only when you remind me of the past. "

"Did you know Ackermann had a sister?"

"No… He said there had been a family tragedy, but that it was a long time ago."

"How long?"

"Late seventies maybe, or early eighties," she frowned, "I don't know –"

"His sister was murdered."

"What?"

"Thomas told me. And he also told me that Ackermann thinks it could be the same man who killed Kara."

Fumbling for the switch, Halle turned on the light and sat up in bed. Her mouth felt sluggish, her head pulsing. "But that's not possible."

"Why not?"

"If his sister was killed then, that would make the killer --"

"In his late fifties or early sixties." Luis interrupted. "If he was a fit man, he could still be active. In fact, he'd be the same age as Hugh Ackermann and Simon Porter." Halle's lips moved but nothing came out as Luis continued to talk. "It's possible."

"But Jimmy saw the killer at the meet --"

"He saw him from a distance, in fog," Luis replied, "He couldn't see his features, or tell his age."

"The police Identikit photograph was of a young man --"

"But was he the murderer? He was *seen* with Sente Fleishman before she was killed, but he could be innocent," Luis paused, picking his next words carefully. "D'you believe there's an expose?"

"Kara wouldn't do that to us –"

"You sure?" Luis countered. "It would be killing two birds with one stone. Taking revenge on her mother and exposing me. When Kara thought I was her father, she could stomach the Famosa lifestyle, but not now. Apparently, she'd been talking to Ivan Holt at the gallery and trying to pick Jimmy's brains --"

"She *wouldn't* write an expose," Halle said, moving over to the window. It was still dark outside, the garden lights blurred with rain. "Maybe she was just threatening to write it --"

Luis's voice had an edge to it. "Bullshit! If she wrote it, she had help."

"*You want to think the worst of her!*" Halle said shrilly. "You hate Kara now –"

He ignored her and pressed on. "She had help from Hugh Ackermann or Simon Porter –"

"*Porter?* Why?" Halle asked, her voice wavering. "The Famosas are his best clients! Why would he want to see us ruined?"

"He wouldn't, would he? He wants to make money from Kara's kidnapping because there's a book and film in it," he paused, adding, "Whether she gets rescued or not –"

"She's my child!" Halle screamed.

"But not mine," Luis replied, his tone ruthless. "So, if Porter *does* have Kara's expose, and it talks about things we've hidden – and want to *keep* hidden - he's going to suppress it."

A suspicion entered Halle's head and lodged there. "He wouldn't…"

"What?"

She couldn't say it, couldn't put the thought into words. But why not? The secret was out. Hadn't she seen the postcard written to her daughter, the words that had tumbled the whole house of cards?

"What wouldn't he do, Halle?"

"I don't know."

"Say it, Halle, tell me what he *wouldn't* do –"

"Kill Kara!" She snapped. She was unravelling, her world shifting underfoot as she clung to the phone, knowing that the conversation was leading to an inescapable place.

" -- but I didn't say Porter would kill Kara."

Halle was confused, floundering. "Ackermann wouldn't kill her either–"

"Who said anything about killing Kara?"

"Does he know?"

Luis kept his voice quiet, almost kindly. "What d'you mean, Halle? Does *who* know *what*?"

"Does Jimmy know that you aren't Kara's father?"

There was a long pause before Luis replied. "Yes. I told him."

"Why would you do that!" she said, panicking. "You know that Jimmy would do anything for you. He chose the business over his own family -- "

"Nobody asked him to."

"You knew the effect it would have!" Her voice was wavering. "You turned him against his sister –"

"Half-sister. It was you who divided this family. You and Kara on one side, me, and Jimmy on the other. You did it, Halle. Whatever happens is *your* fault."

The threat winded her and left her struggling to reply. "Don't hurt her, please… Punish me, but not Kara."

"You need to calm down," Luis said softly. "You're confused, Halle, very confused. Have you been drinking again? Or smoking too much weed? You should be careful; you're older now and your tolerance isn't what it used to be." His cruelty was chilling. "Just tell me why Ackermann would side with Kara."

"I don't know," Halle said plaintively, stumbling out of the bedroom and moving downstairs.

In the library, she flicked on the lamps and moved to the bar, reaching for a bottle of vodka and downing a couple of mouthfuls. Her hands were icy against her skin as she drank again and glanced out of the window. The bodyguards had changed shifts and two other guards were patrolling the property outside, but there was no one moving around inside, the servants and housekeeper keeping to their own quarters. Becoming steadily more drunk, and befuddled by sleeping pills, Halle staggered around the room. And the more Luis talked, the more anxious she became.

"Maybe Ackermann wanted to rein Kara in? Maybe *he's* suppressed the expose to protect you? Or us."

"Us?" Halle repeated blindly, "Why would he need to protect us?"

"You know why."

"I don't know!" She cried, clinging to the glass. "What did we do, Luis? What did we do?" Her eyes came in and out of focus as she turned and glanced at the clock, which was striking the hour. Three in the morning… But that wasn't right! Hadn't the clock by her bedside said 5.45am when Luis rang? "I can't think…I can't think straight anymore."

"You're stressed, worried about your daughter."

"Yes, yes."

Luis urged her on. "Why would Ackermann want to protect us? Or, is it Simon Porter? Perhaps he wants to protect all of us?"

"*All of us*?" She repeated, watching the lights going on in the garden. Someone was walking around, approaching the house. "*Stop it, Luis!* Stop it! I don't know what you want me to say --"

"Hush," he said quietly. "Don't think about it. Forget the past, it's done with. Your memory's bad, very bad. You've always been confused, and now you're drinking again it's worse. You should see a doctor or a psychiatrist and get things sorted out in your mind –"

"I'm not mad!"

"No, Halle, just muddled. Go back to bed, let me handle it –"

"Handle what?"

"This whole mess."

Her fingers clenched around the glass. "Don't do it, Luis –"

"Do what?"

"Don't punish Kara," she whimpered, "please, Luis, don't hurt her. Don't hurt my child."

87

St Martin's Lane,
London.

"You bastard!" Anna screamed, striking out at Simon Porter and pushing him backwards. He fell awkwardly onto his leather chair, his legs splayed out in front of him. "I had to ask the cleaning woman to let me in because you'd changed the bloody locks!"

He was struggling to compose himself, trying to smooth his jacket and tie. "It's over –"

"The fuck it is!" Anna snapped, "I'll tell you when it's over. I left my husband for you --"

"You were bored with Peter; it was your decision."

Her rage was threatening to overwhelm her. The humiliation of not being able to get into the agency had been bad enough, but to have to bribe the way in to see her lover was unbearable.

"I want an explanation."

"You lied to me."

"When?"

"You're Hugh Ackermann's cousin," Simon said coldly, believing he had the upper hand. "And you never said a word. We talked about him often, but you never mentioned you were related. So why was that, Anna? You fucking *him* now?"

She lunged forward, but he ducked away, wagging his finger at her, "It's over! I can't have you here anymore. I'll give you a payoff, your salary --"

"You know where you can stuff the salary!" she roared. "I've been invaluable to you, Porter. You think that just because you're doing a deal for Kara's book you don't need me anymore? You wouldn't *have* a bloody deal without me! It was Thomas who got you in there -- "

"The Famosa family are my clients."

"Thomas was Kara's lover!" Anna retorted, "It was his blog that kept the world interested. *He* made you important again, you creeping bag of shit." She tossed a pile of newspapers at him. "Lucky another woman's been killed, isn't it? Just in time to reignite a failing story. I wouldn't put it past you to do yourself if you thought you could get away with it."

"I'm not a murderer!"

She laughed. "You're right there; you wouldn't have the balls. You'd rather change the locks to duck a problem, wouldn't you? But you're not as good at hiding secrets."

He paled, the colour leaving his face. "What?"

"That shook you, didn't it?" Anna replied, her malice impressive, "I listen at doors, I always have done, ever since I was a kid. My parents used to tell me off about it, told me I'd grow ears as big as a donkey. But you know something? One day I knew, I just *knew* that I'd hear something important," she picked up her bag, her expression smug, "and I did. I heard you talking to Halle about the old days --"

He had paled, obviously shaken. “You’re bluffing!”

“Am I?” Anna replied, burning with spite, “Your laptop has some pretty interesting files on it. I imagine you thought you’d hidden them well.”

“How dare you pry into my things!”

“But I thought you were an open book,” she sneered. “Talking of books, have you told Luis you’ve got Kara’s missive?”

His face was waxy, colourless. “I was going to tell him. I’ve nothing to hide.”

“*Everyone* has something to hide!” She leaned over the desk towards him, “You don’t keep your laptop with you all the time. There were a couple of occasions when you slipped up. Big mistake that. Treat someone badly and they’ll want revenge. Might even help themselves to that secret expose.” Her mouth was so dry she could barely speak, “Does Luis know about your late-night chats with his wife?”

“Halle is my client!”

“Maybe it’s more than that, Simon. You were both young once, and you used to visit the Famosas in the States, didn’t you? When you were all on the way up, just starting to get rich and powerful.” She paused and pointed to a painting on the wall above Simon’s head, “That’s an Oscar Kokoschka, isn’t it? Or *is* it?”

Unnerved, he blundered unconvincingly, “What are you suggesting? You’re insane --”

“No, Halle’s the crazy one. And Halle’s always been close to you, hasn’t she? The question is, *how* close?”

His face was as grey as his suit. “What d’you think you’ve got on me?”

“I don’t *think*, I *have.* Secrets, some from a long time ago and some more recent. One in particular that could be very dangerous if it came to the attention of Luis Famosa." Her eyes glistened with spite, "You think I'm bluffing? You're right about one thing, Simon, I *am* Hugh Ackermann's cousin, and like him, I fight dirty."

"You've nothing on me!"

"Would you like to gamble on that?" Anna queried, "I mean, come on, Simon, are you really *that* stupid?"

88

Maida Vale
London

The doctor examined Peter de Souza and confirmed that he had had another mild stroke. Nothing too serious this time, he told Thomas, but it would delay his progress. Then he asked if he'd had a shock.

Thomas ignored the question and asked one of his own. "Is he going to recover?"

"Time will tell." The doctor closed his bag with a sharp click of the locks. "Look after him like you always do, and we'll see how it goes. It's his speech that has been affected the most, he can't talk at the moment, but it should come back in time. Look, I won't lie to you," the doctor continued, "your father's very sick. He needs peace and quiet. Stress is the real killer here."

Thomas remembered the words after he had shown the doctor out and moved back into his father's bedroom, Peter staring at him, unblinking. There were questions in his eyes, questions, and accusations. His son had been called a murderer by some thug. His own son was a killer. What he had suspected was true…

“You’re going to be alright,” Thomas told him, Purchass’s visit hanging over both of them as he avoided his father’s gaze and opened the window.

He knew Peter was watching him but didn’t turn round, he couldn’t face him. On the street outside. an AA van was pulling up next to a stalled car, a woman was looking agitated, her voice raised. What should I do? Thomas thought helplessly. Run? No, he couldn’t run, he couldn’t leave his father. He couldn’t go to the police either. So, what *could* he do? Carry on, he thought blindly. Live knowing that he had killed a woman. Live with the guilt. Live with his father staring at him, the accusation always in his eyes. Live under the scrutiny of a killer who had framed him; knowing that if he slipped up, Purchass would kill Kara and expose him.

Slowly, Thomas turned from the window and moved over to the bed, avoiding the look his father was giving him. Judgmental. Forgiving. Accusing. Hopeful. His hand went out to his son, Thomas took hold of it and knelt by the side of the bed.

“Don’t worry, it’ll be alright,” he began, but the words were fake, and neither of them believed them. Peter de Souza didn’t want platitudes, he was clinging to life, his brain and body shattered, his mind tormented. But he was still a father and still loved his son, his hand reaching out for the notepad by his bed as Thomas watched him write.

The question was simple:

Did you kill the nurse?

Thomas read the words, then shook his head. “It was an accident. But he saw what happened. He mutilated her and framed me for the other murders.”

Peter then wrote:

Kara?

Thomas nodded. “She’s still alive, but if I step out of line, he’ll kill her.”

With effort, Peter scribbled again, passing the paper back to his son.

You’ve done enough for me.

Save yourself.

“I can’t,” Thomas said, gripping his father’s hand. “I *can’t* save myself. And he knows it.”

89

Still enraged, Anna de Souza sat at a table outside a street café off Bond Street. She had told Simon Porter that she had the ammunition to blow him out of the water, but it was only partially true. Much of it had been bluffing, the knitting of half-heard sentences and muffled innuendoes. There *were* secrets and something sinister, but Anna had only uncovered the bare bones of the corpse, it needed fleshing out to ensure its resurrection.

She needed backup. But who could she make into an ally? Her son was rejecting her calls and the thought of approaching her cousin was dismissed instantly. She had promised Hugh Ackermann fame and fortune, and now Simon Porter had dumped her - something her relative would revel in.

Anna crossed her legs and sipped the coffee she had ordered. It was bitter, but appropriate. Whatever happened she wasn't going back to her old life. Not tending to a sick man for the rest of her days. Bugger that, Anna told herself. She might as well crawl into her grave now because that's what it would feel like.

Her anger cooled slowly, malice taking its place. It had all been so perfectly planned, but now it was falling apart, and she was being shut out. Simon Porter headed back to his whey little family, whilst she had nowhere left to turn and no man waiting to console her.

In the end, it would be *his* choice what happened next. If Simon Porter didn't pay her off – not with a wage, but with something much more substantial - she would expose him. Anna smiled, reassured. Yes, there was always an escape. Men didn't like the world to laugh at them, but mistakes and secrets – however old – seeped out.

Six feet might be deep enough to bury a body - but for a reputation?

Not nearly deep enough.

90

St Martin's Lane,
London

Simon Porter slammed his office door closed and locked it, ignoring the quizzical glance of his secretary. How could Anna de Souza have found out? He thought, turning to his laptop. Dear God, she must have been quick. He only left it unattended when he went to the cloakroom. Often not even then. How had she accessed it? He thought, sick with panic. She didn't know the password, but somehow, she *had* known and read the files. But how could she? They were encrypted! He paused, sweat trickling down his back, his shirt clinging to him. *The files were encrypted*, he repeated to himself, they were safe. Then he remembered how Anna had told him that even doctored files could be accessed and how he had laughed, making a mental note of something that might prove profitable at another time.

Panic was making him unsteady on his feet. What if she had copied the files? Taken the laptop when he was asleep, snoring after sex, or when he was in the lavatory with his pants down… *The files were encrypted,* he told himself again, sobbing, his hand over his mouth. She hadn't accessed them. She might have stolen them, but she hadn't read them. After all, she said she had 'overheard' things? That wasn't the same as reading them, was it? But then she said she *had* got into the laptop…

Fear was making him shake, little mewls of panic coming from him as he bumped into a chair and overturned it. The sound of the fall brought his secretary running.

"Are you alright, sir?"

"I'm fine. I knocked something over --"

"D'you need help?"

"No, I don't need help!" he snapped, immediately softening his tone, "It's alright, honestly, nothing to worry about."

But when she left, he loosened his tie and sat down. He was waiting for his heart to give out; the shock would kill him, would finish him off. But what did it matter? He was ruined. Anna de Souza had uncovered his past, long buried, long forgotten. But *how* had she done it? He asked himself again, rummaging around his office, taking the back off his mobile and then prising open the landline phone. She must have planted listening devices, he thought. Bugs, there *had* to be bugs. Or microphones. That was it, there were cameras. Perhaps they were in the walls. Or under the desk. He clambered beneath, searching for anything unfamiliar, then climbed onto a chair and reached into the lightshade overhead. He found nothing, only the chattering of his own conscience and the acceptance of exposure.

Slumping back into the chair, he checked his pulse. It was steady. How *could* it be steady when he was finished? When everything he had built was being undercut, when every secret was dancing out from the wings like a chorus line of devils. He checked his pulse again, angered. He was a broken man with a heart that wouldn't even let him off the hook.

If only he'd never met Anna de Souza. He wasn't a womaniser, he had enjoyed a stable family existence, but she had seduced him and taken a hammer to his life. If he had stayed at home his past would have never been upturned. No one remembered the past - except for the times Halle had called late at night, usually after she had drunk too much. But those calls had gradually petered out, both of them comforted and reassured.

Until Anna de Souza came into his life. Then the calls had begun again, over, and over, Kara's kidnapping making Halle ever more unstable, ever more confused, ever more the girl he had known so well in the past.

91

Chelsea Wharf
London

Finishing his lunch, Hugh Ackermann watched as his secretary took the empty plate away. She said nothing, which was why he liked her. Discreet, efficient, and monosyllabic. The perfect woman. Reaching down to pull up the sock on his left leg, Ackermann paused, surprised to find himself looking at a pair of feet through the knee hole of his desk.

The feet were mute, as was their owner, waiting for Ackermann to re-emerge. "How did you get in?"

Luis shrugged. "Your secretary has a bladder. I took my chance when she left her desk." He took a seat facing Ackermann. "Can we talk?"

"Must we?"

"You think the man that killed your sister also killed Kara? We have a lot in common."

"And Thomas de Souza has a big mouth," Ackermann retorted, adding slyly. "You never worry about him? de Souza, I mean, he's not reliable."

"In what way?"

Ackermann ignored the question and asked one of his own. "Do you never wonder if he was involved? With Kara's abduction, I mean. Or with the murders, come to think about it."

"Have you got something on him, or just want me to suspect him? I know you've got him watching me."

"And I imagine he's spying on me for you."

Luis smiled thinly. "I'm tired of all the jerking around. Tell me about your sister."

"No."

"OK, I'll tell you what I know. Miriam was killed in the same way as the other victims. Her eyes were mutilated, and the killer was never found. Am I right so far?"

Ackermann had all the animation of a stuffed bear. "Go on."

"You've been trying to find out who killed her since the late seventies, with no luck. Then Ellie Chadwick was murdered. The mutilation of the eyes reminded you of Miriam's death. But then it came closer to home, didn't it? Kara was kidnapped and had a finger severed. Her eyes weren't mutilated, but they were bright blue like the other women. So, you wondered - *was it the same killer?"* He stared at Ackermann. "Am I right?"

"Don't piss about, get on with it."

"Why did Kara's abduction have such an effect on you?"

"You've just answered your own question. It reminded me of Miriam."

"There's more, isn't there?" Luis probed, "Kara used to stay with you in London. There's a rumour she was sleeping with you, but I don't buy that. I think you were working together."

"We had a dog grooming salon in Devon, but keep it quiet," Ackermann said, deadpan. "You don't know what you're talking about, Luis, so don't come here and try to throw your weight around. We go back a long time, there's no way you can hurt me without me hurting you. Stop trying to make a pile of bullshit into a chocolate snowman." He made a point of looking at his watch. "I've got a meeting --"

"With Thomas?"

"You don't need to know."

"His mother visited your office the other day. Why would she do that when she's in league with Simon Porter?"

"She came about some work."

"At your dog grooming salon?"

Ackermann smiled, impressed by Luis Famosa's research.

"Where's the expose?"

"Ah, the famous expose," Ackermann replied, "I don't know anything about it."

"We should work together –"

"On what?"

"Finding Kara."

Ackermann sighed, the sound coming from deep inside his chest. "Your son buggered it up. Missed catching the killer."

"Yeah, he did. As did Thomas de Souza." Luis changed tack. "Why did Kara steal the Gustav Klimt?"

"How the hell would I know?"

Rising to his feet, Luis walked around the office, pausing before an Egon Schiele. "You've bought some good paintings from me. Ever think of the old times in Vegas?"

There was a bite in the words, a nip in every syllable. "I never look back."

"That's a lie; you're obsessed with your dead sister," Luis replied, "That's why we should join forces to catch this bastard. You want him as much as I do. You want him because of Miriam *and* Kara." Luis returned to his seat, smoothing his trouser leg, "Why is Kara's death so important to you?"

"Why are you so anxious about the Klimt painting?"

Luis had hit the wall. Ackermann wasn't going to confide, and he knew it. "The murders are mounting up. The killer's confident, thinks he's got everyone fooled." He paused, holding Ackermann's stare. "That murder of the nurse was reckless, he could have been caught red-handed, but he risked it. He *has* to kill."

"So?"

"He's hungry. Which means he'll start looking for another victim. Unless …"

"*Unless?*"

"The other murders were incidental. Say he took Kara because of the book and the other women were just window dressing. A single murder gets limited attention; a few fall into the serial killer bracket. A murderer could hide the real victim that way."

"What about Miriam? She was killed decades ago, where does she fit it?"

Luis's voice was steady, but the words were incendiary. "Maybe the criminal went to prison. Or he was committed and only just came out and started again. Or maybe your sister was killed for other reasons. By a man who would only kill once."

Ackermann said nothing, merely rose to his feet, opened the door, and waited until Luis Famosa walked out.

92

22nd December

Purchass was looking at the calendar on the kitchen wall. December, with a grinning Santa and a pile of drippy kids. It was over a month since he had killed Ellie Chadwick and weeks since he had kidnapped Kara Famosa. Oh, yes, there had been the nurse's death. That had been satisfying, but too short-lived. Not like the killing he had been planning for decades.

He relished the details of his master plan. First, there would be the keeping in the barn, the prolonged torture, and then the final money shot of death. He knew that he had been clever with Thomas de Souza and was lucky to have a scapegoat. But then again, Purchass didn't really want anyone to have his glory; he needed another killing of his own. And if the police ever suspected him, he could point the finger at blog boy and fit him up for all the murders. Cornered and angry, Thomas de Souza was trapped. The only person who could expose Purchass couldn't say a word, he was as hog-tied as a pig waiting for the knife.

Thoughtful, Purchass hunched over the fire in the grate. The coal was poor, and the kitchen walls yellowed from smoke and nicotine. Purchass had never smoked, but his father and his brother had. Poor fat Sean. That's why he had died so young: blubber heart, lungs like pig's bladders. Purchass remembered Sean in his coffin and Kat picking her nose when she thought the priest wasn't watching, and then that fucking stupid ritual of taking a handful of dirt and throwing it on the coffin. Kat had done it, giving Purchass a hard look until he bent down and picked up some dry earth. Paying his respects, he threw it on the coffin lid, but in reality, he was imagining cramming it down his brother's fat throat. Sean, bloated like a beached seal, sweating ooze and fat into the cheap coffin, stinking out the soil around him.

She had been careful when they got home. With no backup, no brother to support her, Kat's spite was neutered. And besides, Purchass was much bigger than her now. Taller, stronger, meaner. She could have backed down, but she didn't. She went on the hunt instead, bringing back men and fucking them in the barn.

You have to help me on the farm, he had told her.

Piss off, that's your job.

We need more money, Purchass had replied.

If you won't work, get on your back and charge for it.

And she did. She knew that he crept round the side of the barn and peeked through the slats. Watching her under some man and grunting, looking in his direction whilst his face burned, and he jerked himself off. Come summer, she was back in his bed at night, mocking him in the morning when the sun snaked up over the barn roof.

A lot of the animals died off that year. Purchass didn't feed them enough, he also neglected the fields, spending most of his time watching his sister. But she was getting fat and didn't wash enough, her clothes were stiff under the arms with old sweat. The men soon stopped coming to the barn and there was nothing for Purchass to watch. Only the flies caught in the spiders' webs hanging down over stables which held no horses, next to fields which grew no crops, and a barn which was emptied of cattle. And then the money ran out and Purchass broke into someone's house and stole some cash, whilst Kat – lazy, fat Kat – was giving it away in the nearby town to anyone who wanted it. Up against doors, down alleys, and picking her nose at the same time. Only her eyes stayed the same. The only thing that did. Blue as irises.

Purchass roused himself. The memory was a bad one, it was best left behind… He wanted a woman. That was the only thing that would help to put Kat out of his mind. It was all the Yank's fault, that bitch in the barn talking about his sister and how she came to visit her. *As if, as if!* But then he wondered if it was true because he had been hearing Kat's voice a lot lately, and thinking that maybe – just maybe – she *had* come back.

He needed to get his mind clear. And he needed a woman… Purchass glanced back at the calendar. It was the 22nd of December, which meant there would be women everywhere, all shopping for Christmas and buying all kinds of tat from the airport duty free. Women waiting at Arrivals or Departures. Women coming and going. Women pre-occupied, struggling, glad of a helping hand from a friendly member of the airport staff.

And one of them wouldn't live to bring in the New Year.

93

"Mr Famosa."

Luis turned, watching as Anna de Souza hurried towards him. The afternoon was coming to a close, the dying light backed up by streetlamps, the smell of pasta leaking, uninvited, through a restaurant door.

"I need to talk to you," she said, as she reached him, "I can't get my son on the phone."

"What d'you want?"

"A glass of white wine would be a start."

In silence, Luis walked her to a nearby hotel, both of them taking a seat at the bar. Downing half her wine, Anna breathed in, then turned to her companion.

"I've got the expose."

His expression didn't change, the black eyes steady. "What expose?"

"The hatchet job Kara did on your family," she went on, "I've got it. Well, I haven't actually got it, but I know where it is." Her eyebrows rose. "Aren't you going to say anything?"

"You told my son that there was no expose."

"I said a lot of things when I was with Simon Porter. I lied." She shrugged. "But not now. I don't owe that bastard anything."

"He dumped you?"

"Enjoy the moment, Mr Famosa, you won't be smiling when you read the book."

"Have you read it?"

"Not yet," she admitted reluctantly, "I thought it would be encrypted, but it's a newer version of an older file, and Simon didn't get around to it. He slipped up badly there. I've printed out a hard copy --"

Luis frowned. "Why didn't you put it on a flash drive?"

"Because I had to take my chance when I had it! Simon was irritable, he thought I was downloading one of his client's manuscripts, so he didn't question why I was at the printer." Her expression hardened. "Look, I got the bloody file, didn't I?"

"Why was Porter irritable?"

"We'd had an argument, I'd spooked him."

"How?"

"I was bluffing," Anna replied, finishing her wine and signalling to the waiter for a refill. "I pretended I knew things about him that he wouldn't want to be made public."

Alerted, Luis probed. "Like what?"

"Just hinting about his past," she went on. "I was angry, I threatened him." Luis could see that she was regretting her candour and suddenly tried to backtrack. "I knew he had told you that he *didn't* have Kara's expose. I suppose he was worried that I'd tell you --"

"You have," Luis replied, continuing. "So, where's the book now?"

"I hid it. I had to, I was going to take it home, but before I could Simon started an argument, and I had to hide it."

"Where?"

"You think I'm going to tell you that!" she snorted. "I can get it, but I have to get into the office before the cleaner comes. I don't have the key anymore, so we have to break into the agency and grab the book."

"We?"

"What?" Anna asked, puzzled.

"Breaking and entering?" Luis shook his head, "I don't think so."

"You won't be caught! I know the alarm code, so I can stop it before it goes off." She hurried on, trying to convince him. "Simon changed the locks, but we can jemmy the door –"

"Really?"

"What's the problem?" Her expression was steely. "Don't you want the expose?"

"If there is one, I'll destroy it."

"Fine, that's no skin off my nose. I don't care. But Simon's scared of you, he'll have a cardiac arrest when he knows what I've done." She smiled, leaning towards Luis. "You're welcome to keep the private Famosa secrets; I won't say anything – but only on one condition."

"What's that?"

"That you fire Simon Porter and let me handle the film and book deal about Kara's abduction." She put up her hands to prevent his interrupting her. "Simon has a deal ready to go. I drew up the contracts with him. And besides, Thomas is my son."

Luis smiled coldly. "You want to involve Thomas?"

"We'll need him for promotion. His blog was very touching, and when the press junket starts, we'll need him to play the 'doomed lover' role. He knows Kara better than anyone, and photographs well." She paused and toyed with her wine. "You dislike me, don't you?"

"You're a type."

She nodded. "I am indeed. I'm a bad wife and a poor mother, but I can spot an opportunity a mile away. This is yours."

"And if I don't agree to help you?"

"I'll go public with the expose."

Luis drained his glass, his voice emotionless. "You're blackmailing me?"

"No, just helping you to make up your mind. You can hardly go to the police and complain, can you? Not if you want to keep the expose under wraps."

"Why aren't you working with your cousin on this?"

Luis could see that she was wrong-footed, but she didn't miss a beat. "So, you know I'm related to Hugh Ackermann?"

"I've enough money to find out who belongs where, and to whom. Besides, Ackermann might want his own chance of revenge." He paused, adding. "These killings have brought back his past."

"His past?"

"You didn't know about his sister's murder?"

Her eyes flickered. "Of course I knew!" She lied, "but it was something the family never talked about. However, as my cousin brought it up, I wonder if he told you the whole story. Did he happen to mention that he was arrested the day after they found his sister's body?"

94

He was waiting at the corner of the street as Thomas walked past and Purchass fell into step behind him. Hearing the footsteps, Thomas turned. He had known before looking who it was. "What d'you want?"

Purchass gestured towards an old vehicle. "Get the fuck in!" he snapped. "Hurry, or someone will see us."

The van smelt of oil and grease, a pile of empty crisp packets were on the floor, and a plastic gorilla swinging from the rearview mirror as Purchass started up the engine. In silence, he drove for several minutes, then stopped by the side of a children's playground, turning off the engine and turning his body to face Thomas.

"How's your Dad?"

He said nothing, his fists clenched.

"... my old man died a long while back, early eighties. Used to be a fighter. "

"What d'you want?"

"Well, fuck me," Purchass replied, "I was trying to do a bit of bonding there, and you cut me off. You shouldn't do that; we're partners, after all."

"We're not partners."

Purchass lurched forward, holding a hunting knife to Thomas's throat. He could see the pulse thumping under the skin and sensed the blood moving. "Oh, but we are partners, and we have a job to do, blog boy. I don't want to have to worry about you, wonder if you're going to talk --"

"You threatened to kill Kara and murder my father; why the fuck would I talk to anyone?"

"True," Purchass agreed, sheathing the knife, "but I've been thinking. The nurse's murder was an accident, and when I asked if you enjoyed it, you looked shocked. That got me worried, thinking that you might start getting a conscience. All that 'being damned' stuff which makes men go soft, scared, so they want to confess, get forgiveness." He glanced out of the van window. "My mother was religious, but my father beat it out of her. She turned out worse than him in the end. Cut him with a bread knife, got him down to the bone. Fucker deserved it."

Silent, Thomas listened, thinking of his father. The night nurse was sitting with him, Thomas promising to be back soon. The previous night he had slept by his father's bedside, on guard, finally slipping to sleep around five. Not knowing that Peter de Souza had awoken an hour earlier and was watching him.

Thomas thought of his mother then, of all the messages Anna had left on his mobile, the ones he had ignored. He thought of his past, but mostly he thought of Kara. About her confession on the beach, under the sun, making him complicit in a secret. Perhaps one of many she had included in the Famosa expose.

He wondered if the book would ever be published.

He wondered if he would ever see her again.

And he wondered if he would get out of the van alive.

95

St Martin's Lane
London.

Waiting until past ten, Anna de Souza parked her car and walked towards Luis, startled to see a burly figure standing beside him. Then she realised that Luis Famosa would not have attended alone or risked himself – even for a book that could ruin him.

"Aren't you coming with us?" She asked as Luis returned to his Daimler and gestured to his silent companion.

"Tell him what you want him to do."

"But you have to do this with me –"

In reply, Luis raised the car window as Anna turned to the bodyguard and headed for the agency, the man following. Around them, restaurants and pubs were heaving with activity, but only a few people were out on the street since the snow had started. Heavy and sticking, even in London, slush under the passing cars, white and wonderful on the rooftops.

Signalling for the man to follow her, Anna moved down to the agency's basement entrance, her mobile ringing and displaying Luis's number. "What if Porter's still there?"

"The bastard never works past seven," she snapped, turning back to the guard, "Well, go on, break the lock! We've got thirty seconds before the alarm goes off."

Sitting in his car, Luis listened in on the phone line. "What if there's a chain on the door?"

"I don't remember any chain!" Anna replied, urging the bodyguard into action. "*Come on, get on with it!*"

He worked fast, jimmied the door, and pushed against it– but it didn't open.

"There *is* a bloody chain!" Anna said exasperated, watching the guard slam his foot against the wood. Both of them could hear the humming of the alarm begin inside, its soft purring due to erupt, giving its thirty-second grace before it sent a message to Simon Porter's home – and the nearby police station.

"Jesus!" Anna said, panicking, "Kick the door in!"

The seconds were ticking past. Luis was composed in the car, his voice steady. "What a fuck up."

The guard kicked at the door again. It strained against the chain, but didn't give way, Anna looking up to the street anxiously. "**Hurry up**! Someone will hear!"

But the door still wouldn't budge, and the seconds kept passing.

Finally, Anna grabbed the man's arm. "We have to go!"

"Not before you get what you came for," Luis warned her from the car. "Don't let me down."

Distraught, Anna turned back to the bodyguard.

"*Kick it! **Harder!*** **Harder!"** She snapped. He struck out at the wood again, the chain finally snapping as the door gave way. Pushing past him, Anna reached the alarm just as it was about to go off, punching in the numbers and holding her breath. A moment passed. Another. Then the humming stopped. Silence. Blissful, thundering silence.

"Now find what you came for," Luis ordered as Anna flicked on a lamp and moved over to the wall behind her desk. There was a mesh cover over the radiator, Anna lifted it off and reached into the darkness. Her face was expectant, than puzzled, bringing the lamp closer and staring into an empty space.

"The book's not here!"

Luis was still in the car, listening on his mobile. "Look again."

"It's not here!" Anna repeated, "I hid it here. He can't have found it!" She paused, thinking. "The cover came off too easily. It was stiff before; I had to struggle to loosen it but just now it came off straight away." She slammed the lamp down angrily, "That little toe rag must have found it! Jesus, why did I tell him I'd got the book?"

"I don't know," Luis replied curtly. "Why did you?"

"You think I made all this up! What purpose would that serve? The expose was my way to get revenge." Her rage faded into disappointment. "I shouldn't have threatened him. Simon knew what would happen if I went public --"

"Went public about what?"

"About him! Simon Porter has his own secrets - like tax dodging for a start." She struggled to calm herself and then noticed some blood on her hands. "Damn it, I must have cut myself."

Looking down, she realised that the carpet around her was also spotted with blood, hearing footsteps approaching as Luis walked into the agency. He looked from her to the floor, then followed the blood trail from the office into the cloakroom, pushing the door open. He immediately closed it before Anna could see what was inside.

"Don't go in," he warned her.

"Like hell I won't!" She said, pushing past him, and then stopping in the doorway.

Simon Porter was sitting on top of the wash hand basin, both wrists slashed. Although dead for a while, blood still dripped from the ends of his fingers, and from under his backside jutted the corner of a piece of A4 paper.

"Jesus…" A strange guttural sound came from her as she backed away, Luis approaching the corpse. Carefully, he leaned the dead man to one side and slid the piece of paper out from under him.

It was the title page of a book.

The Famosa Family
By Kara Famosa.
PART ONE

96

Hatton Cross Underground Station
Piccadilly Line, London

With Purchass leading and Thomas following, they arrived at the underground station and walked down the steps into the shoal of passengers. There was an itchy queue of people waiting to buy tickets, others using the self-service machines, and a man eating a burger by a Fire Escape. Half-hearted evidence of Christmas spotted the concourse; a plastic wreath hung over a staff entrance and moulting pine tree propped up against the tiled wall with a box of cheap decorations at its base. Above the sound of movement and talking came the weary twang of carols. It was hot, too. Men flagged in coats and leather jackets, women with damp faces struggled with bags, a child fractious, refused to go down the escalator. And, in amongst them, stood Purchass, sucking a mint and nudging Thomas with his elbow.

"Her."

"What?"

“That redhead,” Purchass said quietly, both of them watching a woman walk towards the barricade which led to the station beneath. “She’s the one.”

“What are you talking about?” Thomas asked, knowing only too well but praying he was wrong.

He wasn’t.

“We’ll get her tomorrow.”

Thomas could feel his stomach churn, people bumping into him, the music distorted in his head as he glanced at the man beside him and then at the exit. Could he run? Make a break for it? His gaze moved over to the traffic police. Should he tell them? He *could.* He could tell them now, explain everything, and they would have to arrest the freak. Keep him locked up, away from his father, from Kara, and from him.

But if he was locked up, he’d talk.

He would tell them about Sente Fleishman.

And the other killings.

But he wasn’t involved in those! Thomas thought helplessly. He couldn’t give details about Ellie Chadwick’s murder or Kara Famosa’s kidnapping because he was innocent… But who would believe that when his DNA was all over the German nurse? And if the police checked for anyone else’s DNA, Thomas *knew* that Purchass wouldn’t have left anything at the scene. Even if they did believe Thomas’s story, then what? He wasn’t going to escape justice because Purchass would claim that he was his *accomplice.*

Which was is why he was still standing next to Purchass as he chose his next victim.

“D’you like her?”

Thomas said nothing.

“… Soft sod, aren’t you?” Purchass sneered, crunching down on a mint. “I’ve got a barn; we can take her there. String her up and keep her for as long as we like."

He was going to throw up, he knew he was. Thomas could feel the acid on his tongue, the taste of vomit, Purchass catching hold of his arm, his mouth only inches away, the meat breath hot on his skin.

"Relax! Look normal. You don't want to get caught, do you?"

Numb, he looked down at Purchass's hand. It was thick-fingered, coarse, and with dirt under the nails. Hands that mutilated, tortured, and killed. He couldn't spend the rest of his life connected to this man, hounded by him. He couldn't watch his father deteriorate whilst the threat hung over them. He couldn't survive the stress for much longer. Neither of them could.

"Is Kara still alive?"

Shrugging, Purchass stared at him. "Maybe."

Maybe...

Did he *really* think they would kill a woman together? Thomas wondered. A woman with a home, family, and friends. It was madness. He had abducted Kara and was now destroying Thomas's life... But what kind of life was it? He had murdered a woman, too. He was as guilty as the man beside him... No, Thomas told himself, the nurse's murder had been a fluke, a hideous accident. This was different, and he wasn't going to stand by and watch another woman die.

The redhead was crossing the concourse. She was young and slim, passing close by them, glancing over to Thomas as she did so.

He had known before she looked at him that her eyes would be blue.

97

St Martins Lane,
London

Back in his car, a shaken Anna stared blankly ahead. "We should call the police."

"And risk it coming out about the book?" Luis asked, studying her. "Didn't you suspect anything?"

"Why would I? I didn't know he'd kill himself. Jesus," she paused, "you think me threatening him tipped him over the edge?"

"You said he had other problems."

She wasn't listening and carried on. "I just wanted the book; that was the only reason I came back. I wanted revenge, not bloodletting."

Luis leaned forward, giving his driver instructions. The man turned the car around and headed towards Park Lane. "Why did he kill himself?"

"How would I know!"

"Because of what was in the expose?"

"I don't know!" Anna snapped, "I told you; I didn't read it."

Luis loosened and then refastened his watch strap. "Who else knew about the book?"

"I don't know."

"You were fucking Porter; you knew what was going on. Love was never going to get in the way of business, was it?"

She ignored the question, thinking ahead. "The cleaners will find him in the morning. They'll call the police."

"And they'll find your fingerprints everywhere."

"I work there; of course, my prints would be there. What about him?" She jerked her head towards the driver.

"He's wearing gloves."

"What about *you*?"

"I visited the agency recently, that clears me."

Glancing out of the car window, Anna turned her back on him. "Did you touch anything in the cloakroom?"

"Only Porter's body."

She shuddered, a shape in the semi-dark. "There was no one on the street outside. No one saw us enter.

"They could have heard *you* break in –"

"No," she shook her head, "It's just business offic-es above and on either side. Besides, there was too much noise coming from the pub for anyone to hear anything… I think we're OK."

"Why did Simon Porter dump you?"

"He didn't dump me!" Her vanity was still in place. "We had a disagreement, but we made up later. We had sex, actually. Then I went to a private viewing in Mayfair. People can vouch for me. I was there until just before I met up with you. The gallery was stuffed

with people, no one would have noticed that I left or that I've returned."

"You planned this, didn't you?"

She smiled at her reflection in the car window. "I'd love to say I did, but I can't claim any credit. I just came here with you to get the book –"

"*You came alone*, Anna," he interrupted, "You're not the only one with an alibi for tonight."

98

Chelsea Wharf
23rd December

Christmas, Ackermann thought, what an inconvenience. He knew he had to give his staff time off, wish his secretary the season's bloody greetings, and then retire to his house to wait until the pap of the season passed. But it hadn't always been like this, he remembered, for once memory getting the upper hand. When he had been a kid, Christmas was longed for. Poverty didn't seem to affect the meeting up of family, the exchange of petty gifts, or the meals shared.

As rain dribbled down the office windows, Ackermann looked out over London. The view seemed oddly uninspiring, or maybe that was just the weather, with snow predicted again. Up North, the snow used to come down every winter, with its sharp white elbows leaning on the terraced houses, with their outside toilets and coal fires. there was no central heating then, no showers, just a bath in a tub in front of the fire once a week. He had hated getting into the scummy water because his father had always used it first, and then his sister, Miriam, while his mother hung the laundry on a clothes rack overhead.

Ackermann took off his glasses, letting the blurred vision take him away from London and back home to the place he had grown up. A place he had since grown to hate. A place he had left after Miriam died.

A knock on the door disturbed him, Ackermann was surprised to see his lawyer enter. He was expecting the usual Christmas dross, but David wrong-footed him.

"There's been another death."

Ackermann took in his breath. "Another woman?"

"No, Simon Porter."

"Simon Porter?" Ackermann repeated, "Are you sure?"

David nodded. "I've just heard. It's on the news. Apparently, the cleaners found him. He'd committed suicide --"

Ackermann waved him away. "Get out!"

"What?"

"Get out!" He repeated, "I've got a call to make."

But Anna de Souza wasn't taking calls. Her phone was on voicemail. Thoughtful, Ackermann leaned back in his seat. Had Simon Porter *really* killed himself? Or did his cousin have a hand in it? He had heard about her breakup with Porter, but surely, he wouldn't have committed suicide because of that? Ackermann let out a long breath. Had Anna driven Porter to kill himself? No, he decided, blackmail was more her style. So perhaps she had uncovered something about Porter's past and, by extension, *his.*

Grim-faced, Ackermann thought of his last conversation with Luis Famosa and how he had intimated that *he* might have been involved in Miriam's death. Bastard, Ackermann thought, he had some balls coming out with that. But then again, he had also brought up the subject of the expose... Ackermann frowned. The bloody expose hung over all their heads. Had *that* been the reason for Simon Porter's death? He might have tried to control it, pretending to be interested in selling it, but actually making sure it never saw the light of day. Either way, he must have read it - and not said a word to anyone. Not even his old friends who had kept their mutual secret so diligently.

Angry, Ackermann drummed his fingers on his desk, thinking. Perhaps Anna had seen the book and threatened Porter with going public? If so, it meant there was something in the expose which had made Porter prefer death to exposure. If he was right, Ackermann knew what it was. And if Anna knew about it, how long would it stay hidden?

Unnerved, his hand went out to his phone, punching in a number. "Have you heard Simon Porter's committed suicide?"

"Yes," Luis Famosa replied, emotionless, "what about it?"

"Why did he do it?"

"How would I know?"

"It's very convenient, him topping himself. There are a few people who'd have liked to have seen Porter dead. Including you."

"Why would I want him dead?"

"If he had Kara's book that would be a motive," Ackermann replied. "If you killed him, you killed the expose."

"Maybe he didn't have it. Maybe *you* do. Maybe I should kill you?"

"Don't tease, Luis, you're not the type." Ackermann countered. "Porter's death *must* be connected to

Kara's murder. He was handling the expose and now he's killed himself." He paused, thinking aloud. "Why didn't Kara tell you she was writing a book? Or was it just a threat?"

"Could have been."

"You know as well as I do that if Kara *did* write about the past, we're both in the shit."

Luis refused to be drawn and changed the subject. "Your cousin told me something interesting - that you were arrested the day after they found Miriam's body. Did they charge you with her murder?"

Ackermann breathed in, his upper body massive in a heavyweight brown suit. "Watch it, Famosa, you're treading on dangerous ground. That's almost an accusation."

Behind him was the London skyline. His secretary had left for the holidays, as had all the staff on the other floors, all bound for the car park, train station, or underground. On their way to families and friends, to shopping, conversations, arguments, lovemaking. The building would be mute and deserted until the New Year. Empty corridors with nothing but echoes, lifts silent without freight.

Ackermann could sense Famosa on the other end of the line, listening and waiting. He knew he wouldn't back off.

He didn't, instead he repeated the question. "*Did* they charge you with your sister's murder?"

And in his empty office, where he couldn't be seen by his inquisitor, Ackermann nodded.

99

New York
23rd December

Jimmy Famosa had considered telling his father what he was planning but decided against it, choosing not to have Luis on his back. Climbing out of the yellow cab in front of the brownstone, Jimmy paid off the driver and mounted the front steps. Using his key, he let himself in, he then turned off the alarm and stood for a moment in the chilled hallway.

The furniture was webbed in dust sheets, white cotton statues without character, the clock unwound and silent. Obviously, Halle had had no intention of returning. Not for a while, at least. She had slipped into the English countryside instead, with bottles of Chablis and twists of marijuana. They talked over the phone regularly, but at times, she was barely coherent, repeatedly saying Kara's abduction was her fault without explaining why. If she even knew.

Moving on into the kitchen, Jimmy glanced about him. The fridge was empty and cleaned out, the sink shining with not even a drop of water left. Creepy. He had never seen the house like this and could barely recognise it. Before, the rooms had been in constant use as the Famosa's informal work address, with secretaries, PR people, hairdressers, and florists, all coming in and out at different times.

Making for his sister's rooms, Jimmy hurried along the top corridor and paused at Kara's bathroom. The room was unchanged. Her shampoo, cap off, still stood in the shower, a torn pair of tights dangling out of the wastepaper basket. On a glass shelf, make up - with a coating of talcum powder - gathered dust, Kara having scrawled a reminder on the mirror – *get cigarettes* – the words written in electric blue eyeliner. He wondered fleetingly if she had had time to buy the cigarettes. If she had even smoked one before she was snatched.

Closing the bathroom door, Jimmy moved into his sister's bedroom, searching the drawers and cupboards. In her walk-in wardrobe, he took out all her clothes and shoes and felt around the back, knocking on the wood and hoping for the dull reply of a hollow. Nothing. He tried the floorboards, but there were no uneven or lifted boards and he continued into Kara's study.

She had never been a good student and was not a natural academic, so he suspected Kara had been helped in writing the expose for which he was looking. Not the original manuscript - if it existed his sister would have stored that at the bank – but he was hoping to find a copy. It hadn't been on Kara's laptop. He had looked there when she first went missing, but he knew that if she had hidden something, it would be well hidden. Focused, he glanced around, searching in all the usual places, and the unusual. He checked the pockets and linings of her clothes and searched inside her books, among the myriad DVDs and CDs. And found nothing. Her shoes were next, each studied, the heels tried. As he continued, Jimmy became ever more intent on finding something that might be a threat to the Famosas - and the business he had put before his own family.

He turned back to Kara's desk, searched it again, and then paused. After the failed second meeting with the kidnapper, Kara's flight bag was found lying next to the dead pig, splattered with gore; Detective Jameson taking the bag and its contents to be examined. The next day, he emailed both Luis and Jimmy with a list of Kara's recovered possessions. Make up, phone, wallet. But there had been none of her clothes and no Gustav Klimt painting. No rolled-up canvas, no broken frame. No trace of a missing masterpiece. And then Jimmy remembered something else that *hadn't* been there – his sister's flash drive. And Kara had definitely owned one. He remembered it because he had teased her about its Hello Kitty cover.

Hurriedly, he began to search again. Think like your sister, he told himself. If Kara wanted to hide something, where would she put it so none of her family would find it? Or wouldn't want to look? Hopeful, Jimmy moved back to the bathroom, opening the glass-fronted wall cabinet and staring at the medicine bottles, and the packet of contraceptive pills. He picked it up and shook out its contents. One sheet of pills – and a photograph of the Gustav Klimt painting Kara had stolen the day she was abducted.

100

London

Ackermann was staring at the Satsuma vase placed on the mantel above the fireplace in his office. Its symmetry pleased him as he thought of Thomas de Souza's accusation: *"I know your secret; you're Kara's father."*

He was certainly keen to discover who was, Ackermann thought amused, moving over to the vase and gliding it a centimetre to the left. What a blow it would have been when Kara discovered that Luis Famosa wasn't her father, especially since she had once admired the buccaneer Cuban. Then the realisation of her mother's adultery - and the fact that Halle had disguised her deceit for twenty-odd years - would have compounded the betrayal. Passing off another man's child as her husband's had been Halle's masterstroke. Until someone betrayed her.

Sighing, Ackermann reached into his desk drawer and took out a pair of nail scissors. He then pulled on his overcoat and headed for the back stairs, making for the only place he was certain would be open two days before Christmas.

The Chapel of Rest.

101

Maida Vale
London

When Thomas returned, Peter de Souza was sitting in front of the television, blank-faced. He nodded a welcome but waited until he heard the nurse leave before trying to talk.

"Someone - came -"

"What?"

Impatient, he reached for the pad, writing:

Someone was nosing around on the back stairs. I heard him.

Thomas read the note and turned to his father. "When?"

Half an hour ago.

Could it have been Purchass? Yes, Thomas thought, by using the van, he would have had plenty of time to get to the flat before he returned.

Peter reached for the pad again, scribbling hurriedly.

It was him. I saw him through the window when he left. He looked up at me.

Thomas read the words and then glanced back to his father. His eyes were rheumy and moist, his skin waxy as he gripped the pad, a little spittle coming from the corner of his mouth.

"I can work this out, Dad --"

Peter shook his head.

"I can!" Thomas insisted, "and I will."

His father scribbled one word.

How?

"I don't know. Yet." Thomas replied, his voice measured. "Just trust me."

He might have been fooling himself, but not his father, as Peter stared at him, unblinking. Thomas could imagine what he was thinking: that their lives had been hijacked, their futures depending on the whim of a murderer. It wouldn't be over in a month, a year, or a decade. They would be living under a threat forever. Yes, Thomas knew what his father was thinking because he was thinking it, too.

Then he remembered the redhead in the Underground station. She had passed by him within inches, and Thomas had wanted to warn her because she was suddenly Kara, walking towards something terrible, which only he could prevent. But he had said nothing because he couldn't. Instead, he had watched her go. Listened as Purchass mapped out her abduction and death. Listing all the obscenities he – *they* – would commit. Because, as Purchass told him repeatedly, he had no option.

Thomas felt his father's hand resting on his, Peter de Souza watching his son, the writing pad on his lap, pen poised.

He'll never let go of you.

"He will."

Peter scribbled his reply:

No. It's never going to stop.

"I'll stop it!" Thomas snapped, "There must be a way to get us out of this."

Desperate, he put his head in his hands, his face averted from his father. An hour earlier, Purchass had outlined the plan - the abduction to take place on Christmas Day. And so it would get maximum press coverage, he was going to tip off the papers anonymously. Show them that the killer was back. Set up the chase which would lead – as with Ellie Chadwick and Sente Fleishman – to murder, and Thomas was supposed to be part of it.

Had he been a free man, he would have handed himself into the police. But he couldn't abandon his father or Kara because he was afraid of what Purchass would do in retaliation.

Glancing up, Thomas heard the sound of his father's pen moving rapidly over the paper, Peter handing him the notepad.

Only one way out.

Thomas read the words and frowned. "What d'you mean?"

Peter turned back to the pad. There was a long pause, and then he wrote something. But this time, he hesitated before showing Thomas.

"Let me see."

Peter shook his head.

"Come on, Dad, let me see."

He took in a long, laboured breath, then passed the pad to his son. On it, he had written just two words.

Kill him.

102

Chapel of Rest
London

Leaving him to pay his last respects, the undertaker backed out of the private room where Hugh Ackermann stood looking into Simon Porter's coffin. When he was sure the man had gone, Ackermann bent down towards the corpse and stared into the face. Porter had been embalmed, the blood siphoned off, fluid replacing it and pumping up his veins to mimic life. But the embalmer hadn't made allowances for Simon Porter's spectral pallour, he had been too heavy-handed applying the concealer, and now the grey-faced agent looked – Ackermann thought incredulously – like a drag queen.

The fact that Simon Porter was going to be interred in a Catholic cemetery also surprised him, the agent's rejected wife having organised the burial. Either she was very forgiving or glad to see him six feet under. The room was bitterly cold, but Ackermann wasn't staying. Instead, he took out the scissors in his pocket and carefully snipped off the corner of the thumbnail on Simon Porter's left hand. Sliding the clipping into a plastic bag, Ackermann then put it in his pocket just as he heard the door open.

"Is there anything I can get for you, sir?" the undertaker asked. "I know this must be difficult for you. Especially at this time of year." He was all muted concern. "Were you close to Mr Porter?"

Ackermann turned away, his shoulders heaving. Noting his obvious distress, the undertaker watched sympathetically as Ackermann put his handkerchief up to his face and hurried out.

He never thought for a moment he was laughing.

103

Although smarting from his previous comments, Ackermann invited Luis Famosa to his offices in Chelsea Wharf on Christmas Day. It was easy for Ackermann, he had no family, but Luis accepted the invitation like a person who would do anything rather than be alone. If he had already visited Halle, he didn't say, and Ackermann didn't ask, both men drinking expensive scotch under the baleful gaze of an Oscar Kokoschka portrait.

"You do a lot of travelling, don't you? Still, having a private plane helps." Ackermann said, staring at the window of his office and getting to his feet. Still talking, he wet his finger and rubbed a mark on the glass pane. "Mind you, you could still get a DVT, whether you go private or commercial."

Luis Famosa nodded. "I know."

"About DVT's?" Ackermann replied, "Well, it's in all the papers these days… Did you check up on my arrest?"

"You knew I would. You were arrested on suspicion of your sister's murder. Released without charge."

"Because I didn't kill her."

"The murderer was never caught."

"Which means it could still be me?" Ackermann scratched at the mark on the window with his fingernail. "I admit that I'd have killed my sister's murderer if I could have found him. I still will - when I *do* find him.

Sighing, Ackermann moved away from the window and sat down hunched over his desk, his shoulders massive, his face deadpan. "You been talking to Thomas de Souza?"

"Why would I?"

"He thought I was Kara's father! In fact, he was prepared to blackmail me about it." Ackermann said, drily amused. "But he was wrong. Maybe he started wondering if Simon Porter was her father. You know someone tipped Kara off that she wasn't your kid?"

"How d'you know that?"

"Halle told me."

Luis's eyes flickered. "When?"

"A week ago."

"When did you last talk to my wife?"

"A week ago."

"So, you don't know."

"Don't piss about, Luis, know what?"

"Halle's in The Priory –"

Ackermann took in a breath. "The psychiatric place?"

"She's messed up. Back on the booze, tablets, weed, anything and everything. She's feeling guilty."

"For what?"

"A mistake," Luis replied, "Halle made a bad call; *she* tipped off the police at the kidnapper's first meet. She blames herself for not getting Kara back."

"She told you this?"

He nodded. "That's why she's falling apart, can't cope. Imagining things. She even jumped out of a window thinking someone was coming for her." Luis sighed. "We both know Halle was never stable. Too many drugs messed up her mind. And her memory."

"*Her memory*?" Ackermann's eyes were magnified behind his thick glasses. "What did you do to her, Luis?"

"Not what you think."

Confrontational, the two men faced each other, Ackermann the first to speak again.

"Did you *never* suspect that Kara wasn't your daughter?" He leaned back in his seat. "Remember how it was back then? Vegas, when we were younger. Simon Porter was there trying to get work as a literary agent and failing, and I was still hanging around Halle and that artistic crowd we mixed with. Well, the crowd *you* mixed with - I was never accepted, stuck out like a sore thumb – but I was still hoping Halle would turn to me. And when you two broke up, I thought I had a chance. She was distraught, you were fucking your mistress, but she still loved you, not me. Never me. Who could blame her if she took comfort elsewhere?"

"*Took comfort*?" Luis repeated. "With you or Simon Porter? Or others?"

"It's a long time ago and a lot's happened since then."

"A lot," Luis agreed. "So, you don't regret anything?"

Ackermann's expression hardened. "Halle rejected me, I live with it. We all found our own way in life."

"I got rich," Luis replied, "Simon Porter got respectable, Halle became a trophy wife, my son became a money man, and Kara got abducted."

"Was it planned, or merely bad timing?"

"I'm not here for riddles --"

"But this is all a riddle," Ackermann interrupted him, "A riddle that began a long time ago, in the seventies. My sister was popular with the boys - I think that's the expression - and I was her tiresome, protective older brother." He paused; in the distance, someone was ringing church bells. "It was Christmas then, too," he remembered, "She said she was going out for an hour. But she never came back. Her body did. But not Miriam." In silence, Luis let him continue. "After the police found her, they questioned me. I was violent back then. Now, I hire violence if needs be, but I don't personally indulge. They thought I'd overreacted because my sister was promiscuous. But they were wrong. I wouldn't have hurt her."

"Is there a point to this?"

"Anna de Souza was playing with you, Luis, making you suspect me. Crafty bitch. I should know; she's family, after all. I was arrested on suspicion of murdering my sister, but the charges were dropped. I was arrested again for beating up her boyfriend," Ackermann sighed, a walrus in a brown suit. "Pity of it is that I got the wrong man. It turned out he wasn't anywhere near Miriam when she was killed. A few years later, he committed suicide. Or so the story went."

"If he's dead, how could he kill the recent victims and abduct Kara?"

"*If* he's dead," Ackermann said flatly, "but I don't think he is. The murders are too similar, even so long apart, to be the work of two unconnected killers."

"What was the name of the man your sister knew?"

"Dave Kelly."

"*Dave Kelly...*" Luis repeated, then shrugged. "Means nothing to me."

"Me neither," Ackermann agreed, "and I couldn't find anything on a Dave Kelly. No records, no birth certificate, no death certificate. I spent good money trying to track him down, but it turned up nothing. It was like he never existed. Until the other day." Ackermann paused, in no hurry to confide. "Like I say, I've been after the killer for decades and have talked to hundreds of people, police too. Spent money, wasted money on people who tell you anything for a bob or two. Went over every inch of our hometown looking for clues. Found nothing. Then I remembered that the year before she was killed, Miriam had a temporary job in the rag trade district of Manchester. She was only there for a week. But I wondered if it was there that she first met Dave Kelly. So, I went back, turned up some old contacts who remembered those days and asked around. Finally, a woman got in touch." He pointed to the phone as though emphasising the point. "She wanted money, of course."

"For what?"

"To tell me that Dave Kelly had been a packer on Peterloo Street, but only stayed in the job a few days. He was married, which I'd guessed. That's one of the reasons I'd warned Miriam off him --"

"And?"

" --the woman hadn't made the connection when my sister was murdered because Dave Kelly had used a few different names. It was only when she read about the recent killings that something reminded her about Kelly, and she rang me."

"What other names did he use?"

"David Whiting, Patrick O'Hara and Declan Purchass."

"Have you checked up on those?"

"Working on it," Ackermann paused, the city church bells were still ringing in the distance. "It's Christmas, people are off home now so I'm having trouble getting the information."

"Even if Kelly used other names, so what? He's still dead."

"Maybe," Ackermann conceded. "Maybe not. Maybe only Dave Kelly's dead. Maybe Patrick O'Hara - or Declan Purchass - are still alive. Or maybe they had children. The Manchester woman told me something else. Kelly *did* have children. Two at least." Ackermann let the inference do its job.

"Father and son both killers?"

"It's happened before. And it would explain everything, wouldn't it?" Ackermann replied. "Old man dead, son continuing the family business. That's why the killings were so similar, even decades apart."

"Have you told the police?"

"Is that a serious suggestion? I'm not having my search buggered up by the police." Anxious that he had said too much, he glowered at Luis, "Don't even think of muscling in, *I'm* going to catch this bastard."

"I want him as much as you do."

"I doubt that. Kara's only been gone for a month; I've been on the rack for decades." Ackermann took in a breath, uncharacteristically emotional. "The only women I've ever loved – my sister, Halle, Kara – all taken from me."

Luis looked unconvinced. "Why care so much about Kara? You said she's not your child."

"She isn't, but she reminds me of Halle." Ackermann paused, reverting to his previous theme. "After Miriam was killed, nothing happened for years. There were murders, yes, but no victims with their eyes mutilated. Then Ellie Chadwick was killed in *exactly* the same way my sister was. And then Kara was taken. It all happened within weeks, and all the women had the same bright blue eyes. Unusual enough for people to comment."

Luis stared into his glass of whisky. "The kidnapper cut off Kara's finger, he didn't damage her eyes."

"You know that for sure?" Ackermann replied shortly, "D'you even know if she's still alive? He didn't take the ransom; what's that about? Because he didn't have a living victim anymore? Or because he wasn't *supposed* to take the money?"

Luis glanced up from his glass. "You think Kara was kidnapped for a reason?"

The question ricocheted around the room. "*Was she*?"

"You tell me."

"There's only one reason it could be," Ackermann's voice was steady, but his heart rate was speeding up, "to stop the book being published --"

Luis shrugged. "Could be."

"—and if she *was* taken deliberately, it would have been organised by someone with a lot to lose. Someone who was exposed in the book."

"Like you."

"Like you." Ackermann countered. "After all, Kara isn't your daughter; there's no bond now. You might even welcome her absence to get back at the wife who cheated on you." He continued steadily. "But there are other candidates. What about Halle? You told me she called the police, perhaps it wasn't to help her daughter, but to keep her secret. Or maybe it was Simon Porter, with the help of my bloody cousin." He shook his head, "No, Porter's out of it now. So, what about Jimmy? Your son's done a lot of shit-shifting for you, hasn't he? Even gave up his family for the business. Perhaps he didn't like the idea of being exposed by his *half-sister*."

"If there *is* an expose."

"If there is, how many of the Famosa secrets are in it? Iffy financial dealings, the Las Vegas casino, the property, the hotel, your art collection, plus the gallery in New York. All those paintings you've sold and auctioned – and all those rumours about forgeries." Ackermann's voice remained a monotone. "You were lucky there, Luis. Your associate went to jail on your behalf, but there are still rumours doing the rounds. I see them on the internet. And now a lot of people are wondering if this kidnapping is fake – pretty much like the Gustav Klimt painting that Kara stole."

Luis didn't rise to the bait. "You think it's a forgery?"

"I'd bet my life on it," Ackermann replied, "and Kara knew it; that's why she took it, as leverage to pressurise you."

"If only she'd been that clever," Luis smiled without warmth, "I could have done with someone that smart. No, she took the Klimt for spite," he emphasised the word *spite*. "Like writing the book to spite me."

Ackermann sensed a chink in the Cuban's armour and pushed hard. "*Did* you have her abducted to shut her up?"

"No, but I wish I had," Luis replied, rising to his feet and looking down at Ackermann. "Halle has an excuse to be forgetful, her brain's addled, but yours isn't." His tone became warning, "Don't threaten me. We made a deal in the past, and we've stuck to it because it worked. So, we carry on the same way--"

"And what happens if the book *is* published?"

"It can't be published if it never turns up. It's missing, like Kara," Luis shrugged, "Maybe neither of them will ever be found."

104

Purchass was worrying about Thomas de Souza. Could he *really* trust him? Even threatening his father, taunting him with Kara, could he stop blog boy panicking? Kicking open the back door, Purchass stomped down the steps and walked towards the barn. Snow was due any time. A white Christmas, he thought, staring across the yard to where a cat foraged in amongst the hedgerows. She was intent, digging away, scratching at the earth as Purchass walked over. Kicking the animal out of the way, he bent down, looking into the hole, a pair of broken glasses glinting in the light. Kat's glasses, peering up at him from the dead earth.

What the fuck are you looking at, freak?

Purchass jumped, startled by her voice, then hurriedly reburied the glasses and moved on into the barn. His sister had taught him all about sex but nothing about affection. She might have touched him, but she would just as easily scratch his back or pull out a chunk of his hair. Bitch passion, she had called it. Bitchy, bitch passion.

'*You'll never want another woman.*'

I hate you, Kat.

'Sure you do,' she'd replied, fat and white as unmade bread.

'Sure you do...'

Weighing the rope in his hands, Purchass flung it over the beam in the barn and tied it fast. Couldn't have his new toy slipping off, could he? A smell came to him, the smell of unwashed clothes and sour breath. But it wasn't him this time. It was Kat.

'Tie it tighter, she'd insisted, can't touch the ground.

Feet should swing. Tie it right!'

I am doing.

'Get ready,' she'd sneered,

'I haven't got all day.'

The rope swung in front of him as it had in the past, Purchass looking up. His gaze moved along the rafters above the hay loft. Empty now, only a stack of pornographic magazines and a tin of old biscuits. He had liked it up there, in a spot where he could look down and watch the rope and what was on the end of it. He would read a little, then eat his biscuits. Digestive, plain. Chocolate made him fart.

The rope had been pressed into service for so long, that part of it was wearing thin. Kat had warned him about that and told him to make sure it didn't snap when he was least expecting it. It was old rope; Purchass had told her we should get new. But she had said it was a waste of money and grumbled about being bored.

A little while later, she decided that she wouldn't go out and asked Purchass for money. He gave what he had, and she made some comment about him being a mean fucker. Then she'd gone into the barn and put the rope around her neck, and he had gone behind her and started lifting her up. Just enough, her toes still touching the dirt ground, and Kat had sighed and played with her breasts, glancing up at him in the hay loft where he climbed to get a better view. And that electric stare, freed from her glasses, that blue heat of her eyes, had fixed on his. She was all white blubber. At the end of a rope, like a seal at the end of a fishing line. Ugly, her hem riding up over her cottage cheese thighs, her clothes yellow with old sweat. Hanging like a side of bad pork.

'Let me down, freak. I want my money.'

For what? He had wondered. What was she going to spend it on? Besides, she had money from men all the time. It should be a freebie for her brother. He could imagine what she'd say about Thomas.

'Get rid, he's a liability.

Get rid; he'll get you if you don't.

He wants the girl back.

Yes, her! The girl with eyes like mine.'

Then the memory faded, Purchass jolted as he heard a sudden noise coming from above, and then he saw her, Kat – his missing sister, Kat - sitting on the edge of the hay loft, looking down at him. She was crooning, pointing to the sleeping girl below, Kara Famosa, curled up under a stinking blanket. Confused, Purchass stared up at his sister. Her eyes seemed startling, ridiculously blue; her head tilted to one side.

'Lo there.'

He nodded, like he was facing a judge. "Kat?"

'Do him in.'

"What?"

'Blog boy.'

"He's my scapegoat."

'Get rid of him. You're a fucking idiot, get rid.'

"But I need him."

'What about her, moron? What are you going to do with ***her?***

She'll never take my place.'

She was laughing, swinging her legs.

'None of them can ever take my place.'

"You're not real," Purchass whimpered, "you're not real…"

'Fuck you, freak. Fuck you!'

He ran out of the barn then without looking back, just as he had done that boiling summer day when he had left his sister hanging from the rope. Toes pointing to the floor. He'd loosened the rope and watched it slide over the rafter.

But when he came back, she had wet herself and was swinging limply with a broken neck.

105

THE GOAT'S INN
London

If Carol Humber's husband had warned her not to say another word to the police, the other witness was more than eager to talk. She was sorry, she explained, but she'd been away for a few days.

"I wished you'd stayed in touch," Detective Sandley said, trying not to be curt, "I didn't know you were leaving London."

"Sorry, I didn't think to mention it," she shrugged, her thin shoulders wrapped in a cheap jacket. "It was only when I came back that I found out the police were looking for me."

"It's fine," Detective Sandley continued, voice tight, "When we last spoke, you said that you thought you could identify the man you saw here the night Sente Fleishman was killed –"

"Yeah, I think I could," she agreed, "but maybe I was wrong."

"Wrong? Why would you say that?"

"He wasn't anything like that Identikit picture you put out. I saw it on the internet and thought maybe I'd was confused, and the other witness was right –"

"No, you weren't wrong!" Detective Sandley interrupted quickly. "That was *her* impression, but that doesn't mean it was accurate. People see things differently. That's why I'm asking you to work with us to do another Identikit image."

"Like I said before," the thin girl replied, I'll do what I can to help."

Rising to his feet, Sandley took the girl's details, thanked her, prayed a little, and hoped a lot. After the failure of the first Identikit, he had thought he had nothing, but now there was another witness. Someone who could identify Sente Fleishman's killer.

At last, Sandley thought to himself, they were getting somewhere.

-o0o-

Motionless, Thomas had stared at the latest headline glaring out from his laptop screen.

> ***...New witnesses able to identify the man last seen with murder victim, Sente Fleishman...***

There was a new witness who could give him away... Thomas slumped into a chair, reading the headline. But there had been nothing else, no mention if it was a man or a woman, just that they had seen him the night the nurse was murdered. They had talked to the police, were doing a new Identikit, and within hours they would be drawing media interest - because even if their name wasn't mentioned in the headline, it wouldn't stay secret for long. And if the Identikit looked like Thomas de Souza, his life was destroyed.

So, in the twelve hours since the news broke, Thomas changed his appearance. Because *this* time, the witness might have seen him, and the Identikit might splash his face across the media and internet, a million nosy onlookers reporting sightings and he couldn't run or leave the UK. he couldn't leave his father helpless, and Kara abandoned. He was pinned like an insect, wriggling but not free. Waiting for the new Identikit to be flashed up on the news or for the police to arrive at the door.

He had cut his hair short, almost to the scalp, hadn't shaved, and kept his clothes inconspicuous. Jeans, t-shirt, hoodie. But he couldn't do anything else except wait for Purchass to get in touch. Without contact with him, he was stuck in limbo whilst a criminal decided his fate. While he waited for the Identikit to be published, Thomas stayed home, going out late to get food and avoiding his regular supermarket. No one took notice of a man trudging, head down against the bitter winter weather, but Thomas was alert. Avoiding eye contact, he skirted crowds, knowing that walking amongst them might be the kidnapper, waiting to make his move. Perhaps crossing the road, perhaps on the street outside. Or maybe he would track Thomas to an alley, attack him in some underpass, or drive a knife into him as he waited to cross at the lights. Was he on foot? Or driving? Was he distant? Or close?

Would he see the bastard coming?

On edge, Thomas studied the shoppers around him, the condensation on the supermarket's windows blurring the view outside. It didn't matter; he knew he had nowhere to run. The police would publish the Identikit, and then he would have a target on his back.

Unless he outwitted them.

And forced the kidnapper to show his hand.

106

Chelsea Wharf
London

Ackermann was reading the latest newspaper account when his phone rang, his secretary immediately putting Thomas through.

"What d'you want?"

"I didn't do it."

Slowly, Ackermann levered himself upright in his chair. "Didn't do what?"

"I didn't murder the nurse, Sente Fleishman. I'm not the killer. I was set up."

"Who set you up?"

"The man who killed and mutilated her; the man who kidnapped Kara."

At last, Ackermann thought, at last. "Who is he?"

"I don't know –"

"Christ, de Souza, stop wasting my bloody time!"

"**Why don't you listen**!" Thomas shouted, "The kidnapper's been following me, he was watching me that night, saw me meet the nurse in the pub, and he saw what happened afterwards."

"Which was?"

"She wanted me to stay with her. I was drunk, and when she kept on at me and grabbed my arm, I pushed her away. I didn't mean to hurt her, but she was also drunk and lost her footing. Her head struck a bollard," Thomas paused, reliving the moment and realising how it sounded. "I didn't mean to kill her, but he saw what happened –"

"There are witnesses."

I know."

"One of them is called Carol Humber. She's an office worker. Her husband has told her to keep her mouth shut. That's why the Identikit doesn't look anything like you --"

Stunned, Thomas took a moment to reply. "How d'you find that out?"

"I find everything out, sooner or later. The other witness is called Kim Shaw. She's pretty mouthy. If she says she saw you, she'll tell everyone," Ackermann cleared his throat, "You're in trouble. But then I think you know that."

"I've told you; it was an accident!"

"So go to the police."

"That's your advice!" Thomas snapped, "They'll lock me up. Get the witnesses in, gather together all the evidence they have about Sente Fleishman, find out Kara dumped me, and that I was asking about Ellie Chapman up in Manchester. I'd look like a pretty good suspect then, wouldn't I? Even if I managed to convince them I was innocent, it would take weeks, whilst the real killer's free." He paused. "You know more than you're letting on. Tell me what you know!"

"I don't know anything for sure. Yet."

Exasperated. Thomas pushed him, "Look, I'm not ringing to cry on your bloody shoulder, but you said you wanted the man who killed your sister. At least, that's one reason you're after him–"

"What's *that* supposed to mean?"

"Come off it! You're not trying to find Kara because you're such a good friend of the family. You've got your own motives, and I'm guessing Kara put some of them in that book."

He could hear Ackermann's breathing accelerate and waited for him to reply. When he didn't speak, Thomas continued, "I know who the killer is and who abducted Kara. The same man who framed me. And if you want him, I can give him to you." Ackermann remained silent at the end of the line, Thomas sighing, "I haven't told Luis Famosa. You don't want him in on this, do you? You two are rivals; I'm betting you're working together. Am I right?"

"We might be pooling our resources –"

"You've got information, haven't you?" Thomas interrupted him. "I'm risking my life; you can give me a name at least."

Ackermann was about to refuse, then changed his mind. Why not let de Souza take hold of the rope if he could hang the kidnapper with it? "There were three men, three names, I'm looking into - David Whiting, Patrick O'Hara and Declan Purchass."

"*And?*"

"I've just got the results from my investigators; no records on David Whiting or Patrick O'Hara – they were fake names – but Declan Purchass *was* real. Career criminal, violent, suspected of murder, but nothing proved."

"And?"

"He's dead."

The blow hit Thomas hard. "What about family?"

"Two, maybe three children, but none I could trace. There's only so much information a lot of money can buy."

"But people don't just disappear –"

"Want to bet on that?" Ackermann replied sardonically, "They could be alive or dead. They could live in another country or live off-grid somewhere under a different name –"

"Not if any of them had a job."

"You think your serial killer has a job?" There was a dry laugh down the phone. "As what?"

"He could be a casual worker –"

"Like Santa Claus at Christmas?" Ackermann sneered. "Who cares what his real name is? I just need my hands on him."

"Because of Kara or the book?" Thomas asked, hurrying on without giving Ackermann time to reply, "I can trap him for you."

"You're going to risk yourself just to help me out?"

"No, because I need you, and you want that book." Thomas replied, "which you'll only get it if we get Kara back. And that's only possible if we can catch the man who's got her. *I* can make that happen. *I* can trap him."

"Why should I believe you? You could be lying. You could be coming after *me."*

"Why? What have you done? Whatever it is, I don't care." He could feel Ackermann wavering on the other end of the line and persisted. "I need your support, your backup. You help me, and I help you. We get Kara home, and you get the book." His temper flared. "Come on, Ackermann, stop pissing about! I'm offering you a deal you can't refuse."

107

Stubbing out his roll-up, Purchass narrowed his eyes. Shit, de Souza was clever; he had even fooled him for a while when he first left the house. All the hair and expensive clothes were gone, blog boy was just one other sap in the crowd. Which made him damn near unrecognisable… Purchass clenched his teeth, anxious that he might have been outwitted. Would the second witness now recognise the transformed de Souza as the man in the pub? They would all know soon enough when the police published the new Identikit. And even if the disguised de Souza managed to make everyone think twice, people *would* recognise him. He was handsome, Purchass thought meanly, people remembered good-looking men.

Hands deep in his pockets, he was sucking a peppermint as he followed Thomas towards the Underground station. Where the fuck did he think he was going now? Purchass wondered, standing by a newsstand and watching as Thomas crossed the concourse and headed towards the public toilets. They were under renovation, the frontage covered in scaffolding and sheeted with white plastic, thick enough to obscure whatever was going on behind it.

Ducking under the cover, Purchass called out: “Hey, de Souza!”

Thomas immediately stopped walking. “Where are you?”

“Stay there,” Purchass watched him do as he was told, “Good boy. This is a good spot, no one can see us here.” He moved closer. “Now lift up your hands –”

“What?”

“I’m going to take the mobile out of your jacket. The one you thought you were going to record me on.” He reached into Thomas’s pocket and took the phone, his voice friendly. “That’s better, I can relax now. You’re in deep shit, aren’t you? Not only does everyone think that *you* killed those women, but soon your face will be all over the news.” He could see Thomas move and step back. “*Stop jiggling about!* I’m armed, just in case you think you might have a go at being a hero --”

“Why did you do it?” Thomas interrupted him. “Why set me up?”

“Because I could. Because even with all your advantages, *you’re* the one on the run now, not me… By the way, nice job on the hair.”

“I could go to the police –“

“No, you couldn’t, or you’d have done it already.” Purchass retorted, “Besides, there’s a new witness who’ll identify you.”

“I could tell the police about you --”

“What about me? You don’t know who I am, what I look like, or where I live. You go telling the police about me, and they’ll think I’m just a figment of your

imagination," he laughed at the phrase, "that you're just trying to cover up your crimes."

"*They aren't my crimes!* I would never hurt Kara --"

"I believe you. I read what you wrote about her in your blog. But she *did* dump you, didn't she? And that would count as a motive." Purchass put another mint in his mouth and looked around. "You should keep your voice down, or we'll be overheard. And then what? No one to look after Daddy then, hey?"

"The new witness -"

"The one who saw you?"

"Maybe they saw *you.*"

"We played this game before. *You* were the one with the nurse in the pub --"

"But you were outside, where you could have been seen." Purchass was listening, unsettled, as Thomas kept talking, "Maybe someone saw *you* in the alley-way? Why are you so certain it was *me* they saw? It could just as easily have been you."

"It was you –"

"Maybe, or maybe not, " Thomas retorted, "we're both going to find out soon enough."

108

Pushing past the lawyer, Anna de Souza stormed into Ackermann's office, David Gates following behind. "I'm sorry, sir, the lady was most insistent –"

"Yes, she usually is," Ackermann replied dryly, "Leave us."

Having spent several minutes bending to examine a chinoiserie fire screen, Ackermann straightened up with difficulty, his bulk impeding his movements as he ambled behind his desk. "What the hell do you want, cousin?"

"*The police are after my son!*" Anna said, flinging a copy of the Evening Standard onto the desk in front of him. On the front page was the new police Identikit. "Look, it's Thomas, it describes him, and they've got his name --"

"That part's new."

Her eyes fixed on him, her voice shrill. "*New?* What are you talking about?"

"If you paid a bit more attention to your son, you'd know," Ackermann replied, curious to hear what Anna had to say. "The police are looking for Thomas de Souza because they suspect him of being involved in the deaths of two women and the abduction of Kara Famosa."

Stunned, it took her a moment to recover. "*Thomas?* Are you mad? My son's not a killer!" She sat down, frantically reading the article, then throwing the paper to one side. "The nurse was mutilated! He couldn't do anything like that! He's not the type --"

"He has your genes, Anna, and Christ knows you're the type."

"You really think Thomas could kill?"

"It doesn't matter what I think, it's down to the police." Ackermann lifted his right hand, counting off the fingers. "One, there was a note found in Sente Fleishman's bag. It was short and to the point – *Thomas de Souza, The Goat's Inn pub at 11.00* - Two, Thomas was seen that night with the nurse. Three, the other victim's eyes were mutilated in the same way hers were. Four, Kara was mutilated –"

"You're mad!" Anna exploded, "he loves Kara –"

"But their affair didn't work out, did it? She dumped him. Maybe he took it badly, brooded on it," Ackermann replied, leading her on, "What if Kara broke his heart? That's a motive, if ever I heard one --"

"Thomas isn't capable of killing anyone, let alone Kara. My son was the one who was negotiating for her release. He even went to meet the kidnapper after Jimmy Famosa buggered it up –"

"Ah, but Thomas didn't find Kara's body, did he? Just a dead pig," Ackermann took off his glasses and began to polish them with his handkerchief, "and despite his heroics, he didn't catch the kidnapper. Unless…"

"What?"

"... Thomas killed Kara and then staged the pig thing." Ackermann was enjoying himself, tormenting his cousin, the woman who had previously tried to dupe him. "Be honest, everyone knows your son's had a run of bad luck and lost everything. But Thomas is clever enough to find a way out. He might be over-emotional, and we all know he has a temper --"

"What are you suggesting?"

"He's disgraced, broke. Think about it, Anna; it would have been a very smart move. He could have kidnapped Kara and then gone to New York to comfort Halle and throw suspicion off himself --"

"And leave Kara behind somewhere? *Don't be bloody stupid*!"

"Maybe he had an accomplice?" Ackermann countered, pausing. "You're wondering now, aren't you, Anna? Your son went from being a big hitter to an abject failure overnight. It could turn a man's mind something like that." He could see her confidence falter as he continued, "His life's fucked up, and you left him to nursemaid Peter de Souza like some bloody servant –"

"This isn't my fault!"

"Nothing ever is!" Ackermann roared, "Did you plan the abduction together?"

She stared at him, dumbfounded. "Don't talk nonsense! I'm not a criminal and neither is Thomas --"

"So why has he disappeared?"

"He's gone?" The words shook her, *"Thomas abandoned his father?"*

Ackermann nodded. "Yes. Your husbands in hospital being looked after whilst your son goes on the run.

"I DON'T BELIEVE IT!" Anna cried frantically. "Thomas wanted to marry Kara; he wouldn't hurt her. He wouldn't hurt *anyone*."

Ackermann pointed to the newspaper.

"We'll know the truth when they catch him, won't we? In the meantime, get ready, Anna, because soon you're going to have all the publicity you've ever craved. Think of the press interest in you and your family," he watched the colour leave her face, "if you play clever and keep businesslike you can make a killing – if you forgive the expression. I mean, Simon Porter's dead, so now *you* can sell the film rights, the book, etc. They'll all be up for grabs - and at the same time everyone will want to know *all* about the mother of a serial killer."

"You bastard!"

Amused, he put up his hands. "I think you should go to ground, Anna, hide away somewhere."

"You really think I'm going to abandon my son?"

"Why not?" Ackermann replied, "You've got form."

109

One down. One to go.

Tucking himself into a doorway, Thomas punched out a number on his phone, the station clock reading 10.15pm.

It was answered immediately. "Hello?"

"It's Thomas de Souza."

A moment's pause. "Where are you?"

"I know who he is. The man who killed those women and kidnapped Kara. I know who he is," Thomas flinched as a pedestrian brushed into him, almost knocking the phone out of his hand. "Are you still there?"

Luis Famosa was hanging on every word. "Yeah, so who is he?"

Thomas ignored the question. "Look at www.santaslaughter.com, he's advertising the next killing. And he wants me to help him."

"Help him do what?"

"Murder," he paused, wondering if Famosa would speak, but when he didn't, Thomas continued, "He'll kill me if he finds out I'm setting him up."

"Walk away from it."

"I can't. He's forcing me to do what he wants, or he'll kill Kara and go after my father. I need your help to stop him."

"How d'you know it's the right man?"

"He's got Kara, the book, *and* the painting."

There was silence on the line, Thomas wondering if he had overplayed his hand. Had Ackermann already contacted Famosa and told him that *he* had been approached? Thomas had been banking on their mutual distrust; both men wanted the killer for their own reasons. But were they allies now?

"Go to the police."

"I can't," Thomas replied. "You wanted to catch the kidnapper; I'll give him to you. But you have to help me."

"Where are you?"

"Piccadilly Circus."

"Is he with you?"

"No. I'm meeting him later, at 11.30pm, Ealing Broadway. He wants us to snatch the woman tonight."

"What woman?"

"He's got his next victim lined up, a redhead. He thinks I'm going along with it, but if he finds out I've spoken to you I'm finished." Thomas was talking fast, rallying Luis to action, "I'm going to Ealing Broadway now. Get over here as quick as you can."

"And if I don't?"

Thomas took in a long breath. "If you don't, Luis, I'll know who organised Kara's kidnapping."

110

When the phone rang it took a few seconds for Purchass to answer. He was disorientated, unnerved by what he had just witnessed in the barn: his sister sitting on the mezzanine, watching the sleeping American girl. His sister, Kat. So, Kat *was* back. Kat was watching. Always Kat.

"What d'you want?"

"I was wondering about the redhead," Thomas answered, "maybe we *should* go after her."

"I thought you didn't like the idea."

"I do now. Now I've had a chance to think about it."

Purchass paused, how strange that as soon as he had mused about getting rid of de Souza, his potential victim was having a change of heart. *Or maybe his sister was wrong*? Purchass thought triumphantly. Maybe Kat had it all wrong. Like the length of rope. All wrong.

"This won't change anything, you know."

"How d'you mean?"

"You're still my puppet. You do what I want. For as long as I want."

"Yeah," Thomas agreed, "but remember, you need me."

Purchass reacted violently. *"How the fuck d'you work that out?"*

"I'm the only person that knows about you -"

" - and I'm the only person who knows about you."

"We need each other."

"Maybe. Or I could kill you." Purchass replied, unnerved by Thomas's unexpected volte-face.

"*Why* would you kill me? You wanted a partner. Well, now you've got one."

Purchass was caught off guard. "I don't get it."

"Like you say, you have the upper hand. I don't want to die, so I might as well agree to what you want."

Thomas's voice was abrupt and challenging. But Purchass was too wily to believe his sudden change of heart, and tried to feel him out. "This is a bit sudden. I don't buy it –"

"Buy *what*?" Thomas countered. "The nurse's death was an accident. Now I want to know what it would feel like if I meant it. If I *really* killed a woman."

"I kill her."

"OK, OK," Thomas agreed, "You kill her, I'll help."

A soft laugh came down the line, Purchass amused. "You're a fucking liar."

"*What!"*

"You're not really up for it, you just want to make sure I don't come for you or your father."

"You could have done that already," Thomas replied, "You could have killed me after the nurse's murder. But you didn't, you framed me instead, which left you in the clear. You didn't kill me because you wanted something from me. Like you do now." Purchass didn't reply, forcing Thomas to continue. "You still want the redhead?"

"Yeah…"

"You know where to find her?"

"Yeah. Go on the web in a couple of minutes and you'll see it."

"What?"

"Look at the website www.santaslaughter.com." Purchass was mirthful. "You get it? It reads two ways – either Santa Slaughter or Santa's Laughter. Talk about clever."

He could hear the shock in Thomas's voice. "You've put it up online?"

"Yeah, I've advertised it. *'A killing will be committed tonight, by the same man who murdered Ellie Chapman and Sente Fleishman and kidnapped Kara Famosa.*" He laughed, knowing that Thomas would feel the rope tightening around his neck. "And no one knows it's me."

"I'm announcing *my* next performance?"

Purchass was excited, geared up. "Seems so. How are you liking it, being a fugitive? I saw the Identikit, it's a good likeness of you. Should get you found quick –"

He could sense Thomas's antagonism. "So do we go after the redhead?"

"Why the hurry? You're on the run –"

"To where! Where can I go?" Thomas snapped. "You've got me over a barrel, and I know it… I'll help you and do what you say, in return for you helping me."

Taken aback, Purchass hesitated. "What the fuck are you talking about?"

"I tell you that *after* we kill the redhead."

"After?"

"Yes, after."

Purchass paused, thinking, then finally agreeing. "Are we going to do it?"

"Yes," Thomas agreed, "but on one condition, I want to talk to Kara first."

"Piss off!"

"Just let me talk to her and then I'll do whatever you want," Thomas hurried on, his voice urgent, "Please let me talk to her. Is she there?"

"Yeah."

"So let me talk to her. Or have you killed her?"

Purchass laughed down the line, leaving the house and heading for the barn, the phone connection intermittently breaking up, then finally a woman's voice. Hesitant, nervous.

"*What d'you want*?"

Hearing her voice, Thomas shouted out to her: "**Kara!** It's me, it's Thomas, can you hear me?"

Purchass was watching her, crying, sobbing, and gripping onto the phone.

"Come and get me, please, Thomas, *I'm afraid*." her voice faltered, dropped almost to a whimper. "If anything happens, don't forget me. Keep the last photo I gave you… please don't leave me here," She was shaking, openly weeping with Purchass getting impatient.

"**That's enough!"** he snapped, cutting the connection, and turning his attention back to Thomas. "You got what you wanted, now give me what I want."

He could sense Thomas's anger down the line. "Where are we meeting?"

"Oh no, I'll come for you." Purchass said firmly, "Eleven o'clock, Ealing Broadway Station. Don't be late."

111

He could hear her voice repeating in his head, Kara talking, alive. Then he thought of what she had said:

> *'... I'm afraid. If anything happens, don't forget me. Keep the last photo I gave you ...'*
> 'Keep the last photo I gave you.'

Thomas had known that when the Identikit was published, he would be a marked man and had organised some supplies. Having packed some food and money in a holdall, he had been about to leave home when he moved back into his room and pulled open the drawer of the bedside table, taking out a small suede photo case. Inside was an image of Kara taken only months before. He had received it unexpectedly through the post, the gift confusing him as it was not for any anniversary he could remember. Had Kara just sent it as a memento? Perhaps, but then again mementos weren't really Kara's style.

Thomas looked at the photograph case again, remembering her words over the phone: '*... don't forget me...Keep the last photo I gave you...*'

He turned the case over in his hands; soft, pliable suede, the frame gold, with the initials **KF** imprinted on it. Abducted, injured, and fearing for her life, why would she have mentioned something as trivial as a photograph?

His hands moved slowly around the casing, taking out the picture and finding nothing. But she *was* telling him something, Thomas knew, running his fingers over the suede and then pausing over the embossed initials. Reopening the case, he tore back the lining. And there, hidden under the **KF** initials, he drew out a tiny metal object that, for a moment, he couldn't identify. Then he realised what it was - a miniature, state-of-the-art memory stick.

A sudden noise outside startled him, Thomas put the memory stick into his inner pocket and ran down the stairs, avoiding the front entrance and instead headed for the back door. Checking that there was no one on the road who might see him, he hurried out into the rain, head down, making his way away from his home and into the crowded anonymity of the city streets.

112

Purchass ran over the preparations in his mind. The barn was ready. He had the rope, the bucket, and the sticky tape. No screaming. He couldn't take the screaming. He hoped blog boy wasn't going to turn out to be a disappointment. He was enjoying taunting him, just like he was enjoying the reaction to his online posting.

The police were playing it down about the internet posting, just muttering about a lunatic making mischief. *Making mischief,* Purchass liked that, sounded old-fashioned, almost childish. But soon, the predicted murder would be real. He'd start with the abduction, might even post some footage of the victim tied up in the barn. He liked that idea and found it stimulating, because this time he was going to spin it out and having an audience would just add to it. He'd make sure that he didn't show her face, naturally. Wouldn't make it easy for people to recognise her, for some other fucking family to come after him.

He could imagine Luis Famosa reading about the predicted murder. Foiled again, Purchass thought, smirking. That bloody Cuban and his dumb son didn't have a clue who he was. Both of them running around and finding out nothing. '*No bloody good being rich if you're thick as shit* ' his old man used to say.

He thought of his father, remembering Declan Purchass and the sounds coming from the barn, the sounds that his mother dismissed. He remembered Kat watching through the slats in the side, and the noise of the frightened horses whinnying and kicking out at the decrepit stalls.

No one dared to go near to the barn then. Not when the old man was alive. His brother Sean had been a teenager and was allowed in sometimes, Kat sucking her fingers as she watched. But not Purchass; and he had so wanted to know what was going on in there. His mother had died the previous winter, Declan was left with nothing and no one to fear. So, he went feral. All of them living off grid, on their wits. He beat all his kids, but that wasn't enough. He went to prossies, but that wasn't enough; and before long he was taking what he used to pay for. His weight plunged, a chest cold turning into pneumonia.

Purchass wanted him dead. They all did. He sat on the old couch in the kitchen and coughed up phlegm, wiping it on the arms of the sofa when he ran out of cloths. His face narrowed, cheeks inverted cupolas, eyebrows drawn down over his eyes, a knife always in his belt.

Terrified, Purchass avoided his father and skirted the barn. At night, he put his head under the pillow to smother the sounds because they always came in the dark. He dreamed of escape, wary around his siblings, wondering if one day he would end up in the barn himself, in the hateful wooden building where the women disappeared. Or in one of the fields, buried under sodden lumps of earth.

Useless fuck, Kat had screamed.

Useless, useless, ugly fuck.

There had been three of them in the farmhouse that winter. The two strongest bullying the weakest. Purchass tried to keep to his room, ignoring the sounds from the barn at night. Moans and whimpers into the early hours. From his siblings came the sly looks, whispers that he would be next. He wasn't strong enough, they said, nothing more than a puny kid. The runt of the family. But at the end of the winter only one of them remained.

The derelict farm Purchass inherited had long ceased being a working property. He left it to ruin, and nature obliged. The barns became decrepit, the lane leading to the property so overgrown that there was only a narrow access left, tucked amongst elder trees that had grown high, buckled, and knotted together in a hard arch. There had never been other properties close by - because of a problem with flooding and because it was so remote - so the Purchasses had outlived their neighbours long ago. As the elder trees grew and the encroaching vegetation enveloped the farm, Purchass came and went like a mirage. He paid no tax, no cheques were passed, no Giros collected, nothing to prove he was a living man.

But the silence played tricks on him, and through an old, criminal contact of his father Purchass had got casual work in Heathrow, sliding under the radar, no questions asked. Once, he *was* pulled aside, but the fake papers served their purpose. Besides, his foreman paid him a pittance and always in cash. Dispossessed amongst the myriad travellers and staff, Purchass had turned the airport into his fantasy hunting ground. The place where he could watch and choose who would go back to the blasted farmhouse.

Purchass looked at his watch.

Meet blog boy at 11.30.

Ealing Broadway station.

A hunting we will go…

113

Just as Ackermann got into his Jaguar, Thomas moved forward and grabbed the door handle. "The meet's now at 159, Dover Street," he said, talking rapidly, "It's a building site. He's got it all planned. Look on www.santaslaughter.com – he's advertising the next killing."

"Confident bastard."

"You've got no news? No name?

"Like I told you, it's Christmas, and no one's working."

Thomas was still holding the car door open. "We can trap him, but I can't do alone; I need backup. You want him, so come and get him." Cautious, he looked round at the deserted car park, anxious that he hadn't been seen. "*Don't* let me down –"

"What time are you meeting him?"

"11.30pm. He's bringing the woman with him."

"Who is she?"

"A redhead he picked out the other day."

"You said you had something else for me."

Thomas nodded, thinking of what he had read on Kara's memory stick. All the secrets she had accumulated, germs of deceit and lies, a hot house, festering, stewing, secret history. "Yes, I've got something for you."

"What is it?"

"Kara's expose," he could see Ackermann flinch, putting out his hand.

Immediately Thomas stepped back. "No chance. You only get it if you help me. So don't let me down."

"As if I would," Ackermann replied dryly, reaching into his pocket for a brown envelope and handing it to Thomas.

Cautious, he looked at it. "What's that?"

"Compliments of the season. I'm glad I got the chance to see you. I might have missed giving it to you later." Ackermann jerked the car door free, Thomas ducking back behind a concrete pillar, his voice low.

"He thinks I'll help him murder the girl, but I'm not killing anyone."

Ackermann wasn't so sure he could say the same.

114

159 Dover Street
London, 11.00pm

All he had to do was to hold his nerve and stay focused, Thomas told himself as he looked down the street, watching for anyone approaching or for the sound of footsteps. No one came. It's early, he thought, inconspicuous in a black hoodie as he glanced at his watch again, keep calm.

He had spent the day alone, walking along the Embankment, moving in the crowds around Piccadilly Circus. It was better to be amongst people, alone he would have been more easily seen, or noticed. He hadn't been hungry, but he had bought water, downing several bottles to slake his thirst. Did fear make a man thirsty he had wondered, as the daylight faded fast, the evening striding towards his meeting with Purchass.

A few times, police cars had passed him - but their attention was on the streets or the pedestrians hanging around the pub doors, drinking - not taking any notice of a man walking alone. A man who had expected to be stopped, or threatened; a man moving with purpose to kill time. Every moment Thomas had thought about his father, about Kara, Hugh Ackermann, and Luis Famosa – and the kidnapper. And every moment he had wondered if he would survive. And now, within a matter of minutes, it would be time.

Had the killer snatched the redhead already? Yes, he thought, he must have, and she would be terrified. Just as he was. Afraid that his betrayal would be found out and Kara and his father would suffer for it. Then he thought of the memory stick and what he had read. The book that threatened to expose the truth and set the Famosa clan against each other. A clan that was disintegrating daily. Kara painted as the enemy, Halle befuddled, admitted into a clinic; whilst on the opposing side stood Luis and Jimmy, resolute together. Or were they?

From what Thomas had read it was clear that each Famosa had their own agenda. Everyone one of them was keen to find the kidnapper and find out what Kara might have told him. Reputations, careers, and fortunes were resting on it; so many uneasy nights, sweating palms, so many old sins on the edge of exposure. And all of them were captured on the tiny memory stick tucked into Thomas's pocket.

Restless, Thomas stared at his watch. It was 11.10pm. He breathed in, steadying himself as he waited. No one came. Not Ackermann, nor Luis Famosa. He was on his own, waiting for a killer, with no support or backup. Unnerved, Thomas scanned the street, minutes ticking past until 11.20pm. Then 11.30pm. Baffled, he stepped out into the empty street, looking around.

The killer was late.

No, he wasn't.

He was on time.

He was just somewhere else.

In the instant that Thomas realised he had been double-crossed, he heard the sound of a police siren coming down Dover Street towards him.

115

Amused that Thomas could be so easily duped, Purchass thought of their earlier meeting on the building site. Honestly, was it likely he would believe such a rapid change of heart? It didn't work like that. Not if you were a real killer. That didn't come over you all at once. A slow, planned murder was like cancer. You didn't know it was in you until it was running amok. Then it was too late; it was in your cells, your muscles, your eyes. It was a part of you. That was how murder took a man over. One bad cell multiplying, feeding off old fears and memories, getting fat and getting strong. Chewing into the body until the body belonged to the cancer, the brain following suit until the killer was riddled with murder cells. You didn't become a killer in a day. It was a choice. When all the other chances for a normal life had shut you out.

Purchass knew how it worked and that was why he hadn't kept to their meeting. And why, for his further amusement, he had rung the police.

Turning down a side street, Purchass entered Thomas's number.

He picked up instantly. "You set me up!"

Purchass could tell he was angry. He could even – faintly - hear the sound of the police siren in the background.

"Relax, they'll drive past."

Thomas ducked back into a doorway. The police car came close, to the end of the street, then moved on.

"There you go, I told you. They've gone now." Purchass said, laughing.

"What the fuck was that about?"

"I just made an anonymous phone call. Said I'd seen Thomas de Souza at Piccadilly Station, about to get on a train. Sent the stupid sods off in the other direction –"

"Why do that?"

"I wanted to check up on you before our meeting. Make sure you were alone."

Thomas took in a breath. If Ackermann or Famosa *had* turned up, the kidnapper would have seen them and made a run for it.

"Where are you now?"

"Coming your way," Purchass replied. "Just go back to the building site and wait for me there."

116

He was out of his league and knew it. The police were searching for him, Ackermann and Luis Famosa knew where to find him, and so did the killer. Suspecting an arrest or an attack, Thomas moved back under the plastic sheeting on the building site. The knife he had bought with him was in his back pocket and while he waited, he wondered why Luis Famosa hadn't shown up. He hadn't expected him to, but he *had* thought Ackermann would arrive. Then again, perhaps Ackermann had gone to Dover Street, seen the police, and been spooked… Thomas kept watching and waiting. Ackermann *would* come, he told himself. He wouldn't be able to resist, would come for the expose that Thomas had promised him.

Reaching into his pocket, Thomas checked that the memory stick was still there. Not the original - he had bought a new one and downloaded Kara's book onto that - ready to give to Ackermann in return for backup. For the backup which never materialised. Angry, and braced for an attack, Thomas moved further under the plastic sheeting, the dry odour of concrete dust choking in the stale air. Ghoul-shaped poles and yawning slabs of bricks made jagged landscape patterns, whilst above him, rain dripped through the scaffolding skeleton, the streetlamp barely making an impact on the darkness as he walked towards the back of the site where they had talked earlier.

He could see a Portakabin and an overturned worktable, bags of cement piled high beside a stack of wood. The silence was ominous, Thomas knowing he was watched. But if Purchass was there, he wasn't giving himself away. Above his head the rain continued to drip through the holes in the plastic, forming a murky puddle in the middle of the building site. Then suddenly he heard footsteps behind him and turned.

"Hello, there," Purchass said calmly, holding a woman whose entire body was wrapped in sacking, tied with rope. "I have to say that I didn't hold out much hope for you..." he went on, pressing a knife against the woman's breast, "... never thought you'd go along with it. But there you are, I was wrong."

Thomas kept his voice steady, "Don't hurt her."

"It's a bit late for that," Purchass replied, "and don't give me orders. Remember who's holding the fucking knife. I've been looking forward to this because I want to show you how it's done. Step by step. You can join in whenever you like. Are you ready?" He tightened his chokehold, the woman jerking but silent. *Gagged,* Thomas thought, she's gagged. "We start with the abduction."

"Are we going to do it here?" Thomas asked, playing for time. Ackermann and Famosa had bailed on him. After Purchass killed the girl, he would hardly let his witness live.

"What?" Purchass blinked, surprised by the question.

"What if someone sees us?"

"Like who?" Purchass looked round, "I don't see anyone."

"Someone could pass by at any time. It's a busy area," Thomas blundered on, "and I thought you wanted to make it last, show me how you do it step by step."

"Yeah, maybe I did –"

Well, you can't do that here."

Taken aback, Purchass paused, staring at him. And then his gaze suddenly shifted. He was no longer looking at Thomas but at someone *behind* him.

Someone who had just brought down a block of wood on Thomas de Souza's head.

117

The blow stunned him. Falling to his knees, Thomas caught sight of Ackermann and felt someone ripping open his pocket and grabbing the flash drive. But in his greed, Ackermann had lost his advantage and taken his attention off Purchass. It was a costly mistake; Purchass reacted fast and threw the woman over his shoulder. In seconds he was weaving his way through the scaffolding, escaping out of the back exit of the building site.

Clambering to his feet, Thomas followed, Ackermann's accomplice trying to stop him. But Thomas was younger and faster, knocking the man out of the way and keeping his sights on Purchass. Caught off balance, the bodyguard fell back against the stacked bags of concrete, the top layer falling down on top of him, Ackermann cursing as Thomas left the site and ran out into the street beyond.

He could feel the blood trickling down his neck, adrenalin pumping and driving him on. That, and the knowledge that Ackermann had cheated him, kept Thomas on his feet. Although a big man, Purchass was surprisingly fast, barely handicapped by the weight of the girl as he weaved through the backstreets, crossing Piccadilly and making for Hyde Park.

The park gates were still open as Purchass ran in, Thomas narrowing the distance fast. Under the winter branches they sprinted, swerving off the gravel pathway into an unlit bank of trees. And there Purchass stopped running. Thomas stopped, too, watching as Purchass lowered the woman from his shoulder, putting his arm around her neck in a headlock.

"**Who the fuck was that!"** Purchass shouted. "You tried to trap me!"

"No! I don't know who they were!"

"Liar!"

"I'm not lying," Thomas replied, "they took me by surprise too." He touched the back of his head and grimaced, showing Purchass the blood on his hand. "It wasn't the police."

"You tricked me --"

"No, I didn't," Thomas repeated, his gaze moving to the girl, motionless under the sacking. "We have to move on, we can't stay here. *Come on*!"

Uncertain, Purchass looked around him. His plan was floundering, and the park was open ground; at any time, someone could see them. Confused, he dragged the girl backwards into the bank of trees, Thomas following.

"We can't stay here!" he snapped, "For Christ's Sake, we *have* to get her out of here."

There was a space between the trees, a small clearing, moonlight playing hopscotch through the branches.

Breathing heavily, Purchass turned to face Thomas. "I'll ask you again - *who was that?"*

"I don't know."

“Don’t lie to me!” Purchass hollered. “You must know.”

“You don’t get it, do you?” Thomas replied, “You pissed off a lot of people when you kidnapped Kara Famosa. Her father, her brother, and a few others. They all want to find out what you know. What Kara told you.”

Purchass frowned, baffled. “What the fuck are you talking about? The stupid bitch never told me anything. What the hell was she *supposed* to have told me?”

“You said she confided in you –”

“And you believed me?” Purchass said, amused. “Shit, I was just playing with you.”

“No one hired you to kidnap her?”

Purchass looked almost affronted. “*Hired me?* Are you pissing about? I just snatched her at the airport. It could have been anyone.” He shook his head, aggravated. “I’ll tell you one thing: I made a mistake snatching Luis Famosa’s kid. Got the bloody world after me. My sister would laugh at that. She always said I was stupid.”

Calmly, Thomas pointed to the girl. “Let her go.”

“*Let her go?*” Purchass repeated, amused. “But you said you wanted us to kill her together.”

“Let her go, and you can make a run for it.”

Purchass shook his head, his tone regretful. “*She* can’t escape, and *you* can’t escape, I’ve got the upper hand - and it’s round both your throats.”

“It’s just a matter of time,” Thomas replied, “they *will* catch you –”

“But they *haven’t* caught me, have they? They don’t know who I am. They’re looking for *you*. And no one’s on your side, de Souza. No cavalry for you, chum, it’s over.” He tightened the choke hold around the woman's throat. "Look at her! Go on, look at her. Tiny, easy to handle --"

"Just let her go."

"You keep saying that, but she's not going anywhere, and neither are you! But you *could.*" Purchass said slyly. "You *could* just walk away now. But that wouldn't be your style, would it? Your conscience wouldn't let you. And if you *did* back off, I'd come after you," he tapped his foot on the ground, impatient, "So let's get on with it. We're going to kill her. And this one's got to last." His arm tightened around the girl's throat, her legs kicking frantically.

"Alright, alright! We'll do it your way" Thomas put up his hands to calm him. "But, like I say, we can't do it here."

"Then get the bloody van! It's parked on Dover Street."

"OK, OK," Thomas agreed, his gaze returning to the victim, "you picked the girl because of her eyes?"

Purchass frowned, then nodded. "Yeah, I like blue eyes."

"They all had blue eyes, didn't they?"

Purchass smiled. "Yeah, all of them."

"Sente Fleishman, Ellie Chadwick, and Kara Famosa. Her eyes are really blue. I fell in love with her eyes. Those blue eyes…" Thomas kept talking knowing that Purchass was listening. "I never saw anyone else with eyes like that. It made Kara stand out. I guess that's why you spotted her…" Once more, Purchass nodded. "Was she staring at you?"

"Fuck off!"

"It's OK, I understand. Really, I do." Thomas said soothingly. He could sense a shift between them. Purchass becoming less aggressive. "Kara stares a lot. Did she stare at you with those blue eyes?"

"Drove me mad!"

"Drove me mad, too," Thomas agreed, moving forward. "Kara can do that, get under your skin. I love her, but she could annoy me with those big eyes, staring. She tried to boss me around too. Bosses everyone around --"

"She tried it with me."

" -- but it wouldn't work," Thomas said calmly, "not with you. Women shouldn't tell men what to do."

Purchass was listening, nodding. "She's a fucking handful. And she stares a *lot.*"

"She does, she does. Some women do that. Especially women with blue eyes." Thomas was talking gibberish, but it was connecting with Purchass, so he continued, waiting for his chance. "Like I say, I've ever seen such blue eyes. Have you?"

'Stop staring, you fucking freak.
What are you looking at?'
Blue eyes, weirdly, madly blue
Sweat stains under the arms.
Broken glasses that the cat dug up…

Purchass's attention wandered, Thomas saw the shift in him, but was unaware a memory had come back; of Purchass's sister creeping onto his bed. Creeping like a white toad, come open-mouthed and hot. Eyes closed. Only open when she looked at him. And then heat, burning hot. Her eyes staying open even when she was swinging from the end of the rope. Even later, when he dropped her in the hole in the field, even then. It was a hot night, so hot. Not dark, just coming into dusk. No birds, no animals around. Fields, burnt yellow ochre, sky white heat and Kat lying on her back in the earth, in the black earth where he'd dropped her.

Her eyes were still open as he shovelled the dirt on top of her. He thought she would flinch, but she didn't, even though he knew she wasn't quite dead. Close, but not dead. He shovelled the earth around her, leaving her face clear, until the end. Then the dirt hit her eyes and – finally - she blinked.

'Freak, fucking freak
I can still see you.'

And then, as Thomas watched, Purchass lost control. He wavered, confused, stumbling on his feet, and taking his chance, Thomas moved. He rammed his whole body weight against thc victim, sending her and the killer backwards, the girl thrown out of reach as Thomas grabbed the knife which had fallen from Purchass's hand and drove it into his stomach as far as it would go.

118

Breathing heavily, unaccustomed to exertion, Ackermann got back to his car and locked the doors. Then he drove to Chelsea Wharf, parked in his personal space, and inserted the memory stick he had stolen from Thomas into his laptop. His chest was on fire, his pulse unnaturally fast.

Bugger de Souza's interference! he thought, because of him the killer had got away. But Ackermann consoled himself quickly. It was OK, he would catch up with the murderer another time. He had the expose, and that was the important thing.

His breaths rasping, Ackermann stared at the laptop screen. But nothing came up. Angry, he reinserted the memory stick. There was nothing on it. Just a blank. Thomas de Souza had bested him.

Enraged, Ackermann slammed his hands against the steering wheel, then started up the car again. His mind – usually so focused – was befuddled with frustration, and when he headed for the exit, he took the wrong turn, following the up arrow instead of the exit. He realised too late what he had done and had no time to react when a van came towards him, colliding with his Jaguar and sending him backwards down the ramp.

Losing control, Ackermann clung onto the wheel, but it was too late. His foot jammed on the brake, the car spun round - and a second later smashed into the concrete wall beyond.

119

Blood was gushing out from Purchass's stomach as he screamed, his hands pressing against his guts as Thomas leaned down to the woman and pulled off the sacking. He saw a slight figure in filthy clothes, her hair soiled, her face engrained with dirt. It was only when she opened her eyes that he recognised her. And knew he had found Kara Famosa.

Taking hold of her, he tried to wipe the dirt from her face, talking gently then clasping her to him as the police arrived. Her response was muted, her head resting on Thomas's shoulder, her voice barely audible when she finally spoke.

"Why are *you* here?"

Shocked, Thomas glanced at her, then followed her gaze as Luis Famosa approached them.

His face was expressionless. "Thank God you're safe, Kara –"

"*Safe*?" She glanced at Thomas defiantly. "Did he help you?"

"—the police are here to help you." Luis interrupted, ignoring the question, and turning to Thomas. "You don't have to worry, I've explained everything. I can vouch for you."

"*Vouch for me!*" he said bitterly. "You weren't even going to show up, were you?"

Luis shrugged. "I'm here now."

"Waiting to see who survived?" Thomas retorted, glancing towards the police, one officer leaning over Stan Purchass, feeling for a pulse, and then calling out:

"He's alive!"

Luis was still staring at Thomas. "I have a lot to thank you for," he said, glancing over to the police as they surrounded Purchass. Thomas was also watching, kneeling next to Kara. She was silent, rigid with *what?* Terror, or anger? He couldn't tell, reluctantly allowing one of the police officers to lead Kara towards a waiting ambulance. He was about to follow when another officer stopped him, noticing the blood on his hands.

"Did you stab that man?"

"I did," Thomas admitted, "he killed Ellie Chapman, Sente Fleishman, and kidnapped Kara Famosa. That's the girl in the ambulance."

"And you are?"

"Thomas de Souza," he replied, noting the jolt of recognition in the policeman's face "I think you've been looking for me."

120

Stan Purchass was admitted to hospital under guard. No one took any chances with him. Although the stab wound had perforated his gut and caused massive internal bleeding, he was handcuffed to the hospital bed and kept under sedation. Yet Kara refused to stay in hospital, and however much Thomas tried to convince her to remain, she would have none of it, and wanted to leave the day after being admitted.

"I have to get out of here!"

"You need medical treatment –"

"I've *had* medical treatment."

"You need to talk to someone –"

"A shrink?" She shook her head. "Stop telling me what I want! Or what I need! *I don't want to talk*! Don't make me talk, Thomas, not yet. I can't tell you what he did, what it was like. I can't, so let me be. I'm doing OK. They've checked me out, treated me. Done all the tests, I'm not going to collapse." Her lips closed together tightly for an instant before she spoke again, "You know what I *really* need, Thomas?"

"Tell me."

"I need the truth." She reached out, touched his arm. "You found the expose?"

"You wanted me to."

"I did," she nodded, "did you tell Luis?"

"No."

"My mother?"

"No, Halle isn't convinced that it even exists." He paused before adding, "She's in The Priory, it's a psychiatric clinic –"

Kara reacted violently. "**Why?** Why did they put her there? It was Luis, wasn't it? He did it, of course he did. Who else would do that?"

"She was drinking heavily--"

"He made her drink!"

Thomas kept his voice steady, "Halle needed help. She was confused, taking too many pills, smoking –"

"*But she'd stopped all that*!" Kara said helplessly, "She hadn't touched anything for years. No weed, no booze… why would she go back to it?"

He took it carefully, step by step.

"Your mother was desperate from the moment you were abducted, Kara. She couldn't handle not knowing what was happening to you. I went over to New York to stay with her, but as the weeks went by, she wanted to come to England to be closer to you." His voice was measured and gentle. "You were kidnapped in London, and Halle didn't want all that distance between you. She wanted to be nearer --"

"And my brother?"

"Jimmy tried to find you, as did Luis," Thomas replied cautiously, "they hired people in the States and they both came to the UK."

"Oh, I'm sure they did." Her tone was sardonic, "father and son, working together, as always." She was sitting upright, stiff backed. "I want to see my mother."

"I'll take you to her, but first let me make some calls. There's a lot of press outside, waiting for you, and I don't want you to face that now. So just stay here a little longer --"

She flinched, crossed her arms. "Don't let that bastard Luis Famosa come near me!"

"I won't."

"You promise?" For the first time she sounded vulnerable, afraid.

"I promise," Thomas reassured her, "he won't get to you."

"Oh, he'll find a way --"

"You're wrong, he won't get past me," Thomas replied emphatically. "I'm taking you home later, but for now, stay in the hospital. You're fine here, no one will bother you." He stroked her cheek. "It's over; no one will ever hurt you again."

She lowered her head, her voice inaudible.

"I can't hear you, Kara, what did you say?"

"I said that I knew you'd come for me." She glanced at him, then glanced away. "I knew you were the *only* one who'd keep looking, keep trying. When I thought I'd die there, I knew you wouldn't give up. And even if I *had* died - even if only my body was found - I knew that, somehow, you'd bring me home."

He bent down, kissed her forehead, then moved to the door. "I'll take you to see Halle later, but first, I have to organise something. I'll be quick. Trust me."

"I do," she said, nodding, "I always do."

121

"You said that Kara is going to stay with her mother in Hampshire?"

"When Halle's better, in the meantime Kara's staying with me."

Surprised, Anna de Souza looked at her son. He was forthcoming for once, having been evasive since he had rescued Kara, and consistently dismissive of his mother. However much she tried to inveigle her way into the situation, Thomas blocked her, as he had Luis and Jimmy Famosa.

At Kara's insistence, after her belongings had been examined by the police, they were returned to her. But only on the agreement that it was temporary. Nodding, she took the soiled flight bag and went to her hospital room, locking the door behind her. Barely a minute later she came out and returned the bag to a waiting officer.

He was surprised. "You don't want to keep anything, miss?"

"I just needed some clothes," she said distantly, "you can do what you want with it now."

When she was alone again, Kara stared at the jeans and jumper she had taken from the case, along with a hairbrush. The brush she binned immediately, holding the clothes up to her nose, surprised that they still smelt relatively clean. Clean enough to wear - but she wasn't intending to do that, Thomas already bringing new clothes and a pair of boots to replace the ones left in the sodden barn. Hesitating, Kara's right hand rested on the folded red jumper she had taken from the bag… Since she had been admitted she had showered incessantly, washing, and rewashing her hair, the smell of the barn still on her skin, in her mouth and nose, however many times she rinsed her face. The barn was clinging to her, she could still hear the broken doors flapping in the wind, the pig snorting and jerking for a few instants after Purchass had dropped the anvil on its head…

Stop it, she told herself, *stop it* and think of something else. Her attention turned back to the jumper, still folded tightly as it had been when she first packed it, and then, holding her breath, she unfolded it. It was still there, small, undamaged, the Klimt portrait she had stolen. For leverage.

Thomas had made certain that neither Luis nor Jimmy would get their hands on Kara's possessions, neither her wallet nor her flight bag. His interference was resented, and Luis arrived at the hospital with his English lawyer, both summarily blocked by Thomas. As for Anna de Souza, her extravagant floral bouquet intended for Kara was waylaid, and her persistent questions were ignored. Until, suddenly, she had been granted an audience with her son, the balance of power upturned.

"So, tell me, Thomas, what about the Klimt?" she asked, feigning nonchalance.

"Burned."

"Burned!" She parroted. "Who burned it?"

"The killer," Thomas replied, the lie already in place, "The police asked Kara about it, and she told them that Purchass had burned it."

Deflated, Anna took a moment to recover. "So when will Halle be ready to leave The Priory?"

"How would I know? I'm not her doctor." Thomas retorted, "But when she does go back to Hampshire, Kara wants to go with her."

"And in the meantime, she'll stay with you," Anna pursed her lips, trying to disguise her pleasure and failing. "She needs you now, more than ever. And with your father still recovering in hospital, you two won't be bothered and can get reacquainted in private."

"Reacquainted?" Thomas replied, turning away from her.

Since Purchass had been arrested, and her son publicly lauded for his bravery, Anna had posed as the doting mother. But the lawyer Thomas had hired to keep the press at bay had been canny enough to put a leash on Anna and, despairing at being cut out, she had appealed to her son.

"I knew you could never have killed anyone, Thomas," she crooned, "I'm so proud of you."

"For what?"

"Oh, come on, you're a hero! There are so many people desperate to talk to you --"

He cut her off. "I'm bringing Dad home next week."

"*Your father?*" Anna repeated, nonplussed. She had hoped to keep Peter out of the way, allowing Thomas to monopolise the limelight that she would be organising. Talks of a book deal and the acquisition of film rights had already begun, Anna taking over Simon Porter's old connections. "Are you sure that's a good idea? Your father could get better care in a private clinic –"

"Will you pay for it?"

Anna hesitated, then smiled. "Naturally. I mean, I wouldn't want Peter to return home when you're going to be so busy." She changed the subject deftly. "We have a lot to talk about, all kinds of plans to get in motion. Everyone wants to interview you, and of course they want to speak to Kara –"

"Kara is talking to no one." Thomas interrupted her, his tone warning. "Understand me, Mother, Kara is struggling. She's in a very fragile condition. She could have been killed –"

"But she wasn't!"

He ignored the comment and continued, " – She needs time to recover, and she needs peace. She's not to be disturbed by anyone."

"People want to hear her story!" Anna persisted, frantic at the thought that her biggest coup might be slipping from her grasp, "And they want to know about *you*, Thomas, how you outwitted her kidnapper --"

He sighed. "I know the story, Mother, but I'm not giving interviews."

"*What!"*

"I'm not giving interviews," he repeated, "Not today, not tomorrow. Never. I'll talk to the police about Purchass, but not the press. And I don't want you talking to Kara either."

"Now, just a minute, Thomas! I'm your mother! --"

"Who used her son for her own ends!" He retorted, "I was agreeable once, but now Kara's safe, I want nothing to do with you or your deals. Because that's what it's all about - deals, money, power. You think you can take over from Simon Porter? I doubt it, he has a wife who will be quick to throw a spook in your wheel."

She reeled from his hostility. "Is this revenge for leaving your father?"

Thomas smiled wryly. "*Revenge?* I don't give a shit anymore. I care about Kara. She's recovering and she needs to be left alone –"

"She'll be staying with you, that's hardly alone," Anna replied tartly. "For God's Sake, Thomas, it's a huge story, you can't blame people for wanting to know what went on. The Famosa family attracts interest and curiosity..." Her eyes narrowed, her tone becoming suspicious, "what are you hiding?"

"Nothing."

There was a moment of hopeful realisation. "*Have you got the expose?*"

"There isn't one –"

"Bullshit!" Anna snapped. "Simon Porter had a copy --"

"Oh dear, you slipped up there, didn't you? Thomas smiled, "Did he dump you before you could get your hands on it?"

Stung, she retaliated. "There *is* a book –"

"No, there *isn't*." Thomas lied, "There's no expose. No book to incriminate the Famosa family or expose their supposed corruption. And Kara never colluded with Simon Porter."

"I don't believe you!" Anna shouted, beside herself, "Don't lie to me! I have a right to know. I was the only one who supported you. The only one who believed you were innocent --"

"And I'm supposed to thank you for that? I *was* innocent."

"Don't act aggrieved!" She snorted, "You sound pathetic. And don't pretend you were pressured into something you didn't want to do. When all this started, you were keen enough to help --"

"I was, because of Kara. I could even tolerate your involving me to impress your lover. '*...Thomas knows Kara better than anyone. He still loves her, and he's my son, he'll do anything we ask...*" He parroted, then paused, seeing his mother's embarrassment. "You're right, I didn't mind. I was more than willing to talk about Kara, to write about her, to do anything to find her. But now I *have* found her I don't want any more to do with you --"

Stubborn, Anna persisted. "There are people wanting to sign up a book deal *now*. There's talk of a film, a series. How can you be **so** stupid, Thomas? Now Simon Porter's out of the picture, we'd have a clear run --"

"Why did he kill himself?"

She was dismissive, "Who knows?"

"Was it because of your affair?"

Anna shrugged her shoulders. "People don't kill themselves because of adultery–"

"Christ, how wrong you are!" He snapped.

"Look, Thomas, I don't know why Simon Porter committed suicide, and frankly, I don't care. He was a weak man and I'm not sorry he's dead." She touched Thomas's arm, changing the subject. "We shouldn't fight, it's stupid. You love Kara, you *saved* her, it's a miracle that she survived. It's a wonderful, heartwarming love story, so why can't you talk about it?"

"I'm warning you, leave her be."

Anna shook her head, her temper barely contained. "You're hiding something! I can sense it. I can read you, Thomas, you're my son. What do you know that you aren't telling me? *There* ***was*** *a book, wasn't there*?" Her voice speeded up with panic. "I'm *begging* you not to make any hasty decisions. This is the opportunity of a lifetime. We can make a fortune out of this story."

"*We?*"

She didn't miss a beat. "*You* can settle down with Kara and buy a house together. You're a hero, Thomas. You've got it all, the looks, the courage, and the girl." Exasperated, she stared into his face. "Most people would kill to be a celebrity."

"Not me."

"Give me *something,* please!" She begged, distracted. "I won't involve you or Kara if you really don't want me to. Just tell me one thing - *where's the book*?"

"In your head, Mother," he replied, moving to the door, "nowhere else."

122

Pre-empting Kara's visit, Luis called to visit his wife at The Priory. Still on her medication, Halle alternated between euphoria and trepidation, the news of her daughter's rescue making her an unwilling celebrity at the clinic. Having anticipated some injudicious statement to the press, Luis had quickly intervened, setting a guard on Halle's room, his concern more to protect the Famosa empire than his troubled wife.

Having hoped to see Kara, Halle was taken aback at the arrival of her husband, Luis extravagantly – and publicly – showing concern, greeting the press with urbane thanks for their concern. Once inside his wife's room he changed, became distant, inquisitive. "I hear Kara is coming to see you. She should stay in hospital –"

"I want to go home, Luis."

"New York or Vegas?"

"Hampshire…" she said wistfully, "I was thinking that it's quiet there, and I could spend time with my daughter," she winced at the word 'daughter,' wondering how Luis would react.

He did react, but not in the way she expected. "*Did* Kara write an expose?"

"I've told you; I don't know –"

"You sure about that? Thomas de Souza's throwing his weight around, even blocking me. For now, anyway."

"He saved Kara's life."

Luis nodded. "Yes, he did. I wonder what else he saved? Maybe a missing painting and a book. The one you don't know anything about. The one with secrets in it."

"I only cheated on you once --"

He brushed the words aside dismissively, "I'm talking about Las Vegas."

"*Vegas*... you want to talk about Vegas?" Halle said, her voice tremulous, "why now?"

"You look worried," he replied, bending down towards her. "Has the clinic recovered your memory?"

"I don't know what you mean…" she blundered, perched on the edge of the bed. "… I don't remember anything clearly now."

"Yes, you do," he replied, sitting down, his leg touching hers. "Let's concentrate, shall we? We were young when we were first in Vegas… Is it coming back to you, Halle? Concentrate, think."

She could feel his hand grip hers. "Kara never knew about that time. She couldn't have, Luis, I never told her, never said a word –"

"Even when you were drunk?"

"How could I? *I'd forgotten everything!"* She repeated helplessly, "I forgot --"

"Try again, Halle." He squeezed her hand tighter.

"*You want me to remember*?"

"I want to know what you *do* remember," Luis replied, "just in case you slipped up and your daughter knows more than you think… Go on, Halle, take me back. You know when."

Mesmerised, she stared at him, then glanced towards the door. Outside she knew he had placed a bodyguard; not to protect her, but to keep her cocooned, obedient. Silenced.

"There were four of us …" Luis began.

"I don't remember."

"… Simon Porter, Hugh Ackermann, you …"

"And you."

"That's right, Halle, and me."

She nodded, avoiding his gaze. "But there was another person."

"Yes, you see, you *do* remember," he increased the pressure on her hand, "and that person wrote anonymous notes to all four of us."

She nodded again, like a child. "Yes, I'd forgotten that. Yes…"

"We got them, so did Porter and Ackermann. We compared the letters, the warnings. It went on for years. Then someone sent Kara a postcard. Told her I wasn't her father."

Halle flinched. "That was two years ago –"

"You remember?"

"Yes… but there's been nothing since…" She glanced at him hopefully. "You think it's over?

"No."

"So, who *is* it?" She asked, her voice wavering. "Who's after us?"

"I am."

Jolted, Halle stared at her husband. *"What?"*

"There was no witness, just me."

Confused, she shook her head. "I don't understand --"

"I knew the only way to stop any of you going to the police, or turning on each other, was to keep you scared.

If you were all threatened, you'd club together, and make sure the secret never got out."

"But I never said anything!"

"Oh, I think you did, Halle," he replied, his tone bleak, "Simon Porter's dead, Hugh Ackermann's running scared, and I have a wife who's suddenly got her memory back."

"I didn't say anything…" Halle repeated, her voice dropping. "I never said anything. I'm sure I didn't. I didn't…" her words stalled. "*I don't remember*!"

"But you've just told me you *do* remember."

She turned to face him, pleading. "But I can *forget,* Luis! I can forget. I did it before, and I can do it again." She smiled uncertainly, feeling his hold tighten, her fingers crushed together. "Believe me, I won't say anything."

"*Can* I trust you?" he asked, stroking her hair, and then tapping her forehead hard with his index finger. "What's in there, Halle? A whole flock of crazy birds, cawing and flapping around. How do we get them to keep quiet?"

"I can keep quiet."

"Can you? I have to know if I can trust you, Halle," he replied, "I have to be certain of it."

She nodded again, urgently trying to appease him. "You can trust me, Luis, you can… I don't remember anything, I really don't. And I won't say a word - what *can* I say when I don't know anything?"

He relaxed his grip, then kissed her upturned palm. "I've got a new doctor for you, Halle, someone who understands your problems." Rising to his feet, Luis looked down at his wife. "You just need to stay here a bit longer. You understand, don't you?"

She nodded dumbly. "Yes, I understand…I won't say anything, Luis, I promise… I promise…"

123

St Thomas's Hospital
London

He had expected the dying Hugh Ackermann to be diminished, shrunken. But he was still impressive, massive, filling the hospital bed in a single room of the Intensive Care Unit. Attached to a drip, an oxygen mask over his face, he was breathing noisily as Thomas walked over to his bedside.

Slowly, Ackermann opened his left eye and stared at his visitor. "You came."

Thomas nodded, reaching for a chair and sitting down. "And you nearly had me killed."

"Well, you did for me," Ackermann replied, pushing away the oxygen mask. "You got the expose?"

"Yes."

Ackermann rolled his eyes, one weighty arm flapping uselessly at his side. "You look at what I gave you in that envelope?"

"It says that the Gustav Klimt painting that Kara stole is a fake."

"No comment?" Ackermann said, almost amused.

"I already knew."

"You're a lying bugger!"

"No, I *did* know," Thomas insisted, "because I've read the expose."

"That fucking expose!" Ackermann replied, exasperated, "I knew it existed. Good reading, was it?"

"Action-packed… You know, I really thought you were Kara's father. Even when you denied it."

"Not me. Not Simon Porter, either. Mind you, I *did* wonder about that myself, I even went to the trouble of taking a bit of his fingernail and having his DNA checked against Kara's. No match." Ackermann coughed, touching his ribs and wincing. "I smashed into a fucking wall! The Jaguar's a write-off. Like me." He paused, stared at Thomas, "Go on, tell me what you know."

"First, I'll tell you what I *don't* know. Finding out that Luis wasn't her father would have shaken Kara and made her turn against her mother. After all, she'd idolised Luis --"

"He's a bastard."

Thomas shrugged. " -- Maybe, but she still loved him. But when she realised she wasn't his child, something shifted. She felt betrayed and disappointed; the elegant, sweet-natured Halle was an adulteress; her half-brother Jimmy was Daddy's errand boy; and Luis, well, perhaps Luis was what people had always intimated."

"Get on with it!"

"I don't think Kara ever intended to get the book published. It's not even finished. It was more like a personal diary, something a teenager writes, working out their feelings on paper. But the more she dug, the more she found, and then the water got so murky she couldn't see anything clearly."

"Go on."

"She charmed the New York gallery manager, Ivan Holt, flattered him and asked questions about the Famosa collection. He was happy to oblige, but slipped up a couple of times, mentioned some art works stored in Connecticut and Las Vegas, and then told her all about the employee who had been jailed. He'd been suspected of dealing in forgeries, but when the rumour mill started around Luis, he fell on his sword to protect his boss." Thomas paused. "No doubt he was paid well for the six years he spent in prison."

"And Luis was cleared."

"Yes, but it must have given him a scare. He had a lot to lose. How many paintings had Luis sold over two decades? He had a personal vendetta against the art world, the elites who had made a Cuban casino and hotel owner feels like ignorant upstart." Thomas sighed. "Luis was clever, he made sure that there was nothing criminal about his businesses in Vegas – that would have been too obvious – but art was respectable. And financially safe. No one loses money on art. And if you can sell a *forgery* for the price of the real thing, you're laughing. Certainly, Luis would have been. There's nothing as ruthless as a man with a chip on his shoulder."

Ackermann coughed, shifting his position on the bed. "What else?"

"You were all running after the expose, weren't you? You, Luis, Halle, Porter. None of you knew what Kara had written. You didn't know who'd abducted her, or why. If it was a stranger, a random kidnapping, or if one of the four of you had organised it. And if so, was it because of the book? Maybe Kara had bargained with her abductor and told him things to buy him off? And what about the Klimt, why had she stolen a painting that was due for auction in New York? It was going to be a triumph. There was a global audience for it; Luis was riding high than ever –"

"And Kara could topple him."

Thomas nodded. "That's what he feared. That's why all of you had to find Kara. You *had* to get the Klimt back and stop the book coming out."

Ackermann stared at his visitor, unblinking. "What's the worst a man can do?"

"I'm not here for riddles --"

"But this is a good riddle," Ackermann interrupted him. "You're right, we *were* all afraid of the expose and didn't know if the kidnapping had been set up to silence Kara. No one was talking. We'd hidden so many secrets for so long, that no one could communicate without lying. I suspected Simon Porter. I imagine he suspected me. I even wondered about Halle – could she kill her own child?"

"*Could she?*"

"Who knows? Nah, I doubt it. I met her a long time ago, in London. Upper class English girl, pretty, silly, took risks with herself, but she was a sweetheart, just easily led. I didn't see her for a while, then our paths crossed again in Las Vegas, where she was doing some modelling and a lot of drugs. She wasn't like you see her now. Not elegant; she was an opportunist searching for a man to rescue her. Halle always looked classy, but she was giddy, one of those girls that can end up dead."

"So where did Luis Famosa come in?"

"We did a deal."

Surprised, Thomas leaned forward in his seat. "*You and Famosa*? I thought you were rivals."

"That's what we let people think, but when I realised, I could never get Halle for myself, I was happy enough to hang around on the Famosa periphery. Grabbing bits of time with her, hoarding conversations, imagining what would have been like if she'd chosen me. Pathetic, hey?" He laughed mirthlessly. "Yes, it was embarrassing, but dancing on the rim of the Famosa circle was enough."

"And you were dealing in art whilst you were in Vegas?"

"I dealt everywhere, I just spent more time in Vegas when I visited Luis and Halle. I've been a 'dealer' since I was a snot nosed kid, only we didn't call it that then; I was always picking up stuff and selling on. And I learnt fast, by the time I was in my twenties I could spot a good piece with my eyes shut. God knows how, I don't know where the skill came from, but I've got a sense for it. My hands go cold when I see something valuable and they only warm up when I've got it."

Ackermann was in a talkative mood, Thomas pushing his luck. "But if Luis was always regarded with suspicion by the international dealers, how come you weren't?"

"I'm a Northerner, too thick and too ignorant to worry them. That's how I got where I am, they never expected a moose in a suit to collect Japanese Noritake China or even understand Egon Schiele." He paused, amused, "I've always liked the Viennese painters."

"Did Luis ask for your advice?"

"On buying and selling, yeah. He built up his collection fast, put his money in art. Property, jewellery, cars - they lose money - an Old Master never does. So, if Luis wanted my advice on a piece, I gave it to him, especially when he began collecting ceramics for the Famosa gallery. I charged him a fee, or a consultant's percentage, and in return I got a *special* deal on anything I bought from him."

"Did you buy a lot from Luis?"

"I bought, he sold. At other times, I sold, he bought."

"Tight."

"As a duck's arse," Ackermann coughed again, waving aside an offer of water. "Oh, let me talk. It's time. I want to get it out."

"Where did Simon Porter come into this?"

"He was the agent for the Famosas. Sly, grey faced bastard, with that English accent which fooled everyone. He was ruthless, like the rest of us. Only Porter was ruthless in a different way."

"How?"

"He'd known Halle for a long time, and she invited him to Vegas, told him he could become an agent for all the big names there. You know the kind of thing, making deals for the autobiographies of the mega famous. But Porter didn't look the part, or sound the part, so he went back to London. Did well on his home turf, and always profited from his connection to the Famosa family."

"D'you think he'd have Kara killed?"

"To make sure the expose never got out?"

Thomas nodded. "Yes."

"You've read it, what d'you think?"

"Not damaging enough to kill for. But then none of you knew that did you?" Thomas asked, his tone ironic, "I still don't know the real reason why you're all so scared. There has to be something else, something you've all hidden for a long time. What is it?"

Ackermann made a low sound in his throat. "Why would I tell you?"

"Because you *want* to tell me. And you need a father confessor."

It was a clever ploy, and Ackermann appreciated it. "You know that you can't prove what I'm about to tell you?"

"No, I don't suppose I can."

"It was in the late nineties, in Vegas. Halle and Luis were having trouble in their marriage. Their fortune was building, like their profile, Halle was dressed by the best and she looked beautiful," he trailed off, wistful, then continued, "but Luis was fucking some other woman and it turned out that she was his long time mistress and that she'd had his kid. You can imagine how Halle took that. She was crushed, couldn't believe it, and she went off the rails. Always been unstable and it was too much for her. She started drinking a lot, and smoking enough weed to keep herself permanently stoned. And Luis was encouraging her, because it made her easier to handle and he likes to bully people. His son's the same; Jimmy's devoted to his mother, but she's always going to come second to Luis."

"Why didn't Halle walk out?"

Ackermann turned his head to meet Thomas's gaze. "If you ever think of feeling sorry for her, don't bother. She knew what she was doing the day she took up with Luis Famosa."

"He was a crook?"

"He was as he is now. A vindictive, charming, cultured thug. He's no scruples. But, in his defense, he loved her. He always protected her. It was in his blood. The family was a closed unit."

"Then what happened?"

"Time passed, Halle got sober and became the perfect wife. They were well known, admired, Luis's reputation iffy, but it only seemed to add to his aura. All of us – Simon Porter, me, Luis, and Halle - were all were doing really well and making serious money. Then suddenly Halle wanted to move, to live in England. She was tired of New York and hated Las Vegas, probably because it reminded her of bad times. Her parents were old, and she wanted to spend more time with them. Of course, Luis didn't like the idea. He brushed it off. He needed to divide his time between his businesses in New York and Vegas and it was when they were arguing about it that the whole business of the fakes became public."

"And one of his men went to jail." Thomas replied. "But that cleared Luis, didn't it?"

"Not completely. Rumours stick like shit to a blanket," Ackermann said, rolling over onto his back and looking straight up at the hospital ceiling. "Christ, it was hot that year. Every day hotter than the last. Even the air conditioning was struggling. You got out of your car and the heat hit you, sucked the air out of your lungs. I hated it. Even the Famosa villa with its shady garden and gigantic swimming pool couldn't make up for the bloody heat." Ackermann breathed in, then exhaling before continuing. "He'd been around for a long while --"

"Who had?"

"Freddy Rakins."

"Who's he?"

"He was the unluckiest genius who ever drew breath." Ackermann paused, looking back. "Rakins and Luis had known each other for decades; they were friends long before Luis became a big hitter. And whilst Luis was business savvy, Rakins was a brilliant painter. But he was greedy. Greedy like you couldn't imagine. And alongside his greed went his talent – he could copy anything. I mean *anything*. A Turner, a Picasso, a Caravaggio, no problem, and he had a particular liking for the Viennese painters; Oscar Kokoschka, Gustav Klimt and especially Egon Schiele." Thomas was listening, Ackermann talking in his slow monotone. "Luis had wanted to buy a Gustav Klimt and loved the female serpent paintings. He said they reminded him of Halle, and was very vocal about it. Everyone knew Luis admired the painter, so it burned him even more when he was bested at an auction in London. Two dealers who had had it in for Luis for a long time joined together and drove up the price. Luis was loaded, but he couldn't match what two major dealers could bid working as allies. Then again, he probably *could* have matched them, but he knew they were screwing him over, so he decided he'd get revenge his own way."

"Rakins?"

"Too right. They left it for a year and then Rakins faked a Klimt – a studio oil sketch for one of the serpent paintings. It would have fooled the artist himself. Luis claimed that he had found it in Vienna, and refused all offers. He wasn't selling. People presumed it was because he loved Klimt and wanted to keep it in his collection, but it was because it was a forgery."

"But at that time Luis *was* selling other fakes?"

"Too fucking right, he was! Rakins's work was good enough to con dealers and auction houses. There were a lot of them, fake Goya etchings, Rubens portraits, and a couple of Pre-Raphaelites over the years."

"And no one suspected?"

"No, Rakins was *that* good. And Luis was careful, he wasn't going to risk the Famosa empire after the previous rumours had died down. Even cheating the art market wasn't worth losing everything." Ackermann gazed into the distance. "Rakins was a wonder, he could forge blindfold, and he was handsomely paid. He bought property abroad, and some vintage cars, but never settled in Vegas. During those years he spent a lot of time with the Famosas, Halle liked him, and the kids – they were young then – thought he was fun."

"What happened?"

"Rakins gave up forging."

"Why?"

"Said he was bored, wanted to 'develop his own style' - with the help of a lot of dope. He was a genius forger, but not an Old Master, and his big plans came to nothing. Soon, the stacks of money he'd made were gone."

"So, with Rakins out of the picture, Luis stopped dealing in fakes?"

"Like hell! Rakins was a busted flush, but Luis had found replacements. He was using a couple of painters via an anonymous contact. It was safer."

"And Rakins got jealous?"

"Rakins got broke. He asked Luis for a loan, and for work, and came over to the Famosa property that night. We were all there, Luis, Halle, me, and Simon Porter, visiting from London. We all heard the conversation, Rakins pleading for money from Luis, and Luis refusing. He was cautious because Rakins had become reckless, a drunk, a junkie with a big mouth. Then Rakins got nasty, started an argument, said he could expose all of us, Luis in particular. It got ugly then, Luis told him to fuck off, that he couldn't prove anything… But he was worried; we could see that. Especially when Rakins didn't back down and turned to Halle instead."

"Did she help him?"

"God, it hurts…" Ackermann touched his chest, wincing. "It's nearly over, isn't it? How long have I got?"

"Long enough to finish the story."

"You've turned into a hard bastard," Ackermann replied, glancing away. "Rakins was trying to push his weight around. He never realised the danger he was in. He'd been drinking and smoking weed and was unsteady on his feet, yelling, weaving about. Halle tried to calm him down, but he was out of control and picked a fight with Luis. They were shouting, cursing each other, Luis telling Rakins that he wanted him to leave. He didn't need another drunken addict in his house, he said. That was the flashpoint – because then Rakins let rip and told him that he'd slept with Halle."

"Jesus."

Ackermann's voice began to speed up. "It was so fast. Luis lunged at him and Rakins fells backwards, hitting his head on the side of the pool, before going underwater... He never got out again."

"*Luis killed him?*"

"He thought he had. We dumped Rakins in the car, but the poor sod came around a few minutes later and started fighting. He was going crazy, and Luis panicked, pushed him out of the car, and he hit the road at speed -"

"Was he dead?"

"I didn't know."

Thomas kept staring at Ackermann's profile. "You were driving?"

Ackermann paused. "Yes, I was driving. I'd seen what had happened in the back seat and I stopped and reversed. Rakins was still alive, unconscious, barely alive..."

"And you left him there?"

"Think about it," Ackermann replied, turning his head to look at Thomas. "Rakins was going to expose us. He'd forged a lot of paintings and if we took him to hospital he'd talk. He'd ruin Luis, Halle, me, and Simon Porter. He wasn't going to survive anyway –"

"How d'you know that?"

"He was bleeding like a stuck pig, his head was split open. He was hallucinating, babbling, his eyes unfocused, his limbs flailing around. He *couldn't* have recovered... And if we told people what had happened, who'd believe it was an accident? Everyone would think that Luis had killed him deliberately to keep him quiet about the fakes. There were a lot of people who'd been duped, a lot of angry dealers and auction houses." He grimaced again, the pain increasing. "And besides, Rakins had slept with Halle – who'd have believed that a jealous husband hadn't murdered him for that?"

Thomas stared at the dying man. "Luis *did* murder him."

"It was an accident --"

"Until he was pushed out of the car." Thomas interrupted him, "Did you just leave him there?"

"I drove back to check, but he *was* dead by then, it was over... Look, think about it, we were all panicking. Simon Porter threw up, crying to himself, Luis pacing up and down... It had been an accident, but we'd have lost everything if we'd reported it. If Rakins's body was found there would be questions – all of them leading back to us."

"What happened to the body?"

"We buried it."

"Where?"

"I don't remember –"

"Liar."

Ackermann smiled bitterly. "You think I'd lie after I've told you this much? I *don't* remember where we buried him. Just that it was in the desert. There's a lot of it around Vegas." He stared at Thomas; his eyes emotionless. "Halle knew what had happened. She was hysterical and drunk, Luis ignored her, but I gave her enough booze to get to sleep. In the days afterwards she was silent, kept to herself… The rest of us made a pact, we swore we'd keep quiet because if it came out, we'd be finished."

"And Halle said nothing?"

"She slipped out of reality for a while. And Luis knew that being his wife, she couldn't be forced to testify against him. Her adultery had caught him by surprise, but they carried on, muddled through, and gradually things settled down. Luis's business was safe, and he thought he was home free. We all did. So, when it came out about Kara writing an expose, the shit really hit the fan."

"Especially after Luis found out that Kara wasn't his daughter." Thomas interjected. "That would have put an entirely different slant on things, wouldn't it? A *daughter* exposing the family secrets is one thing; a woman who hasn't a blood tie to the Famosas could be dispensable." He sighed, holding Ackermann's gaze. "Just in case you were wondering, Kara didn't know anything about Las Vegas."

"She didn't know?"

"No, she didn't, and she wasn't holding it over all of you. The abduction was random, pure chance. Purchass snatched Kara at Heathrow Airport. He didn't know who she was. He could have picked the woman standing behind her. He just took her because of the colour of her eyes."

Ackermann was finding speech difficult. "What *was* in the expose?"

"That Halle had cheated on Luis and Kara wasn't his child. That the Famosa fortune was partially based on sharp practice, that Jimmy launders Famosa property money abroad, and that in amongst the genuine pictures Luis collects and sells, there is a lucrative sub-industry in forgeries --"

"*There must have been more!*"

"In a way, there is. Kara didn't expose a murder she knew nothing about, but she exposed all of you for who you truly are. It was only after she was kidnapped that she suspected it might have been arranged because of her book. Then she wondered *who* had organised it. Was it Luis? Or Jimmy, the brother who would not take kindly to sharing the Famosa fortune with a half-sister. Or is it Simon Porter who is eager to control the threatened expose? And lastly, you. You also had a lot to lose."

"I would never have hurt her --"

"But she didn't *know* that, did she?" Thomas countered. "She was being held captive, abused, endangered by her abductor and the very people who were supposed to love her. She was already suspicious of Luis and her brother, and that's why she took the Klimt. As a bargaining chip, in case Luis threatened her. He had a big event coming up. The auction had already attracted a global audience; the grandiose event that he had so generously handed over to Halle. Not in her honour, but as his alibi."

It was Ackermann's turn to be confused. *"Alibi?"*

Thomas nodded. "You see, if the painting was discovered to be a forgery, *Halle* would be the scapegoat."

"What are you talking about?"

"Luis Famosa has a long memory, and he holds grudges. The painting Kara stole was the Klimt, which attracted global attention and was due to be auctioned at the Famosa Gallery in front of the art world's grandees and the media. Halle was to be the guest speaker and whilst she was holding the auction, it was planned that the Klimt would be exposed as a fake by Luis himself --"

"I don't believe you!"

"-- in one fell swoop, he would rid himself of an unstable wife and clear his reputation should any further forgeries emerge." Thomas paused, his voice expressionless. "It was a clever plan."

"But there's no painting left to auction!" Ackermann blustered. "Kara took it."

Thomas shook his head. "No, she didn't. She'd really done her research. Ivan Holt, the manager at the Famosa Gallery, was flattered by her attention and let down his guard. After all, he thought she was the boss's daughter, so he allowed her access to the gallery storerooms, not knowing how much of the forgery sideline Kara had already discovered. Or maybe Holt didn't know about it himself - after all, Jimmy Famosa keeps a tight watch on everything - but based on what she *had* found out, Kara suspected that the auction painting was a fake."

Ackermann tried to raise himself in the bed, his face ashen. "What *are* you talking about?"

"Kara knew that Luis and Jimmy wouldn't care if they never found *her,* but they'd never stop searching for the forged Klimt. They had to find it to protect themselves." Thomas paused for a moment before continuing. "If Kara succeeded, the trick that Luis Famosa was going to pull on his wife was going to backfire on him - courtesy of the woman he had once believed his daughter."

124

St Thomas's Hospital,
London

The day was closing in, rain was giving way to dusk and the hospital windows were running with water. Outside, the branches of winter trees ducked and dived in a hostile wind, Thomas turning on the lamp by Ackermann's bed. It wasn't difficult to imagine how formidable Ackermann would have been once, an impressive opponent in full health.

"Get on with it," Ackermann said, glancing at Thomas, "let's hear all of it."

"Simon Porter killed himself because he thought the murder was going to be exposed in Kara's book."

Ackermann frowned. "But if he'd read it, he'd have known there was no reference to what happened."

"You forget," Thomas replied steadily, "the book wasn't finished."

"Shit..." Ackermann took in a painful breath. "Fear killed Simon Porter? Funny that, he never had such of an imagination before."

Thomas studied the dying man. Ackermann's colour had changed, his breathing laboured.

"So, who *is* Kara's father?"

Ackermann's winked. "Who d'you think? Rakins, of course. Poor dumb Freddy Rakins...That's one more reason we couldn't go to the police. It was a double betrayal, you see. Not only had Rakins fucked Luis's wife, but he's also passed off his bastard as Luis's daughter. Nobody knowing that would have believed the painter's death was an accident."

Rising to his feet, Thomas pulled on his coat. "Anything else you want to tell me?"

Ackermann grimaced, "No. But look out for Halle, will you? I mean, I imagine you and Kara will get together now, but Halle needs someone."

"She's as guilty as the rest of you –"

"No, she isn't." Ackermann replied, "Look at her sometimes. When she's pissed. When she's walking around, mumbling to herself, trying to pretend, to forget, but knowing what we did, and wondering if staying quiet was worth it. There's no peace left; no reason to sleep, no reason to wake up. Watch out for her, please. Don't do it for me, do it for Kara."

Thomas nodded. "I'll do what I can. As for Luis and Rakins –"

"You can't say a fucking word! I'll deny everything, say it was the ramblings of a dying man. There's no proof, no body, no genius forger buried under the sand. Rakins's gone, it's like he never existed. It's old news, no one cares."

"No one cares?"

"No one."

"Then who wrote to Kara two years ago, telling her that Luis Famosa wasn't her father? Who was that?"

"Good luck finding out," Ackermann said dismissively. "That's your problem now."

"I'm not staying quiet about the forgery, or Freddy Rakins," Thomas said, determined, "Luis will have to answer for both."

"You think?" Ackermann countered drily. "Just tell me one thing - who's got the real Klimt now?"

Thomas lied. "It's disappeared."

"Sounds about right. You know, I'd put money on the fact that as soon as Kara was rescued Luis had at least half a dozen lawyers on the phone. Three in New York, three in Vegas." Ackermann moved his position in the bed, grunting with effort. "If Kara *does* expose the forging, he'll deny it, say it's her revenge for being cut out of the Famosa family fortune. He'll claim that Halle is crazy and that her daughter suffers from delusions too, compounded by the appalling kidnapping she suffered."

"He wouldn't get away with it."

Ackermann raised his eyebrows, his expression sarcastic. "You can't take on Luis Famosa, you'll lose. Give it up, before it ruins your life. David might have killed Goliath - but that was only a story."

125

Two weeks later, Purchass was discharged from the prison hospital. Then, three months after that, he went on trial and pleaded guilty to the murder of two women and the mutilation of three. The world's press – who had never tired of the case of Kara Famosa – descended on London, the details spreading across the globe. Enjoying his infamy, Purchass gloried in the title of serial killer. Ellie Chapman and Sente Fleishman's photographs reproduced alongside his own, yet his particular pleasure lay in being the kidnapper of Kara Famosa.

Although he had enjoyed having Thomas de Souza as his scapegoat, Purchass soon dropped the idea. It was true that Thomas had killed the nurse, but it had been accidental, whereas he – Stan Purchass – had mutilated her deliberately, as he had done with his other victims. Thomas was just in the wrong place at the wrong time; he didn't *mean* to kill her. He hadn't plotted her death. He didn't have the makings of a real killer.

According to prison reports, Purchass was an exemplary prisoner. He was willing to be interviewed and quick to agree to work on a book, agented by Anna de Souza. She had set up her own agency, Simon Porter's old premises put up for sale. Yet although she was inundated with offers for the story of Kara Famosa, Thomas vetoed everything, determined to protect her.

At first, Kara's recovery had been swift, then, only weeks later, she crashed into a depression that left her mute for days. In order to get the best treatment, she was admitted to The Priory where Halle was staying, the two of them forging a bond that even Luis's interference couldn't break. It was Halle who found a purpose in supporting Kara; and Kara who found a purpose in supporting her mother.

And, all the while, Thomas visited. He came not as a hero nor a lover but as a friend to both. It was too soon for him to consider Kara as a partner, and as Kara recovered Halle began to stabilise. With her daughter's emotional support and Thomas's backing, Halle began to question her treatment; Luis saw the shift in his control and resented it.

"I don't want you interfering in my family's affairs," he said, confronting Thomas at the Priory when he had visited his wife. "I'm very grateful for what you did for Kara –"

"I don't intend to stop interfering."

Although taken by surprise, Luis remained expressionless. "I would back off, Mr de Souza."

"Really?" Thomas countered, "Well, I don't intend to, Mr Famosa."

The gauntlet was thrown down; Thomas waited for the reaction. His father continued to recover in hospital, and Kara moved in with Thomas, both of them protecting their privacy as best they could, although the press was determined not to abandon either of them. Contrary to what he had hoped, Thomas's reserve incited *more* interest, Anna determined not to be ousted from the story. So, she turned her attention away from her son and courted Purchass like a Renaissance diplomat, flattering his ego, and only realising when she had been working with him for weeks that Purchass had an ulterior motive.

He wanted to see Thomas.

Anna asked her son to visit the prison.

Thomas refused.

Purchass then said that unless they talked, he wouldn't cooperate on either the book or the proposed film. Finally, curious and eager to conclude their connection, Thomas agreed to the meeting.

They faced each other across a Formica-topped table, a guard on either side of them, as Purchass tapped his stomach.

"You nearly killed me," he said, without rancour. "You learnt fast."

"You didn't teach me anything."

"Yeah, I did. I taught you to hate. I set up my killer kit and changed you." Purchass smiled, his tongue flicking over his bottom lip. "When our paths first crossed, you were soft. No backbone. Just a rich boy that wouldn't say boo to a goose. And I changed you. Just like I said I would. I turned you, deep inside. You wanted to kill me. And you damn near did," he leaned over the table, "that was impressive. I felt proud of you."

Thomas refused to react. "I wanted to ask you something –"

"Ask me anything, blog boy."

"When the police dug up the land around your farm they found bodies. I imagine that might even find others when they keep looking. How many women did you and your father kill?"

"I dunno. Between us? Plenty," Purchass said impatiently. "Look, some of those bones were farm animals! They weren't all human. They got mixed up –"

"Who was the first?"

Purchass rolled his eyes, hotly impatient. "I don't want to talk about it! I want to talk about you –"

"Come on, you ask me to visit, I'm here. Now you can do something for me. Who did you kill first?"

"My sister."

Thomas nodded. "With the blue eyes."

"Yeah," Purchass agreed. "I hated my sister. Or did I love my sister? Who knows? She was a right bitch. She made my life a misery. And she *had* blue eyes," he paused, watching Thomas, "That American, your girlfriend, she said she saw Kat. Said my sister went to talk to her. But she was lying - you know how I know? Because Kat came to me later and said that no other woman could take her place."

"So?"

"Don't you understand?"

"No."

"Me neither." Purchass said, laughing, "By the way, what was all that crap about the painting?"

Thomas was almost caught off guard, but reacted with a wry smile. "It was a bluff. The thing's a daub, bought off the internet –"

"And the bitch said it was worth money." Purchass replied, disgusted. "Women are born liars." Then he suddenly straightened up in his seat. "No, tell me the truth; how did it feel when you stuck that knife in me? My own fucking knife too! How did it feel?"

"I didn't feel anything."

"Don't lie! You wanted me dead. You wanted to kill me. So, come on, tell me. How did it feel when you knifed me?"

"What d'you want me to say?"

"That you felt *strong*," Purchass replied, taking a deep breath down into his lungs. "There's no other feeling in the world like it, is there? And after you've felt it, you're changed."

"I'm not a murderer. I didn't mean to kill the nurse –"

"No, you didn't, and I'm glad you got away with it," Purchass said, amused. "Pays to have a good lawyer, hey?" Thomas got to his feet, Purchass watching him as he continued to talk. "It'll never leave you now, that feeling. Knowing that life's there for the taking, and you're the taker. Go on, you can tell me, didn't it feel good?"

"No."

"*Liar!*" Purchass replied, banging his fists down on the table. "Liar! You won't admit it, even to yourself, but a little bit of Purchass is in you now. He's deep inside, but he's clinging on. Just waiting for another chance."

126

Time passed. Winter left London and a nervous spring began. Thomas de Souza's unwanted celebrity had done him one favour, and he returned to banking: not at his old firm, but at a rival's. Yet, whilst people admired his skill, they were more intrigued by his fame. It had been proven that the murder of Sente Fleishman had been an accident with no malicious intent. Thomas de Souza had been drawn into a sick game and had been manipulated by a lunatic, so they were willing to give him a second chance - but no one ever forgot the reputation that walked alongside him. Thomas was not like his contemporaries, nor did he pretend to be. He did not answer intrusive questions, and none were asked, especially if they concerned Kara Famosa.

Still recovering from his last stroke, Peter de Souza was moved from the hospital to convalesce at a nursing home, Thomas taking over the in Hampstead with Kara. He had not said as much, but had intimated to his mother that he might – *might* – be prepared to work with her if she promised to keep her distance from Kara. Annoyed but willing to accept his terms, Anna was convinced that she could manipulate her son and – with clever planning and a little time – could uncover the real story of the Famosa kidnapping.

Ah, but the gateway was not to be breached; it was bolted, locked down, and behind its fortress entrance Thomas watched over Kara. He watched over Halle too, just as Luis did; the two men were deeply distrustful of each other, Luis afraid that Thomas knew too much about his past; Thomas brooding over secrets that were not his own, but in his keeping.

He longed to expose Luis and Jimmy Famosa, but knew that in doing so he would be propelling Kara back into the burn of the spotlight; where she would panic and shrivel like a moth. In his final hours Hugh Ackermann had predicted the inevitable. As soon as Kara was rescued, Luis had hired a bevy of lawyers, all poised to bat away accusations, or any threat of the expose becoming public. The two camps had divided naturally: Thomas, Kara, and Halle on one side, Luis, and Jimmy Famosa on the other.

The unfinished – unseen - expose that Kara wrote was placed in a bank vault, secure and untouchable. Just as untouchable as the story Ackermann had told Thomas. Of the people that were present that portentous night, Simon Porter had committed suicide, Ackermann was dead, Halle was hospitalised, and Rakins – greedy, feckless Freddy Rakins – was buried and forgotten.

But not by Thomas. He wanted to see Luis Famosa destroyed, wanted to force him into admitting that he had murdered the man he had employed as a forger. The man with whom he had cheated the art world, deceived collectors, and swindled auction houses. The man who had become troublesome, deciding his own end when he had bragged about sleeping with Halle Famosa.

Thomas didn't know *how* he could bring Luis to justice, but he brooded on it. Just as he brooded on how he could punish his cruelty. When Luis had discovered that Kara wasn't his own flesh and blood, she became disposable, her death preferable to the truth becoming public. So many stories, Thomas thought. So many secrets, so many versions of so many lies, a garbled twisting of multi-headed, and invincible serpents.

For some unknown reason, Kara never wondered about her real father; it seemed to be a topic she had dismissed. She never asked her mother about his identity and Halle kept silent. But Kara and Thomas talked endlessly, both waiting to see if they would rekindle as lovers, trauma making any firm decision premature. Instead, Kara visited Halle, or kept to the house, avoiding contact with people. And all the time she was recovering, her hatred for Luis grew.

"You know I swapped the paintings?" She said one evening, bringing up the subject after months had passed.

Surprised, Thomas stared at her. "I know you *stole* the Klimt."

Getting to her feet, Kara left the room and returned moments later with the picture. The picture everyone believed Purchass had burned. She laid it down on the coffee table between them and gestured to it.

"D'you know what this is?"

"The Klimt fake that was due to be auctioned in New York."

"No," she said quietly, "This is the *real* Klimt."

Staggered, Thomas looked at the painting in front of him. "*This is real*?"

"Yes," She nodded. "Luis thinks the one at the gallery is the real one. He thinks I took the fake." Staring at the painting, she ran her index finger over the gold leaf, pausing at the outline of the woman's face. "It was odd the way it happened. I'd found out that Luis had some of his best paintings copied. He has a few forgers on his books– I don't have names, but I bet Ivan Holt could find out. Or the police…" Thomas listened in silence as she continued. "Luis would buy a picture by Chagall and have it copied, then exhibit the forgery. Or sell it for the price of a genuine Chagall. Doubling up on the profits." She stopped for a moment, thinking back. "I'd been travelling and came back home, but I was pissed with Jimmy's attitude. He'd found out I wasn't Luis's daughter - I could tell from the way he acted towards me. Even the way he spoke, it was obvious."

"What about Luis?"

"He was cold, distant, and travelling a lot. I was glad to avoided him as much as I could and kept away from New York, but I was already working on the book." She paused, thinking. "I don't know if I really intended to make it scandalous, but the more I found out, the more I wanted to expose the whole Famosa fiasco. I was torn about continuing with it, wondering if it was fair. They are family, after all. Was what I'd found out enough of a reason to go public? But then they *gave* me the reason – Luis and Jimmy – they gave me the perfect excuse to blow them out of the water." She glanced over to Thomas, her expression defiant. "I overheard my brother talking to Luis. They were on the phone so I could only hear Jimmy's side of the conversation, but it was easy to work out what they were talking about. Ivan Holt had told me about the extra security for the Klimt painting, and then Jimmy started reassuring his father." Her tone became bitter. "*…You've told her, Halle knows what to do…*' he said, then added *"She's giving the talk about the need to check out a painting's provenance, especially as big a name as Gustav Klimt…"* Kara held Thomas's gaze as she continued. "I kept listening then, wondering why they were pressurising my mother into giving a speech that *Luis* would have usually given. He loves the limelight; it would be his big chance to shine. We all knew that Halle didn't like giving speeches, they scared her. Then I heard Jimmy laugh, and he said *'…no, she's no idea…it will be as big a surprise to her as everyone else…'* And then I knew what they meant."

"They were setting Halle up?"

"Yeah," Kara agreed. "They were going to try. And I couldn't let those bastards do that to my mother." Her voice hardened. "If the auction had gone ahead, can you imagine what would have happened? Halle would have given her anti-forgery speech and then the Gustav Klimt would have been exposed as a fake in front of all the biggest dealers and the world's press. She would have been crucified - and Luis Famosa would have got his revenge."

"So, Luis thinks he's got the real Klimt?"

"He does - *but can he be sure*?" her eyes flickered. "I know what he'll be thinking - What if it's not real? What if it's a fake? And believe me, Luis Famosa will *ache* to know. He will look at it, stare at it, in its velvet-lined safe, and wonder. He can't sell it, he daren't, but the gambler in him will want to risk it. It will nag at him. It will eat away at him, and I'll watch. That's *my* revenge, Thomas; I want to break him as he broke my mother."

-o0o-

Months passed, and nothing more happened. From London to New York, a peace descended. And gradually, all the players finished their performances, rolled up the media caravan, and moved on. Until one day in late April when Detective Jameson called to see Thomas at his office. He was surprised at the change in him; the angry man he had last seen had been transformed into a sleek London banker, his manner cordial but suspicious,

"I've got some information which will be of interest to you."

Thomas raised his eyebrows. "What would that be?"

"I've been talking to a woman called Lydia Nash; she worked at the coroner's office in London where Sente Fleishman's body was taken." He paused and noticed the shift flinch in Thomas's expression. "She was the private secretary to the coroner, Dr Butler, who performed the autopsy on the nurse. Apparently, he died last month, and Miss Nash retired."

"I'm sorry, what's this about?"

"There was a mix-up at the hospital, a temp returned Ms Nash's files, accidentally including some of Dr Butler's case notes. One of the cases was Sente Fleishman." Thomas's right hand tightened on the arm of his chair as Jameson continued. "Ms Nash hadn't attended the autopsy on Sente Fleishman, but – like everyone else – had heard all about it. She told me that if she'd been working with Dr Butler the day the body came in, she'd have read the notes and known sooner –"

"*Known what*?"

" -- that Sente Fleishman wasn't killed by the blow to her head. It fractured her skull, but it was an injury from which she would have recovered --"

Thomas interrupted him. "*What else did the notes say?*"

"That if someone had called for an ambulance when they found her, Sente Fleishman would still be alive today."

"So that means…" Thomas stared at the detective, "… that I didn't kill her."

"That's right," Jameson agreed, "Sam Purchass killed her. You're innocent."

127

Asking him to visit her in secret, Thomas drove to Hampshire to see Halle. She had finally left The Priory and returned to the country house; her appearance fragile but with a flicker of spirit revived. There were guards around the property when Thomas arrived, the old housekeeper was as welcoming as ever, and showed him into the morning room where Halle was sitting, stiff-backed, at the window.

"I have to tell you something," she began, without preamble or any hesitation. New drugs? Therapy? Thomas wondered, or some other urgency to confide?

"I'm ready to listen."

Her eyes widened for an instant, as though she was getting her surroundings into focus, her white hands toying with the cuff of her jacket. "You'll hate me –"

"No, I won't."

"You will because you should. You see, I remembered something important." She put up her hands abruptly. "No, don't say anything! I can't do this if you talk. You have to be quiet. I remembered something important, Thomas. You have to let me remember."

What *do* you remember? He wondered. Vegas? Luis, Ackermann, or even Simon Porter? And he hoped, unexpectedly, that she was not remembering the death of Freddy Rakins because he didn't want her to remember that or tell Kara.

"I sent the postcard…"

Thomas frowned, not understanding what she meant. "What postcard?"

"The one I sent to Kara two Christmases ago." Halle paused, avoiding Thomas's gaze. "It was a very short message. It simply said that Luis wasn't her father. And then it wished her Happy Christmas." She stopped talking, crying silently, tugging at the cuff of her sleeve. "I only remembered it this morning. I don't know why, I just remembered –"

"*Why* did you send it?"

"Because I wanted her to know," she looked up, held Thomas's gaze, "I couldn't tell her face to face. I didn't have the courage, so I sent a postcard. And it was such a terrible thing to do that I blanked it out as soon as I'd done it. *I forgot.* Even when I found the card, I thought someone else had sent it. I kept wondering who, and why they'd be so cruel, and all the time it was *me!* I did that to my daughter! My own child –"

"Where's the postcard now?"

Reaching into her pocket, she handed it to him.

For a moment, Thomas studied it and then tore it into pieces. "See how easy it was to destroy it? Now let it go, Halle. Forget about it, *really* forget about it. It doesn't matter --"

She wasn't listening. "I was feeling so much better, my mind was clearing, I was getting stronger. *I really was!*" She said urgently, "I had a new doctor, and I could even stand up to Luis. Then I remembered the postcard –"

"*What postcard?*" Thomas interrupted her.

"The card I sent to Kara."

"There is no postcard, Halle –"

"*There was*!" she contradicted him. "I sent it."

He shook his head. "Think carefully." He warned her. "If you want to lose your daughter, choose to remember. If you want to keep her, choose to forget."

For several seconds, Halle stared at him, then nodded.

-o0o-

London

As expected, because of the new evidence, the case of Sente Fleishman was reopened. The postmortem was re-examined, and Stan Purchass was put back on trial for the murder of the German nurse. The eight other bodies found on the farm premises and in the surrounding fields were still being examined, but the remains of Kat Purchass were discovered under the outer steps leading from the farmhouse kitchen. Her DNA confirmed her connection to Purchass, and rumours began to circulate that another body – of a middle-aged man – had been recovered under an apple tree. The corpse was old and had been dismembered, the tree's roots crawling in and amongst the mouldering bones.

The world's press descended on London again, details spreading across the globe. As for Purchass, he gave interviews, talked to psychiatrists, and said that the prison food was good, but he worried about what would happen to the farmhouse. What happened was that it was demolished after the police had finished examining every inch of it - and the surrounding grounds. When they concluded their search, the flattened, burned site was cordoned off. A week later, someone left flowers on the ashes. And a week after that, someone else was holding a séance to contact the spirits of the dead who had perished there.

When Purchass heard, he laughed: "You know what Kat would have said? "*You're all freaks, fucking freaks.*"

Thomas never visited Stan Purchass again and avoided his mother's repeated pleas for interviews.

"But you've been proved innocent!" She said jubilantly, "There's an inspiring story in that. God knows, if those notes hadn't turned up, everyone would still think you were a murderer. Honestly, Thomas, you could sue the hospital for negligence. The papers would love it."

He wasn't interested in talking to or suing anyone; he was at peace. Knowing that he hadn't killed Sente Fleishman lifted the incessant guilt that had grumbled inside him, even in sleep. Any moment of peace or respite had been sabotaged by the memory of the nurse falling, the sound of her head striking the iron bollard, and the sick horror of believing he had taken a person's life. It had made Thomas wonder how the likes of Ackermann, Simon Porter and Luis Famosa had lived with the knowledge for decades, and how Luis could so easily have compounded one murder with the death of a child he had once believed his own.

Thomas didn't understand, and he didn't forgive.

And he waited.

Because he knew that, one day, he would find enough proof to expose Luis Famosa. One day, there would be evidence, irrefutable evidence, enough for him to step forward with what he knew. And what he had heard. If it took him a month, a year, or a lifetime, he didn't care. He would watch. He would wait.

And he would annihilate Luis Famosa.

POSTSCRIPT

Las Vegas
USA
Two years later

Purely by accident, an overturned truck had uncovered something in the desert sixteen miles out of Las Vegas. As the driver scrambled out of his wrecked van, he noticed that his tyre was spinning and that something was sticking up out of the sand. Curious, he moved closer and realised he was looking at a bone. A human thigh bone.

The police dug up the rest of the skeleton. They put it in a body bag and took it to the morgue, where the pathologist pieced it together over the next twelve hours. There was no flesh left, only some remnants of clothing. But no wallet. No driving license. No passport. Nothing to say who the man had been in life.

Suspicious, the police wondered if he had been a murder victim, the killers taking away any identification documents and leaving their victim to rot, which he had done, for decades. He was then put in the morgue with a John Doe tag, the police checking back on missing persons and coming up with nothing.

And so, Freddy Rakins would have stayed lost, except that the pathologist had noticed something about the corpse's teeth. His dentistry looked European, and just before his death it seemed that he had undergone some extensive treatment in the USA. The police checked it out, and finally a Las Vegas dentist - long retired – reviewed his records and came back to them with the name of a man that he had seen as an emergency patient, back in 1998.

His file named him as Freddy Rakins. A British artist who had once lived in Vegas. Once they identified Mr Rakins and searched for any information about him, they checked the internet and then the local papers, finally coming across an old newspaper cutting and a photograph of him. He had been handsome and tanned, and was raising a glass to the person taking the shot. The only person not in the picture.

Freddy was smiling. Living the good life as he posed with friends - Simon Porter, Hugh Ackermann, and Luis Famosa.

Printed in Great Britain
by Amazon

50106368R00341